LAST PAGES

Published by Prospect Park Books
2359 Lincoln Avenue
Altadena, CA 91001
www.prospectparkbooks.com

Distributed by Consortium Book Sales & Distribution
www.cbsd.com

Library of Congress Cataloging in Publication Data is on file with the Library
of Congress. The following is for reference only:
Last pages / Oscar Mandel
ISBN 978-1-945551-51-2 (paperback)
Subjects: Literature; poetry; essays; plays

Book design by Amy Inouye
Cover illustration by Hans Pape (1895-1971)
Printed in Canada

LAST PAGES
Stories, Drama, Poems, Essays

Oscar Mandel

PROSPECT
·PARK·
BOOKS

ALSO BY OSCAR MANDEL

Fiction
Otherwise Fables*: (Gobble-Up Stories. Chi Po and the Sorcerer,
The History of Sigismund, Prince of Poland)

Poetry
Otherwise Poems*

Drama
Collected Plays (two volumes)
Amphitryon (after Molière)
The Virgin and the Unicorn: Four Plays
Two Romantic Plays
Reinventions: Four Plays after Homer, Cervantes, Calderón and Marivaux

Non-Fiction
A Definition of Tragedy
The Book of Elaborations
Fundamentals of the Art of Poetry

Translations and Critical Studies
Philoctetes and the Fall of Troy
The Theatre of Don Juan
Five Comedies of Medieval France
The Ariadne of Thomas Corneille
Seven Comedies by Marivaux
Prosper Mérimée: Plays on Hispanic Themes
August von Kotzebue: The Comedy, the Man
The Land of Upside Down (LudwigTieck)

Art History
The Art of Alessandro Magnasco: An Essay in the Recovery of Meaning
The Cheerfulness of Dutch Art: A Rescue Operation

*Published by Prospect Park Books

CONTENTS

Essays

Epilogue

A word to my imagined readers

A GLANCE at the title of the last essay in this volume should give away the meaning of "Last Pages," which, in turn, may suggest why the contents of my book are so shockingly heterogeneous in genres, in matter and in tone. I emptied my drawer and poured out what lay in it. Apology is useless. The voices are many. The author is one.

STORIES

TWO GENTLEMEN OF NANTUCKET

A Romantic Episode of the American Revolution

1

A BROKEN WINDOWPANE was the only blemish on the Weamish residence in Sherburne, one of the finest houses on the island—certainly the finest on Main Street, and one of the few in town made entirely of brick. As he sat that morning in his upper-story library writing a letter to his widowed mother, Judge Thomas Weamish frowned in anger and pain each time he looked up at the glassy wound. To be sure, rosy-cheeked and chubby in his morning robe and slippers, he appeared more like a man accustomed, at the lovely age of forty, to cheer than to distress. Yet these were distressful times, and Weamish was conscious of them as he concluded his letter, written in a consciously elegant hand, with frequent dippings of the pen into the inkwell. "For the rest, my dearest mamma, the weather today is all radiant sun, as if to invite a swift return from the mainland of one whom not a few among the natives of the island call the queen-mother of Nantucket. Speed, speed to these shores again, for our human storms require a hand such as yours that knoweth how to chide the weak and chastise the guilty. Ever your devoted son, Thomas. Mailed at Sherburne, Nantucket. Tuesday, the 20th of June, 1775."

He dried the letter and rang a little silver bell. Jenny the motherly housekeeper came up from the kitchen.

"Jenny, when the post boy comes by, tell him I have a letter for him," said Weamish.

"I will, Mr. Weamish. And I thought you'd like to know, sir, that I saw Josh Mamack dragging down the street."

"It's about time! Catch him and send him up at once."

When she was gone, Weamish rose from his chair, letter in hand, and took it to an unbroken window for a better light. He was rather proud of his epistolary skills and unwilling to fold and seal the letter without re-reading it. This he did, half aloud, with subdued but eloquent gestures.

"Dearest mamma," said the letter; "God grant that this missive find you in the full enjoyment of your customary health and cheerful spirits. Need I tell you how sorely you are missed by all your friends in town? To fly to an ailing sister, a despondent and helpless brother-in-law, in the midst of an embattled Boston, within hearing of cannon fire, insulted daily by a rabble of treacherous and unprincipled villains, who, like froward children, dare to question the mild authority of a monarch beloved of all his rational subjects; to rush, I say, to a sister and brother cruelly expelled from their ancestral home at Cambridge; to nurse them in their affliction; to comfort them for the loss of property, familiar grounds and acquaintances; all this proves you a Saltonstall, the proud daughter of a governor, and sister-in-law to a royal Councillor of Massachusetts. But let me descend from these heights and commend myself to Dr. Brattle and to your dear sister, my aunt. Pray tell them they acted wisely in taking shelter at Boston under the victorious wings of his Excellency our governor and general, who, if reports tell true, hath recently beaten the impudent rebels out of Charlestown, and will now drum them handily out of the entire province. Alas, how I wish that I myself could wield a sword in these stirring times, rise to defend my king, and scourge the contumacious mob! But the robe enjoins its own duties, the law hath its own heroes. My sphere, at the moment, is our dear county of Nantucket, and here I mean to sustain his Majesty's mild rule and enforce his just decrees. What if you and I, my dear mamma, permit ourselves, in the intimacy of our household, to nurse the virtuous hope that Governor Gage will see fit presently to call me to his side, perhaps into his Council, to serve my king in a wider and nobler field of activity? I make no secret of my feelings. I do not care if a hint should come to the governor's ear that Thomas Weamish, who suffered for his king in the time of the Stamp Act, and who now once again beholds his windows shattered as the reward of his loyalty, that this same Thomas Weamish burns with a noble ambition to sacrifice his repose on the altar of our cherished colony. But you, my dear mamma, will know better than anyone how to convey these not unworthy sentiments to General Gage. Speak to him apart at the next assembly, when music hath made him cheerful. For is it fitting that a son of yours should pine away in a rude colonial outpost, among uncouth whalemen and Quakers, distant from elegant society—"

But the door opened again at that moment and Jenny entered, followed by Joshua Mamack, carrying tools and a sack. "Here's Josh, Mr. Weamish."

The Indian took off his cap with a respectfully cheerful "Good day to you, sir."

Weamish gave the man in return a sarcastic "Well well, Mr. Mamack; very good of you I'm sure to call on us at last."

The Indian looked dumb and scratched his head. "Never mind," said the Judge; "I'll attend to you in a moment."

He sat down to fold and seal his letter, which he handed to Jenny. After she had left, he turned to the Indian and pointed tragically at the broken window-pane, the sharp edges of which remained as if to bear witness. "Here, Mr. Mamack, here."

"Yah. I seen it," said the Indian. "Near same one they break nine years ago. Mamack good memory. I seen it from the street days ago and I brung the replacement. Here."

Mamack produced the bright new pane from his sack. The Judge examined it.

"Very well, Mr. Mamack, but why has it taken you four days to find your way here?"

Mamack had learned long ago that this looking dumb of his was the canniest way to cope with the white world. "Find my way?" he asked.

"To answer my summons, Mamack," Weamish shouted. "Am I to sit in this room for an entire week while the wind whistles through a broken window?"

"I mean to come right away quickly, Judge—"

"But?"

"Well—"

"Well well well! Well what?"

"Well—I got five kids to feed, I got a position in the community—"

The Judge's cheeks puffed and went from his customary rosy to red.

"A position in the—! A carpenter—a glazer—a jack Indian with a position in the community! So this is the new spirit blowing over the land! And what has your precious position in the community to do with my broken window, Mr. Mamack?"

"Yah, I was only talking, Judge. I fix that window fast."

"I insist that you tell me!"

"Well—"

"Well?"

Up to this moment, Mamack had been looking down and sideways as though interested in the Judge's carpet, but now he gazed slyly into the Judge's face: "Well, the folks around here see you comfy cozy with Sergeant Cuff and Mr. Applegate—"

"Aha!"

Just then, in the distance, came the sound of a fife and drum. It had become a familiar one to the Sherburne folk from the time when, months ago, thirty Redcoats, commanded by Sergeant Alexander Cuff (detached from the nth Regiment of Foot) had landed on the island to keep the peace. Mamack became a little bolder.

"There's a heap of bad feeling on the island, Judge," he said, "like a wind, speak East, speak West, a cold wicked wind. But I don't meddle none in white man's business. I don't sit down into no committees."

"Committees, eh? I assure you I know all about their rebel committees."

"They know all about you that you know all about them," replied Mamack with a grin. "They say you and Mr. Applegate hush hush at night, in the dark, only one candle, you write names with ink in a book."

"Rubbish!"

"But maybe they write names too, eh?"

"Let them!" The military note was coming closer. "We have ways," he added, "of slapping their writing hands. As for you—"

"I better fix that window. Big storm step out of sky any day."

"Not yet! Tell me, have these patriotic gentlemen tried to keep you from mending it?"

"They call a small meeting about it, sir."

"A meeting! A meeting about my window!"

"Small meeting, Judge. A bowl of cider and a pipe in Swain's tap room. I said to them, I said, 'Gentlemen, who am I? Josh Mamack, Pokanoket tribe, honest worker, no rum hardly ever, I must mend the Judge's window, not decent to keep the Judge in draft.' And they said, 'Go, friend, go in peace.'"

"So now it's the rebel committee that runs Nantucket! The magistrates and the selectmen no longer count. Tell me, Mr. Mamack, while you gentlemen were guzzling cider and puffing on your pipes, was not the vandal's name mentioned by chance?"

"Who?"

"The window breaker's name!"

"The window breaker? O Lord—I don't know—"

Weamish, who had been standing, now sat down behind the desk and spoke with the voice of a judge addressing a sheep-stealer. "Mr. Mamack," he said, "I am the chief magistrate of this county."

"I know, sir. We're mighty proud of you."

"I order you to speak. Who broke that window? One of the Coffins? Young Macy? Coleman? Hussey's children?"

"How would I know? How would anybody know? But I have an idea, Judge."

"Aha!"

"Because as I said it's near the window what break when you was stamp distributor."

"What of it?"

"I better fix that window. I talk too much."

That the Indian was hugely though slyly enjoying himself escaped the good judge, who now slammed the desk and knocked over a small British flag set in a silver base.

"Don't go near that window! Finish what you were about to say!"

"Yes, sir. I figure the moment I come in, I says to myself, by cod, Mamack, it must be the same Spirit which done it in sixty-six. Spirit, he smashed like he was trying to tell you, 'Watch out, Judge Weamish, the people don't have forgotten!'"

Mamack uttered these words in his best sepulchral tone.

"Spirit be damned!" Weamish now trembled and blustered at the same time. "Rogues and rascals! They will not forgive a man for carrying out British law."

By this time a squad of Redcoats was nearing the house, and Weamish took comfort in the drum's rat-tat-tat.

"Thank God for Sergeant Cuff!" he said. "Thirty-odd Redcoats will suffice to curb these Sons of Liberty."

"We don't see so many soldiers since the French War," said Mamack, who now brought out his most innocent tone. "How long they purposing to stay, Judge?"

But this time he was disappointed. "Forever, damn it!" Weamish replied. "Go mend that window!"

"Yes, Judge," and he began to work, while Weamish went to another window, and opened it to wave at the Redcoats in the street below. There were ten of them, led by Sergeant Cuff himself, a tough-jawed man in his fifties, carrying a sword hanging from his shoulder and a pistol wedged into his belt. He had halted his men just beneath the window. It was evidently the Sergeant's wish to greet the Judge.

"Proud looking lads!" shouted the Judge down into the street. Mamack also peered out the broken window.

The street was wide enough to allow for a little complimentary drill with musket and bayonet, to the sound of drum and fife, honoring the Judge, whom the Sergeant saluted by taking off his cocked hat and waving his sword, while shouting commands. A horse-drawn cart rumbling by, driven by a pair of disapproving Quakers, gave the soldiers a squeeze, but Weamish waved, Cuff saluted, and Mamack thought he would try again when drill and drum were over and the detachment marched away.

"What's your opinion, Judge? They going to hold down the harbor? Put a few fellows in jail? Take our ships away from us?"

"We'll see," said Weamish smugly, and he could not help adding (because one does sometimes boast even to an underling), "Sergeant Cuff has orders from Colonel Montague at Boston to make no move without my consent."

Mamack let out a whistle. "One day, Spirit tell me and tell me sure, one day you going to be Royal Duke in London. Mark Mamack's words, your mummy, she be the proudest lady from here to Boston."

Weamish inspected Mamack's work. "I see you're almost done. Good."

Now, catching sight of a gentleman on horseback trotting down Main Street at leisure, he opened the intact window again and called out.

"Mr. Applegate, do dismount and pay me a visit. There's a cup of chocolate for you if you don't mind finding me in my morning *négligé*."

John Applegate, a wealthy Tory landowner from Concord,

was on the island for what he hopefully called a "short visit" with his relatives the Rotch family, his property, perhaps his life, having been threatened at home by the Rebels. His wife (they had no children) had remained in timorous charge at Concord.

Looking up from his saddle, he replied to the Judge's invitation, "Thank you, my friend, but I've no wish to intrude on preparations for your elegant visitors."

"What elegant visitors, Mr. Applegate? This is Joshua Mamack, a common laborer."

"Mamack indeed!" cried Applegate with a laugh. "I mean the two ladies who came ashore from the New York packet this morning."

"I know nothing about it! Two ladies? I beg you, sir, do come up for a moment and explain."

"I will," replied Applegate, dismounting and tying up his horse. Jenny had already opened the door, and he climbed the stairs into the library.

"Sit down, sir, sit down; two ladies? I'm dumbfounded."

"Well then, I am the bringer of good tidings, or so I hope. I was at the wharves early this morning, hoping the Boston gazettes had arrived. Colonel Mayhew and his sparkish nephew were overseeing the unloading of I do not know what merchandise, while two ladies, most elegant ladies—and I have seen some in Boston—all frills and ribbons—came ashore, escorted with many a flourish by the captain himself—Frobish by name, I know him well. I heard them babble to each other in French. A gig was waiting for them, though 'tis only fifty paces to Swain's Inn. A mighty load of luggage was loaded into a cart, and off they all drove. I do not think that the Mayhews saw them. But to the point. Frobish told me that the older of the two ladies had asked for directions to the house of Judge Thomas Weamish. They will undoubtedly be calling on you before long."

"I'm speechless!" cried Weamish. "Allow me, sir, if I may—"

"Oh, I'm off!" said Applegate with a chuckle, "but I'll stop by this evening for news." A minute later he was on his horse again.

"Jenny! Jenny!" Weamish shouted over the landing, "Two French ladies are calling on me! Come up at once!"

The excitement was understandable. The chronicles of Nantucket do not report any previous visits to the island by Frenchwomen, elegant or otherwise.

Jenny came up the stairs.

"Hurry down again and tidy the parlor! French ladies! Perhaps they speak no English."

"The parlor is always tidy, Mr. Weamish.," said Jenny peevishly.

"Well, prepare a collation. And use the silver, not the china. Hurry while I dress. And let me not hear any farmhand familiarities when they come."

"I don't know what you mean, Mr. Weamish," said Jenny even more peevishly, as she descended the steps. About to rush into his dressing room, Weamish became aware of Mamack again, who had been watching rather more attentively than attending to his work.

"That will do for the day, Mamack," cried the Judge. "Go down to the kitchen, have Cook give you something to eat and drink, and come back tomorrow."

Without waiting for a reply, Weamish dashed into his dressing room. His clothes and wig had been laid out as usual by Jenny, and it did not take him long to dress and scent himself—a little more generously, perhaps, than usual. Mamack had disappeared by the time Weamish returned to his desk, where he busied himself, or tried to busy himself, with some legal papers.

After a while, he heard a carriage approach his house and stop at the door. He peeked down through the window as two women descended from the chaise, which was being driven by old Moses. The elder of the two knocked at the door. As Weamish gave himself a final preening, he heard Jenny, fussy and flustered, invite the ladies into the parlor. Then she called her master, who took hold of his dignity coming down the stairs as he entered the parlor, closing the door behind him.

"Allow me to welcome you in my house," he said; "I am Judge Thomas Weamish."

"And I am Aimée de Tourville," said the lady, raising her head. "This is my daughter Madeleine. I hope you will forgive this unannounced intrusion. I have come to you from the inn without changing, because the matter is urgent."

Madame de Tourville spoke with a surprisingly slight French accent. Her daughter, it may as well be reported here, had none.

"Pray sit," said the Judge.

2

THE FORTY-FIVE-YEAR OLD Aimée de Tourville was not simply fine-looking; she had eyes and lips that showed her, even to the most obtuse observer, to be a creature of high spirits. She was probably more attractive and more striking in her dark-haired maturity than she had been as a young girl. Her daughter, growing up under that radiance, showed more reticence in looks and dress, as well as an intelligence that kept to few words.

Who were these women?

Candor is best. The Marquise Aimée de Tourville was in fact Aimée Binette, only child of an honest Lyon locksmith, who married her off, naturally enough, to a Lyon jail-keeper named Jean Pichot when she turned seventeen. High luck befell her two years into her marriage when the Vicomtesse de Brion was incarcerated for poisoning her husband instead of only crying over his brutalities, as the law required. Before the vicomtesse was hanged, Aimée spent hours, days and months in the lady's cell. That bold woman taught the whip-smart turnkey's wife to speak, walk, sit, behave and even think like an aristocrat. As a result, even before Monsieur Pichot died, she easily became the mistress of an aging nobleman, a relation of the vicomtesse, who had occasionally called on the lady in her cell. Aimée had taken over her father's rather successful key-shop, but the baron enabled her to live at a station higher than what selling keys, even many keys, would have allowed.

Intimacies with the baron—the aging baron, as mentioned before—satisfied only a fraction of Aimée's large capacities for pleasure. Though ever kind and charming to the gentleman (Aimée had a heart) she became the mistress of one of her much younger clients, a sturdy sergeant by the name of Christian Deudon. A couple of years later—in 1752, to be precise—the baron was called to Paris by the king and Madeleine was born, tenderly

acknowledged by both the baron and the sergeant. The girl was
destined so to resemble her mother, physically speaking, that the
question of who was her father would have been impossible to
resolve by the method of comparison. Aimée never did resolve it.

In the last days of the year 1756, the sergeant slapped his
lieutenant's face. This pre-Jacobin act obliged the couple and their
baby to flee to Montreal, where Aimée taught the sergeant what
she knew about the business of selling keys and repairing locks.
But unable to bear the cold, Deudon, though sturdy, succumbed
to a weakness of the lungs. He left mother and child a dented
sword and a tunic with braids out of which Aimée made a pretty
skirt for the baby.

In 1760, during a dreadful winter in the first year of English
rule, mother and daughter nearly froze to death. But this low kind
of death was not meant for Aimée. General Thomas Gage had
given an order—in French and English—that beef was to sell at no
more than ten sous the pound. Aimée had not been in Montreal
long enough to deserve special favors from the butchers. To keep
her baby alive, she ran from one to the other, an ounce here, a slice
there, sometimes as far as the Arsenal, knee-deep in snow or falling
on the ice. Yet somehow she was always dealt the worst cuts, meat
that stank in spite of the cold, never a bite more than her ration,
and her pittance handed over the counter with sour distrustful
faces. Pretty soon, however, she noticed a detail. Every butcher
displayed an alms box for the hospital or the Ursulines that no
eye could miss. Aimée thought, "How wonderfully generous they
all are! Everybody's freezing and starving, but never a trip to the
butcher's without a few pious coins into those boxes." One day
she saw one of the good ladies of Montreal drop a coin and throw
the butcher a wink. That wink was sufficient. Aimée sent a note
to Monsieur Maturin, who was Gage's secretary, named herself,
humble widow of a late sergeant in the light infantry, the butcher
got ten lashes, the alms boxes disappeared, and Aimée quietly
entered the Governor's service, sending elegant and witty notes at

a regular pace concerning the doings and the temper of a restive French population. The two called it "taking the pulse" of the people. They also took that of each other.

Presently General Gage was transferred to New York. Aimée, though she kept her little étage in Montreal (one never knows), followed soon after. That was where the key-shop *persona* disappeared once and for all, and where the Marquise de Tourville settled with her daughter in unpretentious but comfortable quarters, enjoying a monthly retainer quietly paid by the British crown. Tutors gave little Madeleine lessons in French and English. Aimée herself mastered the new language with ease. As a Frenchwoman she appeared in New York, and made sure that she so appeared, as the natural enemy of England and the admirer of the Sons of Liberty, very active in New York in the years of the Quartering Act, the Stamp Act, the Townshend Acts, the Tea Act and other offenses to colonial interests. Aimée's social life was thoroughly American. This was not difficult for her, because the Patriots, in New York and elsewhere, were decidedly among the "best people," among whom she moved with the brilliant grace that was natural to an uprooted aristocrat. On two occasions—one in a drawing-room, the other in a ballroom—she was thrown in with French nobility—a count and his wife, and then a baron; but she had foreseen such meetings, and had memorized from the *Armorial général de la France,* while still in Montreal, all that she felt she would ever need to sustain her personage with *panache.* A few of the "best people" just mentioned were compelled to move from drawing-room to prison as a result of notes from Aimée to Gage. But her personal meetings with Gage remained, needless to say, rare and discreet: New York, in those days, was poorly lit at night.

When Gage became Royal Governor of Massachusetts—in the year 1774—Aimée continued her work in New York, but she received regular dispatches from him. She did not much care that Madeleine, now grown into a much-admired but very uneasy young woman, was acquainted (somewhat vaguely) with her game,

disliked it, feared to talk of it with her, and was openly charmed
and thrilled (such is youth) by the ideals of Liberty. Indeed, her
unconcealed sympathies helped Aimée's work. Aimée herself, need
one say it? thought both parties fools for whipping themselves into
states of political excitement, but fools, she believed, were manna
for the clever.

   By 1775, rebellion in and around Boston was at a boil. Gage
sent Aimée on a mission to Nantucket for which he believed her
to be well suited.

3

WEAMISH HAD TAKEN a seat facing the two women. Aimée brought a sealed letter out of her reticule, and invited the Judge to break the seal and read. Weamish obeyed, cried out "From Governor Gage!" and sprang to his feet. Aimée was amused.

"Do read it, sir. I know its content, of course, but shall be glad to hear it in so many words. Don't fidget, Madeleine."

The Judge began to read. "The person who has given you this letter is the Marquise Aimée de Tourville—"

"Marquise!" uttered Weamish, gaping but delighted.

"Come, my dear Judge, we are two-legged animals all the same. Read on."

The letter continued as follows: "The Marquise de Tourville" (and here Weamish, still erect, bowed to Aimée), "accompanied by her daughter" (and now he bowed to Madeleine), "is sent to the island of Nantucket with verbal orders that you are requested to obey without question. She will name the gentlemen who are the objects of our present concern and inform you of the high importance we attach to her mission."

This was followed by a noise of something falling outside the parlor door. Aimée pointed and Weamish strode to the door and bruskly opened it. There stood Mamack. "What were you doing behind that door?" thundered the Judge. "I dropped my chisel," said the eavesdropper sheepishly, picking up the tool and dashing out of the house.

"War, Judge Weamish, war," said Aimée.

"To be sure; although an untutored Indian—"

"Will you be so kind as to sit beside me?"

"Certainly. And allow me to assure you at that you will be punctiliously obeyed."

"Here is the heart of the matter," said Aimée; but at this point

Jenny, not accustomed to knocking, entered holding a large tray. "Chocolate and buttered buns," she announced.

"Get out! Not now!" the Judge roared.

"Tut tut," said Aimée, "why not now? Madeleine, you haven't said a word all morning. Do you fancy a little refreshment?"

"I should love a cup of chocolate," said the girl.

The ceremony of serving and partaking was properly performed and Jenny had left, closing the door behind her, when Aimée resumed.

"Here, as I said, is the heart of the matter. My daughter and I have been sent to Sherburne to investigate Colonel William Mayhew and his nephew Nicholas. You look surprised, Judge Weamish."

The Judge had in fact opened his mouth wide.

"Surprised?" he cried, "oh, not I!"

"Can it be that you entertain no suspicions in that quarter?"

"I do entertain suspicions. This island is a hatchery of rebels!"

"That is more than I can say," said Aimée, looking sharply at the Judge. "My instructions are limited to the two Mayhews. Are they presently on the island?"

"They are, my lady; indeed, they were seen at the wharf where you and your fair daughter disembarked, looking for their mail. Tell me, Marquise, what are they guilty of? I'll proceed with every severity known to the law."

"Who said they were guilty of anything? I spoke of suspicions. You know of course that Colonel Mayhew fought side by side with Colonel Washington in fifty-nine. And with General Amherst at Montreal in 1760. Fought *for* the Crown, to be sure, and against us of France. But *that* is neither here nor there."

"Precisely," said Weamish. "Neither here nor there. And allow me to inform you, Marquise, that Colonel Mayhew has a brother serving at this very moment in the congress of traitors at Philadelphia."

"A cousin, I believe."

"Though he himself laughs at the matter, babbles about his loyal relations in Boston, and tells the world he has been a peaceful merchant for a dozen years. 'Mayhew & Mayhew': a thriving commercial enterprise."

"That brings me to the nephew," said Aimée.

"Dashing Nicholas!"

"Yes. Soldier, sailor, captain's mate on the *Lively*, but before that, a special commendation by General Forbes in fifty-seven though he was a mere lad. Has killed many a Frenchman and Indian. Sometimes, to be sure, I feel that I am betraying my people by so firmly supporting King George, but these brawls are of long ago, and wounds do heal."

"Indeed, indeed," said Weamish, trying to follow these delicacies of feeling.

"To the point. It appears that Colonel Washington is to be appointed by the Rebels to a particularly brilliant post of command. This cannot have reached you yet."

"I assure you, Marquise, that we receive prompt and accurate intelligence here."

"Then you know that the Rebels who now besiege Boston are anxious to enlist capable officers to lead their ragged bands."

"They'll never find them."

"Perhaps you will put two and two together. Or, if inconvenient, one and one."

"Of course. A terrifying plot—"

"What terrifying plot?"

A diversion seemed advisable. The Judge turned to Madeleine.

"Sugar, mademoiselle? "

"Thank you," said Madeleine.

"You too, mademoiselle, you too no doubt hate rebellion."

"I am unable to hate," replied Madeleine, looking boldly into the Judge's eyes.

"Noble words!" Weamish exclaimed. And, turning again to Aimée: "You were saying, Marquise?"

Aimée sighed. "We believe—that is to say, Governor Gage believes—that Colonel Mayhew and his nephew have both been secretly approached to play a considerable part in the siege of Boston and beyond."

"No wonder. The Mayhews, as I intimated just now, are considerable men in Nantucket."

"That is precisely why I am ordered to proceed with caution. Before risking a popular uprising, I must have proof, proof, proof that they are plotting to escape from the island. We hope that the rumors are false. My mission here is to take accurate soundings and to instruct you accordingly. Fortunately, if I may repeat myself, as Frenchwomen we are thought to be the Yankees' natural allies and Britain's natural enemies. As such, it will be easy for me to make friends with the Mayhew gentlemen, and many others. Living quietly at the inn—what is it called again?"

"Swain's Inn, mamma," said Madeleine.

"Thank you, my dear. There we shall find occasion to chat with the natives, place a few questions, distribute a trifle of coins, and meet the Mayhews themselves. As the old one's a widower, and the young one a bachelor, both are sure to be found in a tap room. I expect to have all the facts within a week. Our story will be a simple one. My daughter has not been well. Witness her pallor. New York in summertime is stifling. Our physician has recommended a cure of fresh ocean air, and we have complied. Naturally we have begun by paying our respects to the chief magistrate of the island, but that call is to be understood as purely formal. We must hint left and right at our sympathy with the Whigs and keep our distance from yourself and other Tories."

"This is a disappointment for me," said Weamish, looking at Madeleine. "You land on this poor island of ours—diffusing the radiance of Versailles—music in the gardens—ridottos—rank and fashion—and now you dash all my hopes by telling me that we must be strangers."

"I have not been at Versailles since 1758, my dear Judge,

the year my husband, may God have mercy on his soul, took his regiment to Canada."

"You followed him."

"Of course. I am a Fapignac!"

"Ah!" cried Weamish, looking meaningfully again at Madeleine. "Poor child!"

"Poor child indeed," said Aimée; "at the age of three she was fatherless in Canada."

"The horrors of war."

"The Marquis was carried off by the cold weather."

Madeleine was gazing deep into her cup.

"Bitter, bitter," said the Judge. "What can I possibly do to comfort you during your stay? Needless to say, I would have offered you my house."

"True American courtesy, Judge Weamish. But the neutral ground of Swain's Inn, where we have been shown fairly comfortable apartments, will be a more favorable place for my mission."

"Confortable enough for our islanders, I daresay," said Weamish. "But, my dear ladies, you cannot conceive what it is for a man of breeding to live among whale-men, Quakers, farmers—with never a ball, a concert, or a play to relieve the tedium. I am—if I may take the liberty of mentioning it—the grandson of a governor."

"Governor Saltonstall, is it not?"

"Yes."

"I am told that your mother, Mrs. Weamish, is presently in Boston."

"To my sorrow, she is. Nursing her sister and her brother-in-law, both refugees from Cambridge, and sadly come down since their flight."

"What is the news from Boston? We have been on board our wretched vessel since Saturday."

It was the Judge's turn to take the upper hand. "Ah Marquise," he exclaimed, "I am in a position to give you news of capital importance. A magnificent victory at Charlestown."

"Under Gage's command?" cried Aimée happily though only vaguely aware of where the place was.

"Indirectly, madam. He dispatched General Howe across the bay to give chase to the villains who had occupied the hills overlooking Boston. Their leader, a firebrand named Joseph Warren, was left dead on the field, and the Whiggish dogs were driven from the peninsula licking their desperate wounds."

"I pray they can still be reconciled," said Madeleine. "Your country is so beautiful—so plentiful—I feel that God has meant it for peace."

"They shall have peace shortly, mademoiselle," was the Judge's reply. "Our generals are making ready to sweep the province clear of rebels. They are a loose collection of shallow rascals, all brave enough behind their fences, but routed by the first volley of our muskets. They cannot enlist respectable officers—ah, you said so yourself, Marquise. This is June. We shall have peace before winter, I assure you."

"Good. Now let me speak of Sergeant Alexander Cuff."

"Reliable, I hope!" exclaimed the Judge.

"Undoubtedly. I must meet with him as soon as possible. I have a letter for him as well. You and he must be the only persons on the island privy to my mission. May we meet again in this very place tomorrow at eleven o'clock in the morning—I, you, and the Sergeant?

"Of course."

"I shall pretend to be strolling as a newcome visitor would, and knock at your door, or ring the doorbell, when I see no one in the street. I am leaving it to you, sir, to advise the sergeant."

Just as they were all rising from their chairs, a series of strong knocks at the front door was heard, the door was opened, and Jenny came hastily into the parlor. "Begging your pardon," she cried, curtseying, "but there's Mr. Mayhew, the young one, in the hall, wanting urgently to see you, Mr. Weamish."

"Splendid!" cried Aimée; "have him come in. What luck!"

"Yes, madam," said Jenny. A moment later, Nicholas Mayhew appeared, tall, lean, hale and resolute. He seemed to bring with him, from the outside, a wave of fresh air. "Judge Weamish," he said, doffing his hat (the Mayhews wore their own hair, slightly powdered), "where is our mail? I know you are entertaining distinguished visitors; I took note of their vehicle; pray accept my sincerest apologies." And here he bowed and addressed himself to the ladies. "I am Nicholas Mayhew, gentle ladies, often called Young Nick, my bad temper was given me by the devil, I was not consulted." And he swiveled again to the Judge. "Sir: myself and my uncle are expecting important commercial letters from the mainland. Three weeks have gone by without a single message. Today the New York packet arrives." Now again to the women: "And by the way, allow me to report that I happened to see your trunks safely delivered at Swain's Inn." Then back to Weamish. "Today, I repeat, the packet from New York puts in. Several sacks of mail emerge from the captain's cabin. Your constable George Hackbutt removes them. Now sir: I make no accusations, but I demand of you, as chief magistrate of this island, whether orders have been issued to seize, withhold, or destroy our mail, merely because it is universally known that a Mayhew, of whom by the way we know next to nothing, is sitting presently at the Congress in Philadelphia."

Weamish winked significantly at Aimée and said, "My dear Mr. Mayhew, calm yourself."

"I am enraged, but in full control of myself."

"Sir," said Aimée to the Judge, "will you introduce us to this most *sympathique* gentleman?" This was soon done, Nicholas declaring that he was honored, and Aimée hinted that she sympathized with his anger.

"And so do I," said Weamish. "Nothing is being withheld *here*, Mr. Mayhew. What is confiscated in New York, or intercepted on the way, I cannot tell. My orbit is limited to these few islands. Come, sir, sit down with us. I predict that you shall have your letters before the week is over. Let me propose something a fillip stronger than warm chocolate."

Opening the door of a sideboard, Weamish produced a flask of rum and several tumblers. Nicholas took a chair, saying, "Judge Weamish, if I'm not mistaken, this is a product of contraband."

Weamish laughed. "Justice is blindfolded."

"A little concession to the good life, eh?" said Aimée.

"Ah, how else can a gentleman survive? Nothing but sperm oil, tar, pitch . . ."

"All the same," said Nicholas, "your worthy ancestor made a pretty thing out of your despised sperm oil. Manufactured sperm candles," he added, turning to the ladies, and then, in a mock aside: "A fortune!"

The Judge gave his mouth a deprecatory bend. "To be sure, he said, we colonials must be content to derive from trade and industry."

"Don't apologize, sir," said Aimée, "I have lived on your continent long enough to value the spirit of commerce."

"This is true elevation of mind! Ah, how I feel the absence of my mother. She is worthy of your acquaintance, Marquise."

"Let us drink to her prompt return, shall we? Shall we, Mr. Mayhew?"

"With pleasure."

The glasses clinked, the Barbados was drunk or, in Madeleine's case, tasted.

"Thank you," said Weamish, adding—rather shrewdly—"and now, I propose a toast to His Excellency, Governor Gage. Will you join us, Mr. Mayhew, in spite of your cousin?"

"Of course I will. Let it be noted that the sympathies of Mayhew & Mayhew are universal, for it is trade that makes us what we are. May Tom Gage live to be a hundred!"

"As Frenchwomen," said Aimée, lifting her glass, "our good-will can hardly fly towards the English, who are now occupying our beloved Canada. But in the interest of peace—I have it!

Madeleine, you shall not toast, but half of us will, in the interest of universal love. To Tom Gage!"

"And to his brilliant victory at Bunker Hill!" added Weamish. Nicholas frowned.

"What brilliant victory?" he asked, setting down his glass.

"He doesn't know!" cried Weamish. "Come, come, you're jesting, sir."

"No, I protest. No jest intended. At Charlestown you mean?"

"I do mean at Charlestown, Mr. Mayhew, on Saturday, three days ago. Nonsense! You do know! Wait. Jenny! Jenny!"

Jenny came to the door; Weamish ordered her upstairs to his library—his "chambers"— to fetch the *Gazette and Post-Boy* lying on his desk. When she returned with the paper, Weamish opened it for Nicholas to read. The young man did so, half aloud, half mumbling.

"So that's the battle, is it?" said Nicholas in conclusion. "Upon my word, the engagement is so differently described in *The Spy* that I become confused."

Whereupon he produced a gazette of his own that stood out from one of his pockets.

"Rubbish!" cried Weamish. "*The Spy*! A well-deserved name. How came you by it, Mr. Mayhew?"

"I found it crumpled on the floor of the Custom Collector's office."

Aimée could say with perfect sincerity, "You pique my curiosity, Mr. Mayhew. Tell us more. What *really* happened at Charlestown?"

"Perhaps this Rebel sheet is lying, Marquise, but it reports that over a thousand Redcoats were killed or maimed."

"How dreadful!" cried out Madeleine, her hand rising to her mouth. A quick thought came and went in Nicholas' head as he glanced at the girl. "A lovely loving lass!" But Weamish was saying, "Stuff and nonsense! The Rebels were driven from the peninsula!"

"The writer," said Nicholas, pointing with his finger at the article in question, "manfully confesses it: an admission which throws some flickers of likelihood upon the rest of his account. And if the rest be true, the British are broken at Boston."

"Pah! Your gazette cannot impose on a rational observer. Trust me, my kindhearted mademoiselle, the rabble is not born that can slaughter the king's army in fair battle. But do I detect a note of glee in your voice, Mr. Mayhew?"

"Nothing of the sort. Long live King George, third of the name, and long may he rule over England."

Another opportunity for Aimée.

"I perceive," she said, "that my daughter and I must keep our opinions to ourselves while residing at Sherburne. Before you came in, Mr. Mayhew, and before I knew, indeed, where the Judge's allegiance lay, I spoke rather too freely in favor of liberty."

"They being French, you see," Weamish thought it wise to add. "But oh, had ever England a sweeter enemy?"

"You are a charmer, sir. I am beginning to feel quite at home in Nantucket."

"You will all remain for dinner, I hope. I shall give Jenny orders at once."

"Not I, thank you," said Nicholas. "I've accounts to settle with Obed Coffin—that's our cooper, Marquise, if I may use the low word."

"And we had better unpack and dine quietly in our rooms today, which we have barely glimpsed. Another time, Judge."

They were all rising from their chairs, when Jenny broke in again. It was decidedly a lucky day for Aimée, who was pondering, amidst all the niceties, the best way or ways of meeting and befriending her major prey; and there he was, being announced, and entering the room with a bow and a handshake with Nicholas. That he and the latter were related was immediately clear: a firm jaw, the straight shape of a nose, in both men, were sufficient to establish the resemblance. Introductions were made. Mayhew expressed the hope that the ladies would spend the summer on the island. "Not so," said Aimée; "as soon as my Madeleine is restored to full health—she's a delicate child, unlike her mother, who's as sturdy as a jailer's wife—we move to our place in Montreal and the good fight for our French liberties under the heavy-handed British yoke. But pardon my outburst. I am sure, Colonel, that you came on business."

"I did indeed. First, to have a word with the Judge about another wearisome dispute concerning a sack of forbidden tea, and second, to take Young Nick home, to pore over our bills of lading."

"Upstairs, to my library, sir," said Weamish. "Will you wait for us, my dear ladies?"

When the two men had left, Aimée shook her head. "Do remind me, Nicholas—may I call you Nicholas?"

"No, Marquise—unless you allow me to call your daughter Madeleine."

"Shall we petition her directly? Well, my child?"

"You may call me Madeleine, sir," said the girl shyly.

"This is a high privilege."

"Now Nicholas," said Aimée, "tell me about this wearisome tea. Why such pother about something so very quotidian?"

"Have you forgotten, mother?"

Needless to say, she had not (that naive daughter of hers!).

"I forget what I've forgotten. I know so little about your politics, Nicholas. This tea...."

"A symbol, Marquise, nothing more. Our brothers in Britain granted themselves a monopoly of the tea trade in the colonies—"

"Ah, now I remember."

"And the colonies object."

"You men! If you cannot make war over the gold mines of Peru, you will do it over a tea leaf."

"Tea leaf is perhaps unjust, Marquise. Our Whigs speak of Liberty."

"Are you a Whig, Mr. Mayhew?"

"Like yourself, Marquise, I forget. I attend to my bills of lading."

"You disappoint me. Or rather, I hope you are using discretion in front of two strangers, and there I commend you. I, who am here simply *de passage*, may freely confess that my heart pounds to the drums of liberty. But I pray you do not mention this to Judge Weamish, who, *entre nous*, appears to be an ultra on the Tory side."

"I promise to keep the peace between you and our excellent magistrate."

"Yes," said Aimée, who believed in reinforcing a won position, "were I a man, I would swim away from this island if need be and make for the hottest sector of the battlefield!"

"You too, Madeleine?" asked Nicholas, looking at the girl with some tenderness.

"I am an obedient daughter," she replied, smiling.

Upon the Judge and Mayhew reappearing, the little party finally broke up, with promises of further delightful meetings. Outside, as the Mayhews were helping the two ladies into their little carriage (Old Moses had fallen asleep sitting on the box, reins in hand), Nicholas exclaimed: "Why not an excursion as soon as you are both settled? While my dear uncle inspects barrels, sacks and hogsheads, I propose to take Old Moses' place and show you our windy island."

This was all the more readily accepted as it proved to Aimée that no immediate plot of escape existed (if any existed at all), and that her instructions to Sergeant Cuff could safely wait till tomorrow. After more niceties, uncle and nephew walked away while the chaise carried Aimée and Madeleine to the inn over the unpaved but decent Main Street. None had far to go. Swain's Inn looked at the waters just above the North Wharf, and the Mayhew residence, with its considerable counting-house in the rear, stood nearby in Oak Street. A chaise, in these circumstances, was meant for dignity rather than for convenience.

That Aimée and Madeleine were the only guests at the inn would have surprised no one in Nantucket. Visitors to the island were almost invariably relations or business friends, and these were given hospitality in homes as a matter of course. Swain's Inn catered principally to drinkers and diners, whether on the occasion of "important" meetings or without noble pretext. That was where Mr. Swain's chief interest and profit lay. Still, the house had some fine rooms, occupied, after all, now and then by a voyager and his family. The elegant strangers, greeted with homely courtesy, could count on sufficient comfort.

As soon as the two gentlemen were alone among passers-by, with most of whom they exchanged tippings of the hat, the Colonel said to Nicholas, speaking casually as if the subject were merely the weather: "The captain of the New York packet told me that the whale-ship *Enterprise* will be mooring offshore in the *very* near future. A dinghy will enter the harbor. One of the men in it will be our own Henry Wallace. They will ask to be directed to Obed Coffin so they can purchase a few barrels for their sloop."

Here the Colonel took his nephew's arm. "Henry," he continued, lowering his voice a little, "will give Obed important letters for us. That is all the captain knew."

"And here I came storming after the mail!" said Young Nick with suppressed excitement. "Uncle!" he whispered, "They want you in command against Boston."

"They can have me as a private," said Mayhew simply.

General Gage had been no fool to send Aimée on her mission.

4

COLONEL MAYHEW cared about his island's reputation for civilized courtesy and hospitality to newcomers and visitors. Besides, he could not fail to be fascinated by the mother and beguiled by the daughter. Accordingly, the morning after the ladies' arrival—but not unseemly early—he walked over to Swain's Inn and announced himself. Aimée graciously came downstairs, and the two went to sit in Swain's homely but honest parlor. Mayhew wished to know, in his and his nephew's names, whether the two women had rested and whether they found their accommodations satisfactory. "This is no château," he quipped. He found that all was well. A girl had been hired to serve the ladies, and Madeleine, it seemed, already looked healthier than but a week ago in New York.

The main purpose of the Colonel's visit, however, was to invite the ladies to tea at the Mayhew home that same late afternoon. It may be guessed that Aimée accepted with delight. "I do so want to see how you islanders live!" she exclaimed. Mayhew promised to introduce her to several of the leading Nantucket families. "I assure you that they will be as eager to meet you and your sweet daughter as you are to have a look at them."

After expressing her thankful sense of the kindness she was being shown in Nantucket so soon after her arrival, Aimée thought it wise to tell the Colonel that, "unavoidably," (as she put it), she had accepted Judge Weamish's invitation as well, namely for that very morning. "You are indeed becoming one of us!" he exclaimed as he left.

At eleven o'clock, as arranged, Aimée walked, parasol in hand, to the Judge's home, where Weamish and Sergeant Cuff awaited her.

The two men had been in conversation for some minutes in the parlor.

"Why should I be meeting with that Marquise of yours?" the Sergeant had wanted to know.

"You will be told in a few minutes, my friend; be patient," answered the Judge.

Not much interested—he thought that some social flummery was at hand—Cuff turned to the worries that beset him.

"I've but thirty men under me," he grumbled, "and two or three of them sick any day of the week. Everywhere we go we're surrounded by swarms of urchins. The urchins run ahead to warn their elders and by the time we reach a spot it's been swept clear of weapons and ammunition. Now, if your so-called Loyalists showed more spunk—"

"Most of the islanders—*many* of the islanders—are actively loyal, Sergeant. Need I remind you that half a dozen of our vessels are secretly supplying General Gage and Admiral Graves, at great risk to themselves?"

"What of it? You're giving us tuppence with one hand and picking our pocket with the other."

Just then Aimée was announced. She entered, brisk as she always was.

"No ceremony, please. Good morning, Judge. And Sergeant Cuff, no doubt, the man I needed to see." And, turning to Weamish, "Have you informed the Sergeant of my mission? Not yet, I hope."

"Not yet, Marquise."

"A mission? The foreign wench?" thought the nonplussed Sergeant, looking at Aimée in a new light.

The lady sat down, produced another, and gave it to the Sergeant. Unlike the Judge, Cuff did not leap up. He too was being informed that he must comply with any orders given him by the Marquise de Tourville. The notion of a Frenchwoman, noble or otherwise, being placed above him irked the Sergeant, but what could he do?

"Tell me, madam, what are Tom Gage's orders."

"You may or may not be aware, Sergeant, that the two Mayhew

gentlemen are former soldiers and that one of them was a sailor."

"I am not aware," said Cuff; "what then?"

"Well, they are now suspected of wanting to join the Rebels as officers in their army. It is our duty, mine, yours, that of the Judge, to discover whether this is true, and to arrest them if it is."

"And I," Cuff cried out, shooting up from his chair, his sword hitting one of its legs, "not a week ago—damnation!—I was asking the young one to help me find—and he said he would—I'll arrest them at once, damn my eyes! Good day!"

"You are not arresting anyone, Sergeant," said Aimée with perfect calm. "Not until I'm vastly more confident than I am now. Pray sit down again."

But Cuff would not sit; *that* little disobedience was a comfort. "I'm to twiddle my thumbs, am I," he cried, "while your rebels bubble the King of England? The house is burning, says Alexander Cuff; don't wait for the fire engine, man the buckets and pour!"

"What house is burning?" the Judge exclaimed. "You say this after our glorious victory at Charlestown?"

"Judge Weamish: with all due respect, you civilians are dreamers. We got trounced on the confounded hill, what d'you call it. Y'are a fool, let a soldier tell you."

"Sir!"

"A fool! Hang the pussyfooters!" And he looked straight at Aimée, who was now, as it happened, hugely interested.

"Sergeant Cuff, gently, gently will do it. Did we or did we not rout the Yankee mob?"

"First of all, my dear Marquise, with due respect once more, y'are a fool to talk about a mob. That mob bled us white afore they took leave of the peninsula. Y'are a friend of General Gage's are you? Then tell him from Sergeant Cuff, he has heard of me, tell the fine gentleman he'd be wise to clear out of Boston altogether, for he'll never set foot on another inch of Massachusetts soil. The fop hasn't so much as a good map of the country. He pinches actresses at the playhouse while the enemy is mustering. He waits for reinforcements from England instead of peppering the rebels from cock-crow till curfew. When he does fight them, what does he do? Climbs up the confounded hill in a frontal attack, because, don't you see, the enemy is nothing but a cowardly mob, show 'em your teeth and they'll run. Well, they forgot to run. They chopped us into little pieces and strolled away at their own sweet leisure."

"Is this true?" asked the dumbfounded Aimée of the Judge. "Is it then as Nicholas Mayhew suggested yesterday?"

"Aha; Nicholas Mayhew suggested, did he? He'll suggest from the jail-house as of today, him and his uncle, who smirked at me the other day. Without further ceremony—"

"No, Sergeant, I forbid it all the same."

"A Frenchwoman forbids Sergeant Cuff? Ha ha ha!"

Aimée stood up and went, so to speak, nose to nose with Cuff.

"In the name of Governor Gage," she said wrathfully, "I forbid you to arrest them. Disobey me at your peril. But you deserve an explanation, my friend."

Aimée took the Sergeant's hand, led him gently down to his chair again, and pulled her own close to his. "The Mayhew pair, you understand, have committed no illegal act. Arresting them at this point would turn a thousand Loyalists into as many Rebels and possibly get us nothing in return, if the two men are innocent. Governor Gage is interested in winning more hearts, not in making more enemies."

Weamish broke in. "The Colonel is one of our selectmen this year. An old, highly regarded family, with numberless influential relations, here and in Boston."

"When these courtesies are over, Judge, your colonies will have whistled off the King for good."

"In the meantime, Sergeant," Aimée resumed, "you are to set your men on patrol—discreetly—along the harbor, and also at other points from which the two men may try to sail. I myself shall pursue my inquiries. My daughter will be working on Young Nick; I shall attack the uncle. Never fear. I know my business."

"I take my leave," said Cuff, rising again. The tone was surly.

"Don't violate your instructions, Sergeant."

"I shan't touch either of the Mayhews. For the moment. Good day to you both."

And he was gone, slamming the door.

"Bear in mind, Marquise," said the Judge, "that our Sergeant is none too happy at having been posted by his superiors to the fringe of important events. Thoughts such as these cloud his perceptions."

"His perceptions look sufficiently clear to me," replied Aimée, in whose mind the Sergeant's words concerning the action at Boston kept resonating. The Judge's mind was running on other matters.

"Marquise," he said, "to distract us all from the tempests that agitate the land, I have decided to offer a ball in your honor this Saturday. If you would condescend—you and Mademoiselle Madeleine—to grace the soirée, it would, I assure you—"

"Let me cut you short, my dear Judge. Not to be rude—I am utterly grateful for your delicate attentions—but I came to Nantucket with an important charge. And remember: I must not appear cordial in my connection with you. Let us talk about dancing when our work is done."

"I defer to you, Marquise. Stern is the word for now."

5

THAT AFTERNOON Aimée and Madeleine shared a serving
of coffee and various sweet things with the uncle and nephew.
An immediate sympathy made them converse almost as intimate
friends. The two gentlemen had much to say about their ancestors
on the island, their own previous lives, the Colonel as soldier and
Nicholas as seaman, and their taking up the commercial line,
following their forebears, in '63, without however becoming ship-
owners. Aimée, on her side, entertained them with anecdotes
about her grandfather, the second Baron de Fapignac, who had
lost a leg fighting the British at the Battle of Blenheim, but not
without making the enemy pay dearly for that destroyed limb.
"Our antipathy for the English has roots, you see!" she exclaimed.
And later, at an appropriate moment: "Does not your heart beat
to take up arms again, but this time in the interest of Liberty?"
However, the Colonel only replied "Oh, yes," with the voice of a
man giving assent to a vague, remotely interesting philosophical
proposition. Still, it was a beginning.

The Colonel, as promised, made arrangements for the ladies
to meet with other good families of Nantucket. This was not
hard to do. A Marquise walking about town silked in pink and
blue, and alongside her a lovely girl with touches of yellow and
green, aroused enormous interest high and low on the island.
The Quaker women stared, some muttering about whores and
Babylon, others sighing forgiveness. Their husbands averted their
eyes, or pretended to. The Presbyterian ladies, on their side, would
not admit that they were surprised and outmatched in elegance;
the Marquise, as far as they were concerned, was one of their own,
though, of course, a Papist.

Thus the two women were happily received the day after for
coffee in the home of the Starbucks, where the Rotch and Folger

couple were also present. Clearly, they were all Whigs, but they seemed bent, the men on business, the women on Boston fashions. Interrogated about what was worn in France, Aimée had to confess her complete ignorance; *she* was dressed in old things from New York. Mr. Starbuck was a grandfather; Mr. Rotch limped; Mr. Folger was barrel-bellied; evidently, Tom Gage need not fear *them*. By contrast, the two Mayhews stood splendid among them, and (she thought) fearsome.

Still, the conversation could not help turning to the recent fighting around Boston, but listen as she did to undertones and implications, Aimée could find no hint of an intention to volunteer for battle on the Mayhew side, nor of some pertinent knowledge on the side of their friends. She was to find out, in the end, that the Mayhews had punctiliously kept their plans to themselves.

The Starbuck parlor prided itself on a spinet. When it was discovered that Madeleine could play and sing, the young woman gave them Handel's "There in myrtle shades reclined" with such sweetness that the tears swelled in the Colonel's eyes. Nicholas was deaf to music, but his eyes showed that he was alive to other charms a young woman can spread.

6

THE SUN SHONE the next day unperturbed by a few playful cloudlets strewn about the blue sky. Nicholas demanded that he be allowed to drive the French visitors around the island, as had been proposed the day of their arrival. But Aimée had other thoughts. An opportunity of "launching" Madeleine at one of the suspects—obviously attracted to the girl—was too good to neglect. Accordingly, she pleaded fatigue and a mild headache, and the two young people, expressing half-insincere regrets, set off by themselves in Young Nick's carriage, she sitting beside him on the driver's seat.

Young Nick showed the girl meadows and ponds, gardens and well-tended farmlands, a couple of windmills, the old villages of Sesachacha and Siasconset (where they lunched), sheep and cows in abundance, and from a hillock, in the limpid distance, beyond the harbor's lighthouse, two whaling-boats a-sailing. Nicholas gestured toward the east, toward Europe. "They have cathedrals, we have cod, they have palaces, we have peat," he said smiling and chuckling. Madeleine, on her side, was happy to breathe an air freed from the odor of whale oil which only visitors noticed, reminding them of the main source of the island's wealth, and happy in the company of the young man, who spoke with modest pride of the Mayhew family, to which the island had been deeded in 1641.

At Siasconset, they met with four Redcoats who were digging with picks and shovels at the foot of a windmill. Madeleine wanted to know what they were looking for. "Ammunition," said Nicholas, "not buried doubloons!" Of course, he was urged to elaborate, and he did so imitating Sergeant Cuff's speech and manners. "The other day, it may have been a week ago, Sergeant Cuff found me slaking my morning thirst in Swain's tap room. 'Young Nick,' a says, 'you and your uncle must help a fellow soldier. I know y'are kith and kin with the natives here, but then again y'ave travelled, y'ave fought for your King, y'ave killed your share of Frenchmen from the Carolines to Quebec. Now comes the time again to show whether there's blood or muck in your veins.' " Nicholas' imitation of Cuff made Madeleine laugh, and he continued: "That's a mighty diplomatic speech, Sergeant Cuff," says I. Says he, and you must excuse the language, 'True by God's gut—I'm brushing your fur a bit, but I've heard about you, Nick. Before you took to sailing the seas you was an ensign at Montreal—you wasn't shaving yet—and you fought the savages near Niagara Falls when General Amherst was commanding.' And he adds, 'I can name you the officers of every regiment that's been raised since the French wars began in the year fifty-four.' 'Well,' I replied, 'that's all water long ago under the bridge. What's on your mind, Sergeant?' He leans forward and whispers, 'Look you, my friend: sure as my mother bore me, I know there's powder, flints and bullets stowed away in a dozen holes up and down the island. And they're not meant for shooting whales, says Sergeant Cuff.' That 'says Sergeant Cuff,' by the way, was Sergeant Cuff saying it, not I saying it to you. The Sergeant likes to conclude his remarks with 'says Sergeant Cuff.' "

"Well," asked Madeleine, "was he right? What did you say to him?"

"I said, 'Why should anyone be hiding ammunition? Our island is defenceless. Three of your frigates could level every house upon it, and never a man living on the mainland would lift a finger to help us.' "

"You answered his question with a question. That was clever of you."

"And it was clever of you to notice."

"Well, I am a noticer. How did the Sergeant respond?"

"Forcefully. 'You tell this to the whaling crews, young Nick—do—they need to hear it. Because all the same they're making cartridges, and there's many a cache under a windmill or a

meeting-house that could tell a tale on my side.' And that, my dear
Madeleine, is what these men are looking for. I had to promise the
Sergeant that as loyal sons of Britain my uncle and I would make
discreet inquiries and report to him."

"And you did?" asked Madeleine mischievously.

"Enough about politics!" cried the young man as he made
Old Moses trot away from the scene. "Your life interests me far
more." And he questioned her closely—he was, in fact, truly
interested—about her life in Montreal and New York. Madeleine
spoke much of schoolfriends and of the towns; she mentioned that
she was immersing herself in the French classics in order not to
forget her first language; but asked about the Tourville family, she
only laughed and said, "For such high matters, you must query my
mother," and then added, taking refuge in a generalization, "One
can be noble yet poor." Nicholas took the liberty of squeezing
her hand. All the same, "Not Indian-poor" he mused, thinking of
Aimée's silks and brocades.

7

THAT EVENING, Amée questioned Madeleine closely about her excursion with Nicholas. What had she found out? Had he hinted at work to be done by the Mayhew pair on the mainland? No, no hint. That his heart was with the Patriots, of that there was no doubt, but Gage was not interested in their hearts. Madeleine could report on no sign of a projected flight from the island. Aware of her daughter's own Whiggish sympathies, Aimée was not altogether sure that the girl would have mentioned hints and signs. Obvious moves she could hardly, in good conscience, have concealed from her mother, but she might have decided not to hear a word or two uttered by the young man. In the end, Aimée could trust only herself.

By the next day, summer clouds had gathered over Nantucket. A great storm was churning over sea and land. In the early afternoon, heavy raindrops were making the Redcoats watching Sherburne and Madaket harbors uncomfortable. Aimée contrived to be drenched very near the Mayhews' house and asked for refuge with a hundred apologies. She was received with pleasure. The housekeeper Priscilla lit a fire and prepared a collation. Aimée looked around for signs of imminent escape and saw not a single open portmanteau standing guiltily in a corner. In the midst of a thundering storm, she was drinking the chocolate and eating the cake of a well-ordered, peaceful merchants' dwelling. Suddenly a series of violent knocks shook the front door and they heard the voice of a boy who was yelling "Man overboard! Man overboard!" Nicholas yanked the door open; a flood of rain accompanied the boy, who kept yelling "Man overboard! Man overboard!"

With a sudden foreboding of disaster, the Colonel and Nicholas rushed out, followed by Aimée, the Mayhew's clerk Abishai Cottle, who had run in from the counting house in the rear, and even Priscilla and Ruth the cook. Nicholas had just had time to find a spyglass. They did not have far to go. At the wharf, a crowd had rushed to see, in the distance, a rowboat with two seamen at the oars struggling against the waves and at the same time trying to save a fellow seaman fallen into the water and flailing helplessly about. From the nearby inn, Madeleine came running. She had been reading *Athalie* in her room when the clamor had roused her. On her way out, she stumbled against Sergeant Cuff, wiping his moustache after drinking his pint of ale in the tap room. Madeleine ran through the shouting and waving crowd to join her mother. A violent rain was rushing from the black clouds, thunders rolled and fearful lightning zigzagged after the rolling and roiling noise.

Pushing their way to the edge of the dock, uncle and nephew peered into the darkness of thunder, wind and rain. Young Nick trained the spyglass at the head bobbing about the water. "It's Wallace! Damn damn damn!" he whispered into the Colonel's ear, while the crowd shouted "He's lost! Where is he now? He's gone for sure! There he bobs again!" and Cuff cried out "Who'll save him? Dive in! I can't swim! Cowards all!"

Nicholas had not needed Cuff's shouts (which in any case he could not hear across the roaring crowd) to thrust the spyglass, his doublet and his shoes into Cottle's hands and to dive into the water. A great clamor went up on all sides. Mayhew closed his fists in fear. Madeleine uttered small cries. Aimée was speechless. And Nicholas swam and swam, shoving the waves aside. Fortunately, Wallace—Young Nick had not been mistaken—managed to grasp one of the oars. But the two sailors were unable to lift the exhausted man—more used to handling contracts than fighting the ocean— into the boat. It took Nicholas, when he reached the boat, to give the final push that lifted Wallace to safety. He himself was strong enough, of course, to swing himself, with the sailors' help, into the boat as well, and presently they were all on land, surrounding the half-unconscious Wallace lying on his back on the wharf.

A Nantucket constable arrived. He interrogated the two
sailors, who informed them that the man's name was Tom Bates,
and that the three of them had orders to purchase a set of barrels
for the *Enterprise*. The rain still pouring, the crowd began to
disperse, while Wallace was carried by the two sailors, helped by
Cottle, to the entrance-way of the inn, followed by the drenched
Mayhew gentlemen, the two Frenchwomen, Priscilla, Ruth, and
Sergeant Cuff. Now, lying on the ground on a blanket Mr. Swain
had supplied, he was clutching, in his half consciouness, a pouch
that was hanging from his neck, held by strong twine. Aimée had
never been more attentive. "This fellow is at least fifty years old,"
she muttered to herself; "what was he doing in that boat?" ("*Que
fichait-il dans cette galère?*" were the actual words that went through
her head.) Madeleine, instead, saw only Nicholas. "You must dry
yourself, you must, you must!" she kept crying, though she badly
needed drying herself. "I will, my dear, I swear," he replied, "but
first we must take care of this poor seaman."

"Why is he holding that pouch so hard?" Aimée wanted to
know. "Let us look at it."

The Colonel grasped the pouch in an instant, managed to
pry it open, gave a quick look and proclaimed, "It's the picture of a
woman. Naturally! Well! We shall move him to my house, which
by God's mercy is next door to that of Dr. Phelps." And the pouch
slipped into his pocket.

Aimée, who wanted the man to remain at the inn, could
think of no objection to raise, though she strongly felt that
mischief was in the air. Not so Sergeant Cuff, who quickly lost
interest, shrugged his shoulders and returned to his unfinished
pint of beer. The two sailors declared that if Tom Bates proved too
weak to return to their ship, he could remain on Nantucket island
and rejoin them upon their return voyage. And there the episode
ended. The Nantucket folk were used to the likes of it. No one had
recognized Wallace; he was in fact almost entirely unknown on
the island, which he had visited from the mainland but twice in

five years. Only Madeleine remained with tears in her eyes at such danger and such bravery, while Mayhew, Cottle, the extremely wet but hale Nicholas, assisted by Ruth, carried the false Tom Bates to the Mayhews' house, Priscilla carrying the young man's doublet and shoes.

8

THAT EVENING, as Aimée and Madeleine sat at supper in their rooms, and the young woman grew expansive on matters heroic, her mother only muttered, "A strange affair, a strange affair...."

"Why strange?" Madeleine wanted to know. "The only thing strange was the scene of courage we saw."

"Look at you! *Dieu me damne!* You've fallen in love with that American Leander."

Madeleine's tone was playful. "Why do you say that, mother? Didn't you order me to be friendly with the suspects?"

"Pooh! I've never yet seen you so keen to do your duty."

"Don't scold me, maman! You must admire him too. How brave he was! For the sake of an absolute stranger—no one else so much as removed his coat—and he plunges in—swims like a Neptune—"

"Swims like a Neptune! A duck can swim as well. Now we're in love with a fellow because he can swim."

"Have it your way."

"As for being selfless—"

"To be sure. This seaman is a pasha in disguise who will leave his millions to Nicholas."

"He may leave him something more important. Seaman be hanged! You must be blind, my girl! Thank goodness I know how to snap at details."

"What details?"

"You weren't struck by that sealskin pouch? How worried he was about it?"

"It was lovely of him to think of his sweetheart or his wife the moment he came to."

"The girl's determined to be an idiot! To think that I raised you on Plutarch and Tacitus! I don't suppose you noticed how anxious the Colonel was to dive into that pouch."

"You're right; I didn't notice."

"And you didn't think it was odd that a common seaman should be wearing a silk shirt with ruffled wrist bands that peeped out under his smock; mind you, got up like a man of condition when he was out rowing a dinghy to take on a barrel of whale oil or whatever. And that a man his age should be put out to sea in a storm to pick up supplies? Silly details, of course. But details, my dear girl, make all the difference between a master and an apprentice. Without details I'd still be Madame Pichot selling keys in Montreal."

"I would have been glad to remain plain Mademoiselle Pichot, and run your key shop for you, mother. Such a life!"

"You have a low mind. Chin up, curls in place, tidy drawers, and an eye that can pick out a flea in the fur of a dog at fifty paces: that's how a woman makes her way in the world."

"I wish I had your fire—but I can't manage it."

"Well, you're a goose—or a kitten by somebody's fireplace. But not Nicholas Mayhew's fireplace—not if he is what I think he is."

"Namely?"

"A rebel officer in the making. He and his uncle both. So my nose tells me. I'm tempted to look no farther and order the Sergeant to arrest them and ship them off to Gage. But I daren't yet, because if God forbid I'm mistaken, my five hundred pounds are gone and Gage crosses me from his books. Never! I mean to work for him—wherever they send him in the colonies." Here Aimée, buttering a slice of bread, became thoughtful. "Still, if the low truth ever peeps out, as I hope it won't, we'll sail back to France in state and settle in Lyon like pigeons come home to roost. I'll be plain Madame Pichot again. Not so plain, after all, and nicely rich. I'll marry you off to a steady barrister, and I'll engage two or three pretty footmen to keep the dust from settling on me."

"Let me teach schoolchildren instead of marrying the barrister."

"How did I ever beget this marshmallow of a child? Well, dreaming never filled a purse. I must look into that so-called seaman, and you must go on petting Mr. Nicholas. That's not too painful a task, is it?"

"Now it is."

"Twaddle! You're to tickle the truth out of him, d'you hear, whether by godly means or otherwise. Five hundred pounds! Your mother forgives you in advance."

9

AT ABOUT THE TIME mother and daughter were conversing over chops and wine, William Mayhew and Young Nick read the letters they had taken from Wallace's pouch, while the poor castaway was yet half asleep on a sofa in the parlor, well dried and covered with a blanket. Nicholas, sneezing a great deal, had of course quickly changed clothes. The little group had made its way from the wharf to the Mayhew house without incident, escorted by ten or twelve well-wishers. The house on Oak Street was quickly reached, the door sharply shut on unwanted curiosity. As Wallace could fit into into the younger Mayhew's clothing, he was quickly stripped naked, dried, and clad, and gently given some rum to drink. He promptly fell asleep. Priscilla was asked to keep an eye on him while Ruth was preparing supper for all. Abishai Cottle, though never was a man more trusted by his employers, was sent to Dr. Phelps for consultation. Finally the two men went into the counting-house, where Mayhew took the pouch out of his pocket and carefully reopened it. Two sealed letters were in it, both blessedly dry, one addressed to Colonel Mayhew, the other to Lieutenant Nicholas Mayhew. The men spoke low, as if fearing to be overheard.

"You first, uncle; break the seal and read and tell me whatever you wish me to know."

The letter was opened. Mayhew's hand trembled. He read in silence, Young Nick's eyes darted on his. Then, solemnly, Mayhew lowered the letter and said: "It is written to me by *General* Washington. My old friend has been promoted. I am asked to accompany General Schuyler into Canada."

"Into Canada? That *is* news!"

"We took it away from France, and now we must take it away from England. Here are the words. 'Our capture of Fort Ticonderoga on the 26th of May has encouraged the Congress to strike boldly into Canada. General Schuyler has been appointed to lead the northern expedition. He will not pause until Montreal and Quebec have fallen into our hands and our Canadian brethren are embraced into the common cause. Your task, my dear friend, will be to assist General Schuyler as his brigadier.' "

"Brigadier! Dear Friend! *General* Mayhew! This should be sung by a choir!"

"Hush. There's more. Listen to this. 'I entreat you to meet me at Cambridge in the first days of July, for I may as well make known to you here and now what you shall undoubtedly be reading in the gazettes, to wit that the Congress has seen fit to entrust me, for the time being, with the defense of our sacred interests. I am proceeding immediately to Cambridge to take command of the army surrounding Boston.' "

Nicholas jumped up. "Blow, ye trumpets!" he shouted, laughing.

"But not too loud! For at the end of the letter Washington recommends caution and secrecy. 'There is a rumor here that you are being spied upon. The Tory element on your island is strong. Shroud your departure from Nantucket in secrecy.' "

"We will! Uncle—to think Wallace might have drowned!"

"*Your* letter, sir, *your* letter now."

Nicholas had been hesitant about opening his letter in the Colonel's presence—the reason will appear shortly—but now he did so and read aloud: " 'You, Nicholas Mayhew, may, as captain of a man-of-war, by force of arms, attack, subdue, and take all ships and other vessels belonging to the inhabitants of Great Britain. You shall—' and so forth. Just as I had hoped, uncle! My years at sea are remembered. Ah! They can count on me!"

"May God bless our cause," said Mayhew simply, unafraid of expressing high thoughts.

They looked in on Wallace, and discovered that he was now awake and that Priscilla's ministrations had made him perfectly ready for supper and talk. He said much, to begin with, of his gratitude to Nicholas, who reciprocated with like gratitude to the agent. "Indeed," added Mayhew, "impossible to think of you as our agent. As anything except a most precious and reliable friend."

"I don't know what to say, Colonel," said Wallace, much moved. "Mine is a family of humble clerks—" and then his eyes teared, and arms and hands were tightened around three pairs of shoulder.

But Wallace had brought verbal news or commands along with the letters. Again Nicholas had to cry out "Uncle, if he had drowned!" It was now specified that within a week or so the same whale-ship *Enterprise*, under Captain Fleming's command, was to return to Nantucket, but bringing the vessel this time round the island and dropping anchor off the south coast between Weweeder and Nobadeer Pond. Fleming would wait for light signals from the little beach, telling him that all was well and that the two men would be rowing out to the ship in short order.

And vanish from the island for who could tell how long? The three men decided there and then that after the Mayhews' flight to the mainland, Wallace and Cottle were to run the business until peace returned to the land—a matter, they thought, of a year or so, but could one really tell? Wallace was a bachelor. Terms were made attractive to him, and to be sure, the new assignment was a step up for the man. Furthermore, should the Mayhews' flight be successful—and it appeared to be an uncomplicated if discreet operation—it would no longer matter that Wallace suddenly turned from being an unfortunate sailor to an associate of Mayhew & Mayhew.

But it was time for bed. A room was ready for the agent. "Henry," said Mayhew as they parted for the night, "few people know you on the island. All the same, for the time being I recommend more time indoors than outdoors for you."

10

NEXT MORNING proved to be a true early summer day, and after Sunday service, Colonel Mayhew mounted his horse for an innocent ramble to the south shore, followed by Josh Mamack in his cart, loaded already with logs and twigs for the future blaze. The two seamen (they had been lodged in a modest inn in Summer Street) met with Obed Coffin that same morning, purchased two barrels (not really needed by the *Enterprise*), and thus completed their mission. A Nantucket lad promptly rowed them back to the ship.

Mayhew's absence was a boon to Young Nick, who had much to hear from Wallace out of his uncle's earshot. Priscilla had set breakfast for the agent in the dining room, but the man slept long and deep. Nicholas was waiting for him at table when he finally appeared, excusing himself.

"Eat and speak!" cried Nicholas.

And here, between fresh eggs, bacon, toast and coffee, is more or less what Wallace reported, halting only at a sign from Young Nick when Priscilla appeared. A Mayhew relation, a certain Mr. Pigeon, presently commissary general for Massachusetts, promised to purchase whatever Nicholas—were he given a brig to command—would capture. "He'll purchase lace doilies for the Army," said Wallace, "if lace doilies is what you take at sea. We were sitting in a private room at the City—that's the tavern of our true-hearted Whigs when the speechifying has made them thirsty—and he was laughing till the tears rolled from his eyes and his belly bobbed like a lifebuoy. Doilies and diapers, he kept repeating, Cousin Pigeon will buy for Massachusetts! You can't miss, Mr. Mayhew."

"He gave you nothing in writing?"

"Pigeon don't put anything in writing except birthday wishes to his mother. So he said, sir."

"But is Fillmore going to believe this in Salem? Verbal promises reported at second hand?"

"The question occurred to me, sir. Pigeon agreed to send a trusted messenger to Salem; the man will tell Fillmore what I have told you. Nothing in writing."

"That will have to do. And Pigeon himself—what are his terms?"

"Ten percent; plus an eighth share in Mr. Davis' chocolate mill."

"An eighth? You didn't agree, did you? A full eighth?"

"I argued; ordered more rum; but Mr. Pigeon is quite above rum. It was an eighth or nothing. 'Young Nick ain't the only cannon in the Atlantic,' says he. I must report honestly, Mr. Mayhew."

"You must indeed. An eighth it shall be. I need him more than he needs me, damn his bloated belly!"

"There you are."

"And on a Sunday the wise man knoweth how to give in order to take. The pieces are falling into place, Wallace! Christ—if we'd lost you yesterday! One missing nail will bring an empire down."

Here Young Nick took a letter from his pocket. It was in the hand of Mr. Davis, owner of the chocolate mill. It concerned Mrs. Applegate at Concord, and informed Nicholas of a very important point, namely that she had the legal power to sell "every blessed acre" which that most Tory of couples owned in and around town. It also mentioned that Mrs. Applegate was suffering many vexations being alone at Concord as the wife of a fugitive Loyalist. One or two more frights, said Mr. Davis, and she would sell for ten shillings in the pound. Davis had her confidence and would buy for Nick when the time was ripe. "I'll make it ripe once I arrive," said the young man, waving the letter. "But not a word... to anyone," Nicholas added, looking significantly up toward the Colonel's part of the house.

Shortly thereafter, Abishai Cottle came in for work, and the three men went into the counting house, mostly to make Wallace familiar with the firm's daily routine. After an hour or so, Nicholas returned to his rooms and prepared to set off for his daily brisk walk along the seashore. He took "staying fit" seriously. Glancing out the parlor window to look at the sky—the June sun was shining and the ground was dry—he suddenly noticed, at the corner of Main Street, Madeleine stopped as if undecided whether to continue her walk (presumably) on Main or turn into Oak Street, where the only possible goal would be the Mayhew place. She stood there for a moment, her parasol twirling slowly, then stepped resolutely into Oak Street. Nicholas jumped back from the window.

A torrent of thoughts raced through his mind. Her beauty, her coming to inquire after his well-being after the great event of yesterday, her inclination for him, but also something grander, something utterly new, as it may happen, once in a lifetime, that at the flicker of some unexpected sight or event, a magnificent world unsuspected until that moment opens suddenly in a man's mind. "The daughter of a Marquise! My bride! Be bold, Nicholas, be bold!"

He had time to look at himself in a mirror hanging in the small vestibule and ascertain that he was presentable, and then the doorbell rang. "I'll open, Priscilla!" he shouted to the upstairs.

"I spied you coming this way, dear Madeleine," he spoke before she said a word. "Welcome again under our roof. Come in, come in, come in!" He led the girl into the parlor and invited her to sit in a comfortable armchair. For himself, he took a footstool and sat at her knees.

"Thank you. I came because my mother and I are ever so anxious about you. After that terrible swim. That storm. So much danger. But you seem to be well."

"You are so kind. I did sneeze a few times. And I slept rather more hours than usual. But you find me fit to swim from here to Martha's Vineyard."

"And the seaman?"

"Still a bit unsteady. My uncle feels that we should keep him until he is quite himself again."

"I hope he is grateful to you."

"Oh yes—but, my dear—" and this seemed like a fair occasion for taking Madeleine's hand in his. She pulled a little but did not withdraw it. Young Nick's voice became very soft. "My dearest Madeleine (if I may), what I did yesterday is an everyday occurrence among us. We live from the sea, and alas we are apt to die in the sea. These rescues are like helping someone from an overturned carriage in Paris."

"And yet, who else threw himself into these monstrous waves—and for a stranger? Don't say any more; I shall believe in you, Nicholas."

Nicholas took the plunge. His voice grew even softer.

"Forever?"

She withdrew her hand.

"Forever? What do you mean?"

"Madeleine—I cannot be near so much beauty—such grace—so much tender regard—without saying 'Forever.' "

He had stood up saying this, taken both her hands, and drawn her gently to him. She only half resisted.

"This is not why I came," she whispered, "believe me—do believe me."

But Nicholas was not listening. He kissed her. She allowed him. She kissed him most tenderly in return. He gently made her sit down again, and again sat on the footstool holding her hand.

"Madeleine," he said, "we have met only three or four times—"

And already she had kissed him! "You despise me!" she exclaimed.

"Angel of heaven! My presumption is what makes me tremble. You will think me rash—brutal—to ask you—after so brief an acquaintance—but war is impatient. Would you be a sailor's bride—take your share of my hardships and rewards—sail with me to the end of the world—"

"I would, Nicholas, and I say it because it can never be. If I came here, it was to warn you."

"You're trembling, my angel."

"To warn you," she repeated. "You have allowed me to guess that you are Whigs, you and your uncle."

Politics at this high moment? Nicholas' eyes opened wide. "Of course, yes," he said somewhat hesitantly.

"Forgive a silly girl, a stranger, a passer-by, for meddling to no purpose. But—beware, I beg you, beware!"

Nicholas was puzzled; the conversation was taking a strange turn, and going astray of his bold purpose.

"How is it you know so much, Madeleine? Because I rattled away about this and that while showing you our island?"

"Yes. And then, I have been hearing rumors, tales...."

"Our tavern's a fine place for that! But rest assured. The island is half Whig, half Tory, and we live in peace."

"True. But with you—there is a difference."

"Why? Why is there a difference?"

How to reveal and yet not to betray? She whispered "Don't speak of... *things* ... before my mother. She—she is quite wonderful, but not always...discreet. Do you understand?"

"I do, trust me."

Madeleine rose as if to leave, but Nicholas gently detained her.

"You shall not go with tears in your eyes." He made her sit again and held her two hands in his. "Calm yourself, lovely, kind Madeleine. I'll not babble in front of your mother, I promise. She is so very lively! I understand. I shall speak to her only about us, Madeleine and Nicholas. Or will you become simple Madelyn in our homely English?"

He had pronounced his own name in the French manner.

"It can never be, Nicholas, never never never."

"Because of your rank?"

"No no no...."

"How little you know about this America of ours! Between you and me I recognize neither moat nor wall. Here we begin fresh, as in a new Garden of Eden."

"I know. But—"

"Don't answer yet. Will you listen to me a little while longer?"

"Of course."

"You land among us for a few days of rest. You discover our unpolished seamen and farmers, so different from the elegance you have known. No fine carriages, no jewels, no mansions—"

"How wrong you are! I—"

"But you haven't probed beneath the surface. Let me tell you my story. When I'm done, you shall lead me proudly to the fearsome Marquise, and I trust that she will give us her blessing."

"Never, my dear, never."

But Nicholas was not listening. It was common knowledge that young ladies feigned reluctance. Besides, he had plunged, and he must, and he wanted to, complete the plunge.

"The man I rescued yesterday was our agent."

Madeleine's mouth opened. She stared at Nicholas and then brought out, "And you knew it?"

"Of course."

Something came into Madeleine's eyes that would have alarmed Nicholas had he not been intent on the plunge.

"We were expecting him with important messages from the mainland. They proved even more important than we thought. I love you, Madeleine. I will tell you my deepest secrets."

"Don't," she whispered." But he was listening only to himself, plunging.

"We have been summoned, my uncle and I, to meet the new commander-in-chief at Cambridge."

"If my mother heard this!" was the thought that crossed Madeleine's mind. But what she said was, "To do God's work."

"I knew you would think so. I am nothing now, Madeleine, but the doors are opening to me. Your Nicholas is now a privateer."

"What is a privateer?"

"Almost a pirate!"

"I understand—a *corsaire*—for your people's sake."

"Yes. But this is only the first link. At Salem a great man is waiting for me. He wants to equip the brigantine which is to sail under my command. My private share of the booty is an entire fifth, Madeleine, nothing to be sneered at. But now comes my second man. A gentleman in a high place in the army, who undertakes to purchase whatever I capture, sight unseen, lock, stock, and barrel. Do you follow me?"

"I think so," said the girl faintly.

"My third man is a banker in Philadelphia. The moment I have got my first two winnings in my pocket, he will advance me, what shall I call it? a majestic sum of money. And then—"

"You will be a nabob."

"We shall see! A year ago, when the Parliament ruined our sea trade, I joined in an expedition against the Shawnees, deep in the West—"

"Did you kill many Indians, Nicholas?"

"Kill or be killed. And they have nearly killed me more than once! At Niagara Falls—but that's another story. In Virginia I met a fascinating person—a Judge Henderson—I can't tell you all the particulars now, Madeleine, but they're magnificent! Henderson bought land from the savages for next to nothing—a few pounds sterling—a sack of trinkets—plenty of rum, too! More land than your French king possesses. Tell me, how well do you know our country?"

"I'm very ignorant."

"Have you heard of the Kentucky, the Ohio, the Cumberland?"

"Yes. They are mountains and provinces."

"They are also rivers. With land in between. A country unto itself. We've given it a noble name—Transylvania—and in that country Henderson is holding a splendid tract for me. No one knows about this, Madeleine, except you."

"And your uncle."

"I should say not! Not about this nor about anything else I
have told you. He has more important concerns. *General* Mayhew
is going to lead an army. You needn't be ashamed of us, you see.
But where was I?"

"Your land, and the savages."

"I am entrusting you with my secrets, Madeleine."

"They will die with me," said the girl, but the image of her
mother's face took space in her mind. She felt a strong wish to stop
Nicholas, but strong too was her curiosity. As for Young Nick,
why, he had never spoken, never revealed, never discoursed, never
had a confidante, and now, joyously completing the plunge before
a charming girl, he exulted in his vision.

"Land!" he cried, holding her hand, "Land and more land!
You and I will be lord and lady! Your princes of the blood will
come and kiss our hands. But Henderson wants hard cash on the
table. And that is why I forged that long beautiful chain."

"You're extraordinary" was all Madeleine would say.

"With special beauties in it. An estate at Concord, a chocolate
mill . . . But we'll not live in Massachusetts, you and I. Virginia is
the place for us."

"Why?"

"Because you'll feel at home there. They will treat you as you
deserve. You'll be waited upon by a retinue of glistening Blacks.
Oh Madeleine, I've been prating like a fool this half hour—sordid
mercantile affairs, but how else could you learn that we are not
unworthy of you? I love you. You are as beautiful—"

"As the chain you forged?" she asked with a sad smile.

"The chain is to bind you with," was his tender reply.

Madeleine gently withdrew her hand.

"Nicholas, I'm a little dizzy."

"And I'm a boor! I haven't even offered you—"

"A glass of water will do. My mother is expecting me for

dinner."

Nicholas called Ruth, who brought a pitcher of water and a glass from the kitchen. "Such marvelous stories," said Madeleine, and again Nicholas failed to hear the sadness in her voice. "Only in America can one hear such stories. I feel so old. Let me go back now to my inn."

"But have I no answer from you? No hint? No kind word? I must be gone within days, and I love you. But are we still not worthy of you?"

Of course, she wanted to cry out, "Are we worthy of *you*?" but she said, "My mind is troubled. Except for this, Nicholas: Your secrets are safe with me. But not with everybody. Remember the one important thing I said when I came to your house."

"Which one, Madeleine?"

"Not to speak—"

"Before your gossipy—"

And she was gone, more troubled than he could guess. He was not untroubled himself as he watched her from a window. "I babbled and babbled," he thought. "Was this a blunder? No, the French are with us. And though I worship her, that was love in her blue eyes too, and love on her thirsty lips, as sure as fish can swim."

11

MADELEINE DID NOT know that her mother, from the top floor of the inn, had seen her turn from Main into Oak street and understood that she was going decidedly toward the Mayhew house, obviously out of concern for Nicholas. She had to admit to herself that this time, Madeleine might do better work than her mother.

Soon after, Aimée strolled to the fruit and vegetable market, where she bought a peach and ran into Ruth, the Mayhew cook who also helped Priscilla in her household chores. Ruth was an elderly, cheerful, chubby, red-cheeked woman born and raised on a Nantucket farm. Being talked to—affably, too!—by a French marquise was destined to be entered as a choice page in the book of her memory. Their talk was of fruit and vegetable, of prices, of market customs, of Ruth's duties, of the fine Mayhew house, and then Aimée asked, "If the Mayhew men decide to travel, will you be going with them?" To which Ruth replied, "Oh no, not I, madam, not at my years!" But Aimée realized suddenly that she ought to have asked "when," not "if." It was too late.

Returning to her rooms, she was glad and eager when she heard her daughter climb the stairs. Let dinner wait! She must hear Madeleine out. "I know where you have been," she said as the girl was taking off her hat. "How is the charming young man?"

"Oh, Mr. Mayhew is quite well. A little sneezing, he told me, no other consequence."

"Did you see the so-called seaman? This is capital."

"I did not."

"Did you notice any signs of an imminent departure? Locked armoires, curtains drawn, a portmanteau or two ready for a journey?"

This was a difficult moment.

"No, mother, nothing."

"So you babbled about swimming and accomplished nothing."

"Oh, I don't know." Madeleine paused and then took *her* plunge. "Nicholas Mayhew proposed to me."

Aimée stared. Was she—No! she was serious!

"Nick Mayhew *proposed* to you? What—what made him...?"

She felt too late that the question was less than flattering, but Madeleine took no notice.

"I suppose because he likes me. He likes my noble lineage too."

"A miracle has happened! Suddenly the girl's an expert! Come here, Madelon!" and she hugged her daughter. "You'll make your fortune after all. I take back the marshmallow. Tell me all about it, and don't leave out the erotic details, you naughty baggage!"

"Well, he wants to marry me. We talked for a long time. He was very wild, very eloquent, but of course my rank made him keep his distance—most of the time."

"If he talked so much, he must have given you what we require to deliver him and his uncle to Gage."

"He did not, mother; he talked of other things altogether. I can tell you that Mr. Mayhew is a man with a very large future."

"A firing squad is not a future."

"I'm not so sure about the firing squad. He has a very keen mind for business, mother. I wish you'd been there to listen to his projects. A brigantine under his command; an estate at Concord; huge tracts of land in the West; a chocolate mill; shiny slaves; bankers urging loans and credits upon him—I tell you my head was spinning. I kept thinking how much you'd have enjoyed it."

"And why was he giving you this inventory?"

"To convince the daughter of the Marquise de Tourville that she wouldn't be taking a dreadful tumble down the social ladder."

"He may have been bragging."

"Such details, such confirmations! No, he was extremely not

bragging."

This prompted Aimée to go to the door, open it, look about on landing and staircase, shut the door again, pull Madeleine down into an armchair, and continue in a voice gone much lower.

"Madeleine," she said, "this is serious. Stupendously serious. I am ready to forestall that British bully of a sergeant and strike. But which way? Aren't we blinding ourselves to the wider landscape? To hear Sergeant Cuff talk, the Yankees are not the sheep we've been told they are. And the Mayhew men prove him right. There must be thousands of these sturdy rogues arming up and down the continent. Providence may have placed the uncle and nephew in our path to show us we were about to commit a terrible sin. If you married Nicholas...."

"You would betray Tom Gage, your employer, your... whatever? Is that quite correct, my dear mother?"

"Quite correct. Tom Gage is a man of the world. And I need to provide for you."

"Thank you, mother. Yet I don't want to marry Mr. Mayhew."

"Why in heaven not? Handsome, rich, a hero, a rebel!"

"A rebel, mother, whom you intend to deliver to a firing squad?"

"A rebel with a ship of his own, and land in the West, and confirmations, is no rebel until I've made up my mind."

"You're a whirlwind, mother! One moment we're arresting Nicholas and the next we're marrying him. *I* say let's leave the island. No plots, no machinations this time, no marriage, no wretched five hundred. Please, mother. General Gage will have other work for you wherever we go."

"There is nothing wretched about five hundred pounds. Yet I may let them go. Tell me, did he go too far, was he gross, is that what troubles you?"

Madeleine smiled. "Far from it. He remained a true gentleman."

"Then I may be obliged to make you change your mind. Or

not. I need time to think. To think profoundly."

Whereupon she rose and rang the bell for dinner.

Afterward Aimée took her wonted nap—it was good for one's complexion, she said—and Madeleine wrote a note she intended to give Colonel Mayhew. She recalled Nicholas mentioning, during their excursion round the island, and a propos of—she could not remember what, that his uncle liked to sit and read, afternoons, by the Brant Point lighthouse, weather permitting. She would give herself a little more time to steady her resolve and then find the Colonel.

The note she wrote was a short one. At ease with her conscience, Madeleine returned to a serene reading of *Athalie*, where she had reached the third act and made little pencil notes of her very own in the margins. For her dream was to be modest Mademoiselle Pichot teaching school in Lyon some day not too far in the future.

12

AT THE MAYHEW residence, the midday meal in the dining room, cooked by Ruth and served by Priscilla, was shared with Cottle and Wallace, and the conversation, discreetly alluding to the imminent departure of the principals of the house, concerned itself chiefly with the business duties of the two others. There was talk of timber and whale oil and pitch and tar and tobacco, orders to fill, merchandise to receive, accounts to settle, customers to please. The Colonel's probity was universally known, and he meant his house to maintain its reputation, as well as its efficiency, during their absence.

After coffee, Cottle and Wallace withdrew for an hour's leisure, and Nicholas, saying he had something particular to impart to his uncle, took the latter to his sitting-room upstairs, inviting the Colonel to make himself comfortable. He looked unusually grave. Mayhew lit his pipe.

"Nothing suddenly amiss, I hope," he said.

"Oh no! Perhaps on the contrary. At least I hope so. I must tell you, my dear uncle, that this morning I spoke at length with Madeleine. I—I am in love with her."

The Colonel smiled paternally.

"You cannot be blamed for that, my fine fellow. Who wouldn't be? You told her so?"

"I did. And I proposed to her."

"That was a tremendous next step. She was delighted?"

"I think so."

"And you will be married when the—what shall we call the thing?—when the troubles are over?"

"I hope so. Perhaps before. However, she did not *quite* give her consent, I mean, not in so many words."

"Perhaps a little maidenly reserve."

"I don't think so. Uncle, she is an aristocrat."

"Ah, I see. And we are but commoners. I see."

"Yet at heart she is ardently with us."

"As is her mother; so that is good. And then?"

"This is the difficult part, my dear uncle. I found myself obliged to speak to her at length about our...our means...our wealth...our standing...our prospects...persuade her that, commoners though we may be, we are not nothing."

"I cannot blame you, nephew."

"And then—I swore her to secrecy. But I needed to say more. It was necessary to tell her everything. She swore—"

Mayhew interrupted, pipe aloft in alarmed surprise.

"You told her about our leap to the mainland?"

"I needed to. The call that has come for us. The important call. Your rank. *That* was important. She was in rapture."

Mayhew puffed at his pipe. Nicholas went on.

"She will not even tell her mother. 'Your secret shall die with me', she said."

Mayhew nodded. There was a rather long pause.

"You may have said too much, Nick," he brought out at last; "but—I believe the girl. Will not even tell her mother, eh? I believe her." Then, standing up, he shook Young Nick's hand. "I judge her to be a fine, honest and very smart young woman. Besides, the time has come for you to be married. I was much, much younger than you when my turn came to the altar. So fine a girl she was, so fine, so honest, and very smart. But so brief our bliss.... However, my boy, there will be a mountain of details. Presbyterian and Catholic. American and French. The Tourville family, unknown to us: who are they? Marriage contract. But of course the chief point is love, the Yes on both sides."

"She hasn't yet said Yes," Nicholas reminded his uncle, smiling.

"A detail! You must attack again."

"I will."

And there, trifles aside, the conversation ended.

Later that afternoon, Josh Mamack was shown in by Priscilla. It was going to be his business to drive his cart twice a day to the southern cove to look for the *Enterprise* anchored off-shore. No one would be suspicious, since Mamack the jack-of-all-trades was ever on the road looking for work or performing it. He would also discreetly transport a solid rowboat to the place.

13

NEXT MORNING Nicholas tried to call on Madeleine at the inn but was told that she was indisposed. He returned home slightly but only slightly alarmed. To some extent it may be said that the young woman was indeed unwell, but the trouble was purely spiritual, it came of reflections about her ungrateful enjoyment of the pampered life she led thanks to the mother she was betraying by her silence. Five hundred pounds! Still, Madeleine was not a brooder. A mission awaited her. When she rose to it that afternoon—a sunny afternoon, the mildest of winds giving a freshness to the land—her spirits were high again. *This* weighed against *that*, she was doing what was right and best.

The lighthouse was clasped round its base by a long circular bench. One could thus sit in the sun or the shade as the day went by. The Colonel, however, was not to be seen when she arrived. She sat where she could watch the harbor alive with all the prosperous bustle that was going to be so cruelly diminished by the long war, and where she saw again the waters in which, so recently, a handsome young man had leaped to save—not a stranger, but a needed business agent of his.

Deep in her thoughts, she was almost surprised by the very person she had been waiting for. The Colonel had arrived, book in hand. His face lit up, as one says, when he saw and greeted her. She invited him to sit beside her. Doing so, he quickly decided not to speak to her of what was, after all, not yet an engagement. She on her side intended to keep the conversation as light as possible before coming to the point. After replying to his inquiry about the well-being of her charming mother, she asked him, "What is your book, Colonel? Perhaps a treatise on whaling ships?"

"No," he replied with a smile; "guess again."

"The poems of some refined but ailing gentlewoman of

Connecticut."

"Not quite."

"I give up. You must tell me."

"Well, I must be honest with you. It is a manifesto."

"Ah, that's dangerous."

"More than you think. It came in the same bottom that brought you to Nantucket so recently."

"Come, tell me what it is."

"The author is one Thomas Jefferson."

"Read to me, Colonel. You have reason to believe that you are safe with me. Safe, safe, safe."

"I know it. I know *everything*. You understand me."

She nodded. He leafed through the little book. "Here's some passable rhetoric," he said, and he began to read, his voice becoming more and more powerful as he went on. " 'The common feelings of human nature must be surrendered up before his Majesty's subjects here can be persuaded to believe that they hold their political existence at the will of a British Parliament. Shall these governments be dissolved, their property annihilated, and their people reduced to a state of nature, at the imperious breath of a body of men whom they never saw, in whom they never confided, and over whom they have no powers of punishment or removal, let their crimes against the American public be ever so great? Can any one reason be assigned why one hundred and sixty thousand electors in the island of Great Britain should give law to four millions in the States of America, every individual of whom is equal to every individual of them in virtue, in understanding, and in bodily strength? Were this to be admitted, instead of being a free people, as we have hitherto supposed and mean to continue ourselves, we should suddenly be found the slaves not of one but of one hundred and sixty thousand tyrants.' "

"I like that!" cried Madeleine. "Who is this flaming orator? Is he a friend of yours?"

"I don't know the man."

"Do you think he is in jail?"

"No; for I've been told that he is presently a delegate in Philadelphia. But you see now, do you not"—and he looked intently at her—"why my nephew and I *must* go."

"I do, I do! What else does this delegate say?"

"Many wicked things—oh, if I were George the Third, I should not sleep easy until I did see Mr. Jefferson in fetters." Mayhew was leafing again. "For example: 'By an act passed in the fifth year of the reign of his late Majesty, King George the Second, an American subject is forbidden to make a hat for himself of the fur which he has taken, perhaps, on his own soil—an instance of despotism to which no parallel can be produced in the most arbitrary ages of British history.'"

But this time the Colonel failed to impress, for Madeleine burst out laughing. "Stop! Here I think your Mr. Henderson begins to foam at the mouth! What? Not to be allowed to make your own hat is a piece of brutality without parallel?"

"I shouldn't have read you this passage. It is followed by a weightier one on the manufacture of iron. Wait. Here is one you must hear."

"With pleasure. You read so beautifully!"

"Thank you. Let me boast that I sing in our choir on Sundays. But here it is. 'The abolition of domestic slavery is the great object of desire in those colonies where it was, unhappily, introduced in their infant state. But previous to the enfranchisement of the slaves we have, it is necessary to exclude all further importations from Africa. Yet our repeated attempts to effect this, by prohibitions and by imposing duties which might amount to a prohibition, have been hitherto defeated by his Majesty's negative, thus preferring the immediate advantages of a few British corsairs to the lasting interests of the American States and the rights of human nature, deeply wounded by this infamous practice.' Does this not touch you? 'This infamous practice.' Such words are quite beyond faction—we'll say no more about the beaver hats."

These words had in fact moved Madeleine more than the Colonel suspected. She asked him, softly: "Had you the opportunity, would you not engage in the slave trade yourself, Colonel Mayhew? It is so very profitable."

The response was an indignant "I—in the slave trade? I would raise my tent in Muscovy or turn heathen before I'd handle a man like a bale of merchandise."

At this, with the utmost gravity, she asked: "But is there not pleasure in being waited on by glistening black slaves?"

"Is this you speaking, Mademoiselle?" asked the Colonel, deeply grieved.

But she placed a reassuring hand on his arm.

"God forbid," she said, and then she took a deep breath. "I was quoting your nephew."

Mayhew lowered his head, and one of his hands went to his brow. Perhaps her words had not come to him as an overwhelming surprise.

"Can you not forgive what must have been a flip word or two?" he brought out, raising his head. "Nicholas has such splendid qualities. And I believe in my heart that you will not be sorry to—you will not be sorry."

"I think I would be," she said in a low voice. "And I came to the lighthouse just now, not by accident, but meaning to find you, and to give you this."

She had taken her folded note from a satchel and now placed it in his hand.

"Please give him this for me. Please read it."

He did so. And then he said, "Nicholas is one of best, Madeleine. A plain dealer and a gallant fighter. He lost father and mother when he was a boy. Perhaps he wants the softer counsels of a woman to complete him as a man. But he is generous, quick-witted, exuberant in imagination. We shall need men like him. They will be our especial glory."

"Or your particular downfall."

"No. It must not be, it must not be," and he tried to return the note to her, but she refused with a gesture and quickly moved away.

14

THAT SAME AFTERNOON, Aimée saw to it that she would run into Nicholas. Minding what Madeleine had said to her, she naturally made no allusion to the marriage proposal. She only told him merrily that she was jealous of the excursion through the island he had offered her daughter, and that she desired one of her own, especially to the Eastern end of the island, where the view was said to be superb. Nicholas was happy to assent: not only was the Marquise excellent company, and most attractive simply as a woman, but he wanted to have her on his side when the moment came of Madeleine's "sweet avowal," namely by giving her, as he had given the girl, a large view of his prospects. He had reason to believe that the Marquise de Tourville was poor though noble—this was such a common occurrence!—and if that were the case, she might, in spite of her rank, snatch at the chance of an alliance with an affluent old American family. Ancient rank allied to new wealth: that too was a common occurrence. Besides, he would remind her that the Mayhews had been among the first to Christianize the Indian natives.

Of course, these dreams and intentions were shattered when he read Madeleine's note, which the Colonel reluctantly handed him in the young man's sitting-room, without saying a word.

"This is a disappointment, sir," said Nicholas peevishly. "The young lady is prouder than I thought. But I do not give up so easily. Tomorrow I am spending the day, or a good part of it, with the mother, and I intend to attack again."

The Colonel doubted that his nephew would succeed, but he kept that thought to himself, and only said, "If you speak *very* freely to her, as you did to Madeleine, ask her as well, most solemnly, to be secret. If gossip were to reach Applegate!..."

"I'll be most careful," replied Nicholas, remembering at this

82

LAST PAGES

point Madeleine's warning to the same effect.

If the young man felt less than his hearty self at supper that evening, he showed so little outward change that neither Wallace nor Cottle noticed anything.

Mamack once again was obliged to report that the *Enterprise* was not to be seen from the southern cove.

Next morning, the day announcing itself as bright as anyone could wish, Aimée jokingly sought permission of Madeleine to spend the day with her rejected lover roving, as the girl had done, over the island. "I must pry secrets from him, but also, I want to see for myself why you are in love with him but will not marry him, or so you tell me."

"Mother," Madeleine implored her, "let's have done with the Mayhews and return to Montreal. They are fine people; leave them alone. You've served Gage so well in the past, he will never dismiss you."

"Well," replied Aimée, "perhaps you are right. And yet I want my day with Nicholas. At worst, it will be my holiday."

Madeleine's refusal of Nicholas still puzzled her. Had she been swayed by the thought that her mother was in all likelihood about to denounce the two gentlemen? Or was it something intimately physical and therefore all but impossible to speak of, even to one's mother? Such a blemish might occur even if the party was superbly handsome. That much said, if Madeleine's rejection of Nicholas was truly firm, she Aimée needed to act, she could dawdle no longer: either arrest the two gentlemen—fine people to be sure—without proof of guilt or leave the island as her daughter wished. Forfeiting the reward would be a hardship. Making a mistake about the Mayhews, who might be Whiggish only in their souls, would be worse: an uproar on the island that would infuriate Gage beyond recovery. Well then, she intended to be bold with Young Nick, out there in the pastureland of Nantucket, and teasingly "accuse" him of flying to the Rebels in order to free America. He might jest in reply. But she was a fine reader of tones of voice and movements of face and body, and upon *those* indices she would come to a decision.

Madeleine retired to her room, her book, and the dark thought that had she been a loving and grateful daughter she would have told her mother all she knew. But, stubbornly, self-blaming and self-approving at the same time, she *would* protect the Mayhew men.

Presently Nicholas' carriage stopped at the inn, Aimée took her seat next to Young Nick as her daughter had done. She did so with an air between gaiety and gravity, and he received her with something of the same mixture of emotions, for they both knew that the rejected proposal would sooner or later come up between them. All the same, there she was in all her beauty, brightly dressed and waving her pink parasol, and he welcomed her with a sweet smile. Nicholas intended to drive all the way east to Sconset, where they would find refreshment in one or another farmhouse in that sparsely populated region, but the rogue also proposed to show Aimée the pretty Miacomet pond in the south, from which point he would be able to visit the rendez-vous cove and spy the sea for a glimpse of the much-desired *Enterprise*.

Nicholas loved the island and found pleasurable distraction in chatting about the sights and about the history of these sights much as he had done for Madeleine's benefit and entertainment; repetition did not weary him. "Sheep and cows on land, whales and cod in the ocean," he said; "we do not have much else to offer." Aimée, looking sideways at him, thought, "Yes you do. Handsome men. What is the matter with Madeleine?" All at once, through body and mind, something deep-demanding came and went.

The roads, though carefully supervised by the island's selectmen, were sometimes rough; the earth and gravel could not always remain even; there were jolts; and one of these so suddenly and sharply shook the carriage that Aimée's hand went fearfully into that of Nicholas, unless it was that of Nicholas which took Aimée's hand. It was hard to say, but it happened. It did not last, of course, the two hands went quickly home, and nothing was said of them, but an alteration had happened between the man and the woman, like a sudden pallor or a sudden blush. Then, after a few minutes of silence—the first since their departure from Sherburne—Aimée placed her hand, but this time with deliberation, on Young Nick's arm and said, "We do need to speak, do we not, about our Madeleine?"

But not while hooves and wheels made their clatter. Nicholas stopped the carriage. "We do," he said and, after some hesitation: "What did she tell you, Marquise? What do you know?"

"I know but one thing, Nicholas; that she said No to you. But she refuses to explain, she is as mute as a fish, and I must turn to *you* for an explanation."

"Is the explanation not a simple one? You are noble, we are commoners. Sheep and cows, cod and whales."

"That cannot be the reason, Nicholas; I know my darling girl."

"Then it is my person."

"Yes, if she were blind."

Nicholas smiled at her.

"What then? And will you not help me, Marquise?"

"I will do my best. I am searching my brain. We are noble but poor, Nicholas; perhaps she considered our poverty. Or mine. Marrying into spermaceti candles!"

"You're joking! I offered her riches! Did she not tell you?"

"She did not. She told me *nothing*. Of course I know that the Mayhews are solid. But you must be open with me, Nicholas, before I can promise to intercede. What manner of life did you offer her?"

She needed to know for sure and needed to have it undiluted from the source. That source yielded the forceful flow we know of already. Nicholas, once again, was glad to repeat himself, and Aimée, hearing it all with a variety of details, thought she understood at last why the "little idealist," as she now called her daughter in her thoughts, had refused the amazing young gentleman—for the time being. He lacked poetry. But she, Aimée, could teach him how to infuse a little of it in his declarations. In the meantime, like Madeleine, she could not fail to be impressed. Young Nick, she imagined, would have laughed at her five hundred pounds.

But the time had come, obviously, for *her* plunge.

"Perhaps there was another reason," she said, and now she used both hands to turn his head toward her and stared into his eyes.

"What? What?" he asked, bewildered.

"Perhaps being the wife of a mere merchant was not enough for her. She wanted poetry, perhaps; perhaps she wanted a soldier, a hero, a fighter for Liberty."

"She had that too," said Nicholas quietly.

His answer produced deep in her brain a tumult of triumph and amused anger at her traitress of a daughter.

"Explain, Nicholas, explain! What did you tell her? I am dumbfounded!"

"In a few days," said Nicholas in a low voice, "William Mayhew will be an American general and I captain of an American warship. We may, no we *shall* be arrested if this becomes known. There are spies watching us. Swear that you shall keep the secret, as your daughter has sworn."

"I swear, I swear! And I am proud of you! Fight! Vanquish! You more than deserve us! And Madeleine shall have words from me, trust me!"

Moved by her radiant joy, Nicholas leaned over, saying "It is not the Tourville I wish to be allied to, it is to Aimée de Tourville" — thinking "Lucky were the men on whom...."

Then, giving his horse a flick, he urged the carriage on its way. He had much to say now about deeds to come in the war, but it must be admitted that Aimée listened to these particulars with only half a mind. She had the essentials, and that was all she needed. Instead, her thoughts ran on Madeleine's refusal of the young man. She could find no reason for it and refused to credit it. "Protecting the Rebel from her mother—the minx!—and yet not marrying him, though he has wealth and Rebel poetry and looks! This cannot hold. I allow her another twenty-four hours to accept him, and if she persists like a little idiot—all that land in the West!—I arrest both men and have done." She glanced sidelong at Nicholas, who was just then speaking of captured brigs, "What delicious lips they are that babble at me...."

They stopped for refreshments as foreseen. A Quaker couple of farmers gave them fresh bread, cold meat, and a bowl of milk from, needless to say, their own cow, milked that morning. As Aimée gazed more freely at that handsome face, and that splendid body, and that great air of his, "fit," she reflected, "for any aristocratic salon," she said to herself, drinking her milk, "This is the future, either way we go."

The farm stood at a little distance from the sea. They returned to their carriage and drove to a rise of the land just above the waters. A fairly steep grassy slope led to the narrow beach. Aimée declared that she wanted to dip her feet in the ocean. She took Nicholas' arm and started down. He felt her warmth with a thrill. Then (suddenly resolved) she twisted her foot. She cried out in pain and, still holding the young man's arm—he was crying "You hurt yourself! You hurt yourself!"—she allowed herself to sink onto the grassy slope, moaning gracefully. Young Nick bent down and began to chafe her ankle and foot. She stroked his hair (he had lost his hat). That was more than man can bear. When had been the last time Nicholas had held a woman as a man holds a woman!—and had he ever held a respectable one in his arms?—he abandoned the ankle, raised himself and wildly kissed her lips. Hidden by the slope—but in any event no one was nearby—they abandoned themselves to the acute pleasures of love, without, to be sure, pressing to the end—but oh what felicities can be had short of that end! Aimée knew, and knew how to teach Nicholas.

"Aimée, Aimée," he murmured, "queen of my soul and body,

I am yours body and soul, will you have me as your own?"

It should not be thought that Young Nick had been alone in feeling what hands, legs, lips and tongue can offer; his reciprocations were as welcomed as rain after a long drought. Aimée could be blissful, in love, and strategic all together. The British empire was thrown to the winds. Aimée declared then and there, on that grassy slope, caressed by the playful sea-breeze, that she cared neither for Tourville nor for Fapignac (unlike her proud daughter) and that she was ready to sail the seven seas with him.

"But my age, Nicholas, my age! Ah, if I were twenty years younger!"

"I refuse to listen!" cried Nicholas. "You are a masterpiece of nature. Don't grow a day younger or I shall cut my throat."

Then she called him *Nicolas* and he called her Amy, and at last they rose, she not forgetting to limp, nor to hold on to him, until they came to the carriage and drove off.

Reaching the south-shore cove, he was able to show her openly the place from which he and his uncle would embark. He mentioned Wallace now for the first time—the man who had brought the Mayhews such important news from the mainland. That was not, perchance, the so-called sailor he had rescued the other day? It was, said Nicholas, laughing, and Aimée was able to congratulate herself—once more—on her sagacity.

Driving on, Nicholas spoke earnestly of marriage. Aimée did not object. It appeared that she was ready to give up Montreal and follow the gentlemen—with Madeleine, of course, to the mainland. The "what next" would depend on circumstances largely dictated by the commands the Mayhews were going to receive. But the wedding need not wait. Nicholas was as ready to turn Catholic as Aimée was willing to turn anything—"are we not all Christians?" she whispered with a kiss.

It was, of course, impossible not to speak of Madeleine. Young Nick managed to forget for a few minutes that she, not he, had made the break. "It was an error, a sweet error," he said as they drove away from the cove. "It seemed romantic. But it was too pale, too prim, too strait-laced. I do believe it would have faded after six months. You, instead—you shall romp with me through life. You and I will hold court in a plantation. You'll walk on my arm as my consort. And when we Americans make a king and titles of our own—need I say more? This is the new world, the new life—and you are the lady who is great enough for it!"

Yes, but how to inform the young woman? They decided to let circumstances show them the way.

The horse was stopped more than once on the way home for an exchange of kisses. When they arrived at Swain's Inn, Nicholas decorously handed Aimée down, whispering in her ear, "I do believe it is you who must be the first to speak to Madeleine. It will be difficult, my heart." But he was not to be let off so easily, for as chance would have it, the girl appeared that moment at the door, her *Athalie* in one hand and a parasol in the other, going for a walk by the harbor. However, Nicholas rose magnificently to the occasion. He took Aimée's hand and said, "My dear Madeleine, embarrassment is useless, concealment impossible: I am your new father. I aspired recently to another, more intimate connection, but you gave me my freedom, which I hastened to surrender to this precious lady, your mother, who is, indeed, more precious to me for being your mother."

They all felt that ceremonious behavior was best suited for the occasion. Yet for a moment, it must be admitted, Madeleine gaped. Her mother looked as prim as she was able to look. But the young woman quickly took possession of herself. "My dear new father," she said with a cutsey, "and mother dear, I offer you my tenderest congratulations."

"This is most kind of you," said Nicholas, bowing. "Permit me to withdraw at this time so that I may bear the news to my dear uncle. My dearest Marquise, will you convey all the necessary intelligence to our Madeleine?"

"I will, my lord," said Aimée.

Whereupon the young man jumped back on the carriage and drove off.

The two women waved, and then Aimée, putting her arm around Madeleine's waist, led her forcefully upstairs to her room. Her limp was miraculously gone.

"Put away your book. Madelon! *Alea jacta est*! We've jumped to the other side!"

"With a vengeance!" Madeleine exclaimed. She had time, while climbing the steps, to wonder at the absolute want of jealousy or anger in her soul. Amazement filled, for the moment, all the spaces in it. Was there another woman like her mother in the world?

"Of course," cried Aimée, "I should spank you for hiding from me everything I had to discover for myself. Yes, you betrayed your mother. But you're forgiven, you wretch! Because all my political opinions are turned upside down. I'm as hot a revolutionary now as you've been all along, Miss Twoface. And I'm going to commit a ghastly misalliance by marrying Nicholas Mayhew."

"What will our Fapignac relations say when they get wind of this tragic degradation?"

"Ah, I'm so glad you're taking it lightly. I was terrified—I thought you'd make a great moral scene in front of the inn. Madelon, my little canary, you're not jealous of your old mother, are you? I didn't take him away from you—you practically—I still don't know why—you practically bequeathed him to me."

Madeleine became serious. "I don't want to bequeath him to you, mother, because of what will happen when he learns the truth."

But Aimée was not to be frightened.

"Why should he learn anything so unpleasant?"

"Because those you are bet...because your former friends will see to it."

"No, my girl. I know too many of their secrets. However, I'll secure myself on all sides. You'll see, you'll see."

"I don't think I'll see," said Madeleine sadly. "Mother dear, I mean to return to Lyon."

"What do you mean, 'return'? You have never seen Lyon! You are staying with me. You're a stranger in France."

"What of it? Tante Marie has invited me often enough; there's room for me; I'll take care of her and teach school."

"Nonsense! I intend to fight your destiny, which, if I don't, is to marry a tailor—and be faithful to him."

"I'm sorry I disappoint you, mother."

"Nonsense. Come here." Aimée kissed her. "I love you, I love you. And won't we look fine, you and I, strolling arm in arm on one of Young Nick's plantations!"

More soberly (*dégrisée*, as she put it to herself), in bed that night, Aimée shone a fuller light in her mind on the fateful reality that she had thrown away security of employment and five hundred solid pounds for a wild adventure into heaven knew what. The plain term for this was: a gamble. But a gamble to which charming Nicholas was attached appealed to her. And before she fell into a mild sleep, a concluding thought came to her, half joyful, half melancholy: "my last chance to be young."

15

IT WAS NOT without embarrassment that Nicholas told his story—the essentials of his story—to his uncle. He had found Mayhew deep in study over maps and pamphlets and histories and treatises of war. The switch from daughter to mother did not strike the Colonel as a matter of historic significance. He was a man of large tolerance and wide humor, and he congratulated his nephew accordingly. But underneath the chaff, the news made him strangely glad, he did not know why, and thought no more about it.

Nicholas had represented the new alliance in the light of a rational understanding between a man and a woman, omitting from his story its components of flesh and sudden impulse. Thus he himself brought up the difference in age between the betrothed. "It is not so great," rejoined the Colonel, "whatever the lady's age may be. That will be found out in time, but, gazing at her, I detect no great artifice of concealment; I give her less than fifty years of age. You, my boy, are no longer a youngster, and I hear, besides, that such marriages are the best." "I do like," said Nicholas on his side, "the alliance with a distinguished old continental family, why deny it? Besides, two Mayhew bachelors are at least one too many. As for Aimée's beauty, charm, and wit, a man would need to be blind and deaf not to recognize them."

That beauty and charm shone brighter than ever the next evening. Not much had happened during the day. The *Enterprise* was not in sight. Aimée, a trifle indisposed, as women will be, was busy with paper affairs, among them, she had let it be known, matters concerning the anxious friends supposedly waiting for her arrival in Montreal. She did, in reality, send a terse note to Judge Weamish: "Making good progress." She and Madeleine were invited by the Mayhews for an evening meal. It was fortunate that

socializing with the suspects could be interpreted by the Judge
only as working hard at her mission.

Aimée knew how to overcome, with brilliant and amusing
prattle, an awkwardness that might otherwise have slowed the
flow of words. The awkwardness, in any case, was slight, because
the Nicholas-Madeleine episode had come and gone so quickly, it
could not bear a heavy weight, it could be, if not forgotten, at any
rate ignored. True, the direct exchange of words between Nicholas
and Madeleine was not abundant, but his attentions to her might
well be called exquisite, they were, one might say, the equivalent of
a "pardon me!"—and, on the whole, the party of four soon became
comfortable and familiar with one another at table and later in
the spacious parlor. It became possible for the Colonel to take the
liberty of inquiring, in the most general and delicate terms, into
the Marquise's financial situation during the coming weeks. He
was satisfied that her "people" in New York kept her sufficiently
supplied. No details were forthcoming, and none, needless to say,
were demanded.

The Colonel agreed that when the time came the two women
should board *The Enterprise* together with himself and Nicholas.
Aimée's betrothal to the latter, he said, would in all likelihood
become known—her alliance, that is, to a Rebel fugitive. She
would no longer be the innocent traveller she had been. The Tories
of the island were sure to make her situation a painful one if she
stayed behind. Indeed, she and Madeleine might be kept by them as
hostages. And of course there was the ineluctable fact of Love. The
two gentlemen could not know how important to Aimée was the
matter of a prompt departure from the island—and its jailhouse.
But the argument of Love was sufficient. She could not bear the
thought of being left behind while her dear man sailed without her.
What with the war, God only knew what might happen to keep
them asunder for ages! She even cried a little and held Nicholas'
hand tightly in hers. The Colonel glanced at Madeleine, wishing
he might take into himself the embarrassment he could see she

felt. But this came and went. Madeleine had long since learned to "adjust."

That evening, Cottle and Wallace, understanding that a family meal and parley were intended, went supping at Swain's Inn.

In the house, as the four sipped and chatted in the deepening night, they heard, in the distance, sounds of trumpet, fife and drum. Priscilla, bringing in a decanter of fine port at that moment, thought it had something to do with the annual sheep-shearing feast that had taken place just before the Marquise's arrival in Nantucket. There might have been a betrothal or two, consequent to the feast.

She was wide of the mark.

In front of the Town House on Centre Street stood the tallest and strongest cherry tree of the island—a place of few trees, as everyone knows, and none very tall. Some twenty young islanders had decided to make this a Liberty Tree—a modest offshoot, so to speak, of the famous Boston elm. So they marched to the tree that evening, to the sound of trumpet, fife and drum, and singing bold songs of freedom from tyrannical yoke.

And yet our isle remaineth
A refuge for the free,
As when true-hearted men
First saw it from the sea,

and the like. Lighting a bonfire and dancing round the tree, they stopped long enough to nail a sign to the trunk declaring this to be the Tree of Liberty. But that was only the beginning. One of the lads unrolled a life-size doll looking somewhat like Judge Weamish, dressed in his best garb, and bearing a sign of his own, in cloth, reading "I am King George's flunkey." (To be sure, his stipend was paid by the Crown). More was to come, but in the meantime Jenny, the Judge's housekeeper, had appeared from one street and, from another, Wallace and Cottle, drawn thither by the tumult. With a cry, Jenny ran home to tell the dreadful tale to her employer, who ordered all the shutters closed and promptly went to bed trembling and furious.

A lad now came running and shouting in glee. He had stolen a Redcoat's uniform from the troop's storage house. A huge whoop greeted him. The uniform was strung up alongside the judge-doll to the accompaniment, none too harmonious, of the aforementioned trumpet, fife and drum. But now, from two sides, came the counter-attack. From one street a crowd of Loyalist youths irrupted, shouting Long Live the King, and agitating staves and pitchforks. They were met, and mingled with, ten angry Redcoats headed by Sergeant Cuff and accompanied by Mr. Applegate who had, in fact, alerted Cuff to the outrage committed against His Majesty's uniform. A frantic melee ensued. Heads and shoulders were clubbed, the soldiers pulled down the doll and uniform, tore off the Tree of Liberty sign, the Patriots tried to wrest the trophies from their opponents, two musket shots were fired into the air, and suddenly Mr. Applegate took the Sergeant by the arm and cried "Look at that man! The one dressed like a seaman!" pointing frantically at Henry Wallace, whose face was lit by the bonfire. "That's the fellow Nick Mayhew rescued," said Cuff; "what of him?" "Damn his hide! It's Henry Wallace, who was my middleman in Boston until I saw him come out of a tavern with the arm of that imp of the devil Sam Adams round his shoulder. I gave him the boot that same day, and here he is disguised as a sailor!"

"And living with the Mayhew pair, confound them!" growled the Sergeant. He had, in truth, been busier in the past few days looking for hidden weapons and ammunitions than zealously spying on the Mayhews, but now the Frenchwoman's suspicions returned in force. He marched with two of his men up to Wallace and said "Your name is Henry Wallace and you're under arrest." Resistance was feeble: hearing his name all but silenced Wallace, who was led off to jail forthwith between a pair of His Majesty's soldiers. One of Nantucket's two constables was on guard that night, gently sleeping on a cot, as there was, as usual, no one to watch. He was shaken awake and told to lock up their man forthwith.

While this was happening, the brawl had continued, until the Redcoats and Loyalists succeeded in routing the Patriots by means of shots in the air and blows on the shoulders. The cherry tree resumed its normal aspect, loaded only with its ripening cherries, silence returned to the streets, and Abishai Cottle ran home as if pursued by the English army in order to bring the catastrophic news to the Mayhews.

"Henry has been arrested!" he cried, sinking into an armchair. Priscilla and Ruth came running in, the four conspirators surrounded the gasping fellow, who now told his story from beginning to end, and thus turned the family gathering into a war council.

"Your opinion, uncle," said Nicholas.

Mayhew had quickly recovered his balance.

"We will do nothing tonight, obviously," he said, "but early tomorrow I shall demand of Tom Weamish that he order the release of our business agent, who has committed no crime."

"Yes," said Aimée, "but why did you conceal him? Why, when my valiant Nicolas pulled him out of the sea, why didn't he cry 'Wallace, dearest business agent'?"

"Madame," said Mayhew, "I see that you will prove an important contributor to our struggle."

"I am not without experience in high affairs," answered Aimée demurely.

"Therefore, I answer your question as follows: We concealed his identity because our business affairs are private. The house of Mayhew & Mayhew is negotiating in secret an advantageous contract with a West Indian seller of molasses and rum, and Henry Wallace is our confidential go-between in that affair. I shall slam the table and shout that we've a right to keep our affairs to ourselves."

"But will Wallace keep his mouth shut?" asked Nicholas.

"Sergeant Cuff has him pat. The man can be branded and flogged. We are in danger, uncle."

"Hence no time must be lost. Tomorrow early I must have Wallace released. But at the same time—Cottle?"

"Yes, sir."

"After a bit of rest and food and drink, you are to run to Obed Coffin who must in turn rouse Mamack and all our friends. By tomorrow morning we must have a band of armed men shouting slogans in the streets, in front of Sergeant Cuff's billet and the house of Tom Weamish: 'We are the Minutemen of Nantucket!' and 'Free Henry Wallace!' What do you think, Nicholas, and you, my lady? And even you, Madeleine?"

"Let them also shout 'Protect the Mayhew family!' said Aimée.

"Well, why not," he acknowledged, smiling.

"My idea is somewhat different," said Nicholas, "and here it is. Myself, my uncle and ten armed men will overcome our booby of a judge, use him for a hostage, capture Sergeant Cuff, proclaim at the top of our voices the call we have received from the Congress, pluck Wallace from his cell, and calmly wait for the *Enterprise* to come round, which will be any day now."

"No, no, no! I hate your scheme," cried Aimée. "Your hostage won't stop the Sergeant. He knows perfectly well that you would not shoot Mr. Weamish. And he has five times your ten men."

"We have half of Sherburne!"

"Worse still! You're too young, you believe you're indestructible! But I know better; I've seen too many indestructible youngsters bleeding to death in the Canadian snow! General Mayhew! Speak to us!"

"Let us not begin in bloodshed," said Mayhew.

"Nor end in it!" cried Madeleine, grasping the arms of her chair. Mayhew added, looking long at her: "Let us try my way. Abishai my lad, do you agree and are you ready?"

"I agree, sir, and I am ready."

Soon after he was gone.

"If Wallace breaks, we are done for," said Nicholas glumly.

The two women rose; it was time to go; but as hands were being warmly kissed—Priscilla had already opened the door—Aimée put her free hand on the Colonel's forearm and said, "If you will accept myself and my daughter not simply as helpless female relations but as allies not entirely witless, I propose to give this affair all my thoughts for the next twelve hours, barring a few hours of sleep. May I, Nicholas?" she added, turning to him. "And bear in mind that I am on excellent terms with Judge Weamish. I feel that this may help."

Both men, somewhat surprised by this most formal speech at the door, acknowledged her, absolutely, as their active ally.

16

ABISHAI COTTLE had done good work during the night, for the next morning a considerable band of self-styled Minutemen paraded up and down Sherburne, brandishing cutlasses, muskets, along with less deadly weapons, and shouting their well-memorized slogans. Weamish, still trembling from having been hanged in effigy the night before, remained in bed. Wishing to avoid, for the time being, a nasty and dangerous confrontation, Sergeant Cuff sent most of his men on various expeditions whose aim, as always, was to uncover caches of powder and bullets. He himself and half a dozen Redcoats remained to guard the jail, for one or two aging constables of uncertain loyalty were not to be counted on in case of an attempt by the mob to free Wallace. In the jail's ante-room Cuff received a note from Aimée, handed him by one of Enoch Swain's boys, which read, with intentional vagueness: "The Marquise de Tourville reminds Sergeant Alexander Cuff not to take any action contrary to the prosecution of her mission." The Sergeant had in any event not yet interrogated his prisoner (who, by the way, was making a great deal of noise in his uncomfortable cell), feeling, not unreasonably, that the longer the rascal was left stewing (as he put it to himself), the more amenable he would be to some no-nonsense questioning about the Mayhew pair. In fact, he was prepared to apply the roughest methods to the case. The Sergeant would have liked to arrest the two gentlemen without further niceties, but the yelling along Main Street reminded him that he must work hand in hand, however reluctantly, with the powerful Frenchwoman.

Nicholas, that morning, paid a call on his bride-to-be; he was holding back while his uncle was taking action. Leaving Madeleine to her *Athalie*, the two drove to the southern shore to scan the sea once more for the *Enterprise*. But the ship was not to be seen, the ocean was flat under the June sun.

The Colonel, on his side, failed dismally. When he knocked at the door of the Weamish house, a grave-looking Jenny (well instructed) told him in a low, alarmed voice that the Judge was in bed under the care of Dr. Tupper, instructed to avoid all nervous excitation, to see no one, and to take only milk and toast for a day or two. All Mayhew could accomplish was to request Jenny to inform the Judge that the Mayhews were offended and alarmed by the arbitrary arrest of their commercial agent Henry Wallace. Jenny gaping irresolutely at him, he thought it wise to ask for a sheet of paper and a pencil, on which paper he wrote his grievance, with some sharp words concerning the privacy of his business affairs, for delivery to the bedroom.

At the jailhouse, the Colonel was informed by the British soldiers that Sergeant Cuff had gone to smoke his pipe at the Meeting House on Fair Street. The place had been converted into the Redcoats' barracks upon their arrival on the island, a move (by the way) much resented by the population. There the Colonel found Cuff puffing on his pipe at the front door, enjoying the mild air of beginning summer. He demanded the immediate release of a man who had violated no law and made no trouble, and who was an important member of the firm of Mayhew & Mayhew.

"Sir," said the Sergeant, "I shall keep the man you disguised as a sailor until I have interrogated him."

"Your authority, sir?"

"King George the Third and twenty muskets."

"I wish to speak with Mr. Wallace and assure myself that he is being well treated and decently nourished."

"The prisoner must see no one until further notice except myself."

"Good day. You shall hear from me again."

"Gladly."

With this, the Sergeant turned on his heels, went back into the guard-room, and shut the door *almost* with a slam.

It was then that Aimée rose grandly to the challenge and, that same afternoon, "sold" her plan to the despondent uncle and nephew. She had returned with Nicholas and found the Colonel discussing business matters with Cottle quite without his usual good humor. He now gave them a report of his failures of the day. "Will you allow a woman to save you?" asked Aimée. "If so, kindly come to my rooms, you too Mr. Cottle, after dinner, round three in the afternoon, and hear me out."

It was a somber conference. Aimée, however, amazed the two men. Spending a week or two on the island as a distinguished visitor on her way to Montreal and desiring her daughter to breathe the bracing air of the place before proceeding north, she turned out to be a shrewd, hard-headed, and probably experienced stateswoman (as indeed she had hinted before this)—the word did not seem too strong, especially to the delighted Nicholas. The scheme she now put forth was hazardous. Madeleine looked worried. Various possible objections were raised. But in the end, the plan was adopted, and after Aimée and Madeleine were left alone, the former promptly sent a note to the Judge, ordering (that was her word) an urgent meeting: she, Weamish, and Cuff, at the Judge's house at eleven the next morning. "This," she said to Madeleine, "will pluck him from his bed."

17

AS LUCK would have it, early next morning Josh Mamack came running to the Mayhew house to announce that the *Enterprise* was lying at anchor off the Weweeder side of the island, as planned. No more time must be lost. Abishai Cottle walked to Swain's Inn to deliver the news to Aimée, who asked the young man to assure the Mayhews that she was going to set "the affair" going that very morning.

Arriving at the Judge's house before Sergeant Cuff, Aimée found Weamish in his morning robe and very agitated. "Oh Madam," he cried, "the population is up in arms, I utterly tremble for my life, I was hanged in effigy, the false sailor is arrested, and I am near believing the world is coming to an end."

"Calm yourself, my friend," said Aimée. "Come, sit down. Of course, I am fully aware of all that has happened in the streets, and I know that Henry Wallace is under arrest. You shall see that my having befriended the Mayhews has borne the fruit I wanted. Let us wait for the Sergeant."

"You bring me comfort, Madame. You even know the man's name. With you at my side, Marquise, I shall smite to the left and right. I shall spare no one."

A few minutes later, Jenny introduced the Sergeant into the room.

"Good morning all," he said, sitting down without ceremony, and before Aimée could return his greeting, he said, "Y'are here, Madam, to give me a dressing down by leave of General Gage. Consider it done. I arrested that rascal of an agent on my own initiative."

"What has the gentleman told you about the Mayhew gentlemen, Sergeant?" asked Aimée sweetly.

"Nothing yet. But leave him to me another day or two, and

the truth shall be flogged out of him."

"In another day or two, my friend, Colonel William Mayhew, bearing the Rebel title of Brigadier General, will be on board a sloop—he and his nephew Nicholas—called the *Enterprise* headed to Cambridge."

If silence can be explosive, Aimée's announcement had precisely that effect. As the two men gaped, speechless, Aimée continued: "Henry Wallace landed here with the news and the command to quit the island. And off they'll go, with him or without. You may spare the whip, Sergeant Cuff."

"Od's guts, how did you discover this?" roared the Sergeant, leaping out of his chair.

"I shall reveal only that cultivating a fine friendship with the two gentlemen bore the results I had counted on. I hope that you credit me. If you do not, the event will speak for me soon enough."

"I credit you so thoroughly," said Cuff, "that I'll invite myself to their house unasked, with ten of my men, and march them off to join their accomplice in jail. I should have done it the day you arrived. It was you that kept me, Madam. Od's liver, I smell a vile rebel a league away. Judge, write me out a warrant. We'll do it by the book this time."

Aimée only smiled, two fingers pressing her lower lip. The Judge stared at the Sergeant as if the latter had gone slightly daft.

"Sign a warrant against the Mayhews?" he cried. "Who settled here in 1659? A selectman? And have you seen and heard the islanders? I'll be cutlassed to death. You too."

Aimée became serious. "Judge Weamish is interested in avoiding bloodshed."

"I'm not," shouted Cuff, still standing.

"To each his profession. But a soldier's first duty, as I understand—"

"Is to destroy the enemy."

"Is not to be destroyed *by* the enemy. That's a *sine qua non* for the other."

"The devil of a sinecure it is! Madam, with all due—"

"Sergeant, with all due, arresting the Mayhews in the open is out of the question. Armed patriots are standing guard over their house; Minutemen they call themselves."

"Merciful gods!" Weamish moaned.

"Your life is not safe, Judge; you were right; and yours even less, Sergeant. Won't you sit down again? Thank you. Granted, these yokels are untrained, but they shoot in all directions, and they are philosophical enough to hide behind fences and trees. Must a woman teach you these nursery-school facts?"

"I am taught, Marquise," said Weamish, pressing his hands together as if in prayer; "consider me your devoted pupil."

"Sergeant?"

"The women are in command here. I see we must go by ruses and devices."

"Be patient, Sergeant. I am reserving a capital role for brawn and firepower. Will you both kindly dine with me tomorrow in Mr. Swain's private dining room? Shall we say at one in the afternoon? My other guests will be the Colonel, or General, and young Mr. Mayhew."

Cuff slammed the arm of his chair in high glee: "I'll be there!" he cried; "Madam, I am your friend. Speak on!"

"I may boast," Aimée continued, "that I have the Mayhews in my pocket (to speak plainly) as a Frenchwoman and a friend. They think it wise to have me bring the two sides in the Wallace affair together for explanation, negotiation, and conciliation, and they know that I am here with you for that very purpose. Of course, they have rehearsed their laughable story about secret importations and exportations. On my side, I have discreetly explored the situation of Mr. Swain's private dining room. The large table is round. A fine Dutch tablecloth covers it to about knee-level. A footstool will be placed invisibly under the table where I am sitting. Right outside the dining room is a passageway leading to the inn's parlor. In that passageway I found a door that leads straight to the cellar. That door will be open. Are you right or left-handed, Sergeant?"

"Left-handed."

"Therefore, you will be seated to my right, because I shall be handing you your pistol, your loaded pistol, with my right hand from my footstool into your left hand. May I see your flintlock, Sir?"

The Sergeant handed Aimée his weapon, which she examined with great care—she best knew why. "An old Chaumette, but in fine condition. I could wish you carried a double-barreled weapon," she remarked, returning the pistol to him; "but this one will do, because stopping one man will stop the other long enough to give us the time we shall need. Have the weapon brought to me tomorrow before ten in the morning, hidden in a common bag. It will lie snug under the table. On my left I will seat my daughter, whose presence will help give the affair an air of innocence. Then, to her left, Nicholas and the old Mayhew, facing you, seated closest to the door into the passageway. And, finally, the Judge, seated to your right."

Aimée had stood up to draw an imaginary diagram on a table, with Cuff standing beside her to study it. "And by the way," she continued, returning to her chair, "my daughter and I happen just now to be the only guests at the inn. No stranger will come running. As for Mr. Swain, he is neither Whig nor Tory, his politics are confined to his inn, and he will accept General Gage's money for his pains and for damage, if any occurs. Sergeant, you will invite two of your sturdiest men, and place them within earshot in the cellar."

"Two?" interrupted Cuff. "Why not ten?"

"Good heavens! What becomes of our secrecy? Two, well armed, and loaded with rope. They must come to me a half hour before you, that is to say punctually at twelve-thirty. The cellar has an opening on Mr. Swain's orchard. That is where I will wait for your men and instruct them. When we are all seated at table, after the first course, I shall go ask Mr. Swain to serve the *plat principal*, and

I will see to it that the door to the cellar and that into our dining-room are open, so that the men in the cellar can hear you. When the meat is served, the Judge must rise and propose a toast to His Majesty King George the Third. You rise from your seat, the glass of wine in your right hand, and respond. I do not know what the Mayhews will say but say something they will. I will have stooped to pick up your pistol and, as mentioned before, placed it in your left hand, which is dangling at your side. You will aim it at the younger Mayhew while shouting for your two warriors. Your two men, and you threatening to bring down Nicholas Mayhew, or bringing him down if you must, should suffice to disable the uncle."

"Have you forgotten, Madam, that the Mayhews may be armed?" Cuff inquired. The diabolical woman impressed him, although he still preferred his own quick and simple if violent plan of storming the Mayhew residence.

"You are wise, Sergeant," she replied to his *caveat*; "for to be sure that is the heart of the matter. Therefore, I shall tell the two gentlemen this very afternoon that all arms must be banned from my dinner. At your entrance tomorrow, you must offer to be searched, and demand to do likewise upon them. Bear in mind that they are meeting with you only to secure the liberation of their agent, as they are mortally afraid that if he is not released, he'll betray them. They have no hare-brained scheme of giving their true character away by brandishing pistols."

"Granted," said Cuff. "And then?"

"And then you and your men will tie up the prisoners, hustle them into the cellar, and at midnight, when even the young of Nantucket are asleep, your men will convey them to any one of the ships docked at the wharves, and order the captain to sail immediately to Boston harbor with the two prisoners and their guards. He will be well compensated there."

Cuff was won. "Marquise," he said, "I apologize for my sour words."

"I have forgotten them, Sergeant Cuff. Indeed, I intend to

commend you specially to General Gage when I send him my final report."

Judge Weamish had remained tight-lipped. He wished both his visitors to the devil.

"And what if they resist?" he finally blurted. "Yes! What if they resist? Even unarmed! If they make an uproar? If they rush about? If they knock me down? You would shoot? Shoot a Mayhew?"

"It will save Tom Gage a trial," replied the Sergeant calmly.

"I hope," said Aimée, "they will have wisdom enough to offer no resistance. But your two men, Sergeant, must be prompt. We must amaze the foe."

"We'll amaze them out of their scalp," said Cuff.

"This will not do," the Judge declared, rising from his chair. "The Mayhews are not Trinidad pirates. A bloodbath at Nantucket! No. I say No. Never heard of. Gentler means must be used."

"With a man like Nicholas Mayhew?" Cuff snorted. But Aimée looked kind.

"What is *your* proposal, Judge?"

"Well, I must give it some thought. But...suppose that when the fruit is brought in after dinner, I turn to the Colonel, for as far as I am concerned William Mayhew is a colonel and nothing else; I turn to him and inform him with my severest demeanor that important disclosures have come to my attention. 'Colonel Mayhew,' I shall say, 'unimpeachable revelations have reached my ears; discoveries of the gravest character, conveyed by private informants whom, needless to say, I am not at liberty to name—' "

The Sergeant was greatly amused. "By the time y'are done with that fine Oxford sentence, the rascals will have cut our throats with your fruit knives!"

"No, Sergeant, I believe they will be mute. But to oblige you I shall be more direct. 'In short,' I will say, 'I know that you and your lively nephew are harboring a secret purpose injurious to the peace of this nation and contrary to that cheerful subordination which has hitherto ensured the happiness of these colonies—an attempt, I am told, to escape from Nantucket with the object of joining—' "

"Et cetera, et cetera, et cetera." The Sergeant was still laughing. Aimée looked grave and respectful.

"Laugh if you will. 'But now,' I shall continue, 'your avenues are barred, for Sergeant Cuff has surrounded these premises.' At this terrifying news I shall rise to my feet—no, I believe I am on my feet already—and call upon both Mayhews to renounce their wicked purpose. 'As you hope for eternal salvation of your souls in the world hereafter, and ease, honor, and comfort in your present existence, you now solemnly swear that you shall cease to be the treacherous ministers of satanic rebellion, and that you shall uphold his Majesty George the Third, defend the British Kingdom, and lend the support of your arms to his Majesty's forces.' Why are you still laughing, Sir?"

"Because my bedtime will have come afore y'ave run through that monstrous oath!"

"And I maintain—"

"No, Judge, excuse me. I'm a raw fellow, I know, I ran from school when I was nine, but this will never do. If we allow the Mayhew pair of rogues to slip out of our hands tomorrow, we deserve to be hanged without benefit of clergy."

Aimée had kept her respectful demeanor.

"Your plan would have merit, Judge Weamish, did I not know that the two gentlemen have already sworn an oath to the Rebels. As the person empowered by General Gage, I must go with my plan, and I am happy that Sergeant Cuff endorses it."

"If y'are afraid for your life, Judge," said Cuff, "you can pretend to faint the moment I aim my pistol at Mr. Nicholas. But I *will* shoot if I must."

"I am as fearless a man as you shall find in Nantucket," said Weamish with a quiver in his voice. "You'll not see me flinch."

The Sergeant rose from his chair. "Well," he said, "that concludes our palaver. I'll see to my side of the plan. You, Madam, shall receive that *loaded* sack tomorrow after breakfast. The two men will be posted in the cellar. If I'm obliged to open fire, let the ladies dive under the table. I will have ten more soldiers patrolling about the wharves with orders to come running if they hear a shot. That should pacify any rabble that may object to our procedure. Are you staying, Marquise?"

"No, Sergeant, I'm coming with you. Don't forget the toast, Judge; loud and clear, so the soldiers can hear you."

"Yes, Marquise." The tone was decidedly unfriendly.

"Your two men," Aimée reminded Cuff, "must report to me in the orchard at twelve-thirty sharp."

"They will."

The Judge rang for Jenny and called for her to open the door for his guests, whom he pointedly did not accompany down the stairs.

When Aimée and the Sergeant were outside, she took his arm and said, "The Judge might be prudently indisposed again tomorrow. You may do well to call on him on your way to Swain's Inn."

18

THAT AFTERNOON Aimée was busy inspecting those parts of the inn that needed her deep look and helping Mr. Swain and the cook set the table. She wanted the best china, silver and crystal. Mr. Swain was alarmed. He was also worried about the barrels and bottles and crockery in the cellar. Arrests were going to be made—he did not know and did not care who was going to arrest and who was going to be arrested. He did care, however, for her assurances that anything broken would be paid for, and, more concretely, for the ten-pound note she slipped into his hand, demanding, at the same time, perfect secrecy under pain of severe penalty from "the government"—she did not specify which. She paid especial attention to the orchard, the entrance to the cellar, the hiding places in it (since four Patriots, ensconced there in good time, were to overwhelm the two arriving British lads), the steps leading from the cellar to the corridor on the main floor, and the door that opened thence into the dining room. Everything seemed to be in order. "However, if the Sergeant," she reflected, "decides after all to send me a swarm of Redcoats, we are undone." But Aimée was an unflinching optimist. The dinner itself was going to be excellent though plain: a tureen of soup, followed by a joint of mutton (with *garniture*) lying on a platter, alongside of which would be placed an impressive carving knife (she chose it carefully in the kitchen) destined to do—whatever work was needed.

While these preparations were taking place, the Colonel sent an urchin from his home with a note to Madeleine (who was by now studying *Esther*) begging her to meet him, that afternoon, around such and such a time, at the lighthouse, if it was not too much trouble.

Book in hand, he was sunning himself on the same bench where they had sat so recently, reading and thinking. Ever since the fateful storm that had brought Wallace ashore, the weather had favored the island with its kindest gifts of sun, harmless clouds and gentle winds. The great white clouds, on this last day of June, made it possible to set oneself to the sun without that furnace in the sky proving a bother. Had Madeleine been really ailing, her stay at Nantucket would already have lifted her back to health, in spite of that well-known scent of whale oil from which only a breeze, rightly oriented, could offer some protection.

She saw the Colonel from a distance, nose in book, and sat smiling next to him.

"Are you still reading Mr. Stevenson's pamphlet?" she asked him without even a "Good afternoon." Their mutual smile supplied that greeting.

"No; Mr. Jefferson's pamphlet is read; but this one is on the same subject, and I took it down from my shelf thinking of you. It is in a way even more interesting."

"Because?"

"Because it was born on this very island, and because it predates Mr. Jefferson considerably. I found it very moving."

He handed her the well-worn little book. She read the title page aloud. " 'Elihu Coleman, of Nantucket. 'A Testimony Against That Anti-Christian Practice of MAKING SLAVES OF MEN'. In very large letters!"

"The date is here," said he, pointing.

"1729! So long ago!"

"Aye; I was seven years old then; but I remember Mr. Coleman. He was a Quaker minister and, for this modest island of ours, a learned man. The Mayhew family prayed in the Presbyterian meeting house. Then as now. We felt something of a superiority over these prim Quakers, and I for one can approve of no religion that bans music. Yet now I am proud of old Mr. Coleman. Few men before him, if any, had spoken out against slavery. All Christianity was content to emulate the pagans in their vilest practice. But not old Mr. Coleman of Nantucket, bless him."

He had almost forgotten why he had "summoned" Madeleine.

She was turning the leaves, on which the cloud-teased sun was shining. "This is pretty," she said, reading aloud: " 'Now although the Turks make slaves of those they catch that are not of their religion, yet (as history relates) as soon as any embraces the Mahometan religion, they are no longer kept slaves, but are quickly set free, and for the most part put to some place of preferment; so zealous are they for proselytes and their own religion. Now if many among those called Christians would but consider, how far they fall short of the Turks in this particular, it would be well; for they tell the Negroes, that they must believe in Christ, and receive the Christian faith, and that they must receive the sacrament, and be baptized, and so they do; but still they keep them slaves for all this.' "

"Yes," said Mayhew, "it is pretty, as you remarked, though perhaps a little wooden in style. And Mr. Coleman did not stray far beyond the obvious, but far beyond the obvious is often an artificial and useless place."

There was a longish silence, and then Madeleine, returning the little book to Mayhew, said softly, "You will struggle to make this America of yours stainless?"

"Without oppressors and without victims at any rate."

"Can this ever be?"

"You are wise beyond your years, but I must believe it. My own happiness will be hobbled as long as I know that somewhere black men are being abused, Indians robbed, other white men persecuted. Oh, this reminds me. Look, here is an old Indian stone pipe. It's one of the very few left on the island."

He had taken the humble object from his pocket.

"It has such a contented look!" said Madeleine. "Is it very old?"

"Perhaps a century; perhaps more. They smoked these long before we Englishmen came. An Indian told me they used a weed they called *poke*, which no longer grows here. It's not really a stone pipe, you know, though they call it that. It's made of a mixture of blue clay and mussel shells, pounded, mixed, and burnt."

"Thank you for showing it to me."

"I would like you to keep it. As a new member of my family."

"I shall take it with me when I return to France and never part with it."

"Return to France? What do you mean?"

"I should have said 'go', not 'return', because I have never been in my country. But everything is decently arranged. I have an aunt in France who has often begged me to come."

"I am sad to think that you will not be with us. With your mother, with Nicholas. But I understand. It is a strange situation. You mentioned an aunt. There are probably many fine relations to choose from. Your mother has mentioned a cousin—a baron Fap... Fap...suddenly I can't recall the name!"

It was a hellish moment for Madeleine. "Fapignac," she brought out in a whisper. Mayhew failed to notice her violent blush, but a thought darted through his mind: "There must be an unsavory secret or two in that family," then quickly dismissed it. It was not relevant to Madeleine.

"Wherever you go," he said, "surely you will return one day to your mother—she holding court, no doubt, wherever Young Nick decides to pitch his tent, so to speak. I will have the happiness of seeing you again. You and I shall visit the charming couple together."

"I will never return," she said decisively.

He was so startled by her vehemence that he reverted to an idea that seemed to have been buried.

"Do you feel the disgrace to the family after all?"

All she could do was hide her face in her hands.

"Forgive me!" Mayhew cried out, "I ought to know you better. But remember that I haven't told you yet why I asked you to meet me here. It wasn't to give you an Indian pipe! I have a very important request to make of you."

"Anything," she said softly.

"It concerns tomorrow's dinner."

"I pray that my mother has made it sure for you."

"Amen. But there is a condition. I ask that you stay away from that dinner." Then he lowered his voice. "Nay, I demand it."

The words were more peremptory than the voice. But when she began by saying "My mother," he rose from the bench in anger: "Let her say what she likes! I am going to tell the Marquise that if you appear at the table, I will quit the game on the spot, happen what may."

She looked up at him. "But if I promise you I won't spoil anything? I have as much courage—"

He sat down again. "Who said you were going to spoil anything? Who said anything about want of courage?"

"Then why shouldn't I be present?"

"Need you ask? Need you ask why I worry?"

They were now looking into each other's eyes. At last she whispered, "I promise," and rose, but wanting to reassure him, she turned about and repeated "I promise" before walking away.

The Colonel remained pensive, gazing at the sea. He had work to do; they might all be sailing in two days! He was about to rise when, to his surprise, he saw Madeleine slowly returning. She sat down next to him again and said quietly: "My name is Madeleine Pichot."

"Pichot? Pichot de Tourville?"

The solemn moment had turned almost comical, and Madeleine was forced to smile. "No. Plain Pichot. It sounds humorous in French."

Mayhew was baffled. "Then you are not the Marquise's daughter!"

"Indeed I am. Her name is Aimée Pichot."

The revelation was enormous, and the Colonel greeted it with an "Ah!" that did justice to the dimension of it. Madeleine continued in a trembling voice: the sudden betrayal was bringing her close to fainting. "We are both in the pay of General Gage," she almost whispered. "Vulgar spies. Mother and daughter. We came to Nantucket on an important special mission, which was to arrest you and Nicholas if we determined that you are plotting to join the mainland rebels."

"That is to say tomorrow, at table?"

The worst, at any rate, was over. Her voice could rise a little now. "No. My mother has changed sides. Madame de Tourville intends to become the noble wife of an immensely rich Yankee."

"And you?"

"For once I wasn't lying. I do have an aunt in Lyon. She is a milliner. The hat shop will be my plantation."

"But is not your father living?"

"I don't know."

"How is that?"

Madeleine had a feeling of sinking ever deeper into mud. And even as she spoke—ideas very different from one another can swiftly alternate in the mind—she thought of how outlandish and outrageous these revelations of hers must be to an innocent, a naïve Nantucket gentleman.

"How is that? Because I don't know who he is, and neither does my mother. Perhaps he is the sergeant who once slapped his superior's face and ran off with mother to Canada, where he died. And where—"

"And where?" Mayhew repeated. "Tell me, don't be afraid."

"She became Gage's. . .intimate."

"So that explains it all. And why did you come to me with this confession? Why now? Why at all? Was it so urgent to save Nicholas?"

"That was not the reason. I don't know the reason."

That was almost a fib.

"Surely you don't wish to harm your mother!" the Colonel exclaimed.

"My mother? Who brought me up, gave me teachers,

groomed me to be something like a lady, shared her thoughts with me, loved me, yes, loved me, loves me!" Tears filled her eyes.

Then why? The thought ran through his mind, inevitably, that she cared for him, and then, as quickly, a modest corrective thought, which claimed to be Reason, whispered, "Nonsense! It is quite simple: she abhors dishonesty." He could now take her hand into his without "nonsense" and say, "Thank you, at any rate, for confiding in me." He dared not, however, keep her hand. But he had said the simple words so warmly that she felt encouraged to continue.

"Then—may I be bold and rash and plead for her?"

"Do."

"Could you bring yourself to say nothing to...to anyone until we are all safe on the mainland?"

"Yes, I could," he replied gravely.

"And when the time comes to speak, could you bring yourself to *whisper* the truth to Nicholas, and turn your backs on us without saying a word to anyone else—?"

"So as to allow her to keep her noble name. Her great weapon."

The girl's cheeks reddened.

"I asked for something wicked; it cannot be; forgive me."

"Oh, I am no slave to virtue myself! And Nicholas, poor boy, can't wish to have it proclaimed from the rooftops that he was duped. My dear, what worries me is something else, something you seem to have forgotten."

"Tell me."

"Your jilted mother—the quietly jilted Marquise—cannot fail to understand how, and who—"

"So be it. I will have told her before you do."

Mayhew took this like a blow. And it made him say, sorrowfully, "Fatherless and motherless girl, adrift in the world."

Madeleine bowed her head. "That is as it should be."

"That is as it must never be. But I sorely need time to think.

You have thrown so much into my head! Mind you, if we come to grief tomorrow, our worries will take on a darker shade of dark. Madeleine?"

"Yes?"

"Remember your promise. You will be receiving an invitation from Mrs. Folger, she of the spinet, to dine with her tomorrow. Will you go, does your promise hold?"

"It does."

"Then let us begin with that."

They said nothing as they walked together back to the town's houses. The Colonel's imagination was busy reconstructing for himself the picture he had been led to entertain of the false Marquise. She was now another woman. True, she had dropped hints before today that she was no Meissen figurine of aristocratic porcelain, and she had given them strong evidence of that fact the moment they had heard of Wallace's arrest, but—a professional British agent! *That* image needed adjusting to! In the meantime, he wisely resolved to unknow, for now, everything he had just learned, and to concentrate his attention on matters immediate. In his mind, the Marquise became, for the time being, a marquise again, and Nicholas—here his conscience gave a twitch—would have to wait.

Walking silently by his side, Madeleine was carrying a terrible and terribly different burden in her thoughts: the consequences of her virtuous, calamitous, irrepressible impulse. Not only was her mother about to be furiously dismissed by Gage (she now suddenly bethought herself that it had been useless begging the colonel to denounce her mother to Nicholas in a whisper, since Gage was sure to trumpet her real identity to the world), she had condemned Aimée to a life of poverty in Montreal. But worst of all by far: the vision of mother turning away with hatred and contempt for an unnatural daughter. As these thoughts became too painful, her imagination turned to another image. She saw herself dropping at Aimée's feet, begging for forgiveness and love, her arms around her mother's skirts, sobbing her life out, irreconcilably hated....

God, what had she done? What on earth had come over her?

The two parted with some awkwardness, but Madeleine felt a little comforted when Mayhew managed to say, "I will not fail you," before leaving her in front of Swain's Inn.

19

IT WAS A BUSY next morning for Aimée. We have seen that she wanted the table elegantly set, mostly to satisfy her own taste for the fine things of life. She gave orders to Enoch Swain and his cook quite without minding that the meal was supposed to end abruptly well before its conclusion. "We'll enjoy the good things later," she thought. She inspected once more the garden, the cellar, the passageways and doors: all was in order. The carving knife in the kitchen received her renewed attention. Mid-morning a package came for her in an innocent wrapping. She extracted from it the Sergeant's pistol, emptied the barrel, and placed the dead weapon on the footstool under the dinner-table that was to be its home until brandished. Madeleine was gone by then, gone, reluctantly, to spend half a day with Mrs. Folger. Pleasant perfumes were already emanating from the kitchen when, at a quarter to noon, Obed Coffin, leading three other sturdy Sons of Liberty, Benjamin Barnard, Samuel Barrett and Shubael Worth, appeared in the garden, bringing rope with them in case the quantity supplied by the Redcoats proved insufficient. As they had arrived in Coffin's cart, seated amidst three of four barrels, they aroused no suspicion from the passers-by. Aimée placed them behind the crates and pillars in the dark of the cellar. At twelve-thirty, two British soldiers appeared in the garden. Not a word was said. Aimée noted joyfully that one of them was a corporal—the only one in Sergeant Cuff's platoon: a minor but substantial piece of luck. Keeping a finger across her lips, she led the way into the cellar where, without great difficulty but with considerable noise, the four well-prepared men leaped at and overwhelmed the astonished two, bound them, gagged them, and took their pistols from them. As they already had their further instructions, nothing more was said, but Aimée gave her wink of approval before climbing the stair into the passageway, where she dusted off her dress and waited for her guests.

Aimée had seen to it that the Mayhews would arrive before Sergeant Cuff, for if the latter had announced himself ahead of them, he might have wanted a word with his men, and blood might have been shed. Aimée was not afraid of blood, but she was averse to it. The Mayhew gentlemen thus arrived a few minutes before the Sergeant, who had called on Judge Weamish and made sure of him. When Cuff and Judge Weamish entered the dining-room, and after polite greetings were exchanged, Aimée asked the Sergeant to relinquish his sword. He did so, placing it on a credenza. After that a good-humored mutual search took place. "No hidden weapons, gentlemen," cried Aimée, "do pat each other, but let us also investigate the furniture," and drawers and cabinets were opened and searched with smiles and jests as to whether it was necessary to search the Judge. The unanimous decision was that it was not. For good reasons neither party showed any interest in looking under the table. In the meantime, Aimée had managed to whisper into Cuff's ear, "The door to the cellar is wide open," receiving from him a nod of thanks.

They sat down according to the diagram. Words were said in thanks to the Lord, and then Mr. Swain brought in an ample tureen of soup, poured it into each person's bowl, filled the glasses with wine, and left the room.

"Before we begin our deliberations," said the Colonel, "let us thank the Marquise de Tourville, our Nantucket visitor from neutral France, "for troubling herself about us from sheer benevolence of spirit. Let us raise our glasses to her."

"Amen to that," said Sergeant Cuff, in high glee at the notion of what *he* knew about the Frenchwoman and what the traitors were ignorant of. Aimée, duly toasted by all present, smiled happily and winked at the Sergeant.

"And now," the Colonel continued, "before I bring up the liberation of Mr. Wallace, my nephew and I want to inquire whether he is being treated humanely in prison."

Cuff replied that he was being treated as humanely as he deserved.

"This means wholesome food, frequent exercise, some company, and comfortable bedding," said Nicholas.

"I'll try to find a pair of rogues to keep him company," Cuff replied, looking straight at Nicholas.

Weamish, who had no appetite, and longed to be at home in his slippers, tried to calm the conversation into normalcy. "Where is your lovely daughter, Marquise?" he inquired.

"She is visiting dear Mrs. Folger and will stay with her till tea-time—oh dear!"

"The fatal word!" Young Nick cried out, laughing. "Well, if Mrs. Folger keeps a few ounces of tea in case one of her neighbor's children should be indisposed, I believe that even our most frenetic Patriots will wink and let pass."

"Strike me dumb," said the Sergeant, pouring great amounts of salt and pepper into his soup, "but this Yankee commotion over tea is the strangest piece of foolishness since Noah loaded his ark with asses. For a tax of threepence on a pound of tea y'are ready to overturn the world. It makes a man mad. Besides, don't I know, and don't the King, Lord North, Lord Germain and don't everybody know that you smuggle in your tea from Holland anyhow? Your merchants, sir, your invoice-scribbling, bill-of-lading tradesmen can't abide to let a halfpence of profit go without raising an insurrection, bawling tyranny, ringing all the church-bells, and setting the whole continent adrift. Pah!"

"Well, this is a proud nation . . ." said the Colonel mildly.

"Nation? Y'are not a nation, says Sergeant Cuff, y'are a British colony, a child, a dependent, you breathe by your sovereign's grace! Too kind a rule has spoiled you, y'are lunatics of freedom, we've given you a leash three thousand miles long and it's time we pulled it in a foot or two."

Cuff's bawling caused the Judge, whose hand kept trembling against his will, to spill his glass of wine. This gave rise to a rapid, friendly and distracting "Goodness!" "Oh dear!" "I spoiled the tablecloth!" "Fiddlesticks!" (from Cuff), "Nothing of importance," "Is your sleeve wet, my dear Judge?" "A tiny bit." "Here's another napkin. We'll spread it neatly over the scene of the crime," "Thank you. . . . Forgive my clumsiness. . . ."

And with that the first course of the dinner came to an end. Aimée rang the bell and Mr. Swain appeared with a kitchen maid to clear the table.

"Excellent *potage*, Mr. Swain," said Aimée. "My compliments to Mrs. Finney. I'm tempted to steal her from you."

"Thank you, Madam. I hope our joint of mutton answers your expectations as well."

"Well, you might let us pass judgment on it right now. And kindly leave the door open. We need a little more air."

Aimée turned to the guests: "I propose that you gentlemen delay your serious discussion till after the pudding. What say you? A peaceful dinner will lift your spirits."

All agreed, and just then Mr. Swain entered carrying the succulent joint of mutton on a large platter, with the tremendous carving knife at the side.

"Place the dish in front of Mr. Nicholas," said Aimée. "He is the youngest here and will do the carving. Thank you, sir, that will be all."

When Mr. Swain reached the kitchen again, he closed its door, nodded at Mrs. Finney the cook, and said "Mum's the word." He also closed the door to the taproom, where a couple of working-men (it was a Saturday) were enjoying a pint.

In the dining room, Cuff turned to Weamish, sitting to his right. "Judge," he said, "before the pudding, and before the meat, let's have a toast to the king."

"Now?" quavered the Judge.

"Yes, now, by the devil!"

There was no way out. Weamish rose, the glass of wine trembling in his hand. Aimée slipped the pistol adroitly at that point into the Sergeant's left hand under the table-cloth.

"Long live King George the Third!" Weamish brought out.

Mayhew and Nicholas stood up in turn.

"Long live the United Provinces of America!" they shouted.

And Nicholas took hold of the carving knife.

The Sergeant shot up from his chair waving the pistol back and forth at the two Yankees.

"I arrest you both in the king's name! Drop that knife or I shoot! Ludley! Harrington!"

And he repeated, bellowing, "Ludley! Harrington!" while Nicholas, by-passing the open-mouthed Weamish who had collapsed back into his chair, advanced toward him from one side, knife in hand, while Mayhew moved toward him from the other. "You're dead!" Cuff yelled at Young Nick, and pulled the trigger.

The only noise was a click.

Stupefied, Cuff shouted, "The French baggage is a rebel too!" to which Aimée replied, "Your servant, Sergeant Bully," while three of the four Sons of Liberty rushed into the room (one stayed below to watch over the prisoners), armed with pistols and rope. The carving knife returned to the platter, the Sergeant was held fast, Nicholas tightly bound him, and he was forced to sit down.

The Judge sat like a man paralyzed.

"Where are my men?" shouted Cuff.

"Safe in the cellar, where you will be joining them presently, my friend," answered Young Nick.

The Colonel now rang the bell; Mr. Swain appeared, glancing round to ascertain how much damage had been done to his property.

"Mr. Swain," said Mayhew, "Sergeant Cuff will join the two men below whom we have already captured, and the three will remain there under guard until supper-time. You and your two women must keep this event an absolute secret. I do not care to say 'or else', but circumstances compel me to say it. Or else! Kindly give them food and drink. Our men will escort them upstairs when, as they say, Nature calls. In due time we will remove and rid you of them. And by the way, nothing here has been broken or spoiled—"

"Save a little wine spilled on your table-cloth, Mr. Swain," interrupted Aimée, who had been speaking softly with the Judge. "Do forgive us all that trouble," she had whispered to him. "Marquise," he replied, "how could this be? What happened? You were sent by Governor Gage! I feel I am dreaming!" "Hush, my ever dear Mr. Weamish; I have had my reasons; but say nothing to anyone about Gage—you understand me—protect me, and I will protect you once I reach the mainland; nobody shall move you from the place in Nantucket you hold so well."

Aimée had given some thought, the day and night before, about her "game" being revealed by the Sergeant and the Judge during the turmoil to come. Her conclusion had been that she did not much care if the Mayhew gentlemen discovered that she had landed on the island of Nantucket as—well, what she had landed as, but had changed sides, knowing the world and falling suddenly in love. Still, she would try, for the time being, to remain an innocent traveller, and later reveal to the Mayhews whatever she cared to make known.

In the meantime, the Colonel was quietly giving orders. "Samuel and Shubael, you will keep an eye on the three prisoners until we return for them. Obed and Benjamin, your mission is to collect some twenty reliable men and meet my nephew and myself at seven o'clock at the Meeting House on Fair Street where the Redcoats are quartered. As you know, they all return there for supper toward six in the evening. Our prisoners will be loaded on a cart; Nicholas and I will produce them to the soldiers. Seeing the prisoners on one side and a band of resolute Patriots on the other, and not much in love with their mission in Nantucket, nor with their leader, they will surrender without resistance."

Mr. Swain, who had been standing anxiously in a corner all this time, asked "Where, sir, shall I send my bill?"

"To Mayhew & Mayhew, my good man," said the Colonel,

"down to the last napkin."

"So much for that," said Young Nick, after their host had left. "Now for the toast that was so interestingly interrupted. Men, take glasses from the sideboard, here is a fine Madeira, let us drink to America!"

"To America!" they all shouted, except Cuff. Weamish, looking at Aimée, added his voice as feebly as possible.

"God save the King!" Cuff bawled in reply, wriggling in his ropes.

"God save the people!" Obed Coffin replied.

"They'll need more saving than you think, you blockhead! You'll miss the king one day, all you raggle-taggle levellers—when high and low are topsy-turvy—when your stage-actors write your laws and y'are ruled by ambitious haberdashers. God save the King!" And then he turned baleful eyes on Aimée. "As for you, scurvy Marquise, traitress—"

"Silence!" cried Nicholas, "You are addressing the future Mrs. Nicholas Mayhew."

Cuff burst out in a homeric laugh.

"Good. She'll sell your scalp to the Indians. Mr. Mayhew, with her as your wife, I'm avenged already."

"Carry the fellow to the cellar, you two," said Nicholas to Samuel and Shubael, "let him confer below with his two henchmen."

"Yes. Remove me from this kennel, you dogs," were the Sergeant's parting words.

After Obed Coffin and Samuel Barrett went out to spread the word as requested by the Colonel, the two Mayhew gentlemen and Aimée were left alone with the Judge. They sat down and looked at him with friendly eyes.

"Thomas Weamish," said the Colonel; "will you be so kind as to accompany me to the jailhouse and ask Mr. Morton to set Henry Wallace free?"

"Yes," said the Judge meekly.

"My nephew and I will be gone from the island by tomorrow night. We shall not meet again for many a stormy day. Will you give me your hand, sir? We are not saints. God knows I have told my share of lies and gone by crooked ways. But all in all, Tom, I am your elder—and a wiser head than sits on your shoulders. Listen to me: we are the better men, believe me, and the future is with us."

"Join us, Judge," added Aimée, because, *entre nous*, the Revolution is likely to become the fashion."

"I promise to think it over ... favorably," Weamish murmured.

"And, wherever I live, in America or France, I shall always keep a set of rooms ready for you and your respected mother."

It may be noted that the uneaten roast on the table and the pudding that never left the kitchen did not go to waste. They nourished the men in the cellar (the door to the garden was kept open for fresh air) and helped them pass the time till they were plucked from their confinement. Bottles of beer were handed round as well, and duly noted on Mr. Swain's reckoning. Aimée walked Judge Weamish home, her arm in his. "Say nothing to Jenny," she advised him sweetly, "and keep everything to yourself, because arousing a few Loyalists will only lead to brutal deeds. Shall we remain friends, Mr. Weamish? Such at any rate is my ardent hope." And indeed it was, and the Judge, pressing her arm, assented and consented.

That evening, the Sergeant, the Corporal and the private were led, hands tied to their backs, and pistols to their heads, to the British quarters, where they were exhibited, in front of some thirty young Patriots, to the dumbfounded soldiers. Mayhew had been right. The lads did not relish their lives on the island, as remote for them as the North Pole, and now, seeing their Sergeant humbled secretly tickled them. They promptly surrendered their weapons to the Patriots. At Young Nick's suggestion, they were made even safer by having their shoes sequestered, to be returned to them on board ship. No one, it was argued, runs away from captivity in his stockings. Sergeant Cuff, of course, was locked up in jail, in

replacement of Henry Wallace, waiting to rejoin his men on the
day they all sailed forever from Nantucket into the grip of George
Washington.

20

JUDGE WEAMISH had, once more, taken to his bed after the frightful dinner in which he had been obliged, he felt, to take part. The alarmed Jenny soon heard the whole story from his lips, perhaps embellished a trifle with respect to his role in it. A trifle—a detail or two—for he knew that she would not believe him if he overdid his heroism. That the Marquise had been a traitress did not surprise the faithful housekeeper. "I never liked the bold looks of her."

From Jenny the tale spread swiftly through the town, confirmed by details Mr. Swain's cook carried abroad. But no practical consequences came about. The Loyalists could only, as one says, gnash their teeth when they witnessed, from a distance, the Redcoats' surrender. Later that night, however, they vented their rage on the Town House Liberty Tree by chopping it down to the sound of joyous huzzas, and several women were seen passing platters and dishes through the windows of the Redcoats' temporary prison, unimpeded by the good-natured Rebels guarding the place. But Nantucket lived on whaling and trade, not politics, and even the Toryish selectmen (there were two of them) shrugged their shoulders in private, at the dinner-table, saying to their wives, "Let the Mayhew pair do the devil's work on the far side of the sea!" They said much the same when, the next day, Mr. Applegate, deeply upset, came round to them urging drastic action.

Still, the Colonel and Young Nick decided that they would leave the island very quietly, very privately, from the south shore as planned. The morning after the capture of Sergeant Cuff, Josh Mamack was sent to the beach to light the fire that told Captain Fleming to expect the Mayhews that very day. He also unwrapped the rowboat lying under some shrubs that was to carry—not the two persons the Captain was expecting, but two more, with

baggage. Mamack, scratching his head, could see that either
another boat was wanted, or else that two separate trips to the
awaiting sloop would be needed.

That second day of July the sun showed fitfully through
racing clouds, causing Mr. Swain, standing protected from the wind
in the entrance to his tavern (he had just finished the Mayhew &
Mayhew reckoning, to be handed to Abishai Cottle the next day)
to look up at the troubled sky and muse, "Thus are some rejoicing
and some sorrowing." Meanwhile, above his head, packing was
going apace, in high good mood on Aimée's side at any rate; she
did not notice her daughter's low spirits. When would she tell her
mother? When, when? "To be sure," Aimée was bubbling, "Tom
Gage will be tempted to shout into the four winds of the continent
who and what we are, you and I, but the letter I mean to send him
the day after we arrive at Boston will stop him cold. I hold two
secrets concerning the dear man that will keep him quiet. I think
I'll leave this petticoat to Mrs. Finney."

The Mayhew residence was a-bustle too, of course. It was the
Sabbath day, but there was no time, this once, for worship. The
only peculiarity worth noting here is that Aimée, though very
busy, ran over to the Mayhew house more than once in order to
help the gentlemen, albeit an outsider might have thought no help
was really needed. It was as if, touchingly, she could not tear herself
away for any length of time from her future husband. Well, she did
dote on him, yet she had another reason.

Needless to say, the Mayhew men were travelling light.
Wallace and Cottle had all the instructions and legal powers
necessary for the furtherance of the family business. Henry
Wallace, that day, was confined to the house with a fever and an
ache in his bowels, not having recovered from his imprisonment.
In the afternoon Abishai Cottle went to borrow Obed Coffin's
cart. Helped by Mr. Swain's people, he loaded it with Aimée's
impressive trunk and Madeleine's modest portmanteau, and then
returned to the Mayhews' residence to help load the two men's

belongings—clothes, linen, dressing case and papers. Thus the convoy that took its way to the southern beach consisted of the cart, driven by Josh Mamack, with Cottle crouched between the trunk and portmanteau, and two chaises, one driven by Old Moses and the other by Samuel Barrett, bringing the four voyagers to the shore. The cart was quickly unloaded, Young Nick chuckling at the sight. "How is it," he asked Aimée, tapping her trunk with his fingers, and then the girl's valise, "that our Madeleine is carrying so much less than you, angel?" "Immaturity, dear," she replied. "Idealism travels light; but when ideals wear thin, property becomes a comfort." "And what am I, woman! your ideal or your property?" "You are—my ideal property," she said kissing him, "and let them all stare!" she thought.

She turned to Mayhew. "The waters look choppy. Shall we have a safe passage, William?" she inquired, wanting particularly to call him by his first name, and adding, demurely, "I may call you William, I hope, from now on?" "Of course," he replied with a warm smile, "and I believe we will be quite safe." "You will call me Aimée, will you not?" "With pleasure, my dear Aimée." Madeleine looked and listened, somewhat surprised at the Colonel's cloudless amiability. Her moment must come on board the *Enterprise*. It was from her, not from the Colonel, that her mother must hear the truth.

But it was time to part. The Colonel sent Barrett and Old Moses home with heartfelt thanks, echoed of course by the others. The mood of the uncle and the nephew differed greatly. Nicholas felt joyful and triumphant, but for Mayhew the hour was solemn, especially when the moment came to part from Cottle. He was about to shake the young man's hand when suddenly he embraced him—a gesture most rare in Nantucket!—saying "Farewell, my friend, my son, farewell." Tears began to fill Cottle's eyes (and those of Madeleine, in secret), but he braced himself to say the manly thing: "We shall guard your property here, Henry and I, like the dog in Hades. When you return, sir, you will find every speck of it as you left it."

"When will that be?" Mayhew wondered, his hands on
Cottle's shoulders. "I fear that streams of blood will be shed before
heaven decides who shall stand and who must fall."

"God forbid," said the young Quaker, "and Heaven cannot
condone the shedding of human blood. But I hear there's talk of
conciliation yet. God willing you will be back sooner than we all
fear."

"I wish I could believe it. But whoever in history gave up
power without a fight? Go home now, Abishai, and may that same
God bless you."

Cottle gravely shook hands all around (Young Nick also gave
him a hug) and departed with his now empty cart.

The late afternoon was windy, the sea neither tranquil nor
dangerous. There would be summer daylight enough for the two
trips to the *Enterprise*. It was decided that Aimée and Nicholas
should go first, trunk and all: no light load! The young man and
Mamack pulled the rowboat to the edge of the water and installed
the lady and her baggage, followed by Nicholas jumping in.
Presently they were on the water, Mamack working the oars and
the other two waving at the Colonel and Madeleine.

A cabin stood near the water, built by and for fishermen who
angled there for cod, mackerel, and herring. The builders, using
simple brackets and planks, had given it a bench along one of the
walls. Mayhew went to sit there and closed his eyes, breathing
deeply as if to store for the future the place's especial perfumes of
water, beach and trees.

Madeleine began to move quietly away, but the Colonel
heard the rustling of her dress and opened his eyes.

"Where are you going, Madeleine?"

"Only a little farther off."

"Why?"

"I—I wanted to leave you to yourself."

"Will you not stay? And sit beside me? From here one can

see the ocean, the land to left and right, our friends on the waves.
..."

She sat down next to him.

"Nicholas and his prize, Aimée and her prize!" he exclaimed
as the couple again waved from the distance. The Colonel waved
back gaily, Madeleine less so. She now confessed that she had
not spoken to her mother. "So I concluded from observing her
cheerfulness," he said with a smile. "But I will, I will before the day
is over!" she exclaimed.

"I beg you, dear Madeleine, to do nothing of the sort."

"So that it will be up to you?"

"Who knows? A poem is tugging at my mind. It begins:

'Let me not to the marriage of true minds
Admit impediment.'"

"Is it yours?" asked Madeleine naively. Mayhew smiled. "I
wish! No it is not, but it speaks to me if I alter it ever so slightly. 'Let
me not to the marriage of *like* minds admit impediment.' Who am
I to play God? Seeing them so snug together, I feel I will never rise
to the high moral plane from which I can pulverize them in a flash
of virtuous lightning. And cause a mother to hate her daughter. No.
Let you and I be still. Let Nicholas enjoy his Marquise for many
years to come! She'll be 'the star to his wandering bark.' "

Madeleine stared at him. He seemed wonderfully serene.

"I marvel at you," was all she could say.

"More likely you are a little shocked by my levity—relieved,
of course—your mother is safe—but shocked. What can I say? I
thought and thought and thought, and discovered that I keep my
fund of rage for very large occasions. This is not one of them."

"I wish I could learn from you!"

"Do you really?"

"Of course. Can you doubt it? I am so ignorant!"

"Beware! I am an old man, fifty-four years old. This means
that I have amassed a huge store of useful knowledge. Even

Madame Pichot's trunk couldn't hold it all. It would take me years to unload it, sort it out, and bequeath it to you."

"If only it could be done in an hour, before the boat returns. I shall sorely need it."

"Impossible. A lifetime is necessary. What is it, Madeleine?"

She had turned her head away.

"Nothing. You wanted to say farewell to your island, Colonel. General."

She began to rise, but he held her back.

"What will you do with your lifetime instead?" he asked.

"Is this not a cruel question?"

"Presently I will give you a chance to be cruel to me in return."

"What do you mean?"

"My wisdom," he said, "I can impart to you in less than an hour, Madeleine. It is my love that would take me a lifetime to unfold."

She said nothing.

"You see," he said, looking down, "now *you* can be cruel to me."

Her voice now was so low that it was hard to hear above the splash of the wavelets on the sand. But he did hear. "My mother is a swindler, a spy, a libertine. I am her bastard, a pauper, a nobody, a daughter who rewarded her mother's care by betraying her. How would you deal with me if I had not almost a pretty face?"

"I would love, admire, and defend you, above all against yourself. I would look after you as long as I live. Your beauty, I confess, has unhinged me to the point of asking you to be my wife as if I were a catch for a girl of twenty-three. But I fancy that your good sense will keep you at a safe distance from me."

"Because I would not disgrace you," said Madeleine.

"Madeleine is always gentle."

"Because I would not disgrace you," she repeated more strongly.

She had been looking away. Now, with a hand on her cheek,

he made her turn toward him.

"Look at these miserable wrinkles," he said. "Think of what they foretell."

But what happened then is that her eyes filled with tears. An immense desolation had overcome her. "Don't abandon me!" was all she could cry.

"Could you bear me as a husband?" he asked, and she flung herself into his arms.

"Care for me! I'll please you, you'll see! I shall try so bravely that you'll be proud of your foundling!"

"Such wild words! I'll care for you like an old hound standing guard over a treasure. But why take me as a husband? Your friend William Mayhew will do it as well, I swear, and he'll slink off the moment you appoint a more tasteful husband."

She held on to him, but now she was smiling. "Are you turning me away already? So soon?"

"Mine then. Mine to the end of my blessed time."

"Yours for as long as my heart will beat."

They kissed, not unseen by the astonished Aimée and Nicholas, who could even make out the girl touching Mayhew's cheeks, eyes and forehead with her fingers. Of course they could not hear her "So fine, so strong, so merry, so wise . . ."

"Wise indeed," he said, "to have bewitched you into my arms and condemned you—"

"To be a lifelong burden to you."

"Yes, as a flower burdens the earth."

"Hold me. Your flower is shivering."

"The sun is setting and the wind is blowing. Is this better?"

"Much better."

They were silent for a while. Then looking toward the sea, Mayhew said, "Look! Your mother is pointing at us."

Aimée and Nicholas were waving merrily again. The two rose hand in hand to the shoreline and waved back.

"Romantic couple!" cried Mayhew.

Madeleine, still looking toward the now distant rowboat, took his arm: "William," she said—and the instant she said it she thought, "I shall never, never call him Bill!." It felt wonderfully strange to both of them that she spoke his first name.

"What, my Madeleine?"

"Surely, in spite of your sweet and most wicked silence, surely Nicholas will discover sooner or later that he married mere Madame Pichot. What will happen then?"

"Why, he'll fume for an hour or two, but his interest will be the same as hers: to bury the truth. I believe he would not even confide the awful truth to me."

Madeleine hesitated for a moment before coming to another painful decision. "My mother was less confident," she said at last. "She took precautions."

She walked to her portmanteau and opened it. She felt as though her mother's eyes were glaring at her from the ocean. But she took out a folder containing several letters and gave it to Mayhew. The Colonel, sitting down on the cabin bench, looked at the first of them and exclaimed, "What's this? A letter to Nicholas from Ezekiel Davis! How did this come into your hands?"

"Mother filched it from Nick's case and gave it to me for safekeeping. I couldn't refuse to take it, though I knew I would be betraying her again."

Mayhew began to read. "Our Mrs. Applegate grows desperate; she has indeed every power to sell the Concord estate. Give us some useful intelligence, true or false, concerning the Tory doings of Mr. Applegate in Nantucket, and our Sons of Liberty shall rattle Mrs. A., I assure you, till she will sell to yours truly, and gratefully too, for five shillings in the pound."

Here Mayhew's hand dropped. He wanted to read no farther and wanted to read no other letters. "Intelligence true or false," he said bitterly. "Five shillings in the pound. Handsome! Good work, nephew."

Madeleine had been standing over him as he read the letter.

When his head sank, she cried out, frightened, "What have I done?"

"You have done well. Once again you have done well," he said, raising his head to her; "I must try to save that woman . . ."

"But I've given you pain—already!" Madeleine moaned.

Mayhew, rising, replied vehemently: "Salutary pain. Don't I know that this letter is but one leaf out of an evil book? Haven't I known it for a long time in some remote corner of my soul that I dared not visit? Thank you for pulling me by the hand and forcing the door open and saying to me in your deeper wisdom than mine, Look look look! Every day of the week, Young Nick—but what am I saying? Every Tom, Nick and Harry will be busy buying cheap and selling dear, abusing the ignorant, hoarding scarce goods, making hyena profits from our war, and sucking the sap out of the land. But now what? Where shall I find the strength?"

"How can I comfort you?" she cried, taking his hand in hers.

They walked to the water-line again and looked at the rowboat, which had become a speck, almost lost by the keel of *The Enterprise* they too would soon be boarding.

"Should we even begin?" Mayhew's question went to her, to himself, to some great Thing at large. And he repeated, "Should we even begin?"

Madeleine, kissing his hand (it was still clutching the letter), said firmly, "Not, at any rate, with your eyes closed."

This led to a long silence.

"So be it," Mayhew brought out at last. "Not with our eyes closed," he repeated after her, pressing her hand and gazing at the *Enterprise*.

The End

Notice

Here is a passage from Boswell's *Life of Samuel Johnson*:

> Mr. Wilkes remarked, that "among all the bold flights
> of Shakespeare's imagination, the boldest was making
> Birnamwood march to Dunsinane; creating a wood where
> there never was a shrub; a wood in Scotland! ha! ha! ha!"

No Redcoats were stationed on the island of Nantucket during the Revolution; no Marquise, fake or real, visited the island, no great officers were recruited thence. All the same, the island is present in my romance in its more or less true character of the time; the lighthouse, the street-names, the wharves, these and other features truly existed. I owe my knowledge of them to a flurry of books and the help of the Nantucket Historical Association, to which I herewith offer my heartfelt thanks. As for the names of my characters, many of them belong in fact to the islanders, often going back to the seventeenth century, and some are still alive in Nantucket families today. And here it is important to declare that I have distributed these names quite arbitrarily. They are real names attached to fictive characters.

Real without qualifications are the words of Thomas Jefferson quoted in chapter XIII; they are taken from his 1774 tract, *A Summary View of the Rights of British America*. Alike real are those of Elihu Coleman of Nantucket in chapter XVIII. And the Nantucket ditty in chapter XV is perfectly authentic too.

WICKEDNESS

1

THE SHRILL, unearthly bleat of the unicorn made itself heard in the Great Hall of Dumfrey Castle, where the earl and his good friend Baron Theefton had been examining a map which Ralf Basset, the earl's steward, had spread on a table before them. The earl and the steward had heard that bleat before, of course, so now, in spite of their undiminished dismay, they could not help enjoying (but the word is probably too strong) the mixture of startled and aghast look they saw in Theefton's face. "There you have it, my lord," said Basset; "you have heard the call of the beast that kills our sheep, our cows, our goats, our hens and roosters, our horses, and even, as if for its amusement, our cats, our dogs, once even a canary."

The Baron looked grave. "I am glad I came. You need help, Umfrey, and here I am."

His visit to the earldom had been delayed for over a month because, gone deer-hunting in his forests, and alighting from his horse, he had been bitten in the shin by the expiring animal and had suffered bandage and bed for weeks. But of course he was immensely curious about the unicorn's depredations in the earldom, heaven-sent, he had no doubt. His own lands were unaffected—another decision, surely, of the Powers above; and he now silently congratulated himself for his tact in not mentioning the dramatic difference to his host.

Unicorn or no unicorn, he had asked to look at that map— the parchment the three men were bending over when the unicorn's shocking bleat had interrupted them—with the notion that he might dare, sooner or later, to demand, no, to suggest one or two very minor "adjustments." His fief and that of Umfrey, Earl of Dumfrey bordered on each other. Theefton had been placing a finger here and a finger there and throwing out little snorts to which the Earl paid, or pretended to pay, no attention. The latter's domains, covering some twenty-six pleasantly rolling hundreds, were half again as extensive as Theefton's. The map also showed in a separate color the unusually fertile possessions which the orphaned Lady Margaret had brought to the Earl as her dowry, namely Wyngham, Brigsley, Tuckbetter and Glaswin Epton. These lay almost puppy-like on the parchment, to the south of both the Earl's and the Baron's domains, as if licking the one and then the other. Theefton's finger also wandered over these. Had he instead of Umfrey married Margaret, they would have been his. Somehow, he vaguely felt, the punishment inflicted on the earldom had something or other to do with this faulty circumstance.

The examination, along with some chat about a forthcoming visit to their shire by King Edward, was suddenly halted by a door thrown open, and the appearance of the Earl's trusted head-servant, Peter by name, holding a gored poodle by its ears, a cake of blood still visible around the wound. The Earl slumped a little, still seated at the table, and moaned "Another one!" Basset, lowering his head, mournfully covered his cheek with one hand, but Theefton jumped to his feet and rushed to examine the poodle: it was, after all, his first encounter with the murders the unicorn was committing in his friend's lands.

"Whose pet is it this time?" Basset asked Peter with a groan while the Baron was palpating the dead dog.

"Mistress Bullen's, sir." Peter was pale but dutifully calm. This was the elderly *dame de compagnie* of the Countess, who (it may be mentioned), had been reading the tale of Holofernes to her mistress the night before this latest murder.

"Has the poor woman been told?" groaned the Earl.

"Indeed she has, my lord. Mistress Bullen is in bed under sedation."

"And my wife?"

"She is aware, my lord. Lady Margaret has been walking in her Garden of Exotics to recompose herself after putting Mistress Bullen to bed. So her maid told me."

In the meantime, Theefton had come to a conclusion. "A clean penetration through the abdomen," he pronounced. "A circular penetration of an inch and a quarter on one side of the beast, and of something less than an inch on the other. Umfrey: that unicorn of yours is no novice."

"Take the thing away, Peter," said Basset.

As Peter was leaving the hall, a servant entered, carrying refreshments.

"Well now," said Theefton, lifting his glass after the servant had left, "let's drink to the destruction of the unicorn. If your men can't catch him, I'll send you the best of mine. Duty of a vassal and friend. And you'll be nailing his horn over your mantelpiece before the month is out. I pledge it."

"My lord," said Basset softly; "you forget."

"Forget what?"

"That a man can never catch the unicorn."

"Of course, of course! What was I thinking? It must be a virgin. Carrying a mirror in her hand. The unicorn looks into it. He can't move away from his image. He follows her. She pulls him into the castle. You kill him."

"Perhaps, my lord, only perhaps."

"Perhaps what, damnation? Why haven't you sent a battalion of virgins into the field?"

"Ah, if life were that simple, my lord! Only a virgin can catch the unicorn, but she does not necessarily catch him. God must decide whether the time is ripe. And here lies the difficulty."

The Earl was becoming more uncomfortable by the minute. "Enough of that," he said with an affected yawn; "we were looking at the map, Harry."

"It can wait. What difficulty, Master Basset? Difficulties are meat and drink for me. The year the King sent me to Norway—but never mind that. The difficulty, Basset?"

"It is as follows, my lord. You send a girl out—"

The Earl stood up. "My wife must be wishing me to be with her." And without another word he left the hall. Basset thought the sudden exit a little strange, but not strange enough to alarm him. The Countess might indeed be in want of a sympathetic ear. So, after watching his master leave the hall, Basset resumed his explanation.

"You send a virgin out, my lord, mirror in hand. A girl of good family. With a reputation. But suppose she fails to catch the unicorn. Perhaps the time has not come. But perhaps, on the other hand—"

"On the other hand?" The Baron was prodding his brain.

"On the other hand."

"I see! I see!"

"A reputation ruined, a family destroyed. It happened, my lord; I can hardly bear to speak of it. And since that fatal day, no woman, no girl dares take the risk."

Master Ralf Basset—but a few words should be said about the Earl's faithful steward. A generation older than his master, a large worry-wrinkled ever-grieving widower with thinning grey hair, the man was known as Probus Basset throughout the Earl's fief for his undeviating and unusual virtue. He did not spirit part of the Earl's revenue into his own pocket—on the contrary, he gave a portion of his wages to the castle's Almoner for the beggars at the gate. He did not appoint his two nephews to lazy clerkships in the earldom. He had reduced the three-days' labor a week the villeins owed the Earl to a single day and persuaded his reluctant master to abolish the detested death duty which obliged a peasant's heir to surrender his best animal to the Earl before inheriting his father's acres. He had saved more than one captured poacher from being blinded and castrated. He was also a great drainer of the fens that spread over a part of the earldom.

Such then was the man who spoke to Lord Theefton. As can be guessed, he had no great opinion of the Baron, but the latter having galloped to the aid of his friend, accompanied only by his valet and his coiffeur, Basset was touched, and he decided to tell Theefton the sad story, which was, briefly, that the Earl's all too ambitious chamberlain, Bruce Bennyworth, had clamored for his daughter Clotilda to be dispatched to capture the unicorn. Lord Umfrey had urged him—almost on his knees!—to change his mind ("the Earl has such delicate feelings," added the steward), but to refuse outright was impossible, it would have been tantamount to official skepticism as to the honor of the Bennyworth family— the ancient Bennyworth family, respected throughout the shire. Clotilda herself protested that she felt unfit for so sublime a mission. But the chamberlain was not the man to be overruled by a mere daughter.

"In short, she was dispatched, and she returned without," said Basset. "It meant nothing. The Immaculate Saint Perpetua, our patroness in heaven, might have failed as well. Heaven is inscrutable. But the people do not make fine discriminations. Even in better circles.... To make a long story short, Bennyworth did not survive the blow. The mother, who had died giving birth to the girl, was spared this wretchedness."

The Earl had returned just before the conclusion of Basset's account. He had endured a "scene" with his wife in her Garden of Exotics. She wanted him to act. Do something. But what? What?

"Umfrey," Theefton cried out, "I have the solution!"

"The solution?" Umfrey's voice conveyed no great curiosity.

"Don't you want to hear it?"

"Why not." The question mark was missing from the Earl's reply.

"Why not send out a girl ten years old? It's so simple, and so sublimely obvious, that it probably never occurred to any of you. A ten-year old girl, carefully chosen, is sure to be immaculate, and would certainly not object to being thought so. And if she failed, no one would snicker."

The Earl and Basset stared at Theefton, who began to fidget.

"You answer him, Basset," said the Earl, shrugging his shoulders.

"Ten-year-old girls have no effect on a unicorn, my lord," said Basset. "For him, a virgin is a girl who might be no virgin if she chose. You see the point, my lord: there has to be merit in it. Otherwise it's like asking a cat not to bark."

"I give up!" exclaimed the Baron; "maybe I shouldn't have come."

2

THAT NIGHT, the hideous bleat of the hated beast was heard again in the distance by those who were not asleep. In the morning it was discovered that Lady Margaret's favorite foal, Purity, had been gored to death. The news quickly spread from the castle to the village, where it was heard with especial satisfaction by Leofa the blacksmith, who had been fined by Bennyworth—fined in public—for botched work on one of the Earl's horses, some weeks before Clotilda's failed sally. Leofa had spread the word that the unicorn had been born, so to speak, of the Bennyworth daughter's evident unchastity. The girl, it must be said, had not endeared herself to the common people by acts of charity or even simple daily affability. They remembered the afternoon when, accidentally pushed by a girl running away from a bully, she had slapped the poor innocent thing so hard she had lost two teeth. This was not known in the castle, where Clotilda showed far more sugar than pepper.

Leofa was a man of powerful stocky built and menacing beard who boasted of a following in the village as its radical voice. It took him no time to gather a small mob, at the head of which, crossing the moat, he marched into the castle grounds, demanding of the guards to see the Earl. Needless to say, it was not the Earl who appeared, but Peter. The Earl's chief servant was not the man to be intimidated by Leofa, but neither was he the blacksmith's enemy. On the contrary. They shared the affectionate services of a girl who "worked," with a few others, in a house where the village drifted into pasture-land.

Peter gave Leofa a warm welcome. It was mid-morning. As it happened, mid-mornings the Earl was nowhere to be seen. It was a time when everyone was busy, including the Earl's wife giving orders, writing letters, and currently hearing out candidates to succeed the deceased chamberlain, whose task, of course, had been to oversee the complicated household. It was the time when the Earl spent his almost daily hour or two in Clotilda's chambers, held and being held in her pink and spotless limbs.

Thus it was Basset who received Leofa in the great hall; Leofa alone; Lady Margaret would have raised a storm had a flock of ruffians been permitted to sully the tiles. Peter, in the meantime, hurried up the stairs to where the Earl lay, and tapping lightly on the door, slipped a brief message under it. A whirlwind resulted. "You will stay here!" growled the Earl, hastily dressing. "I will not!" "You will!" "We shall see!" snarled Clotilda, still in bed. There was no time for bandying reasons. The Earl sped down the stairs. About to enter the hall, he almost collided with Theefton, who had been informed by his valet that the unicorn had struck again. The two men entered the hall as Basset was lecturing Leofa. "Very well, Leofa," the steward was saying, "but you've gone too far this time. What on earth has Mistress Clotilda to do with the unicorn? You know as well as I do that the unicorn appeared weeks before she—to make a long story short, one thing has nothing to do with the other. I have explained the logic of it a dozen times."

On the entrance of the Earl Leofa bowed suitably low but did not chasten his words. "Logic is all right for them what can afford luxuries," he cried out. "The people has got feelings, and the feeling today is that it's time the land was purgated. We demand morality in 'igh places. And there's some in our midst what mutter worse."

Just then Clotilda made her appearance, tall, blonde, large-breasted, magnificent. "What do they mutter?" she snapped.

"That you're not a Christian!" shouted Leofa. "We ain't seen no penitence since the day you didn't do what you was supposed to do. Folk snarl at you in the market and you sneer at folk. Witch!"

The word hit like an electric shock. Clotilda winced.

The Earl should have spoken, of course, and Basset moved to throw the blacksmith out, but the Baron was first. "I'd gladly have one of my men thrash this fellow, Mistress Clotilda, but alas,

I came here practically unattended, and my position prevents me from doing it myself."

"Excuse me, sir," retorted the unfazed Leofa, "but no stranger 'as the right to thrash the common people; that's the prevocative of our own lordship."

"Enough," said Basset. "Here's a shilling, Leofa. Now go away."

"You're a sensible man anyway, Master Basset. I meant no harm. Hoo! Here's Lady Margaret. Mind your manners, everybody."

Lady Margaret was coming from the stables, where she and the best of the grooms had been trying to save Purity from death, but in vain. Infuriated, she was looking for her husband, when, entering the hall, she saw company and caught Basset's "go away" to Leofa.

"Good Leofa!" she said with surprising friendliness. "What brings you to us?"

"We don't like witches," he said, shooting a dark look at Clotilda, "and the people want a return to morality and causes removed. I saloote your lordships with respeck," and he bowed himself out. Clotilda's fists tightened, but she dared not speak.

"What did the fellow say?" asked Lady Margaret as if she had not understood.

The Countess was a fine-looking woman. Not so young as Clotilda. Not so fresh as Clotilda. Not so tall as Clotilda. Her teeth not so white as Clotilda's. Her lips not so full as Clotilda's. Her form not so round and soft as Clotilda's (one of her small breasts was, alas, smaller than the other). All the same, she was indubitably a fine-looking woman with a presence. And she was kin (at some slight remove) of the Arundel.

"Purity is gone," said the Earl weakly, instead of repeating Leofa's words. "I don't know what to say, my dear."

"Of course you don't. Innocently at pasture she was; then all of a sudden gored to oblivion. Is there a God? I ask you. What do you mean to do about it, Umfrey? Ah yes, you don't know what to say! The cup is overflowing at last."

The Baron took her hand in his and kissed it. "My dear Countess," he said, "I was struck dumb. Your favorite foal. I feel as though a child of mine had been gored. I could weep."

"Thank you, Lord Theefton and childhood friend. The simple love of an uncomplicated beast. I saw her born. It's as if the only creature who ever loved me had died."

"Margaret!" exclaimed the Earl in dismay while Theefton muttered tut tut tut. Basset had said nothing all the while, feeling, quite rightly, that the varied expressions of his face and the gestures of his hands were all that was needed for the occasion. Clotilda, instead, could not resist a "Please accept my condolences, Lady Margaret," and was decisively snubbed.

"Well, Umfrey?"

"Father Willibald mentioned an Exorcist a week or so ago, a man who lives in the moors. I have had my doubts, but now Basset and I will look into this, my dear."

"Ring the bell for something to drink," retorted Margaret.

3

FATHER WILLIBALD, the castle's chaplain, was a very old, seldom seen figure who did his holy work for the family and its retainers as needed and was given his meals in his rooms. It was known that he spent most of his hours poring over his breviary and performing various exercises of self-abasement (including the employment of a lash) in preparation for an indisputable admission into one of the higher circles of Paradise. He did, however, care for a little flock of rabbits in the gardens that lay outside the castle moat—not far from the larger space in which Lady Margaret's Garden of Exotics had been built—and he had suffered the loss of two of its long-eared folk from the merciless attacks of the unicorn. Moved into action, Father Willibald had spoken to the village curate, and, following the goring of Purity, the two called for a penitential procession of the village in which, to the ringing of the church-bells, the wooden, prettily painted statue of Saint Perpetua (she held in her right hand a box containing a true nail of the Cross on which Saint Peter had been martyred upside down) would be taken from the church at night, carried by torchlight through the eight streets and market square of the village with suitable chants of penitential psalms, and finally returned to the church. If this failed to persuade God (or the Devil) to send the unicorn to a faraway shire, it would at least tell England that they knew how to do the godly thing.

On the evening of the procession, the Earl stood alone in his bedchamber, watching from a window the preparations in the near distance, and brooding over his sins. How often had he meant to make a full confession to Father Willibald, but failed to do so at the last moment, and thus sinned against by hiding his sin...his sins. The menacing talk by Leofa, who of course spoke for many in the village but undoubtedly for grumblers in the castle as well, weighed on him, and just when the image of Clotilda in splendid undress passed through his mind, with a knock at the door Basset came into the room.

The steward hesitated as he stood near Umfrey, who was interrogating him with his eyes. Candles burning on a chest nearby threw a shadow from Basset's very large presence onto the Earl.

"Speak, my friend, speak," said Umfrey in a low voice. He expected nothing cheerful.

"My lord, I saw our lovely Clotilda weeping and could not let this pass without speaking to you, frankly speaking to you, a master whom I dare almost look upon as the son I never had."

"You *are* almost a father to me, my good man. Speak freely. What is it that troubles you?"

"Your silence, my lord, your silence. The girl is in danger. The scene with that scoundrel Leofa. The aroused villagers. I look in vain for a firmer stand on your part, a public declaration of your faith in the young lady's innocence. Listen to these bells, Lord Dumfrey. Think of your father who wore the cross under the gates of Jerusalem. Think of the founder of your line who baptized the savage Saxons. Think of our faith in you, and then call out to the people, 'As you love me and as you take pride in my righteousness, thus shall you believe in her chastity!' "

The churchbells, as if on purpose, had stopped ringing. To the earl, the ominous silence seemed suddenly to mean: Your turn! Speak! He could bear it no longer. "My righteousness! Why doesn't God strike me now?" he moaned, his head in his hands, turning away from the window and dropping heavily into a chair.

"Strike you, my lord? Our beloved ruler? Why are you saying this?"

"Stop, stop. . .I must speak at last. . . ."

"Speak what, my lord, in heaven's name?"

"Clotilda and I. . .I and Clotilda. . . ."

Basset's mouth opened wide, and unable to stand, he sank, against ceremony, onto a bench at the side of the Earl's chair. "Oh

my God my God my God!" — It was his turn to moan. "Since
when?" he then managed to ask.

"Since. . .the beginning. On the wedding night, I. . .I
shrank. . . ." The Earl's tone changed. "Thank God, I've told you, of
all men. Finally. I was, I am a man bewitched. . . ."

Suddenly Basset sprang up. "Bennyworth!" he cried out. "My
lord, you knew all the time—to put it mildly!—and yet when
Bennyworth made his daughter seek out the unicorn, you relented
and let her go."

"I had no choice! I would have insulted the poor misguided
man beyond recovery if I had refused to send her out. I didn't know
then that people would hound her to the stake. Basset, listen to
me. The unicorn comes of my fault. Comes of my faults. Sit down
again, Basset, forget what I am and listen. I have also committed
the horrid sin of Simon Magus. And more than once."

Basset, not accustomed to ecclesiastical speech, looked
puzzled.

"I have kept from you in a closet great sums of money, ill-
gotten as bribes, yes they were bribes, paid to me for fat livings—
archdeacons and deans and rectors—because King Edward wanted
money from me—I needed his consent to marry the orphan
Margaret—she liked me—I liked—I liked—"

"Her lands."

The Earl said nothing.

A grey thought passed through Basset's mind: I have lived too
long. Night had fallen. The procession was over. The village below
was asleep. The Earl whispered "It is I who brought on the unicorn.
I have exchanged letters with that saintly Richard Rollo. . . ."

"Of Oxford?"

"Yes. He who sees things. . . ."

Umfrey rose from his chair and went to a chest from a drawer
of which he drew two letters, which he handed to the steward.
Basset read them slowly aloud by the light of the tapers. The first
one went as follows: "The Gospels do not mention unicorns, my

lord, the Fathers of the Church do not speak of them, the Councils have not heard of them. It appears that God moves sometimes on the outskirt of his Church, as though wishing for infinite freedom to invent and to act. Thus it may happen (so I believe) that when secret daily wickedness rises in a land beyond its ordinary quotidian, a dark malevolence inspissates the atmosphere, and suddenly the unicorn appears as if in vengeance."

The Earl interrupted Basset at this point and said, "Read the other letter, after I asked him 'Why my shire? Why me? Am I worse than other men? Why not Theefton's lands'?"

Basset turned to the other letter. "God moves in mysterious ways," Rollo wrote. "The arbitrary, the inexplicable and the unforeseeable combine into one quintessential element of His sway. Man must not understand him entirely, as he is meant to understand Nature. No one knows why the unicorn harried Cornwall in the year '14. *Deus absconditus*. But I say: Repent. Change."

The Earl took the letters from Basset and replaced them in the drawer. He was now standing in the dark, looking at the steward.

"What now?" he asked.

Basset was silent for a while, and then he asked, "My lord, what does my poor Lady Margaret know?"

"About?"

"The girl."

"Nothing, I think. But Peter tells me that she has sent Blanche Bullen more than once to speak in secret with that trouble-maker Leofa."

Basset pondered this.

"Clotilda must go," he said.

4

BASSET'S INTERVIEW with Clotilda (who had been treacherously warned by Umfrey) proved disappointing.

They were sitting face to face. The beginning was a simple "I know everything."

But this Clotilda already knew. So she simply nodded. She had decided to be demure, come what may. Basset noticed that no look of repentance appeared along with the nod. He decided to plunge.

"I wish to speak to you about Paris."

"Paris?"

"Perhaps you will smile if I tell you that the capital of France is a place infinitely more amusing than our earldom. We have heard of Paris, but has Paris heard of us?"

"I don't suppose it has."

"As my lord's steward, I can promise you the most comfortable conveyance to the French capital, and the richest entertainment upon your arrival. You will lodge with the Marquise de Vendôme, who is our blood relation there. Shall we say three months with the Marquise? A dream!"

Sweetly, Clotilda replied, "Thank you, sir, but no. I am not going to Paris."

"Dresses, servants, balls, opportunities, if you will let me be very frank, opportunities for an advantageous marriage, what more can a girl want? You are an orphan, my dear. Pardon me for reminding you."

"It would distress me to leave the Earl."

As the note was tender, Basset thought that he might echo the note. "This touches me, my dear Clotilda," he said. "You are in love. It is something I envy a little, as an aging widower who can do no more than remember such feelings. But what of the sin? What of Lady Margaret?"

Very sweetly: "She hates me."

"Oh no! Perhaps she is a little jealous of your beauty, your youth, your vivacity. But be that as it may, you are harming the Earl, you are harming yourself, and didn't your hidden deeds help bring the curse of the unicorn on our heads? Believe me, my child, you will love again. It seems impossible to you now, you feel that all you possess of love has gone irrevocably to his lordship, but you will be surprised, I promise, one year, two years from now, when you discover that a new power to love has replaced the old; the dry well has slowly and imperceptibly replenished itself. Go, my child, leave us for two months, try, and then we shall consider again what to do."

Clotilda had found it hard to repress a yawn during this homily which, in truth, had not come easy to honest Basset, who was trying to judge what discourse might best suit a young female mind.

"No, Master Basset," said the girl, demure as ever, "your words are so very beautiful, but I wish to stay. I have my reasons."

"Something I don't know? Are you—?"

"No I am not."

"Anything else? This amazing passion—"

"Why amazing? I love the earl, I am all his, he is mad about me, and I won't budge, I am going to make my way right here."

Was that too tough? It was too late to retreat.

"Make your way? What does that mean?"

"I mean, love where I love."

"But suppose a terrible scandal breaks out?"

Clotilda began to think that Basset was an idiot. She decided that prudence was unnecessary, but that the dulcet tone should be continued.

"Please, master Basset," she murmured, "you who handle deeds and contracts and settlements all day long! The earl loves me so tremendously, and I love him too with all my might, isn't he bound to do something for me? Even if there's a scandal? Especially if there's a scandal?"

A groan was the response.

The unexpected twist to this conversation was that Clotilda found herself rather enjoying it.

"Oh!" she exclaimed, "pray do not misunderstand me! I would die for the Earl, I'd do anything for him, I'm sure I can never love anybody again, but I'm an orphan, you made a very special point of that yourself. In Paris I may be forgotten. No! I don't like to gamble."

"What are you hoping for?"

"As the Earl's mistress—"

That was too much. Basset leaped from his chair (the girl did not budge), exclaiming "Brazen girl!"

Clotilda now stood up too, and, almost whispering into Basset's ear (she was as tall as he), said "One day I shall live in my own manor."

Whereupon she glided out of the room.

Basset sat down again, crestfallen, and muttering "Poor Lady Margaret, poor Lady Margaret." Then the image of his dead wife drifted into his mind. She had been, when he married her, a year or two older than Clotilda, not nearly so beautiful, but the word for her that rose in his mind at this moment was a tender "innocent"; and then she had died. By some mysterious transition, the image of Kirkstall Abbey in deepest Yorkshire now rose into his imagination. His cousin Thomas had risen from "nothing" to be its prior, a lovely man! He, Ralf Basset, would always be welcome there. A green image of a mild oblate pruning a tree drifted into his mind, and, sitting down again, he fell asleep in his chair.

5

AFTER BARON THEEFTON'S arrival at the Dumfries' castle, Lady Margaret strangely dreamed twice of walking in its nearby wood, discovering the unicorn louring between two trees. Holding a mirror to the unresisting beast, she saw herself drawing it after her, aiming the mirror at it, awkwardly to be sure, from behind her back as she moved toward the castle. But the head of the beast was that of Baron Theefton! Baron Theefton displaying instead of a nose a long whitish-yellow horn! The dream dissolved well before they reached the moat, but what could it mean? A dream dreamt twice so obviously sent from Above?

The day after the second one of the dreams, a minstrel knocked at the gate, informing Peter (by the way) that he had seen two gored cows lying in a pasture a mile off. He was well received, like all wandering entertainers who knocked at the castle gate (the earl was fondest of jugglers), and invited to perform for the company, lords and knights and squires, after supper. He did so, plucking away at his gittern and singing war ballads, crime ditties and love songs "fresh from London." The love songs especially affected Theefton, who began to blubber and cry about his loneliness as a bachelor. Thereupon, suddenly, a great scene opened in Lady Margaret's mind, the insistent dream explained itself, and she all but exclaimed "Come to my Garden!" staring at the Baron who was wiping a tear from his nose. But she must act quickly. Theefton was leaving. A messenger had arrived that morning to warn him that a revolt was occurring among his villeins: they were refusing to do their grinding at his mill; they would not pay his heavy fee; they were going to do their own grinding at home: he must return at once to restore his authority.

Fortunately, Theefton's notion of "at once" was lax, so that Lady Margaret was able to arouse his curiosity about her Garden of

Exotics, doing so by alluding to the lascivious bizarreness of some of her plants. He knew about her Garden, of course, but had not shown any interest in it. Plants! But now he promptly accepted her invitation to see for himself.

The most interesting seedlings of Lady Margaret's collection of faraway plants had been brought to her by her cousin Baldwin on his return from the Holy Land, where he had been slaughtering infidels and, when done, botanizing eagerly. Stopping, shortly after leaving Palestine, at a village called Anazarbos, Baldwin exchanged a sliver of the Holy Prepuce, purchased in Jerusalem, for the seeds in question with a grizzled herbalist who had seen him bent over a sprig, and engaged with him in learned conversation.

Much gratified, Lady Margaret had given these plants their separate place in her hothouse, a fine enclosure kept heated in turn by three churls during the long cold months. The astonishing plants were, just then, in full ardent bloom, near the Garden's entrance, so that, when they entered, the symphony of scents almost overwhelmed the Baron. "We are coming into a strange land, are we not?" said Lady Margaret. "Yes yes," he murmured, "do guide me, and do protect me!" This, of course, with a little laugh, as he permitted himself to squeeze her hand. She withdrew it, but not without the tiniest counter-squeeze, intimating that no offense had been taken—and remembering just then that, in the days of their childhood, when the two families had often met, Theefton had stolen her favorite puppy.

Presently she snipped a leaf off a flowering plant and stroked the Baron's cheek with it. "It has the softest fur, has it not?" she said with a smile.

"Yes. . .amazing. . .again?. . .uncanny. . . . What is the plant, dear friend?" "The *Kalosperma impudens.*" Theefton tittered: "Kalosperma: how do you do?" "But now," she said, "you must observe its flower. Do you see these long, supple filaments, reaching anxiously over the corolla?" "To be sure. What are they, Margaret? I am full of scholarly wonder." He had not called her by her first name since years ago. She pretended not to notice and replied, "They are the stamens." Theefton looked blank. "The male organs." Theefton blushed. "They tickle." The Countess had in fact tickled Theefton's palm with the flower. "Each filament," she said, "bears its bud, swollen, distended with the male particles, namely the pollen, and waiting for a touch to break open, and pour itself out. Poof!" "The little rogues!" giggled the Baron. "And this one?" he inquired of a particularly violent-hued flower and bending over it. "Not so close, my lord!" "What did I do?" cried the Baron, jumping back. "You were inhaling the *Iasonus sceleratus*. Its perfume. . .what shall I say? The Persians chew its petals for—for unmentionable purposes. It seems to me that merely breathing it—" here her voice grew weaker. "The people call it St. Anthony's bane," she murmured. "St. Anthony's bane?" "They say that St. Anthony himself couldn't have resisted the fragrance. And yet," said Lady Margaret, moving to another flowering plant, "this one is even more entrancing. Really shameless. Look at this elongated pistil, erect in the calyx. For a flower!" "Yes, for a flower. . .no shame. . .I hardly. . . ." "We call it the *Priapisca vehemens*. But I'll surprise you, my lord. This is a female flower." "This. . . this thing. . . ." Lord Theefton shuddered as he felt the pistil. "Female?" "Ah yes, Nature is mischievous. Expect anything. The pistil contains the flower's womb. Do feel it again, my friend." "Almost like. . . " "Like flesh, yes."

The Baron brought out a laced handkerchief and wiped his brow. The Garden of Exotics was in every way a warm place!

Lady Margaret's voice went low and, as best she could, insinuating (it was not her natural mode): "When the plant is ready, when the time of desire comes upon it, the time of fruition, why not call it the time of love?" "Ah yes, the lovely time of love!" "The pistil grows, it lifts itself stiffly and yearningly, it seeks and we might even say it calls for the pollen, namely through the perfume it secretes. There is no modesty, no hypocritical reticence here. Come to me, the flower cries, come to me!"

That was too much for man to bear. "And come to me, Margaret!" cried the Baron, flinging himself on the Countess and kissing her passionately.

"My lord!" cried the good lady.

"Come to me, the flower cries. Come to me Margaret, my Margaret! I am your pollen!"

"Harry!"

"Yes, call me Harry, and you—my love, let me kiss you again, my flower, my nectar, my perfume!"

Lady Margaret very prettily disengaged herself, murmuring "Harry, if I had known.... What is happening? Where am I? Since when?"

"Since always! Can you ask? I could bear it no longer at Theefton Castle. Surely you know why I came here. The unicorn was a pretext. Too many years had gone by. Oh Margaret, Margaret, Fate came between us."

"Perhaps, perhaps...."

"Didn't we play together as children, years before Umfrey saw you, and hadn't we celebrated a solemn mock wedding in the rose garden, you were eight, I was nine...."

"How was I to know this meant anything to you? Or that you'd remember these childish promises?"

"Oh Margaret, that was the culmination of my life—at nine—I have remembered nothing else. You were my wife from that holy afternoon forth. You the heiress of Wyngham, Brigsley, Tuckbetter and Glaswin Epton, I the future Baron Theefton—our lands, too, lying amorously flank to flank. But then—miserable times—you were orphaned; the King gave you to Umfrey—to my friend! He an earl, I his vassal. I bowed, I wept, I withdrew, I decayed. But now—look down, ye gods, Margaret is in my arms again!"

However, before he could grasp the lady, she had gently pushed him back, saying in a low voice: "A married, virtuous woman, my lord."

"Bitterness! And I must think of you lying in his bed at

night—or day!—oh God!"

"You mustn't torment yourself, dear friend, on that account; indeed you needn't." She thought it wise to repeat: "You needn't." But hush, we were looking at my specimens. My lovely flowers, my only consolations. . . ."

She began to move away, but Theefton took her arm.

"Wait, Margaret," he cried, "You said 'you needn't.' Why 'you needn't?'"

"It must have escaped me. Don't probe, my dear, for the sake of our happy childhood. Leave an aging woman to tend her griefs alone."

The Baron grew heroic. "Griefs?" he shouted. "You *will* tell me! I'm on fire, I could smash walls with my bare fists, confide in me, here, rest your marvelous head on my shoulder."

She did so, murmuring "Oh Harry, if only I had a trusted friend. . . ."

"Look at me," he replied tenderly. "I would leap into a gulf full of crocodiles to rescue a hairpin that belonged to you! Tell me, tell me what it is that weighs on your soul, beautiful Margaret."

"Hide my face. . .listen. . . ."

"Speak to me!"

Margaret allowed a pregnant pause to intervene before slowly uttering her "I am not my husband's wife."

The effect was tremendous. Theefton's mouth opened wide. "Who. . .who is his wife?" he finally brought out.

"Clotilda."

For a few seconds, Theefton was at a loss. But then—"Clotilda Bunny, Benny? The girl?"

"Yes."

"Is his mistress?"

"His wife."

"I'm lost. Good heavens! Is Umfrey a bigamist?"

"No, Harry" (one had to be patient!). "They are not married, and yet she is his wife, and his only wife." Lady Margaret gave this last phrase a fine stress.

"His only wife! And you?"

She now spoke so softly that Theefton had to bend in order to hear the tragic words: "I am the virgin Countess Dumfrey."

"Virgin?"

"Virgin."

At this, the Baron all but leaped in the air. "And I am Harry newborn, newborn this instant!" he clamored. "I am forming my first thoughts on this earth! I will liberate you! Before God, you are not married, and never were. You revert to me! The Pope shall hear of it! Exact an annulment at once."

"Umfrey will fight it. He has my lands, Harry, he is in love with my lands."

"The villain! I had forgotten your lands."

"I could prove his—but that's too loathsome—a medical inquiry...."

"Odious! I forbid it. But something must be done! I am lashing my brain. Sooner or later it will produce ideas. It always does."

"I have had years in which to produce ideas."

"Margaret! Your eyes tell me you have found the way."

"Perhaps. A hazardous way. I would need all your courage, your—"

"Love! My love! My invincible love! Into my arms! By all the saints in heaven, Harry shall be twined about Margaret like the— name it for me, my soul."

"The *Kalosperma impudens.*"

"Amen. Now; tell me what to do."

"Nothing at first. The first action is mine. I shall go into the forest with a mirror in my hand—"

"And catch the unicorn! Divine virgin, the unicorn will be yours. How did I fail to think of it? You will capture the unicorn, you of all maidens will not fail! For God rewards the innocent. And the world will know that you are no man's wife. Your false husband will be unmasked. The false marriage will be dissolved. Margaret and her true Harry will be joined, stamen to pistil. The archbishop of York will bless their union. And happiness seasoned with revenge shall fill the bowl of our lives. My wife!"

He tried to embrace her again, but she had enough of that. Fortunately, she had seen Basset through the half-open door approaching the Garden. She knew that he was simply going about his daily round of the castle and its grounds; so she greeted him at the entrance with simple friendliness. "Join us, Master Basset," she cried; "I have been showing the Baron my famous plants. I shall leave you with him;" and she walked away with a wink addressed to the Baron.

6

ACKNOWLEDGING BASSET'S slight bow did not keep Theefton's thoughts from flying about his brain. "Margaret is mine! The dear is no Venus, heaven knows, but *tant pis*, Wyngham's grazing lands are mine! The mills of Brigsley are mine! Tuckbetter's corn is mine! The waters of Glaswin Epton are mine!"

So went his whirling thoughts as he put his hand on the slightly surprised steward's shoulder, thoughts accompanied by an overwhelming desire to tell the world his triumph.

"You seem happy, my lord," said Basset, noting the obvious.

"I seem because I am and I am because I love." Whereupon Theefton broke into a ditty.

> *This way, fair maiden, to your lover's arms;*
> *Your lover with impatience sighs.*

Basset's response was sarcastically glum. "You too, sir. The place is being smothered with love. You will tell me, I suppose, my lord, that you are in love with Lady Margaret, who has adored you since childhood."

A torrential glee overcame the Baron. "How did you guess?" he cried in the highest of pitches, joined to an outburst of laughter.

"What?" cried the steward. "I was joking!"

The Baron suddenly became grave. "No, Basset, you were not joking, it's the power of your famous honesty, it gives you prophetic gifts in spite of yourself. Extend your hand to the happiest man in Britain!"

He had taken his hand off Basset's shoulder and was extending it to him. The steward took it as limply as possible, then, disengaging himself, all but snarled (a tone exceptional for the good man): "Love as much as you like, my lord; congratulations; but I trust my poor Lady Margaret has sense enough to see with her own eyes the difference—I say no more."

Theefton answered anger with anger, the limp handshake helping: "I return the congratulations, Basset; she does see the difference with her own eyes—and with her own fresh lips—and with her own plump arms—here in front of the *Pripisca vipimmens* she saw it ten minutes ago."

By this time Basset was hot with anger: "I don't believe it," he almost shouted, "but I admire your telling these fables to me, who have served Lord Dumfrey from the time he was a child."

"Your service be damned, my good man. I know enough to freeze you all in your shoes. I was not in the diplomatic corps for nothing. In Norway—in short, I have plucked the secrets of this house."

"Secrets? Fairy tales!"

"Is the connection between your master and the Benny girl a fairy tale, Master Steward?"

This was a thunderclap, and Theefton enjoyed the effect it had on Basset's face, indeed on the man's body, for he stepped back as if the revelation had struck him a blow.

"Who told you?" he asked in a strangled voice.

The Baron guffawed: "An angel—Lady Margaret."

"She knows? She knew? And she told you?"

"She knows, she knew, and she told me."

Here the irrepressible Baron broke into song again:

> *Your lover with impatience sighs.*
> *Fair maiden, swiftly yield your charms!*

"Yes, Basset, I have culled the secrets of this house. Your loyalty is useless. I know who is the true virgin in this house, and I know who is the false virgin."

"What do you mean, sir?"

"You know precisely what I mean, my good man. At the hour of my choosing, the public will be invited to inspect Umfrey's bedchamber. And I shall address them as follows: 'Your master, good citizens and reverent judges, has failed to perform his conjugal duty even once in the five vacant years of his spurious marriage. Here, however, is Mistress Clotilda.' And all the rest."

Theefton had not been in a better mood since taking his first steps as a baby. He broke into song again:

> *Fair maiden, swiftly yield your charms,*
> *Else your woeful lover dies.*

"As sure as the Pope and King Edward are alive," he continued, "Margaret will be mine, along with Wyngham, Brigsley, Tuckbetter, and Glaswin Epton."

There at last was the essential truth. "Plunder!" Basset shouted. "Wyngham, Brigsley—vulgar plunder!"

"Vulgar?" The Baron was offended. "You misunderstand me. My designs are pure. I love Lady Margaret. I knew her long before Umfrey set eyes on her. We played together as children. I saved her puppy from drowning. We had exchanged oaths in a bower, she was seven and I was eight, the spirits of the woods were undoubtedly listening, we were Aeneas and Dido, only younger. The nymphs and the goblins declared that we should ultimately be united; for these lands, I ask you to note, these lands border upon mine, they are my natural extension. I am amputated without them."

"They also border upon this earldom," Basset retorted.

"They bordered on me before Umfrey knew Margaret. No, my good Basset, this is the beginning of my ascent. The Theeftons are destined to eclipse the Dumfreys. Three weeks and two days after I was born, a bolt struck down the church steeple in Dumfrey Bottoms. The heavens don't speak in vain."

Here Theefton grew poetic:

> *Dame Fortune can whirl*
> *Baron to Earl,*
> *And one more fluke*
> *Turns Earl into Duke,*

he grandly recited. "Shall I make cottage laws," he cried, "do
cornfield justice and harvest ten sacks of corn when I could be
multiplying my estate and branding my name into the chronicles?"

By this time Theefton was addressing heaven rather than
mortal man. Basset understood. "Excuse me, my lord," he said, "I
have work to do on the estate," and he began to move away from
the Garden of Exotics. Theefton detained him, however. "Let's
be friends, Basset. Your master is beyond help. Oh, you can warn
him about me—much good may it do him! I'm galloping into the
future; saddle your horse and ride after me before I'm out of sight.
I need capable and loyal men like you in my service."

And without another word he left. Basset watched him saunter
toward the castle, watched him pluck a flower, sniff it, place it in
his sleeve, and cross the drawbridge with steps so sprightly one
might almost call them a dance.

Feeling too weary to make his daily round, Basset entered the
Garden instead, where he let himself heavily down on a *tabouret*.
He felt surrounded by newly unmasked petty villains. Only the
Countess, he thanked God, was pure. "The unhappy woman," he
reflected, "is looking for comfort, she staggers in the darkness,
and stretches out her innocent hand to a smiling claw! However,
there's still Ralf Basset. I can at any rate warn her and protect her.
Theefton in the ascendant? Not while I have power of speech!"

7

THE DAYS WERE long, but at last night crept over the earldom and Lady Margaret, alleging a headache, left the company after supper. She had quietly given Theefton the task of keeping everybody at the card table or listening to the minstrel, or both, at least until midnight. She told her women to be secret and go to bed. Then she provided herself with a small mirror, wrapped a light cloak around her shoulders against the very slight chill, and, waking up the Porter, who was lying asleep (as usual) on his cot near the gate, she made him open it—without, to his surprise, harshly berating him—crossed the moat, and walked resolutely into the nearby wood. A full moon shone conveniently through the branches, and of course the unicorn presently appeared, for a dream as exceptional as hers had been, one so significantly repeated, does not lie. Needless to say, the unicorn did not wear Theefton's face, and Lady Margaret did not expect it to. Moonlight made its long, deadly horn gleam. The beast (it knew that its mission was ending) looked calmly at her, bleating mildly, and she looked calmly at the beast, slowly raising her mirror to it.

She did not need to walk backward, as she had feared, and as everybody supposed that the successful virgin must somehow do. She simply moved a few steps ahead of the obedient animal, holding the mirror backward, facing the unicorn, who dutifully followed, its bleat changing to an amiable grunting.

Presently the two cleared the wood and arrived at the edge of the castle moat. This was the moment when the unicorn flung to the air its most unearthly bleat. There was no need for the Countess to knock at the gate, for the bleat had awakened the Porter, who had allowed himself to fall asleep again, and who now leaped off his cot to open the gate. He saw the beast within touching distance, growling at him, and ran away. Lady Margaret, followed by the unicorn, began mounting the stairs.

Up in the hall, Theefton had kept the company at cards *and* listening to the minstrel, alleging his imminent departure from the earldom and his wish to see much of everybody before saddling up with his valet and coiffeur. The rest of the company—several knights and pages—had gone to bed. Peter had served those who remained a tasty collation of green ginger, syrups, sweetmeats and spiced wine. The unicorn's bellowing bleat made them all leap from their chairs and dash pell-mell to the balcony. The moon showed them Lady Margaret but especially the unicorn with startling clarity until the two disappeared into the castle.

Achilles could not have shouted Ha! across the windy plain of Ilium more powerfully than did Theefton when he shook the air with "Ha! The virgin has succeeded!" The Earl knew, of course, that Lady Margaret possessed this attribute; so did Basset; but not so Clotilda, who gaped with astonishment at what she had just seen and, especially, heard, for she had assumed that her lover shared his ardors with both women, if less frequently with his spouse. More to the point, however, was the fact that Umfrey did not know that Theefton knew. Hence the fellow's exclamation broke over him like a falling tower. Should not the Baron's exclamation have been one of high astonishment?

"My lord," said Basset urgently, as the Baron cackled with glee, "Lady Margaret will surely be with us in a few minutes. Be strong."

Unfrey was looking round him speechlessly, almost beyond thought. The minstrel had withdrawn into a corner, sensing that here were the beginnings of a fine ballad of his making or, better still, a tale to be conveyed from castle to castle. Peter too was present, half hidden by the minstrel in the same corner and somewhat remorsefully enjoying the unhappiness of his lord. As for Clotilda, she was muttering "This is a plot devised against me," though she could not tell the why and the how, and simply added *in petto* "somehow."

They all had returned to the middle of the hall, staring at

the door through which Lady Margaret would be making her entrance. The Baron was rubbing his hands and snickering. Basset's only thought was that he must be prepared to fight Theefton and protect Lady Margaret.

The lady now appeared. Umfrey rushed to her. He wanted to shout, "Why did you do this?" or "Why now?" or "Why didn't you tell me?" but all he brought out was a not very relevant "Where is the unicorn?" "Locked up in the armory, my friend," and she handed him a strong, large key of complicated wards.

She now perceived the half-hidden Peter and the minstrel. "You two," she snapped, "out, out!" There was no need to tell them twice.

"Dear lady, are you quite safe?" Basset asked her. "Did the beast try to harm you?"

"Thank you for asking," replied the Countess, and then, lancing the Earl with a contemptuous look, "thank *you* for asking, Basset. I felt a moment of terror, for he was growling and ready to thrust at me. But I held the mirror steadfast, and lo! he became meek, and gently followed me. I have not even a stain on my dress, not a spot on my hands, not a wrinkle in my purpose."

"Margaret, my love, my virgin, God has spoken!" Theefton pronounced with high solemnity.

"What is this? What did the fellow say?" Umfrey cried out. Basset and Theefton spoke together, the chamberlain crying out, "My lord, he knows everything" and Theefton: "Brace yourself, Umfrey. Your unmarried wife has confessed herself to me. Capitulate!"

The Earl heard them both. Lady Margaret glared at him, tight-lipped. "Basset," he brought out, "speak to me, explain!"

"Let my lord Theefton explain," said the Countess in that stony tone of hers which always made the servants tremble.

"Brace yourself, Umfrey," said the Baron, speaking in his best solemn tone. "Your unmarried wife has confided the awful truth to me. Leofa will be summoned. Capitulate, or tomorrow morning the man will trumpet the news that Lady Margaret is a virgin, and you a rank and unlawful adulterer."

"Umfrey, do something," Clotilda squeaked. "This is a dirty scheme to ruin me!"

No one paid attention. "Capitulate?" the Earl all but screamed. "The world is coming to an end! How does Harry come into this? How did Margaret—? And why does this blackguard keep chuckling in my face? Basset!!!"

"Oh my lord, my lord," Basset wailed, shaking his head, "he comes into this because he wants your neglected wife and her lands." And here Basset wanted to turn to Lady Margaret, but the Earl prevented him with a cry: "My lands! Never!"

"Too late, Umfrey, Margaret is mine!" Theefton proclaimed.

Had the Baron looked at the Countess, he might have been less sure.

"Harry, what have I done to you?" The Earl moaned.

"You have done that you stole Margaret from me. I love her, she loves me, we were pledged to each other years before you knew her—I was twelve, she eleven—children, pure and prophetic. All is fulfilled. Umfrey, the time has come to yield up your so-called wife, declare the so-called marriage null, and return to the lady the lands you took from her. Speak, Margaret!"

"Not yet," was the curt reply.

In the meantime, Clotilda had moved toward the Earl, who had sat down like a man crushed by a boulder, and whispered to him, "I'll be with you to the end, Umfrey. Only you and I." The Earl looked at her as if a snake had bit him.

"I heard you, girl," said Lady Margaret with a grim smile. "Umfrey, I set you free to marry her."

"I don't want to be set free," moaned the Earl. "I was bewitched. You belong to me."

"You mean Wyngham, Brigsley, Tuckbetter and Glaswin Epton belong to you."

"Precisely," interjected the Baron.

The Earl ignored him. "This is unjust, Margaret. We've lived together for five years, peacefully, in concord. You accepted my deep respect. You can't wish a scandal to break over my head, surely."

"What scandal, my good friend?" said the Baron. "Leave things to my diplomatic experience. When I was in Norway— in short, all that's required of you is a friendly settlement with Margaret, a donation to the church, and a gift to the Pope. I have it! You'll send him the unicorn's tusk in a velvet case, and the story ends with toasts and violins."

The Earl stared. "The man is an idiot. I'm dizzy. Margaret?" he wailed. In response, she offered her hand to Theefton: "My lord," was all she said. Ecstatically kissing the hand, he uttered "My own!" Whereupon Basset threw himself (it was not easy) at Lady Margaret's feet, crying "Dearest lady, listen to me, listen I beg you, don't take refuge with Theefton of all men! Your husband has done you an immense wrong, but he repents—look at his face!—while Theefton desires you only, only for your lands!"

"Slanders!" cried the Baron. "Love, pure love propels me! I defy—"

"Rise, Master Basset, rise," Lady Margaret interrupted. "I believe you."

"Margaret!" the Earl and the Baron both cried out, though in contrasting pitches, one joyful, the other appalled.

On his feet again, Basset was radiant. "Lovely lady, I've opened your eyes, I've saved you."

"You haven't opened my eyes, my good man," the Countess retorted. "I know how to open them on my own, thank you. I understood Theefton's greed from the beginning. He stole my favorite puppy when I was ten."

"He ran away! Finders keepers!" cried the Baron. "And what's more, you fell into my arms in your Garden of Exotics."

"That's a lie," cried the Earl.

"Of course it is," said Lady Margaret. "Attend to me, all of you.

Umfrey, choose," she spoke with ice in her voice. "Either you lock your mistress up in a convent, come to my bed, and give me my rights as Countess Dumfrey, or else I leave you demolished in your ruins, demand an annulment from the Pope and marry myself and my lands, eyes wide open, to your enemy Theefton."

"Protect me, my lord," Clotilda wailed, "show her what you are. Protect the defenseless."

"Go away," said the Earl feebly with the gesture of a man who tries to persuade an obnoxious insect to go sting elsewhere.

"What did you say?" she all but hissed.

The Earl had been sitting. He now leaped up and shouted, "Go away!"

Clotilda fell back, looked wildly at them all and shouted: "Baron Theefton, listen to me! The King demanded a hundred twenty knights from him for crossing into France. He gave him thirty! He said he could raise no more. He bribed the king's clerk. I have the man's name. It's yours, Baron, I have proofs!"

It was the truth. New to the Countess, looking more grim than ever, new to Basset, who sank his head into his two hands. The Earl, like a true lover, had babbled the shameful fact—gleefully at that!—to his mistress in one of those moments. . . .

The Baron was ecstatic. He no longer needed Lady Margaret in his bed! Let the virago fly to the devil! "Clotilda, my roof will be yours," he proclaimed. "As for you, Umfrey, you shall do my bidding, or else you will end your days in King Edward's clammiest dungeon."

Whereupon Lady Margaret stepped calmly to the Earl's side and gently pressured him to sit again. "Let me deal with this, my dear," she said. And, turning to the Baron, "What is it you ask of us, old friend?"

The answer came, of course, as no surprise. "Wyngham, Brigsley, Tuckbetter and Glaswin Epton."

"That is a great amount of land," said Lady Margaret. "But we are willing to give you Brigsley."

"That won't do."

"It will have to."

"How so? Knowing what I know, I can take all of Wyngham, Brigsley, Tuckbetter and Glaswin Epton—and more! In exchange, of course, for eternal silence."

"Knowing what you know will not help you out of our castle, dear Harry, not even if you call your valet and your coiffeur."

"True!" cried the Earl, leaping up. "I'll try him on the spot for treason against the earldom and have his head before he can open his mouth."

"But I'll shout his story from the rooftops!" Clotilda cried out.

"Shut your mouth, girl; we'll come to you in a minute," retorted the Countess. "Well, Harry? Think of the axe. And think of Brigsley's cornfields."

"I'd prefer Wyngham."

The Earl and his wife looked at each other.

"It's yours," said the Earl. "Basset here will draw up the new charter."

Clotilda's fists were clenched: "And I?" she threw out.

The Earl stared at the floor.

'What might you like, my child?" asked Lady Margaret in a tone as sweet as she could make it.

There was a moment of silence.

"To live with the Marquise de Vendôme."

Unnoticed, Basset left the hall.

8

THAT NIGHT, before going to bed, the two reconciled friends, flanked by a couple of halberdiers, carefully unlocked the door to the armory into which the unicorn had been led by the cool-headed Countess. They were the same men she had summoned from the guardroom to help her, even though the unicorn had obeyed her as meek as a lamb. Halberds were at the ready and swords were drawn; but the unicorn had vanished, leaving no trace, not even a hair. The night of the capture, prompted by curiosity, one of the halberdiers had found time, while Lady Margaret was viewing the unicorn from all sides, to fetch a pail of milk for the beast. Not a drop of it had been touched. Nor had the beast, it seemed, felt any "urge," for the floor was immaculate. It remains to be said that the unicorn was not to be heard or seen again in Lord Dumfrey's domains. A week later, however, it reappeared in those of the Duke of Cornwall, which it ravaged for several months for sufficient cause. The history of its depredations there can be found in the *Chronicles* of that house by Hugh of Swinforth.

9

IN THE COURSE of the next day, Ralph Basset and one of his clerks prepared the documents needed for the change of status of Wyngham, famous (incidentally) for its orchards as well as its grazing land. Because the post of chamberlain, held, it will be remembered, by Bennyworth was still vacant, Basset was also kept busy supervising arrangements for Clotilda's departure. On the same day, the relocation of Lady Margaret's bedchamber to its new place adjoining that of her husband was quickly and discreetly accomplished.

Lord Theefton left the next morning. The Earl saw him off outside the castle. Bending down from his saddle, the Baron said in a confidential voice, not to be overheard by his valet and coiffeur on their horses, "You can count on my utter silence, my dear Umfrey." And away the three of them trotted.

That evening, exceptionally because of the new situation, the Earl and his wife supped alone in their wing of the castle. Lady Margaret's aspect was one of placid satisfaction. That of the Earl spoke of sober resignation. Be that as it may, the two conversed amiably of the affairs of the earldom, now that the unicorn had vanished, and also of the proposed replacement for the defunct Purity. Clearly, good times were going to return to the land. While fruit was served, the minstrel was ushered in to entertain the couple before bedtime. He sang old ballads of forlorn maidens and bellicose Scots—the expected repertory—but his concluding ditty, which he announced (again!) as "the latest from London," caused them to stop eating and to stare, just as he wished.

> *When God said*
> *Let us make the earth*
> *What did he do*

He took a heap of dirt

He took a heap of dirt
And made a muddy ball
And that my lads is why
We're muddy one and all.

With this he bowed, the pair complimented him on his originality and fine voice, and the Earl bade Peter, who was attending them, to see that the man was properly rewarded on his journey next day to another castle or manor-house.

Left alone, they were about to rise when, unexpectedly, Basset entered, carrying a thick leather-bound folio, which, bowing to them, he placed on the table between two platters of bones, pits and peels.

"What does this mean, Basset? And what are these papers? Is this a time for business? In the middle of the night?"

But the Earl's words seemed not to reach the steward.

"My lord, Lady Margaret, your next steward, whoever he may be, will find the accounts of the estate in order."

Red-faced, the Earl rose from the table. "Have you gone mad? What is happening to you?"

The Countess had remained seated. She, needless to say, understood. "Where are you proposing to go, good Master Basset?"

"As I believe you know, my lady, the prior of Kirkstall Abbey is my cousin on my mother's side. I propose to ask him for shelter."

"I tell you you're raving!" bellowed the Earl. "In the middle of the night! I need you! The land needs you!"

A strange silence followed as Basset stared into the standing Dumfrey's eyes. The Earl's voice became low and tremulous. He wanted to say, "I am your son, Basset, forgive me," but all he could bring out was, alas, beside de point. "The unicorn is gone. He will migrate to other shires."

"Let him go where it pleases him, my lord; I will not hear him in my cell. Allow me to withdraw. It is almost midnight."

"No, turn back, dear Master Basset, and listen to me," said Lady Margaret, whose voice was now as gentle as feathers. "It was you, Ralph, who caused our fens to be drained, it was you who abolished the death duty that weighed on our peasants' heirs, it was you who saved captured poachers from being blinded and unmanned, it was you who reduced the three-days' labor the villeins owed us to a single day. Tell us, what will you do when you lie month after month in your Kirkstall cell?"

Umfrey stared at his wife with astonished admiration, while Basset remained silent, unable to bring himself to reply "Pray" or, simply, "Nothing."

"May we beg you as a particular kindness to give this a *little* more thought?"

Basset stared at the ground.

"A week? Three days? Till dawn?"

The Earl placed his hand, with heavy meaning, on the steward's arm.

The End

DRAMA

DRAMA

THE FATAL FRENCH DENTIST

a heart-rending tragedy

This is a retouched and revised version of a play inspired (if the word is apt) by a story my wife told me over the breakfast table in the early 1960s about certain acquaintances of ours. The text appeared in a short-lived magazine called *First Stage* in 1965, and two years later it was published by the firm of Samuel French, provider of plays for both amateur and professional stages. It reappeared again in my *Collected Plays* of 1970-1.

Characters
Bill Foot
Mary Foot
Bill Nethergood
Mary Nethergood
Bill Tuttle
Mary Tuttle

Scene One

(A nice American living-room. Mr. Foot is examining a quiz in his newspaper. Mrs. Foot is doing nothing)

MR. FOOT. Newspapers are becoming more educational all the time. This quiz is called "Are You Socially Acceptable?"

MRS. FOOT. It seems a little insulting for them to doubt it, considering we're subscribers.

MR. FOOT. Nonsense. It's scientific. You get points and then they add up the points for you and you find out how socially acceptable you are. The best and second best and third best and the worst answers are printed upside down, so you're not tempted to cheat. Ok, here goes. Question one: When you leave a party, how do your hosts react? (a) They sob; (b) They faint; (c) They grin; (d) They guffaw. *(He makes a mark)*

MRS. FOOT. What are you answering?

MR. FOOT. This quiz is confidential, but so far, I'm satisfied with myself. Two: How do you behave when an unwelcome guest rings your doorbell just as you are settling down for a quiet evening with your wife and/or video-game? (a) You shoot him.

MRS. FOOT. And be thrown in jail?

MR. FOOT. (b) You slam the door in his face; (c) You tell him to come in if he must, but to keep his mouth shut; (d) You make him feel he is the nicest thing that could have happened to you that evening. *(He makes a mark)*

MRS. FOOT. I would not answer the doorbell at all and pretend I wasn't home. It's the best solution, because it keeps you happy and doesn't offend your guest. I think shooting him is simply too awfully overdone.

MR. FOOT. You do go on, don't you, my dear. Question three: What do you do when your hostess serves you a dish you do not like?

MRS. FOOT. I eat everything.

MR. FOOT. (a) You throw it on the floor; (b) You tell her you'll eat it but you wouldn't feed it to your hogs.

MRS. FOOT. Oh, that's a terrible thing to say.

MR. FOOT. Why?

MRS. FOOT. Well, I mean, throwing something on the floor isn't so bad; nobody need notice, especially if there's a low-hanging tablecloth, and maybe a cat or a dog under the table. But to say "I wouldn't feed it to my hogs" is awfully rude.

MR. FOOT. I suppose so, and yet when you look at it sympathetically it really isn't. Let's say the husband overhears me. "I wouldn't feed these asparagus to my hogs," says I. He rises from the table, he's furious, "You've got a nerve telling my wife you wouldn't feed these asparagus to your hogs!" "What," says I, "would you feed them to your hogs?" "Of course not," he hollers. "Well, that's precisely what I said," I reply, and he crumples.

MRS. FOOT. Well, fortunately there aren't any hogs in Queens, so why trouble our heads about them?

MR. FOOT. The hogs are meant as a for-instance, my dear. Let me see, where was I? (c) You eat it but you sulk for the rest of the evening; (d) You wrench your mouth into a wonderful smile and you say—

(The doorbell rings)

MRS. FOOT. Oh, maybe it's somebody exciting at last!

MR. FOOT. Hope springs eternal.

(Mrs. Foot opens the door. Enter Mr. and Mrs. Nethergood)

MR. and MRS. NETHERGOOD. Hello hello hello hello!

MR. and MRS. FOOT. Hello hello hello hello hello!

MRS. FOOT. Wonderful to see you people! Those dear Nethergoods!

MRS. NETHERGOOD. So good to see you two again, plump and ruddy and all.

MR. NETHERGOOD. How are you, Bill?

MR. FOOT. How are you, Bill?

MRS. FOOT. Bill, get the Nethergoods a drink. Sit down, children, sit down, Mary.

MRS. NETHERGOOD. We absolutely can't, Mary dear. You stop those drinks, Bill Foot.

MRS. FOOT. Why? What's the matter?

MRS. NETHERGOOD. We're on our way to a wedding. Bill Lumley and Mary Finkelberg. Do you know them?

MRS. FOOT. I don't think so. Come on, tell us all about it, do sit down, both of you—five minutes, that's all, we'll set the alarm if you insist; I want to hear all about the wedding.

MRS. NETHERGOOD. All right, five minutes, but no drinks, not a thing. Sit down, Bill.

MR. FOOT. All right, but what's the rush? Just another wedding. And what's a wedding these days? A legal requirement for a divorce.

MRS. NETHERGOOD. This is not just another wedding, my dear man. I'll tell you all about it if you swear to take the secret to the grave with you. Bill, you naughty, that goes for you too, you mustn't tell anybody.

MR. FOOT. I don't gossip about people I don't know.

MRS. NETHERGOOD. Well, it's a dreadful story.

MRS. FOOT. Wonderful. Go on!

MRS. NETHERGOOD. The Lumleys and the Finkelbergs had agreed not to invite anybody on either side beyond uncles and aunts. Parents, grandparents, brothers, sisters, authentic uncles and genuine aunts, and that was to be all for the dinner. No cousins.

MR. NETHERGOOD. Mark this. No cousins.

MRS. NETHERGOOD. And that's where the roof caved in. It seems that Bill Lumley's cousin just came back from three years of mission work in darkest Boola-Boola. He's alone in the world, the natives ate his wife, he arrives in America penniless, all yellow with malaria and something shot off, an arm or leg, I don't know which—

MRS. FOOT. So?

MRS. NETHERGOOD. So, Bill Lumley decides to make an exception for the one cousin, in view of the special circumstances. Well! The Finkelbergs go wild. They've got a cousin who almost drowned while trying to leave a submarine before it reached the surface. A tragic case, half a lung taken out, a few medals on the sound side of the chest—so why the Boola-Boola cousin but not the submarine cousin? I assure you the marriage just about broke up. Mary's mother said that without the submarine cousin the marriage was off. Bill's folks answered that one exception was enough, because once you started adding exceptions you'd soon have the hall f ull of them.

MRS. FOOT. So?

MRS. NETHERGOOD. So, Mary said she surely wasn't going to give up Bill because of a cousin who wasn't smart enough to keep the door of a submarine closed when it was under water. And then she asked Bill to give up his missionary cousin. So Bill blew up and then Mary blew up and it was a mess.

MR. FOOT. But they patched it up?

MRS. NETHERGOOD. They did; they decided to invite everybody, including us. But nobody is talking to anybody. Even the bride and groom aren't on speaking terms.

MR. FOOT. A quiet wedding, in short.

MRS. NETHERGOOD. Aren't people just too horribly horrible?

MR. FOOT. The trouble is, they're not socially acceptable.

MRS. FOOT. I always tell Bill if only people were reasonable and did what's right, the world would be a better place.

MR. NETHERGOOD. Bless you, those are almost exactly my words, aren't they, Mary?

MRS. NETHERGOOD. Be quiet, dear, and let me speak. What was I saying? Oh, yes, we absolutely must go. We only stopped in to bid you to a homely f east chez nous.

MR. NETHERGOOD. At Nethergood Manor.

MRS. NETHERGOOD. Next Saturday, dinner at seven. We want

you to meet an exciting dentist visiting from Paris. He's looking into photodontic equipment in the States.

MR. NETHERGOOD. Dental surgery, actually. Top man in his field.

MR. FOOT. How drilling. *(He and Mr. Nethergood enjoy themselves)*

MRS. FOOT. You're an angel to ask us, Mary, and we'll be delighted to come. I simply adore Parisians. France wouldn't be the same without them.

MRS. NETHERGOOD. That's why we're asking only the two of you. We didn't want to scare him with too many strange people. Well—*(she embraces Mrs. Foot)* we've got to run.

MR. NETHERGOOD. Sorry we can't stay, old Billberry, but I'll hold you to a double scotch next time.

MR. FOOT. Great. Say, do you know the difference between a double scotch on the rocks and Siamese twins on gravel?

MRS. FOOT. Do stop, my dear, you're unbearable.

MRS. NETHERGOOD. Never mind, I think he's a love. Well, bye bye now.

MR. NETHERGOOD. Bye bye.

MRS. FOOT. Bye bye.

MR. FOOT. Bye bye.

(The Nethergoods leave)

MRS. FOOT. So here we are again. The excitement's over.

MR. FOOT. I hope they serve broccoli.

(He goes back to his newspaper)

MRS. FOOT (to herself). Me, my husband, and the question why. Maybe something interesting will happen again before I pass on.

MR. FOOT. It says in the paper that according to the best thought of the day, people like you and I live the desperate lives of meaningless automata in a consumer-driven society which has lost touch with the inner springs of a rich and fruitful existence.

MRS. FOOT. Well, the newspapers always make things sound more exciting than they are. It's true that you have your position in the company and we have our friends and our home and our birch tree in the backyard, but I don't think that the paper is right to point to people like us as models of anything.

MR. FOOT. I'd better get back to the quiz.

(The doorbell rings)

MRS. FOOT. More excitement I bet!

MR. FOOT. With this infernal doorbell going all day I'll never find out how socially acceptable I am.

(Mrs. Foot opens the door. Enter Mr. and Mrs. Tuttle)

MR. and MRS. TUTTLE. Hello hello hello hello!

MR. and MRS. FOOT. Hello hello hello hello!

MRS. FOOT. Mary! How lovely to see you again! And dear old Bill with you for a change!

MR. FOOT. Dear old Bill and Mary.

MR. TUTTLE. Dear old Billberry and good old Mary.

MRS. FOOT. Come in and sit down. Fix the drinks, Bill.

MRS. TUTTLE. Don't make a move, either one of you. We're on our way to a funeral and we can't stay but a minute.

MRS. FOOT. What funeral? You scare me.

MRS. TUTTLE. Mary Spiffin's husband—don't you remember Mary Spiffin, at the Happy Orphanage Circle?

MRS. FOOT. Of course I do.

MR. FOOT. You mean Bill Spiffin who was in gaskets?

MR. TUTTLE. That's right. Gaskets and washers.

MRS. TUTTLE. Anyway, this is one funeral we don't want to miss.

MRS. FOOT. And yet you talk about running away without even telling us. No, I'll really be unhappy if you don't sit down for at least five minutes. We'll set the alarm if you insist.

MR. FOOT. Come on, be friendly with the natives.

MRS. TUTTLE. All right, but five minutes is all, I swear.

MRS. FOOT *(to Mr. Tuttle)*. Here, put this pillow behind your back.

MR. TUTTLE. Thanks. Go on, Mary, open the old valves and tell her about the funeral.

MRS. FOOT. Yes! You were saying?

MRS. TUTTLE. Well. About a year ago Mary Bartlett's husband
died.

MR. TUTTLE. You knew Bill Bartlett, the piston man.

MR. FOOT. Sure I remember him. I wrote a policy for his outfit.

MRS. FOOT. So?

MRS. TUTTLE. So—the funeral that Mary Bartlett gave her
husband positively sickened Mary Spiffin. She was so jealous it
was all she could do to bring out a decent condolence. There
was Bill Bartlett lying on an adjustable mattress, satin and
velvet and Venetian lace on the sides of the coffin, looking ten
years younger than what he'd been, and holding his pipe in his
hand! And when I say coffin, I should say triple casket: one of
mahogany, the next of bronze, and the third a genuine Roman
sarcophagus, flown over especially by an antique dealer in Italy.
As for the guests, half of General Motors was there—with a floral
piece by the Chairman of the Board himself—"For Bill Bartlett,
whose pistons shall not be forgot." The eulogy was spoken by
the archbishop, and while the organ played they had birds
twittering I don't know where, it was deep and inspirational
and we all cried. I counted fifteen boys in white standing around
the caskets like so many Cupids, you never saw anything so cute
in your life. And in the midst of all, there was Mary Bartlett
sobbing her heart out and blubbering "If only Bill were alive,
he'd be so proud!" Well, you should have beheld Mary Spiffin.
She was sitting there with her lips pressed together taking it
all in, and swearing to herself (so I could tell) she'd show that
Mary Bartlett a funeral when the time came. But of course you
can't just ask your husband to up and die so you can throw a
big funeral—I don't think Spiffin would have gone in for that at
all because he wasn't the kind of man who approves of making
a show, if you know what I mean, he was really a quiet sort of
man. So all she could do was stare at him a great deal. And then
suddenly he popped off after all—three days ago it was—

MR. TUTTLE. Keeled over while he was having a drink with the boys at the convention of the Gasket Association of America.

MRS. TUTTLE. Aren't men unpredictable? And that was that.

MRS. FOOT. What an opening for Mrs. Spiffin!

MRS. TUTTLE. Exactly. Naturally Mary Bartlett is at the top of her guest list, and I'm dying to see what she's rigged up. Well, we're sitting here chattering with you. Come on, Bill, we'd better be off.

MR. TUTTLE. My dear, you've forgotten what you came here for.

MRS. TUTTLE. Didn't I ask you over for Saturday?

MR. TUTTLE. No, you didn't ask them over for Saturday.

MRS. TUTTLE. I'm in a daze.

MRS. FOOT. Actually—

MRS. TUTTLE. You must join us next Saturday night—two bridge tables, the Simpsons, the Hardys....

MR. TUTTLE. Bridge at the Tuttle Estates.

MRS. FOOT. We'd love to come, it sounds delightful, but I'm afraid we're taken next Saturday.

MR. FOOT. Broccoli and all the rest.

MRS. TUTTLE. What a pity!

MR. TUTTLE. A blow to the solar plexus, old Billberry.

MRS. TUTTLE. Well, I'll ask the Nethergoods.

MRS. FOOT. Oh, but it's the Nethergoods we're going to! *(Mr. Foot coughs)*

MRS. TUTTLE (miffed). Oh, I see. That's odd.

MR. TUTTLE. Yes, that's odd. What's odd about it, dear?

MRS. TUTTLE. Nothing. Are the Nethergoods throwing a party?

MRS. FOOT. Oh no, nothing like that.

MRS. TUTTLE. They usually ask us.

MR. TUTTLE. How about our funeral, Mary?

MRS. FOOT. Couldn't you go a little later, and have a cup of coffee with us?

MRS. TUTTLE (*cold*). No, we can't. Well, good bye, you all. Bye bye.

MR. TUTTLE. Bye bye.

MRS. FOOT. Bye bye.

MR. FOOT. Bye bye. We'll see you, Billberry old man.

(The Tuttles leave)

MR. FOOT. Well, you've did it.

MRS. FOOT. Don't be funny. What was I to do?

MR. FOOT. Why did you have to tell the Tuttles we were going to be at the Nethergoods? Wasn't it enough to say we weren't available on Saturday?

MRS. FOOT. I just saw a little deeper into the situation than you, that's all, my dear. Mary Tuttle was going to call the Nethergoods to ask them over. And what would have happened? Mary Nethergood would have answered that they couldn't because we—oh no, I guess she wouldn't have—*(She gasps)*

MR. FOOT. You guess! You see a little deeper into the situation than me! A nice puddle you've made of it. You didn't think the Nethergoods would have had enough sense just to say, "Thank you but we're engaged"? What a woman! A social misfit.

MRS. FOOT. I made a mistake.

MR. FOOT. A whammer.

MRS. FOOT. I made a big mistake.

MR. FOOT. You've just caused an international incident between the Tuttles and the Nethergoods. And they the best friends in the world. Adored each other, that's all. But the Tuttles don't like to be left out.

MRS. FOOT. But why do you suppose the Nethergoods asked us without asking them?

MR. FOOT. Don't you remember anything? She didn't want to scare the French dentist with too many strange people. Very delicate, I think. Besides, do they have to ask everybody they know? The only trouble is that a famous French dentist would be a nice morsel for the Tuttles, and they'd better not find out about him.

MRS. FOOT. Dear oh dear, what am I to do? How can I clean up this horrible mess? Wait. What time is it?

MR. FOOT. Let me check. *(He goes up to a clock and moves the minute hand)* It's eight o'clock.

MRS. FOOT. The funeral must be over by now. I've got an idea.

MR. FOOT. Tell me.

MRS. FOOT. Just let me do what I have to do. *(She picks up the telephone)*

MR. FOOT. Hadn't you better tell me first?

MRS. FOOT. Quiet. *(Into the telephone)* Hello! Mary? This is Mary Foot. How are you, dear? How was the funeral? A hit? The Governor! And the Vienna Choir Boys! How simply lovely! Yes . . . yes . . . (She gasps) Bill! You have to hear this ! Yes! . . . yes . . . Bill! Listen to this! They had a mausoleum ready for Spiffin, and they rolled him in sitting inside his Hudson Super Six— worth millions—they wheeled the Hudson Super Six right into the mausoleum. Yes . . . yes . . . All they took out was the air conditioning. . . .

MR. FOOT. This will kill Bill Bartlett a second time.

MRS. FOOT. Yes? No! Well, why not? It's a thing you can do only once. That's right. That's right. You're so right. Listen, Mary, the reason I called—we got to thinking, after you left, Bill and me, it sounded a little funny, I mean about the Nethergoods—Yes! No! I mean—of course! I understand perfectly! Of course!— Yes, yes, by all means!—I didn't—I wouldn't—anyway the point is that the Nethergoods are having a life insurance man over from India—

MR. FOOT. What's that?

MRS. FOOT. Yes, that's right—exactly—Hong Kong—ha ha ha, cosmopolitan is the word. Anyway, since my Bill is in life insurance himself, they thought—that's it—naturally—right— awfully technical—indemnity tables and so on, frankly it's going to be a bore for me personally—but I thought—that's right— you're so right—of course—I'm so glad I talked it over with you. Are you lunching at Peewee's tomorrow? Wonderful. About twelve-thirty. Bye bye! *(She hangs up)* Satisfied? I'm a genius.

MR. FOOT. You're playing a dangerous game. You should have consulted me first.

MRS. FOOT. What would you have advised me to do?

MR. FOOT. Book the first flight to Siberia.

MRS. FOOT. Very funny.

MR. FOOT. You'd better call the Nethergoods right away.

MRS. FOOT. What on earth for?

MR. FOOT. Don't you want to tell Mary Nethergood that you told Mary Tuttle that she, that is to say Mary Nethergood, was having a life insurance man from Hong Kong over for the soiree to which she didn't invite her, that is to say, Mary Tuttle? I mean, they see a lot of each other. You'll be feeling pretty sick if Mary Tuttle shakes her curls at Mary Nethergood at the beauty parlor next week and asks "How was your soiree with the life insurance man from Hong Kong?" "What life insurance man from Hong Kong?" "Why, the life insurance man from Hong Kong that Mary Foot told me about! Bang!

MRS. FOOT. I'm going to have to take a chance on that.

MR. FOOT. Why?

MRS. FOOT. Very simple. You want me to call Mary Nethergood.

MR. FOOT. Right.

MRS. FOOT. But if I do, I'll have to admit to Mary Nethergood that I told Mary Tuttle that she, that is to say Mary Nethergood, invited us for next Saturday. Insurance man or dentist, what's the difference? The point is that I'll be miserably exposed, and the Nethergoods will know that the Tuttles know that they, that is to say the Nethergoods, did not invite them, and that it was me who told the Tuttles. They'll never talk to us again.

MR. FOOT. Who?

MRS. FOOT. The Nethergoods, silly.

MR. FOOT. And if you don't call her?

MRS. FOOT. There's at least a chance. Mary Nethergood naturally won't tell Mary Tuttle about the party. And maybe Mary Tuttle will be tactful and proud enough not to let on she knows there was a party. And it will all blow over.

MR. FOOT. Something is bound to blow over. Oh well, hand me the paper, will you?

MRS. FOOT. I'll sit down and do nothing for a while. It's the most restful thing when all is said and done.

MR. FOOT. Where did I leave off? Ah, here it is. "Why, in your personal opinion, is it incorrect to wear a necktie on the beach over your swim trunks? (a) Because this is too conservative for our day and age. (b) Because it shows an exaggerated concern with your personal appearance. *(As the lights go down)* (c) Because the necktie would leave a white streak on your sun-bronzed chest. (d) Because you wish to avoid political and religious controversy.

Scene Two

(Mr. and Mrs. Tuttle are sitting on a bench in a park)

MR. TUTTLE. Look at the birds looping all over the air. Look at the grass cuddling the flowers. Look at the wind nibbling the leaves. Look at the innocent youngsters with sailboats and bicycles. Look at the romping butterflies. Come here, pretty pigeons, here are crumbs for you.

MRS. TUTTLE. If the Nethergoods want to invite a life insurance man from India especially to meet Bill Foot because Bill Foote is also a life insurance man, even though he is not from Hong Kong, why make a secret of it? What is wrong with doing what they did? Was Mary Nethergood afraid I'd be offended just because she didn't invite *us*? Why *should* she invite us? You're not in life insurance, you're in preformed cardboard and you don't export to Hong Kong. Why should we be offended? She must take us for a pair of fools if she thought we'd be small enough to resent her not asking us. Do *I* ask her over every time I have a guest, especially if he is in preformed cardboard? How stupid can a person be? Why didn't she talk to me honestly and say, "Mary, we're having a life insurance man from Hong Kong over next Saturday. I'm asking the Foots, because Bill Foot is in life insurance too. You don't mind, do you?" Instead she had to keep it a secret as though she'd been guilty of something, and when I met her on Thursday and asked her over to our house for Saturday, just to test her, mind you, just to test her, because I knew damn well that she was having her own party with the Hong Kong man and the Foots, she just played innocent and pretended they were going out. I'm glad Mary Foot happened to tell me the truth. I like to know what goes on.

MR. TUTTLE. That pigeon sure was hungry.

MRS. TUTTLE *(rising from the bench)*. Hello hello hello hello!

MR. TUTTLE. Who's coming?

MRS. TUTTLE. It's the Nethergoods!

MR. TUTTLE. Well, I want you to be nice to them. Let's everybody be nice to everybody and everything will be nice.

MRS. TUTTLE. Be quiet. You talk as if I was a hyena. *(Enter the Nethergoods)* Hello hello!

MRS. NETHERGOO. Hello hello!

MR. NETHERGOOD. Hello Billberry old man!

MR. TUTTLE. Good to see you again!

MRS. NETHERGOOD. What an adorable purse, Mary! Perfect for a spring day in the park. Is it new?

MRS. TUTTLE. Bill gave it to me for my birthday ten years ago. Thank you. By the way, we ran into the Foots the other day.

MRS. NETHERGOOD. Oh, how are they? Have you noticed how the park has become full of dirty pigeons?

MRS. TUTTLE. They said they had a lovely time at your place last Saturday.

MRS. NETHERGOOD. I'm so glad.

MRS. TUTTLE. And they enjoyed meeting the life insurance man from Hong Kong.

MR. NETHERGOOD. Life insurance man from Hong Kong? There was only a French dentist.

MR. TUTTLE. A French dentist in life insurance in Hong Kong?

MR. NETHERGOOD. What life insurance? Is everybody going crazy? He's a French dentist, I tell you, or a dental surgeon to be precise. Of course, Bill Foot talked to him a lot, and maybe he has a life insurance practice on the side, but that's more than I know.

MR. TUTTLE. Maybe he needs two jobs to make ends meet. Life in Hong Kong is awfully expensive, you know.

MR. NETHERGOOD. That's true. Or he might be divorced and paying alimony.

MR. TUTTLE. Or he could be supporting an old mother or two.

194

LAST PAGES

MR. NETHERGOOD. Anyway, what with the rate of industrial growth having slowed down to 0.6% per annum in France, I wouldn't be surprised if a Frenchman actually needed two jobs.

MR. TUTTLE. Well, that explains our little confusion.

MRS. TUTTLE. When are you two males going to stop chattering? Who cares how many jobs the man had? The main point is that the Foots had a very pleasant time.

MRS. NETHERGOOD. Well, I don't know where the life insurance story started, I'm sure he is a dentist and nothing else. We had a casual spur-of-the-moment thing at the house. He was going to show pictures of French teeth and I remembered how your Bill came down with a headache watching our World Tour pictures. By the way, will you be free next Sunday afternoon? Could you stop by for cocktails? The Willoughbys will be there.

MR. TUTTLE. Old Bill Willoughby of the Security Federal Union Security Universal Trust Bank?

MR. NETHERGOOD. That's the one.

MR. TUTTLE. Great. We'll be there.

MRS. TUTTLE (frosty). You're forgetting we're engaged, my dear.

MR. TUTTLE. Great. We are?

MRS. TUTTLE (frosty). I'm sorry, Mary, but we can't this time. Our schedule is full. Come along, Bill. It's getting chilly. Goodbye all.

MR. and MRS. NETHERGOOD. Goodbye.

MRS. NETHERGOOD. I'll call you!

MRS. TUTTLE. You do that. (On the way out, soft-loud to Mr. Tuttle) The liars, the simpering liars.

(They leave)

MRS. NETHERGOOD. We goofed.

MR. NETHERGOOD. You goofed.

MRS. NETHERGOOD. You goofed.

MR. NETHERGOOD. We goofed.

MRS. NETHERGOOD. Why didn't you keep your mouth shut when she rattled on about the life insurance man from

Hong Kong? Why did you have to stick your stupid facts into the conversation?

MR. NETHERGOOD. What's the difference? She was mad already, that was as obvious as a pimple on an egg. "I hear the Foots had a lovely time at your house," she says with a snaky smile that would have poisoned you at fifty paces if you hadn't smiled right back. I told you you should have asked them to the house.

MRS. NETHERGOOD. Don't start on *that* again. It so happened that I didn't feel like asking them that time. Do I have to ask the Tuttles every time I have anybody at the house? And I tell you that she wouldn't have objected if it hadn't looked suddenly as though we'd tried to keep the French dentist hidden from her for some evil reason or other.

MR. NETHERGOOD. Or if you hadn't told her last Thursday that we were engaged on Saturday when later she found out that we were engaged because we were having friends at our place.

MRS. NETHERGOOD. Found out! But where in sweet heaven did she find out that we had asked the Foots, and where in all that's holy did she hear about the life insurance man from Hong Kong. I can't figure it out.

MR. NETHERGOOD. Maybe somebody heard about the Foots meeting a life insurance man from Hong Kong at another party.

MRS. NETHERGOOD. That's very odd. Mary Foot has never mentioned it to me. Why should Mary Foot make a secret of a life insurance man from Hong Kong?

MR. NETHERGOOD. Well, then, suppose the Foots had this life insurance man from Hong Kong at their own house along with some other people who happen to know the Tuttles, and suppose they hadn't invited us. That would explain their not telling us about him.

MRS. NETHERGOOD. I suppose so. But behind our backs?

(Enter the Foots)

MRS. FOOT. Mary dear, oh, hello, Bill. There's something I'd better tell you.

MRS. NETHERGOOD. Oh, hello, Mary, hello, Bill.

MR. NETHERGOOD. Hello both!

MR. FOOT. Hello, Bill and Mary. Nice day, pretty birds.

MRS. FOOT. There's something I want to tell you, Mary.

MRS. NETHERGOOD. As a matter of fact, there's something I want to ask *you.*

MRS. FOOT *(apprehensive).* Oh. Why don't you ask first?

MRS. NETHERGOOD. No, you tell me first.

MRS. FOOT. Well, I couldn't get out of it, Mary. I won't go into details, but I had to tell the Tuttles *something,* so I told them you had invited—

MR. and MRS. NETHERGOOD. A life insurance man from Hong Kong.

MR. and MRS. FOOT. How did you know?

MRS. NETHERGOOD *(frigid).* We talked to the Tuttles.

MRS. FOOT. Oh no!

MRS. NETHERGOOD. We ran into them just now, and Mary said to me, "We heard you had a life insurance man from Hong Kong over at your house last Saturday to meet the Foots," she said to me, and naturally Bill said, "What life insurance man? He was a dentist," and then it all came out. Now what I'd like to know, just for curiosity's sake, is why you made up that story about the life insurance man from Hong Kong.

MR. FOOT *(to Mrs. Foot).* I told you.

MRS. FOOT. Oh, shut up. Mary, listen to me.

MRS. NETHERGOOD. You know how sensitive the Tuttles are; you know one can't take a step without treading on one of their hundred toes. And yet you have to blab to them, and tell them a cock-and-bull story about a life insurance man from Hong Kong. Excuse me for saying so, but it's plain stupid, that's all.

MRS. FOOT. Mary—!

MRS. NETHERGOOD. I'm sure you had your reasons for inventing this idiotic figure, but you might have given a moment's thought to the impossible hole you were digging for me. You made me look like a liar, a plotter. Mary Tuttle left here convinced I had told you to make up that story of the life insurance man from Hong Kong. They gave us a frosty goodbye. Two of our dearest friends down the drain. Thank you very much.

MR. NETHERGOOD *(weeping)*. Bill Tuttle, who was my buddy in the army, my chum at the Bowling League, my pal at the Lodge.

MR. FOOT *(to Mrs. Foot)*. I told you.

MRS. FOOT. May I put a word in sideways one of these years? Is anybody going to listen to me? Thank you. I wish you'd realize, my dear, that I invented the life insurance man from Hong Kong exclusively to save your face.

MRS. NETHERGOOD. Well, I never!

MRS. FOOT. I repeat: to save your face. I told the Tuttles it was a kind of business affair—insurance shoptalk between the men— so that she wouldn't be offended at being left out.

MRS. NETHERGOOD. And how did she come to know I hadn't asked her in the first place? Answer that one, if you please.

MRS. FOOT. Well, why didn't you?

MRS. NETHERGOOD. I've heard too much.

MR. NETHERGOOD. Me too.

MRS. FOOT. And why were you fool enough to tell her "Oh no, it wasn't a life insurance man from Hong Kong, it was a French dentist?" How naive can you get? A child would have guessed something and would have confirmed my story.

MR. FOOT. My wife has a point there, you know.

MR. NETHERGOOD. I protest.

MRS. NETHERGOOD. Don't bother protesting. You can't argue with boors. Let's —

MRS. FOOT. Boors? Did you say boors?

MRS. NETHERGOOD. Boors. Without an ounce of etiquette. You're a pair of public hazards, if you want an unbiased opinion.

Come along, Bill, let the Foots enjoy the park by themselves.

MR. FOOT. We will, damn it. Good riddance to the windbag.

MR. NETHERGOOD and MRS. NETHERGOOD. Boors!

(They leave)

MR. FOOT. I guess they don't like us any more.

(Enter the Tuttles from the other side)

MRS. TUTTLE. There you are.

MR. and MRS. FOOT. Oh my God.

MRS. TUTTLE. We heard all about your phony life insurance man from Hong Kong.

MR. TUTTLE. Our eyes are unplugged and the scales have fallen from our ears.

MRS. TUTTLE. All of a sudden he's a dentist.

MR. TUTTLE. A French dentist. Ha!

MRS. TUTTLE. Next time, you and your friends had better get together on the fables you're going to tell your stupid acquaintances. Come along, Bill. I just wanted to let her know we're wise to all of them.

MRS. FOOT. Won't you—

MRS. TUTTLE. Don't worry. I'll put your copy of Love in the Suburbs in the mail for you.

MRS. FOOT (weakly). You can finish it first.

MRS. TUTTLE. Come on, Bill. Let's leave the Foots and the Nethergoods to enjoy a good laugh at our expense.

(They leave)

MR. FOOT. So here we are.

MRS. FOOT (sniffling). I'm sure I did my best. If you hadn't—

MR. FOOT. If I hadn't! I like that! If I hadn't! That takes the prize! I told you a thousand times—

MRS. FOOT. You told me! You're always telling me! You think you're Einstein, don't you? You're always telling me what I found out three weeks before.

MR. FOOT. Keep talking, and if it makes you happy to unload your guilt on me, go right ahead, it's cheaper than analysis, you can tear me to bits to relieve your subconscious frustrations. But in the meantime, don't forget you've ruined six beautiful friendships.

MRS. FOOT. So it's all my fault. You take their side. Everybody else's wife is a pure spotless angel, only your own is a monster. I should have known. *(Tears and moans)*

MR. FOOT. Oh, well, it's not as bad as all that.

MRS. FOOT. Nobody understands me, not even my husband.

MR. FOOT. Sure I understand you. God knows I understand you. Come on, Mary, don't cry in the middle of the park. People are staring. There, there.

MRS. FOOT. Do you love me? *(He wipes her eyes with his handkerchief)*

MR. FOOT. Of course I love you. Who else should I love? Forget those Tuttles and Nethergoods.

MRS. FOOT. We've got plenty of other friends, don't we?

MR. FOOT. I should say so. We've got so many wonderful friends that when we lose a few we don't even notice. Look, Mary, we're in luck, look who's coming our way!

MRS. FOOT. Oh, it's Bill and Mary McGrue!

MR. FOOT. All right, make yourself presentable. We'll ask them over for drinks. Ready?

MRS. FOOT. Ready.

MR. FOOT. Forward!

(They advance into the wings, smiling, arms stretched out)

MR. and MRS. FOOT. Hello hello hello hello!

The End

TWENTY
POEMS

I am printing here the scant eight lyrics I have written since the publication of *Otherwise Poems* (2015). Following these are a dozen poems taken from my previous volumes: *Simplicities* (1974), *Collected Lyrics and Epigrams* (1981), and *Where Is the Light?* (2006). I need to explain that, not having been a prolific versifier even in my most fertile years, each one of my books following *Simplicities* contained, besides fresh poems, repeats from the previous collections, some revised, others not. This process culminated with the 2015 volume. But twelve of my earlier poems were left behind in 2015 for no reason I can ascertain. They are revived here (somewhat "perfected" if I thought fit), beginning with the brief "Should."

The only general observation about my poetry that I wish to record here is the fact that their "I" has never been afraid of not looking "nice."

AFTER LUNCH

Coming downstairs
I saw that my wife, before driving to her yoga class,
had sweetly left lunch on the counter for me.
There was the bit of fish left over from the night before,
not bad if not exciting, the dwarf tomatoes
that made a near-bruschetta on my bread,
and radishes, because she knows I like them
with my toast and butter. The Pavoni, recently repaired,
made me a nice espresso, not far beneath
the famous coffee at Rome's Tazza d'Oro.
Done, I stretched on the sofa in the den
for my usual doze, and there I died.
No doctors, no nurses, no needles, no hospital.
I had my wish.

ADRIANA IN SURGERY

Death saw his chance. He made a dart
Into that gash two inches from her heart.

The surgeon bested him—stanched and sewed so well
The fiend went rolling back to Hell,

Sneering, though, *Arrivederci, bella* from his hole
To my wife's Italian soul,

And to my Belgian : *A bientôt, mon pote.*
Death the polyglot.

[mon pote = pal]

September 2007, March 2010

MISERY

Nothing has changed.
The poor in their torn shirts
Are still stinking of sweat.
The children whose eyes the flies go licking
Suck at empty nipples.
When the earth jerks the buildings
Collapse on three rich men and ten thousand paupers.
The poor pick tomatoes under a raging sun
That would kill the rich in an hour.
The poor dig for wires and nails
From the generosity of refuse.
Nothing has changed.
The poor dream of villas and limousines
And bleeding the rich.
Called up by the rich
The poor machine-gun the poor.
Dazzled by the thugs
The poor will be yelling forever
Heil Hitler! Hurrah Pol Pot!

Maybe another world is gaping at us
Far in a fold of our galaxy
With peaceful, disbelieving eyes.

A BUS RIDE IN PARIS

So: I'm one of the elderly,
another "senior citizen."
It came all of a sudden,
no notice was given.

You say I'm lying to myself?

I swear I never saw it coming.
I was looking the other way.

A woman, not very young at that,
gives me her seat in the bus.
I must be dreaming!
No, it's me she's aiming at!

So what do I do?

I raise a smile that makes me sick,
I sit down, I say thank you.
The bitch!

HORSES

I tell the eight horses
trotting impeccably on the beach
where the sea murmurs its last:
Your beauty is strange —
it existed and exists and alas
will exist without us,
yet only we rejoice in it,
for tell me, wonderful horses, where,
and tell me, dog that watches you passing,
where, behind your eyes, does it lodge,
the ah! that beauty burns into the soul?

FLIGHT 065

Humbly seated in tourist class,
I dream of those who invent these difficult planes,
Of the pilots, the mechanics, and the rest
Who turn the sky into almost our sofa.
But wait—the reliables are everywhere:
"A job well done" is no rarity —
The water in our faucets clean to drink,
Holes in the asphalt decently filled,
The mail that arrives at five o'clock,
Violins almost as good as Guarnieris....
I tell myself as the Boeing tucks me in,
All is not fraud, all is not carnage!
Now and then one dares to breathe.

WHAT HAPPENED

Mother, I was far away when you died.
The other side of the ocean.
And I was ill. It's true.
And I'd left my passport (not needing it)
Even farther away.
And other obstacles.

I'd have whistled them off, bastard that I am,
If I'd been offered, at the other end,
Not this coffin,
But a million.

LE CORBEAU DANS MON JARDIN

On te dit : que tu es noir !
Noire, noire est la chevelure
de mon italienne épouse.

On te dit : que ta voix est rauque !
Socrate grognait cratt-cratt
ses onctueuses vérités.

On t'appelle mangeur de charogne.
Nous autres, nous rôtissons
Ceux à qui nous coupons la gorge.

On te dit : tu portes malheur.
Le malheur, hélas, vint me trouver
avant que je ne te connusse.

Reste dans mon jardin, corbeau,
appelle tes amis, j'aime les malins,
et j'ai vingt choses à vous dire.

SHOULD

Like the tip of a stranger's tongue
in the corner of your eye
the poem
should

ON THE ASSASSINATION
OF JOHN F. KENNEDY[1]

1

First came the special issues of the magazines
With loyal photographs: the old rich times, the rocking chair,
The wife who knew who Dali is, the muscular war,
The politics retouched and smiling, the happy hammer
Of his power, the idiocy of death. Each fifty cents.

The president was dead, tears fell and incomes rose.
Wait, brothers, wait,
My grief has gone to market too.

2

The picture books cost more but they were meant to last.
They used the most caressing words, like strong ideals
And dedicated heart and faith in our democracy.
And those who sold the plaster statuettes (one dollar each),
Their right hand mourned, their left rang up the cash.

The president was dead, laments and incomes rose.
Wait, brothers, wait,
My grief has gone to market too.

---

1 The original title of this poem was "We who do not grieve in silence." It appeared in
1964 in *Of Poetry and Power: Poems Occasioned by the Presidency and by the Death of
President John F. Kennedy*, edited by E.A. Glikes and P. Schwaber, who had asked me for
a contribution.

3

Congressmen deplored into the cameras, the voters saw
Their simple, manly sorrow. Foreign crowns were caught
Bowing usefully toward the poor man's grave.
All were shocked; what's more, they really were.
Alas one could not keep one's honest sobs untelevized.

The president was dead, tears fell and reputations rose.
Wait, brothers, wait,
My grief has gone to market too.

4

Next came recordings, and his voice was heard again
To make flesh creep from shore to shore. A publisher
Withdrew a luckless exposé; a sensitive biography
Recouped the loss. Three journalists retold the terror
Irreversible. We shuddered, covered up our eyes, and bought.

The president was dead, laments and incomes rose.
Wait, brothers, wait,
My grief has gone to market too.

5

When great men breathe their last, their expiration
Swells our sails. Films shall be turned, sermons released,
Memoirs composed and statues unveiled. Pure grief is silent,
And yet pure hardness is too hard for us as well.
We are the double flip-flop varlets of the playing cards.

The president is dead; my poem goes to press.
Grief, brothers, grief
Is my profit, but all the same I grieve.

MY COUSIN STELLA
(shot in Poland in 1944)

I am walking, fed and tranquil, book in hand.
Near a broken wall
a girl lies on the ground
half her face blown out and both her eyes dead open
like two bulbs gone out.

She asks, "Is that the ledger of our blood?"
And I: "It is the tale of Aucassin and Nicolette,
a mild small book
of decent merriment
and songs between
like poppies in a field."

She says: "Bullets made me what I am,
bullets struck me running in the field."

I kiss the crust of blood
then the lady spoke saying
I am Nicolette your dearest
returned from distant lands to

"Howl the world sick
womb howl throat howl howl!"

And nothing else
save, shock on shock, there, where she fell,
a shameless wheat pushing against the crow.

THE HOMBURG-HATTED MAN

Going my corrugated way
I stop two laughing pealing veering
sun-outsunning children about eight.
"You two!" "Yes sir?" (a little downed)
"Five years and then a gavel
chinks the simple cup the boy has been
and crack you will be men."
They stare at me with open mouth
dumb they gauge
the funny danger of the homburg-hatted man,
then crack indeed they gallop to the park,
at fifty yards the cup chimes double loud forgetful
crystal wholly hale.

MIRACLE PLAY

Doctor

I'll speak straight out (you are a man).
We'll pamper you two months or three,
but then—that nugget on your brain—
Yes, yes, it is a tragedy.

Patient

I have a wife, I have a child,
I have a car, I have a lease,
I have a yard, I have a job,
I have such love for all that is!

Angels that night

Our wings will tell you who we are,
Our wands will tell you what we can:
We are the sprites that gratify
The last desire of dying men.

Patient

Please kill my wife, please kill my child,
So I won't miss it, kill the world.
How dare these bodies play when oh!
Under the mud my bones lie curled.

Jesting angels

We promise you, there is no world;
That beauty which you see, you made,
And those who play shall be, we swear,
Invisibly by you unplayed.

God
For each man's death kills all the world,
And each man takes the world to bed.
I am the kindest God of all,
The flesh I kill does not regret.

I AM NO JEREMIAH

Stay with me still
and say no solemn word.
Play me over and again
the rhythms of the leaves
and do not say the wind must brutalize our dust.
O forgetters and unknowers,
I am no Jeremiah
eyeing blasphemous Jerusalem.
I dream a man at sixty may yet curl
his tongue around the berry he has plucked.
I hear the balloting for spruce or fir
among the nationalities of birds. . . .

FOOL OF A FREUDIAN

Fool of a Freudian,
what if God had made it His provision
we should light upon him (glory glory!)
through the bearded figure of a mortal dad?

Fool of a Christian
to believe it might be so.

Three o'clock: on the lake
the sun places a flock of suns,
which a placid wind erases
at three o'clock and three.

ENNUI

A bird trips up a tree,
a clock runs after time,
the Senate throws a law
at sempiternal crime,

Fresh factories steam up.
There's so much progress on,
idleness itself snores louder
and my lids fall down.

SUNDAY TWIDDLING THUMBS,
PEEVISH AS A CHILD

I'm not fond of anyone,
and no one's fond of me.
It's the devil of a joy,
I tell you, to be free!

Should they find me in a pool
of blood tomorrow on my bed,
they'd bury me like a tin can
the way I was, still wet.

My friends (I have a pack)
would say, "So much for wit,
and doing neither harm nor good,"
and talk two days of it.

Maybe I'll give some chocolates
and bestow a compliment,
to buy God willing half a sob
that will be really meant.

THE OSTRICH

Hail ostrich! Noteworthy bird! Head buried softly in the sand
While other creatures, eyes aloft and nerves a-twitter, spy the land

Where gangs of growlers circling close
Grimace their threats of unmedicinable blows.

These others take a stand. They'll live another one, two years
But live, poor things, with bowels melted by indecent fears.

So cancel my appointment, Dr. Gass.[2]
Let come whatever comes to pass.

2 Dr. Lew Gass, family friend.

OLD AGE

Harder, my boy, harder the speech,
stiffer the thoughts that ought to bend,
emotions stiffen into bone,
the rhetoric is bleached.

My poems stick like oil or glue.
To me my cough sounds louder
than the topple of a tyrant's statue,
than the crashing of the galaxies.

EPITAPH

Life has been a heavy broom
And I have been a little dust.
Dust we know must leave the room,
As is only just.

ESSAYS

UNACCEPTABLE POETRY

1

TO PUT IT SIMPLY, I take a poem to be a special form of literature consisting of a set of words, related signs, musical effects and visual strategies, arrayed on the page in what, elsewhere, I have called "limited quanta," which together normally produce *energized propositions*, whose success consists in giving pleasure, whatever else the text may do for the reader or the listener's spirit. A successful poem (and, by the way, a successful work of any art) is one that has lifted its "consumer" from his or her current level of pleasure to a higher one. There is no loophole from this inflexible axiom, no escape door opened by any theory of art. "Please or perish!"

But first, a word about the "related signs" just mentioned. They are the non-verbal elements of language which can be vital to the poem's propositions. Here is a strong example by that prolific humorist Richard Armour (1906-1989):

> That poem is a splendid thing.
> I love to hear you quote it.
> I like the thought, I like the swing.
> I like it all. (I wrote it).

Without the parentheses, which yield the proposition "This is an unimportant detail," the little quatrain would suddenly lose its ironic wit. A far more common related sign pregnant with meaning is a simple exclamation point. Even a comma is capable of yielding meaning and feeling. Here is Shelley's "A Dirge":

> Rough wind, that moanest loud
> Grief too sad for song;

> Wild wind, when sullen cloud
> Knells all the night long;
>
> Sad storm, whose tears are vain,
> Bare woods, whose branches strain,
> Deep caves and dreary main,—
> Wail, for the world's wrong!

Removing the comma from the last line obviously changes the meaning of the word "for"—changes it and thus alters the proposition conveyed by the line.

And the "visual element"? Scattering words over the page, special typography for certain words or letters, unusual spacings and so on are visual maneuvers that many poets indulge in to escape from the standard appearance of poetry as exemplified by Shelley's poem. A precedent can be found in the emblem or pattern poetry of the 17th century, when a poem about angels might be shaped on the page in the aspect of a pair of wings. The *Concise Oxford Dictionary of Literary Terms* mentions a poem by Guillaume Apollinaire called "It Rains," "in which the words appear to be falling down the page like rain." To what extent these games affect, subtly or plainly, the plain or subtle propositions and feelings delivered by the poem is difficult to say. My calling them games suggests that, for me, these are paltry energizers of the text and paltry sources of meaning; but there is no doubt that the poets intend them to be meaningful and/or producers of satisfying emotions.

There is nothing paltry, at any rate, about the musical resources of poetry, especially rhythm and rhyme, provinces of language fully owned by the art of poetry. Armour's quatrain would lie stone-dead without them. And yet I remain uncertain as to what, if anything, these and other musical effects (alliteration, for instance) can contribute to the poem's essential propositions— its intellectual side, in other words. Might a broken rhythm, for instance, be suggestive of an idea? Be that as it may (here I digress), the typical poetry of our times is distinctly unmusical. In the terms I am using here, it is a neglected source of energy for the propositions advanced in the text. Take, for instance, the following example, culled from the *Kenyon Review* dated September/October 2017:

> For many years I lived a normal life. Normal to some. Hotel
> Privilege. Etc., etc., as they say.
>
> But when I became sick,
>
> I discovered what I had always naturally called *I* was no longer
> an "I."
>
> It changed all the time—in fact, utterly receeded as a coherent
>
> notion—according to something happening in my cells that
> noone could identify.

And so drearily on for six pages.[3]

The near-death of music in the American and English poetry of our times is caused, in my opinion, by deep albeit unconscious cultural/historical pressures on mentalities, the same pressures, I believe, which have all but emptied serious music in our generations of delectable melody. (I except the two Russian giants). Technology has triumphed over melody.[4] "The work," an ecstatic critic writes about a new score (2018), "is made of repeated cycles structured like a spiral. The pianos come back halfway through and start the second one, which is half as long as the first. The third is again sped up double time, and the experience could be likened to being propelled in a spaceship toward a black hole. Eventually time breaks down. The pianos float away to heaven-knows-where. Other instruments follow suit. In an exceptional feat of musical

---

3 The author is the recipient of a Guggenheim Fellowship and two Pushcart Prizes and teaches at New York University and Princeton: no amateur! I have religiously reproduced the space corridor between the lines, in case this visual element has meaning.

4 Why one Lied (for instance) by Schubert or Schumann is "delectable" and the next one mediocre is a total mystery to me—and, I believe, to everybody else.

transformation, we wind up in an indefinable new dimension." Take that, Schubert!

But here ends my digression. My concern in these pages is not with the means at the poet's disposal for energizing his propositions, music among them (such music as unsung language can make); it is with the large topic of the propositions themselves.

2

WHAT THEN IS a proposition? Here too my answer is simple: anything that makes sense to the person who is reading or hearing the text. "God is great" is a proposition, and so is "Sunsets are beautiful." "Nevertheless splenetic fixity" makes no sense to me. It is not a proposition.

The notion of propositions applies to the poem as a whole but also, evidently, to any of its parts. This is, again, important in our times because certain highly regarded poets appear to discourse in discrete, disconnected propositions which, to many readers, convey no overall proposition: what we normally call a subject or a theme. But in what follows I will be speaking mostly about overall, or, if you will, central, or governing propositions.

A proposition, need one say it, can be overtly stated in a poem or (as in Armour's quatrain) it can be implied, read between the lines, insinuated—sometimes, as I have said already, by non-verbal means, say removing a word to the bottom edge of the page. Propositions can be easy or difficult of access. People can disagree about them. They may be completely misunderstood from the poet's point of view—but that is simply a risk the artist takes.

Finally, in preparation for what is to come, the obvious fact should be stated here that propositions come to us pregnant with emotions—emotions of all kinds and in all degrees, and sometimes complex and difficult to name; they range from Armour's jolly quatrain all the way to Hopkins'

No worst, there is none. Pitched past pitch of grief....

3

TURN A SEMI-COLON into a colon in a poem, use another preposition, find a synonym producing a sound that you prefer, and you have thereby changed the proposition you began with. This may be splitting hairs, but hairs do split. "Shut the door" is not the same proposition as "Close the door" nor is it the same proposition as "Shut the door!"

We live, however, largely in a macro-world. We can name in words of our own the governing proposition, or subject, or theme, of Shelley's "Dirge" without fatally betraying the absolutely unique meaning and emotion of the text itself. In doing this, we reach out for the *bare, pre-energized* proposition which precedes, or underlies, the energizing work the poet has wrought: "The world's a very bad place and nature itself says so," or a statement in the same conceptual region—mine is complacently gross and naïve—can be taken, in that macro-world of ours, as the pre-energized governing proposition of Shelley's lyric—its theme, as this is normally called, even as we admit that, minutely speaking, only the text itself can speak its absolute, irreplaceable meaning.

I now arrive, at last, to the point that the bare, pre-energized propositions of any poem possess *to begin with* a power of their own (if any) for every particular reader. Propositions like "my love is beautiful," "let us enjoy ourselves while we are young," "duty not enjoyment is the aim of life," "here was a man we thought happy and yet he committed suicide," "the voice of a singing girl deeply moved me," "I am lonely," "my mother ignored me," "Sir Lancelot loved Queen Guinevere yet remained loyal to King Arthur," "may

LAST PAGES

God protect my country," "patriotism is a disgrace to mankind," "a brilliant person ought to beget children," "let poetry evoke moods and not philosophize," "war is exciting," "war is hell," and an infinity of others, exercise a power over most of us most of the time, distinctly greater, need one say it, than a statement like "bookshelves should be at least eight inches deep." Even blandly worded, they are more energetic than the mass of daily propositions that make up the routine of ordinary life. And more energetic whether we agree with them or not; whether they seem true or false to us; whether we have or have not experienced what they report; and whether or not they make us wiser or morally improved. No wonder therefore that poems—even humorous poems—usually form themselves out of these significant and therefore potentially more satisfying raw propositions. All other things being equal (to be sure they never are), the better of two poems is the one whose raw propositions interest us more than those of its rival. Its raw material is, so to speak, in motion to begin with, hence the text will receive more benefit from the input of new energy it enjoys as the result of the poet's artistry.

A reminder: raw propositions are at least microscopically modified by the artist's work on them, but they remain recognizable "behind" the created work.

Need I repeat that however thrilling a raw, pre-poetic proposition is in itself, it cannot ever account as such for the success of a poem? Imagine the most electrifying of all possible ideas: "We shall be happily reunited with our loved ones after death." What idea could be, for almost everybody, more moving and powerful *to begin with*, before literature has taken hold of it? And yet, even this—or any stirring proposition one cares to formulate—is but a resource for the poet. All the perspiration is still to come. If every great theme guaranteed good poetry, the world would be flooded with masterpieces by our best philosophers and scientists. I am reminded here of that clever comic strip, "Calvin and Hobbes," by Bill Watterson, in which little Calvin's imaginary tiger-friend helps him draw a tiger for school, informing the lad as he does so, "The good thing about drawing a tiger is that it automatically makes your picture fine art."[5]

4

WE REACH at last the topic of *unacceptable* raw propositions. A splendid meal cannot be made out of foul ingredients. A superb poem cannot be built out of what I choose to call unacceptable propositions. Unacceptable to whom? I am not about to sneak a dictator into this discussion—some awe-inspiring personage who will decide for us what is and what is not acceptable. Each one of us is his own judge, of course; yet the result is not chaos. We all fall into more or less large and more or less durable groups, however unique we like to think we are. That is why we can speak of the literary canon. Homer is safely canonical. But be that as it may, the underlying principle is valid for you and for me as it is for the culture as a whole: raw propositions (whether governing the poem or local within the poem) weaken or kill the poem for any reader who finds them unacceptable; and this, no matter how the poet has gone about working to energize them.

I am using a vague term like "unacceptable" in order to cover the largest possible territory. But now we need to ask what is in fact unacceptable to readers. Broadly speaking, we *cannot* enjoy poems (or any other literary works, for that matter) whose raw, pre-energized propositions we regard as one or more of the following:

Stupid

Evil (vicious, disgusting, odious, vile)

Boring

Emotionally unbearable

5 Is not Van Gogh's *Starry Night* a greater work than his *Chair* largely (though not entirely) because its subject (its raw proposition, so to speak) is intrinsically far more "energetic" for most of us?

Concerning the first of these poisons: Since no one can enjoy a poem felt to be stupid, it follows that even the stupid (I am shamelessly using the blunt word) feel contempt for what *they* consider stupid. For if we avoid pathological mental deficiency, we find that no matter how low a person's intelligence, that person, just like the brilliant people *we* are, pronounces the judgment of stupidity, whether in people or in works of art. This much said, I trust that the readers who have stayed with me so far will inevitably sneer at a poem like Edgar Guest's "Departed Friends":

> The dead friends live and always will;
> Their presence hovers round us still.
> It seems to me they come to share
> Each joy or sorrow that we bear.
> Among the living I can feel
> The sweet departed spirits steal,
> And whether it be weal or woe,
> I walk with those I used to know.
> I can recall them to my side
> Whenever I am struggle-tied;
> I've but to wish for them, and they
> Come trooping gayly down the way,
> And I can tell to them my grief
> And from their presence find relief.
> In sacred memories below
> Still live the friends of long ago.[6]

Eddie Guest's poetry, of which "Departed Friends" is a fair sample, had just the intelligence needed to gratify a multitude of readers, but for *us* it is too stupid to live.

As an aside, it is interesting to note that the musical elements in "Departed Friends," to wit the babyish sing-song rhythm and rhymes that run counter to the gravity of the theme, contribute to the radical failure of its intelligence—for intelligent readers.

---

6 "Edgar Albert Guest (1881-1959) was a prolific English-born American poet who... became known as the People's Poet. His poems often had an inspirational and optimistic view of everyday life." (Wikipedia). In 1916 he published his first book: *A Heap O' Living.*

Naturally, since there are gradations in our judgment of what is stupid, so there are degrees to which poems are injured for us through this paticular vice. But the truth is that our requirement in this domain is a modest one. The pre-energized basic proposition of a poem need not be impressively intelligent, because so very much depends on the energizing skill of the artist. Like a great chef handed average ingredients yet concocting an unforgettable meal, the good poet can be trusted with modest propositional resources. To be sure, all other things being equal (once more: they never are) the more intelligent we deem the raw proposition or propositions of a poem, the more we are bound to love it. But the evident fact is that many poems on relatively small subjects are lodged in the canon. I could go back to Greece (the *Anthology*) and Rome (Catullus) for any number of examples; but let us hear Robert Herrick in our own dear language:

UPON JULIA'S VOICE[7]

So smooth, so sweet, so silv'ry is thy voice,
As, could they hear, the Damn'd would make no noise,
But listen to thee (walking in thy chamber)
Melting melodious words to Lutes of Amber.

The pre-poetic subject of this poem—"a compliment to a girl's beautiful voice"—is hardly world-shaking. For most of us it is simply interesting and intelligent enough to be energized into a charming poem, unless, preoccupied by wars and famines, the triviality of the matter irritates us. As for one of the "local" propositions in the poem, which I paraphrase by saying that Herrick imagines the very damned stopping their din in order to listen to the lady, for me, at any rate, this is a modestly witty little thought, and for me it is already "something": an invention, an act of the poetic imagination, even when presented in my colorless prose words.[8] And again, nothing earth-shaking has transpired.

7 "From *Hesperides* (1648). "Chamber" should be pronounced to rhyme with "amber."

8 Herrick's poem is of course highly energized by its verbal music; its first line alone is a tiny masterwork in this respect.

Good poems do not require profound thought. In a word: my "acceptable" will do. Trifles can be immortal.

All this time I have been sedulously avoiding the word "true" in favor of "acceptably intelligent." Not, however, because the notion of "truth" offers insuperable philosophical difficulties in the present context, in which "true" means nothing more arduous than "seems true to the reader." The real point is that we are very likely to accept propositions (stated or implied) that appear untrue to us, provided they seem reasonably intelligent, and provided the other conditions I will be speaking of in a moment are also met. The canon at any rate does not care about the truth of what poets say, for it embraces Shelley's

> Rough wind, that moanest loud
> Grief too sad for song;
> Wild wind, when sullen cloud
> Knells all the night long;
>
> Sad storm, whose tears are vain,
> Bare woods, whose branches strain,
> Deep caves and dreary main,—
> Wail, for the world's wrong,

as blithely as Pope's

> All Nature is but art, unknown to thee;
> All chance, direction, which thou canst not see;
> All discord, harmony not understood;
> All partial evil, universal good:
> And, spite of pride, in erring reason's spite,
> One truth is clear, WHATEVER IS, IS RIGHT.

However, I do not mean to suggest that the true/false judgment we pass on the poem we are reading is flatly inapplicable. All other elements being equal (again!), we invariably prefer poems whose propositions we deem true to poems whose propositions seem in error, for the combination "intelligent-and-true" or "interesting-

and-true" is unquestionably more satisfying—delivers more energy, in my terms—than "intelligent" alone.

A minor addition to what I have said so far is that this satifying energy will receive another boost if it happens that the poem is also instructive for us, whether we take this term in the narrow sense of giving out new information, or in the generous sense of the feeling that the poem has made us wiser. "True, intelligent, and edifying" produces more enjoyment than "true and intelligent" alone. Encountering ideas in a poem—or a novel, or a play— which one had never met with is a thrill particularly common for young readers. As we grow older, and our brains store more and more ideas from our various readings—readings literary and far beyond—poetry inevitably declines as a source of instruction and wisdom. Its intelligence, however, remains alive as a sufficient foundation and absolute condition for doing its work of being admirable for us.

5

JUST AS IT CAN be stated axiomatically that a stupid poem is a bad poem, so I posit the axiom that if the morality of the propositions of a poem is odious to us, the poem inevitably sickens or dies for us. Sickens or dies, because here too gradations occur. Now, it may be argued that morality is no longer much of an issue in our times, not, at any rate, with our intellectual elite, not, that is to say, with most readers of this essay. Long gone are the days when writers were asked, or rather required, to inculcate virtue, and when they claimed, or rather pretended, to do so. Oscar Wilde's legislation on this subject seems to have prevailed: "There is no such thing as a moral or an immoral book. Books are well written or badly written. That is all." In obedience to this ukase, such words as "virtue" and "morality" have disappeared from the vocabulary of our literate elites. The reality, however, is that we sophisticates demand morality as fervently as any Victorian clergyman, with the difference that for us good and evil are terms we use chiefly for social and political opinions, not personal ones like, say, chastity and marital fidelity. We are not especially aware of the axiom in question here simply because we have no expectation of reading a poem in our quarterlies or in the numberless "slim volumes" of poetry looking for readers these days, in which the poet tells us (or implies) that Blacks are an inferior race, that homosexuals should be jailed, that Jews are plotting to take over the world, that women should obey their husbands, and so on. Editors would have to go mad to publish a poem (if they could find one) based on the affirmation that "a woman can always be satisfied with devoting herself to her husband"⁹ or a poem that sings of military heroism, glory, conquest. Who, among our sophisticates, would enjoy and extol a poem congratulating the American wars in Vietnam, Iraq, Afghanistan? Where is our Tennyson, the one singing of the Charge of the Light Brigade—of the wretches killing and then dying during the wretched Crimean War?

> When can their glory fade?
> O the wild charge they made!
> All the world wonder'd.
> Honor the charge they made!
> Honor the Light Brigade,
> Noble six hundred!¹⁰

And yet for a large percentage of the population of any Western country (let alone the rest of the world), these "abhorrent" feelings and opinions are very much alive, and many would be disposed, if accidentally confronted by a poem, to delight in finding them expressed in metrical shape. They are abhorrent only, without exception, to the kind of person who, in 2018—I'll pick a random name—can identify William Carlos Williams. For this "us" group,

9 From George Eliot's *Silas Marner*, II, 17.

10 Our moral revulsions do not kill poems when they are masterpieces of the past, like the *Iliad*. This is due to the psychological trick of "taking into account."

such poems would be poisoned from the start—if they existed.

My axiom stands. Morality in poetry, and in all the arts, remains as important as it ever was, even if, in poetry at any rate, it never, or hardly ever, manifests its force. All other elements being equal (as usual), the less moral a poem (from our point of view), the less we will like it, the more moral (from our point of view), the better we will like it. And at the boundary, both phenomena come to their logical conclusions. On one side profound moral revulsion will fatally poison aesthetic pleasure. But on the other side it may happen that a moral stand in a poem so delights us that, overlooking all manner of defects in the artistry, we are aesthetically carried away. I can vouch for this axiom, incidentally, by confessing, at great risk to my standing with the readers of this essay, that the use, so very common in the poetry of our times, of what used to be called foul language repels me and causes the poem that uses it to sicken or die for me.

An interesting side-issue is that our moral revulsion can also poison a work of art not because of the work as such, but because we hate the person who produced it. No good Nazi could feel love for Heinrich Heine's poetry. And, going off poetry, fifty years after the Holocaust, the Israeli Philharmonic Orchestra still refused to play the music of Richard Wagner. At the other pole, a burst of sympathy or love for a person may cause us to be charmed or moved by almost anything whatsoever this person has produced. Take the following little poem:

> 'Twas midnight and he sat alone,
> The husband of the dead.
> That day the dark dust had been thrown
> Upon her buried head.
> Her orphan children round me sleep,
> But in their sleep do moan.
> Now bitter tears are falling fast.
> I feel that I'm alone.

As poetry, this is not *much* better than "Departed Friends."
And yet, when we discover that these lines were scribbled in 1853
by a broken-hearted pioneer (John Tucker Scoot by name) on the
harsh Oregon Trail, a burst of sympathy may well make us like the
poem with a liking we withhold from a best-selling professional
nonentity like Eddie Guest. But, I repeat, this is a side-issue, a
rarity.

6

I TURN very briefly to the next cause of aesthetic death. Poems
can be, and often are, simply uninteresting to us rather than stupid
or morally odious. They bore us. Nothing, we feel, that the poet
can do with his matter will arouse our interest. "Even Homer
nods." One reader may be fundamentally uninterested in minute
descriptions of nature; another in theological speculations;
another in tales about King Arthur. Who reads *Paradise Regained*
anymore? Who can read Wordsworth's *The Excursion* without
dozing off? Boring his audience is probably the sort of failure an
artist dreads most. He prefers rage to yawn. This holds, of course,
for all the arts. I have yawned my way across many a roomful of
"nice" nature paintings in many a provincial museum, and even in
many a museum not at all provincial....

7

THIS LEAVES US with the fourth class of unacceptable
propositions—those that are neither morally revolting nor
stupid, and drastically the opposite of dull, namely emotionally

devastating. In daily life, the unbearable presses upon us, naturally, far more readily than it does in the arts. Most directly, of course, when we ourselves feel the pain. Then comes the pain felt by those closest to us. Then the pain endured by strangers. Then the pain we read about in the newspapers. And finally the pain depicted, sculpted, danced or written about in works of art. In these, as the history of all the arts testifies, we can remain pleasurably excited even when some extremely upleasant emotions—fear, horror, disgust, indignation, shame, pity, gloom, and so on—are being stirred in us. The pain and terror of cancer, the fear of aging, the fright when faced by an armed robber or a rapist, mourning over the loss of a child, the desolation of a financial reverse, anxiety about our careers, a humiliating put-down before strangers, sexual shame, jealousy of a rival, envy of someone's happiness, desperate loneliness, pity for an orphan, and then, in a larger arena, the sorrows brought about by fires, famines, epidemics, wars…. All of these, as everyone knows, can and do deliver pleasure in masterfully energized works of art. The actor playing Othello need not worry that we will run from the theatre as he strangles the lady playing Desdemona in a blaze of poetry:

> Not dead? not yet quite dead?
> I that am cruel am yet merciful;
> I would not have thee linger in thy pain….

We are thoroughly "appreciating" the scene, even as anguish filters into our pleasure. Far from what our feelings would be if we were to witness a real strangling!

Be that as it may, for almost every one of us, even in the world of art, removed though it is from "lived life," there is a border on the other side of which aesthetic pleasure dies. Yes, some spectators *may* want to tip-toe to the exit as Othello kills Dedemona. Just as not every patron of the roller-coaster ride truly enjoys himself, so the grim, the tragic, the pathetic, the shocking work of art may die for the reader, the looker, the listener, no matter how expert the handling of its propositions. There comes a time in the cinema when the spectator, disturbed by a scene of torture, warfare, misery of any sort, rises from his seat and leaves; a time when a reader shuts the excessively sad or disturbing novel and refuses to re-open it; a time when the visitor in a gallery turn his eyes away from too horrifying or even too embarrassing a picture. It is an old story. Around 500 BC a dramatic poet by the name of Phrynichus so upset the Athenian audience with a play concerning a recent victory of the Persians and massacre of the Greeks that he was fined, and the city decreed that no play on that subject should ever be produced again, for the matter was too painful.

I have taken a step away from the topic of unacceptable propositions in poetry for the plain reason that poetry, or at any rate what we loosely call lyric poetry, is the form of literature least likely to fail for us because it has aroused an intolerable emotion. A novel or a play is far more likely to do so. I conclude therefore with a purely hypothetical situation. Your son has recently been killed on the battlefield. Someone shows you a war poem about a young man killed in battle. You try to read the poem, but you cannot go on, you return it half-unread, with tears of anguish in your eyes. The poem is, for you, neither stupid nor evil, let alone vapid, it is simply unbearable. At that frontier of feeling, Art fails and withdraws.

AGAINST CASTRATED ART

1

IN NOVEMBER 2018 David Hockney's harmless painting of a swimming pool with figures was sold at auction for some ninety-million dollars, more than twice as much as Gerhard Richter's *Abstraktes Bild* had fetched a few years earlier; monetary proof, if proof was needed, that figurative art has survived, and indeed was never in danger of not surviving, the onslaught, long ago by now, of the art of sheer shape, color, texture, space and innovative materials, and more recently, the art of "installations," with or without feats of high technology. Figurative art never left the scene, and neither has abstract art. Non-referential art, as it might better be called, is securely alive. Indeed, a glance at airports, office buildings, restaurants, advertising and so on proves that it is downright popular. Historians of later ages, whether they choose to call it a culmination or an aberration or just another movement, will surely pick it as the most *distinctive* manifestation of the artistic life of our Western world inasmuch as there is no precedent for it, no precursor. Although the movement, or school, has had its enemies since its beginnings before the First World War, they have been fewer, if I am not mistaken, than admirers. Either way, an immense literature exists concerning it in general and its practitioners in detail. But it seems to me that the subject is by no means exhausted. It continues to deserve observation and comment. Mine, in these few pages, will be amicably hostile.

To impeach non-referential art, the gravest charge against it must be, obviously, its "decision" to disengage art from the infinite world of objects—from our merest neurons to the farthest star, and from every object mankind has ever fabricated (including works of art!)—its renunciation of the infinity of objects to which our passsionate interest is attached. What is a little less obvious is the fact that *in art the function of this passionate interest is aesthetic.* In other words, it fuses into all the formal elements of the work of art to produce our delight in it. Our moral and intellectual interest in a vessel tormented by a storm is intrinsic in the delight and admiration the depiction of it produces in us as we feel, expertly or naively, that the thing is "well painted." An aesthetic theory which ignores this fact preaches in a vacuum not inhabited by human beings.[11]

Here, as a not wholly irrelevant aside, it may be observed by how much the world "out there" exceeds in interesting things to look at what it offers in interesting sounds to listen to. For mankind, nature produces not only literally fewer sounds than sights, but what is more important, the sounds which it does produce are less beautiful, less interesting, less significant on the whole than the sights. As I look out my window, I see a hill covered with fine trees, a grand museum on top of it which, if not beautiful (alas) is still, in its appearance and suggestions, interesting and significant, and against the lovely blue sky, the coquetterie of a white cloud. By contrast, the noises that reach me are the uninspiring ones made by cars in the nearby freeway and the occasional ugly toot of their horns. Now and then the unpleasant noise of an airplane—an object beautiful to see—descends on me. How many other natural sounds strike us as intrinsically beautiful or significant? The songs of birds, so often praised, are not really beautiful; they have been made beautiful by the visual, tactile, and affective associations of bright plumage, springtime, freedom, and grace of flight. The trickling of a little stream over its pebbles is not a disagreeable sound; but if we abstracted the sheer sound from our view of the flowing water, we would quickly lose interest in it. More decidedly, think of the good-looking dog with his shocking

11 In my essay "Unacceptable Poetry," I discussed the corollary of this fact, to wit that, *other things being equal*, the more morally and intellectually fine the work is in our estimation, the more we will admire it.

bark, the caterwauling of the lissome cat, the uninspiring neigh of the horse. I could go on and on. As for human speech, that of course is as fascinating to us as any sight we know, but hardly for the sound as such. Besides, literature has taken it as its province. Neither painting nor instrumental music is the art which imitates or makes use of language.

But let me return to my subject: My title speaks, somewhat dramatically, of castrated art. But who did the castrating? Not some grim enemy of art; it was of course done, done happily and intentionally and in many cases (as we will shortly see) all but religiously, by the artists themselves, ridding themselves of the infinite resources for giving pleasure that I have dwelled on. The deep question that must be asked is whether the resulting "purification" of art has offered compensation for the loss suffered because of the terrible knife-act. Was visual "imitation," when all is said and done, exhausted after so many centuries of undeniable glory, and in dire need to be replaced by an art which, like music, is—at last! its practitioners and partisans might exclaim—strictly about itself?

Be the answer what it will, it must not be hidden that representational artists inevitably take risks which do not threaten the workers in "pure" art. One does not turn away from a "Composition IV" because it is silly or stupid, trivial, or plain ridiculous, but this happens all too often when we gaze at figurative art. For myself—strictly for myself—I confess that I am offended by the ostentatious will-to-be-different which impels Tintoretto to exploit rather than render certain Christian subjects. The numberless depictions of Jesus as a sweet, pretty, neatly combed youth (the *Salvator Mundi* by Anton-Raphael Mengs which hangs in my local museum is a relevant example) are downright idiotic. I am much inclined to yawn at Poussin's conceptions of antiquity, pagan or Christian. I do not care for the baroque convention of uplifted eyeballs, meant to denote ecstatic spirituality; for me, alas, this rotation too often suggests a condition of advanced imbecility.

I demur before Gericault's *Raft of the Medusa* because it is too muscled and operatic. I am fatally amused when I see Romans and Sabines fighting stark naked in David's masterpiece. The depiction of tethered Angelica by Ingres strikes me as silly. I remain cold to the triviality of Van Gogh's obdurately negligible straw-bottomed chair, in contrast with his heart-breaking painting of a pair of worn-down peasant shoes. The repellent bodies exhibited by Lucien Freud and Francis Bacon look disgusting to me *sans plus*— morally empty, in fatal distinction from the moral force of Otto Dix depicting the bodies torn by World War I or Goya's vision of victims of the Napoleonic invasion of Spain; distinct too, of course, from the scary-humorous bodies painted by Bosch.

Some of the examples I have just given are reminders that objective art has been especially apt to be tormented by ridicule. Baccio Bandinelli's derided statue of Hercules and Cacus on the Piazza della Signoria in Florence is a classic instance; but far more widely known is the contemptuous laughter that barked at the work of the Impressionists in their first generation.

I for one am also repelled by works the subjects of which should, I feel, convey a moral or intellectual dimension but simply stand there, in front of me, without saying anything. Andy Warhol's cans of tomato soup or repetitions of images of this or that celebrity, and Jasper Johns' coat-hanger and target and American flag illustrate my meaning. Compared with the loving still-lifes of the Dutch, where a glass flute, a copper kettle, a loaf of bread sing with joy, they strike me as utterly dull and dumb, let the artists, their admiring critics, the museums and the moneyed collectors say what they will. Only if such works are humorous— like, for instance, the wonderfully witty supersized items made by Oldenburg and van Bruggen—do they instantly rejoin the moral-rich tradition that includes, for instance, the jolly works of Jan Steen and Jacob Jordaens.

I have spoken only for my inexpert self. Everyone to her and his examples. The point here is that the self-castration of non-referent art makes it immune to displeasure caused by moral or intellectual failure. I will be discussing its frequent claims to the contrary in a few minutes. For the moment it is enough to say that moral and intellectual considerations are simply beside the point in a Vasarely, a Stella, a Pollock. Abstract art, in short, can never sink as low as figurative art. I need hardly finish the thought: it can never rise as high.

2

REMARKABLY, even as non-referential art was being born and beginning to thrive, representational art was showing that, far from dying of exhaustion, it had undergone and was continuing to undergo renewals in multiple directions.

To begin with, objects new to the world were, inevitably, entering the pictorial arts: trains, factories, automobiles, airplanes, football players, the Eiffel Tower, machines and machine guns, and so forth. Furthermore, old objects which the tradition had ignored became valid subjects for depiction: Malevich's scissor grinder, the coat-hanger I have already mentioned, a urinal, newspapers, a Swiss Army knife, and so on. Often, too, objects known to the tradition but "kept in their place" were made leading actors in the picture. I have mentioned Van Gogh's chair and shoes. In 1650, a Dutch grain-merchant and his wife, owners of a picture showing a tavern-scene, would have been not a little surprised on learning that a few centuries later the pipe one of the bibbers was smoking would be enlarged to become an entire painting. No need, I think, to mobilize more instances.

But a more remarkable development was bearing witness to the fact that artistic renewal did not require killing the object. A *freedom of play with objects* took place, and continues to do so, that would have astonished—more than that: would have dumbfounded every artist we know of from days immemorial. Picasso's *oeuvre* can stand for this unprecedented exuberance of imagination, and even that does not exhaust the range of play we find in the galleries and museums. As everyone is familiar with this flood of inventivity, there is no need for me to ape textbooks by citing a flood of examples. Let it be enough to note that the flood in question seems to have begun, *grosso modo*, after the pleasantly boring productions of the Barbizon School. That playing with known objects of nature and human fabrications will surely be remembered in the distant future as prodigious, while the morally and intellectually barren tide of abstract paintings, sculptures and "installations" will, I prophecy, receive no more than honorable mention as an interesting but "gone too far" phenomenon.[12]

By the way, a comical by-product of the creative fury that characterizes post-Barbizon art (both abstract and referential) has been the tsunami of Schools and Movements, one more pretentious than the other, quarreling for attention and domination. This too would have astonished our ancestors, and, I am sure, amused them.

3

TO BE SURE, many, perhaps most, abstract artists, and many, probably most of their learned apologists, reject the judgment that non-referential is empty of moral and intellectual interest. After a few sarcasms aimed at "what people are pleased to call objective reality," at "the oppression of the subject," "the figurative obsession," "the dead weight of the object," many artists will tell us that they are in fact committed to metaphysics, deep psychology, history or ethics. Their three patches of round items on a background of squirms merely avoid "outward appearance"

---

12 For a moment, Picasso "went too far" (for my taste) when, during his cubist phase, the figure essentially vanished in some of his paintings; but this was a mere blip in his long *parcours*.

to dwell on "the underlying significance of reality." When two criss-crossing scratches suffice to "portray the inner existential tensions of our age," any blob can be the Summa, and a wiggle becomes The Decline of the West. Here are a few utterances from the Great Names: "The circle...is a link with the cosmos" and "the expression of mystery in terms of mystery" (Kandinsky); "Mystical inner construction" (Franz Marc); "the infinite abyss" and "a true impression of the infinite" (Malevich); "Structures of lines, surfaces, forms, colors . . . try to approach the eternal, the inexpressible above man" (Arp); "a revelation, an unexpected and unprecedented resolution of an eternally familiar need" (Rothko).

The critics are often equally eloquent, if not even more so. Here is one, speaking about the vertical line (called by the artist a zip) that crosses the middle of some of Barnett Newman's canvasses: "The zip may be seen as the Divine Light."

In effect, many practitioners of abstract art want to eat their cake and have it too: destroy representation but catch it back with a title fetched from the world they have destroyed, thus by magic enjoying (they think) the advantages of both worlds. Hence the inventively inflated titles we see on so many abstract works. One piece of post-cubism, constructivism, suprematism, neoplasticism, action-painting, or whatever, may be called, modestly and reasonably, *Composition* or *Untitled* or *Red Rectangle*. Its kindred neighbors on the wall reach higher. One is called *St. Francis Xavier in the Indies*; another, *The Harvest*; another, *The Birth of the World*; another, *Anything Else But Love*; another, *Calvary*; another, *Jazz City*; another, *Pompei*; and then, returning to honesty, *Yellow, Purple, and Blue Rhythms*. Joan Miró named his breezy abstract masterpiece *Tryptich of the Hope of a Man Sentenced to Death*. A painting by Robert Motherwell which ought to be called *Oval and Longitudinal Black Shapes Against Strips of Various Colors* wins from his generous pen the title, *Elegy to the Spanish Republic*. One critic goes so far as to speak of "the tragic implications of reds and greens which jar on one another" in the work of Franz Kline.

Motherwell, by the way, is quoted as saying that "without ethical consciousness a painter is only a decorator." This reminds me that Kandinsky, the Adam of abstract art, informed the public that a straight horizontal line is cold and flat, a vertical one is warm, a diagonal one is lukewarm.

Sometimes pure dithyramb takes over. "The symbol," chants a typical nonrepresentational artist about his own work, "has safely guided my course into the unknown realm of experience. The traveler is just a pilgrim. Sometimes he knows a little more, often a little less, because values change with each voyage. Sometimes one gets a glimpse of the bridge to eternity before it disappears like a rainbow. Somewhere between exultation and despair lies the answer. In one sense my work gives structure and dimension to thought in time." And so forth.

The critical language we find in innumerable exhibition catalogues and scholarly works echoes the claims by the artists themselves. Let us listen to a typical critic: "What [Jasper] Johns has done is to manifest an organizing process at work, which he claims is an effort to articulate the space of the painting by a growth pattern. I would hazard that the extended narrative weave of correspondences represents a dialectical relation between structure and process: a laying out of fundamental principles. I suppose him to be speculating on the origin of things, elaborating a 'code' for the unfolding of a world-order, a skeletal ontological framework that serves as a metaphor for the unity and density of the world."

As every reader of art criticism knows, this kind of "analysis," this kind of blather, is pervasive in the art-world. The less there is to say about a painting, the more is the shop-talk of its authors and admirers likely to bristle with frighteningly sublime verbiage. And why not? If I start with the assumption that my blobs of color and my distribution of shapes have meaning, why not make the largest statements for them that I can put into words? Who can prove me wrong? Let my rival for gallery space and critical attention naively call her work "Composition in Yellow and Green"!

This sort of humbug (by the way) is also pervasive in the world of instrumental music. Since non-vocal music is "abstract" by its very nature, it is not surprising that highly imaginative titles appeared in this realm centuries before the birth of the non-referential visual arts. How long ago I don't know (let scholars tell me), but in my own music collection I find two pre-Bach composers who indulged in this shrewd marketing device. Heinrich Biber published a set of so-called *Rosary Sonatas* for violin which, though nothing else than straightforward sonatas, are adorned with such titles as *The Birth of Jesus*, *The Presentation of Jesus to the Temple* and the like. Johann Kuhnau's equally straightforward harpsichord sonatas are called *The Fight Between David and Goliath*, *Jacob's Wedding* and so on. The fashion grew and became a torrent. Closer to our times (I name at random) we find a *Harold in Italy*, *A Hero's Life*, *The Drowned Cathedral*, *The Painter Mathis* and hundreds of other alternatives to honesty. True, to a feeble degree music can imitate certain sounds of nature: Rameau's hen, Beethoven's storm, Richard Strauss' sheep or the sawing off of his John the Baptist's head come to mind, hence there are occasions—exceedingly rare ones—when titles do fit. But, this extremely rare occurrence aside, humbug prevails just as it does in the Kandinsky world. In our times titles of musical scores have left the hen and sheep and Harold far behind. We are inundated with ingenious and often grandiose titles like Stockhausen's *Ascension to Heaven* and *Cosmic Pulses*, Boulez's *Hammer Without Master*, Philip Glass' *Anima Mundi* and *Prophecies from Koyaanisqatsi* (I have not troubled to identify this redoubtable reference) and numberless others, far more marketable, needless to say, than a drab "Sonata in D major."

4

I SAID, at the beginning of this essay, that my hostility to abstract art is an amicable one. A castrato is still a mensch! Think of those wonderful singers history is enamored of! Well! Abstract paintings and objects can be very pleasing indeed in their minor way— minor in the context of the truly great works, like those that reign over the Sistine Chapel. I am not sure that as an unprofessional lover of good things I can tell why *this* abstract work is hanging in a Museum of Contemporary Art and that one is not; why the first has fetched millions and the second not a dime. But the fact remains that many non-referential works of art are attractive as they beget, much like music, unspecified feelings—of power, of violence, of cheer, of exuberance, of tranquility, and so forth. I for one am especially struck by the astonishing explorations and innovations of so many artists (famous or not) in areas of sheer beauty and charm—beauty and charm without the slightest reference to pretty girls, flowers, gods, any object or event whatever, beauty and charm only through the sheerest manipulations of the material elements at hand.[13] The floating leaves of Alexander Calder and the geometrics of Piet Mondrian spring to my mind, inevitably, as I write these words, but many "installations" I have seen have struck me as utterly delightful (most have not).

In the past, the non-representational was limited to humble decorative effects. In our generations, it has made bold to assign to itself center-stage. Grand claims aside—modesty was never a strong point with artists—it would be foolish to wish that the extreme "logical conclusion" of Cézanne's paintings which created abstract art was an aberration—as can be said, I would maintain against all opponents, of any music in which great melody is not

13 The fact that artists have "splashed about" exuberantly with every material and tool and device that exist in the world is outside the argument of my essay.

the main source of merit.[14] Let me repeat, to conclude, that the greatness of a painting like *Guernica* or, taking a mighty leap across subjects, Fragonard's *Young Woman Playing With a Dog*, cannot be equaled by any work in which the means of art are turned into its end. But this assertion is hardly a call for it to die.

14 The spiriting away of the object in the visual arts and of melody in music is a parallel deserving of inquiry and comment.

CONCERNING IMBECILITY

1

LET ME BEGIN with an epigram I wrote long ago; it was called "The Astronaut ate a piece of consecrated bread on the moon (1969)":

> The Reverend blessed a loaf of bread,
> Aldrin flew it to the moon,
> To prove man is and shall remain
> Half sage, two-thirds buffoon.

The hero of this poem, as alive as I am this January 2018, is colonel Edwin Eugene Aldrin, known as Buzz, who went for a walk on the moon July 21, 1969, an exploit for which he received, naturally, a great deal of attention in the press, which reported the telling little anecdote concerning the consecrated loaf of bread, Catholic or Episcopalian, I don't know which. Our convenient "search engines" provided me with the information that the astronaut is an expert in spatial mechanics, holder of a doctorate in astronautics and author of a thesis bearing the title "Line-of-sight guidance techniques for manned orbital rendez-vous." The contrast between the blessing of the bread and the landing on the moon, relying, needless to say, on very advanced guidance techniques— the contrast, I say, between two worlds so distant one from the other yet wedded under the cranium of the bold colonel was what gave rise to my mischievous quatrain. I ought, I think, to add that the word "buffoon" was imposed on me by the need to rhyme with "moon." The French version of the epigram rhymed "là-haut" (up there) with "idiot," both words pronounced with a final ô (the "t" remaining silent). I mention this because "two-thirds idiot" comes closer to my present concern than "two-thirds buffoon." I will leave the juxtaposition of "half" and "two-thirds" to the attention of literary analysis. For my present concern is simply with the fact (one I am hardly the first to detect) that ever since Noah's Ark, so very expertly constructed to resist all rains and winds and waves, man (I mean of course man and woman, but even the child!) has shown himself to be prodigiously intelligent when he puts his brain in command of his hands, his eyes, his ears, even his nostrils, but more often than not idiotic when that very brain exerts itself to produce intangible ideas, prodded by the desires, the ambitions, the fears, the loves, the hates that make storms in the souls of *homo sapiens*. In other words, Nature has bestirred itself to bestow on mankind an astonishing practical brain (*homo faber*)—having already done much for the apes—that is to say a brain capable of creating, after the sea-tossed Ark, roofed huts and houses, fire and cooking, bread, wool, the wheel, arrows and machine guns, irrigation, sheep-herding, pulleys, automobiles, flashlights, the hydrogen bomb, Aldrin's techniques for orbital rendez-vous, the Internet and the flood of electronic gadgets invented by our outrageously smart electronic gadget engineers; and then, having so to speak done its job, it has so to speak shrugged its shoulders, saying "What is it to me?" when that same brain, escaping from its proper acreage, has invented Hell, Purgatory and Paradise, prayers, incantations, theories of Creation, metempsychosis, the influence of the stars, the Chosen People, the Trinity and Transubstantiation, infant baptism, washing oneself in the Ganges, palmistry, Mormonism, the platonic Idea of the Chair that begets all our chairs, Leibnitz's monads, spinning tables and ectoplasm, a plague caused by the wrath of God, Nirvana, feng shui, no making telephone calls on the Sabbath, reading the future in the guts of a sheep, ghosts, goddesses with eight arms and twelve breasts, fear of Friday the 13th, the divine right of kings..................

Those dots tell you that I could go on for a thousand pages and more if I knew and listed all the simplest superstitions of the Friday-the-13th kind, but the most interesting fantastications of our species are of course those that have played a role in our violent history. A few days ago I was being bemused, in a biography of Martin Luther, by the question that roiled up great passions in intelligent men, to wit, should congregations receive Holy Communion in "both kinds," that is to say, allowed to swallow both bread and wine, or must the wine be reserved for the officiating priest? From this minor sample imagine the all but infinite controversies about phantasms which have bedeviled and often bloodied Christianity in all its forms. Here I take care to omit, from plain fear, any reference to the figments of another religion, soul-filling to numberless millions, whose more enthusiastic followers would gladly cut my throat for mentioning them in these pages.

Let me repeat. Nature, busy creating paramecia and people, and instilling in all its creatures the urge to survive and devising for them the more or less efficacious ways and means for survival, seems to have felt that it does not matter whether we worship Zeus or Jesus. Who cares, says that great It, provided that when people are cold, they invent fire.

Language, that essential gift of Nature to mankind, has generously lent its power to the creation and diffusion of our figments. Take this sentence: "The chief is going to visit you tonight." This is tangible and verifiable.[15] And now another sentence: "Our men found a dead body at the edge of the forest." Equally tangible and verifiable. Now, the words having done the work Nature intends for them (as in "I had better prepare a snack for the chief" and "Is he one of our own?"), syntax gives them freedom to dance into the world of figments. "A dead body will visit me tonight." Thus ghosts are born. Not, perhaps, created by language, but strongly suggested, facilitated, and credited by it; and then spread into the group. A fanciful scenario, yes, but pregnant with truth. Nature, as I said, washes its hands of this side-

---

15 Much can be said (but not here) about the human conception of futurity and the capacity of language to deal with it as effectively as with the immediate.

effect of its gift.

Language, be it said, comes to mankind with the fundamental virtue Nature has urgently given it: it is the carrier of information verifiable by eyes, ears, touch and smell. It is credible. I state this proposition under the mocking grin of the great thinkers of our day who enjoy proving to us that language is ambiguous, muddled, ungraspable, impotent, indeterminate, self-destructive. They write fine books on this topic confident that their books, at any rate, will be truly understood. But the fact is that were language basically ambiguous, our species would have been, bluntly, nipped in the bud. Language would have been a poisoned gift from Nature, like a noxious genetic mutation. When a warrior yelled "We're out of arrows!" his fellows understood him perfectly and acted in consequence. Mankind simply continued this confidence when indulging in its most outlandish speculations, speculations out of reach of its senses, assuring them that this belief or that was so certain (the words said so) that slaughtering those who nurtured another set of words was imperative.

The readers of these page need not be reminded by a mere poet that the propositions we rightly call scientific escape from the extravagances of the brain because they are rooted in what our senses are able to verify—senses which are common to mankind, I might add, because if what I saw as a curve you saw as a straight line, mankind would, again, quickly perish. The predictions of mathematics are confirmed by our shared senses. They inform us, for instance, that such or such an Aldrin object will be in such or such a place at such or such a time, and our telescope-aided eyes or the computer screens we eye (your eyes and my eyes and everybody's eyes) bring confirmation. By contrast, there was no way for Luther to exhibit souls in Paradise, Purgatory or Hell, or to summon the Holy Ghost as a witness at Leipzig, to prove against his great opponent Johannes Eck that God demands bread and wine for the laity, and not bread alone. He had only texts (Scriptures, the Fathers of the Church, Papal decrees, Councils), which, like himself, could provide no sensory or mathematical verification. And who was there to photograph the Virgin when Bernadette Soubirous saw her at Lourdes; and to make sure, besides, the photo was not faked? Samuel Johnson believed the truth of Christianity was proved since so many had witnessed the miracles. The scientific spirit had yet to conquer some of the best minds of the day.

That all we really know is determined by our senses ("empiricism") is a notion launched, as far as anyone knows, by the Greeks, then lost through what someone (I forget who) has aptly called "the failure of nerve," to be revived at long last in the sixteenth century when Francis Bacon appeared. "Everything we know is conveyed to us by the senses: they are our masters," Montaigne wrote in his "Apologie de Raimond Sebond," echoing Lucretius. But then, to be sure, he skidded off the road and amused his readers by denigrating their reliability. "In order to judge the appearances we receive from our senses, we would need an adjudicating instrument; to verify this instrument, we need a demonstration; to verify that demonstration, we need an instrument: thus we land in a vicious circle." And this: "Our senses cannot stop our disputations, since they are themselves fully unreliable (*pleins d'incertitude*)." But Montaigne erred. We have learned and continue to learn to correct the mistakes of our senses, aided of course by instruments and calculations. A cloud may at first look like a camel, a weasel or a whale, but sooner or later it asserts itself as a cloud. Our essentially reliable and essentially unanimous senses uncover and correct their occasional and temporary errors. I say again that we would have perished long ago had this not been the case.

Of course, the history of every one of our sciences is replete with errors and absurdities. I remember the affair of two scientists working in Utah (center of another *homo sapiens* fabulation) who rose to an Everest of fame in 1989 by way of their fantasy-discovery of cold fusion. This episode is pretty much forgotten by now (I am writing in January 2018), unlike that ill-famed Lysenko theory of inheritance, widespread, long-lived, and heavy with consequences. One mirage was driven by personal ambition, the other by political pressure. Cynics (their prestige is great) also inform us that even the purest sciences are driven by the sociological forces of the moment. So be it. All the same, beginning with Bacon—a convenient starting point for our thinking—the essential history of science is one of continuous *correction*. By contrast, the thesis (for instance) that a wafer is the body of Christ could never be corrected, as it could never be proved or disproved. The imbecilities of *homo sapiens* are subject to disbelief and disappearance; they often go out of fashion, but they cannot be corrected. Go prove that Zeus never existed!

Returning to the *songes et rêveries* (Montaigne again) of *homo sapiens*, it would of course be unfair to concentrate our attention on the zany exuberances of the past. In Paris and Los Angeles, well-educated, sophisticated persons are still apt to ask you under what sign you were born. And to tell you that talking to their plants helps them grow. Despite the arrogant march of technology (triumph and tragedy of Western civilization, slavishly copied by the rest of the world), notions not subject to the criteria of "I touch, I manipulate, I see, I hear, I calculate" continue to live almost as strongly as they did ten thousand or a hundred thousand year ago, and a cosmonaut, master of defectless techniques, will always be found craving a priest's blessing on his loaf of bread.

I find, in a newspaper (we are in the 21st century) that in New York, on the occasion of Yom Kippur, certain rabbis slaughtered 10,000 chickens in order to slip their congregations' sins into the helpless creatures. In the same year, according to the newspaper on another day, the Chilean police arrested four persons for throwing a three-day old baby to the flames on a hill in a town near Valparaiso, because the chief of their sect believed the end of the world was at hand and the child was the Antichrist. I am reminded of a passage in Herodotus Book 7 where Xerxes, having crossed the river Strymon at a place called Nine Roads on his way to devastating Athens, had nine local children buried alive as a sacrifice to the gods. This in turn leads the historian to recall "that Amestris, wife of Xerxes, when she had grown old, had fourteen children of noble Persians buried alive as a gift on her behalf to the so-called god of the underworld" (David Grene's translation). "So-called," says Herodotus, who elsewhere, however, gives credence to any number of absurdities begotten by human speculations.

On a far larger scale, though I know that missionaries have been at work in the Far East for centuries, it bemuses me to hear that several million Chinese, picking away at their just-updated electronic tool, are Christians today, untroubled, it seems, by the plain and obvious fact that Jesus had never so much as heard of China, his Father not having taken the trouble of informing the second member of the Trinity that it existed. These good Chinese simply keep away from their brains this troublesome truth they know as well as you and I, and they can do this with impunity as far as Nature is concerned, for they do not fend off or ignore facts of the kind that tell them where there is food and where there is not; and that is all that matters to Nature.

With these godly Chinese in mind, I return for a moment to the past, wondering whether it occurred to any of the vastly intelligent and learned theologians and other philosophers of past ages to scratch their heads over the question what purpose their God might have had in His infinite mind in not manifesting Himself to the multitudes in other parts of the world, in allowing an army of other prophets and religions to exist, in pitting Christian against Christian, theologically and militarily, century after century, heresy after heresy, and in not sending the Son into the world a few centuries before deciding at long last to do so? I finger my Calvin and Bossuet in vain. Inconvenient thoughts often vanish from the mind. Or—they were all too busy fighting to think.

2

MY ADMIRATION for the sciences and the tough scientific spirit and scientific method does not stand without challenge from my own mind. To begin with, the material-physical benefits derived from scientific thinking have been tragic in the sense of this word I explored in my first book, *A Definition of Tragedy*. Each benefit seems to have been balanced by a piece of misery. This has been said so often (about the Industrial Revolution, to give but one instance) that I need say no more about it. But the obverse of this truth is also a truth. Can I, for instance, entirely desire, or even desire at all, that the human brain had never spun the fantasies of the supernatural and the miraculous? The truth is that for every quantum of evil that has fallen on mankind from its imbecilities, an equal quantum of good has been wrought by them: both private and public. Can I wish that men and women, wholly rational, had never experienced the sense of the uncanny, of the poetic (whatever that word may mean), never felt the joys and consolations of religion? "Noël, le premier jour de l'an, les Rois, Pâques, la Pentecôte, la Saint-Jean, grâce à la religion, étaient des jours de bonheur," writes Chateaubriand in his *Memoirs*, remembering his childhood in Saint-Malo. As for consolation, I am reminded of the letter Boswell's father, Lord Auchinleck, wrote him in 1766 about the death of the lord's wife, Boswell's mother: "Notwithstanding her persuasion of approaching death, she was so far from showing any terror that she expressed a pleasure in the thought of it." And he continues, speaking of "her full persuasion in and through the merits of our blessed Redeemer of attaining endless bliss in another world." Even if we suppose an aspect of conventional "theatre" in innumerable testimonials of this kind, there can be no doubt that such consolation did and does exist, and that we who are so very advanced in our thinking are deprived of it. We die in the bitter cold. And the other manifold soothings and pleasures of religion (a priest blessing a bicycle) and of pagan superstitions ("knock wood!") are unavailable to us the tough ones.

No need to belabor the obvious. The death of religion, wherever and whenever it dies, is tragic, just as the living presence of religion, producer of so many woes, has always been tragic.

As for the aesthetic side of the question, can we imagine cathedrals built to celebrate the laws of gravitation or the Bohr model of the atom? Or Bach composing cantatas to sing of robots that clean carpets for us? Science and technology do have the capacity to beget beauty: graceful buildings and bridges, for instance; and Picasso did not need religion to become a great artist. But can I love the scientific spirit so much that, wishing it on *homo sapiens* from the very start, and deploring the imbecilities of our species, I am willing to forego all that we cherish in the arts that religions and plain superstitions in all the continents on earth begot? I once made a little poem on this subject:

> How could grown-up men,
> More gifted thousandfold than I,
> Upon this hocus-pocus
> Cathedrals edify?

> Yet how dry to think like me,
> Hard, straight and pointed as a nail.
> Give Milton his angels
> Lest his iambs fail!

My French adaptation is more specific:

> Qu'ai-je à vous offrir, amis ?
> Esprit droit, pointu et dur comme un clou,
> esprit sans fariboles,
> sans diable et sans dieu,
> Je vous nomme mes cadeaux :

ni cathédrales, ni Dante,
Michel-Ange sans doigts, Milton sans plume,
et Bach muet.[16]

Turbines are fine to look at; but can we dispense with Michelangelo's *Last Judgment?* With Bernini's *Ecstasy of Saint Theresa?* No, I do not want our delusions never to have existed in the interest of Reason.

As often happens to me, brooding causes me to find large servings of truth on both sides of almost any question that frets me, and in the end I can decide nothing.

16 Harrap's translates fariboles as stuff and nonsense.

OTHERNESS

1

WHAT LEAPS to the eye, what is utterly and immediately obvious, is that Reality contains an otherness which is neither time nor space. I emphasize that this fact leaps to the eye, because most people, including most scientists, turn their heads away, unwilling or unready to see it. The fact glares at us! No need whatever to initiate ourselves into the mysteries of quantum mechanics. Time begins with that famous Big Bang, which indeed creates it. But we poor mortals, we know time exclusively as a reality that delivers itself to us *only* as a past, present, and future, while the Big Bang is endowed (for us) only as a present and a future, into the latter of which (incidentally) our wise heads are digging into with ever-growing and, alas, dispiriting success. What is the past of the Big Bang? For us it that for which the word Nothing is simply an escape. An otherness *must* be called in, another "there is no word for it" radically inconceivable for us, since, I repeat, we humans are equipped only for time in its three facets, one of which is an obligatory past. Time without a past is inconceivable. An otherness that begot the Big Bang (if "begot" is not simply another convenient word) forces itself on us.

And *where* was the universe at the "moment" of the Primal Burst, a burst, they tell us, perhaps more rapid than light itself? This question, again, makes no sense, since there was no "where" before the Big Bang, the latter having created it. Saying the universe was born nowhere tells us nothing once more; it is a mere substitute for "we cannot know." Since space did not as yet exist, it is in something not-space that a birth took place; it took place in an otherness unfathomable to the senses, to science, even to mathematics. A literally *metaphysical* otherness, where "metaphysical," this time, does not convey us to God or Gods or other "spiritual" essences.

Again: at the uttermost bound of the universe, which continues to expand at an ever-accelerating speed (they tell us), into what beyond is it expanding? If it creates space as it expands, out of what does it perform the creation? "Out of Nothing." Again the word that has no address. An answer to the question is impossible, for the human brain is unable to conceive of anything expanding other than into a space which already exists.

And the atoms, and the bits that constitute the atoms, and the energy or force that launched them, who or what concocted them? Whence the universe's energy? Neither in time nor in space: in an otherness where our very questions fail, not to mention our instruments and calculations.

We hear talk of other universes impinging on ours, and even of an infinity of universes, but does this mean anything else than, once again, the utter impossibility of our knowing and the need for a sense or several senses which we do not and cannot possess?

The cosmologists, I repeat, turn their eyes away: this subject of mine is not their business. They drive to the end of the dead-end, whipping up their Geneva accelerator, and there they stop. As they must. What scientific investigation can be made of a condition of which one can say one and only one thing: it exists; it leaps to the eye that it must exist. Perhaps they turn away their thinking about this otherness because, consciously or not, they fear it will embroil them in the childishness of religion.

A word in digression about the expression Big Bang. It is childish, funny, good-humored, banal; in short, perfectly American. In pre-democratic times a beautiful and noble name would have been found for the inexpressible magnitude of the event. My "Primal Burst" is a very modest attempt in that direction.

I said that we know with an absolute certainty that an

otherness which is not time and not space *must* exist, inconceivable and inexpressible for us. But is such a situation possible? Clearly, it is. Try to visualize a color beyond the infrared at one end and the ultraviolet at the other. It is unconditionally certain that these radiations would be sensed as colors if we possessed the receptors adequate to them. Let us call one such color "glig." Nothing we do, strain as we will, can make us see or imagine glig. Yet it must exist. Proof that it is perfectly legitimate and accurate to assert that an unimaginable condition *must* exist.

2

I BECOME MORE hesitant when I think of suggesting that our consciousness also partakes either of *an* otherness or of *the* otherness. I have read somewhere that Einstein spoke of an "internal illumination." I also like the term "lucidity," rooted in "lux," because light or illumination is the best available metaphor for this very strange phenomenon. A term like consciousness or lucidity or awareness might be thought of as the successor of that bygone word and concept: the human soul. "Soul" expresses better than these the sense that nothing is more important to us. Survival after death interests us only if, once we are there, we remain conscious. Cruel Dante does not deprive of their soul, their consciousness, their awareness, the most thoroughly damned of his damned. Interestingly too, when Hamlet ponders suicide, the obliteration of consciousness does not even occur to him as a dreaded possibility; all he is afraid of is "what dreams may come" and "the dread of something after death": punishment yes, but consciousness of punishment. Were the two poets "repressing" a condition too awful to turn into words? To Milton, at any rate, the awfulness of that awfulness did occur, for he makes his Belial say, tremendously, when the latter speaks of God spending "all his rage" on the rebelling angels,

> And that must end us, that must be our cure,
> To be no more; sad cure; for who would lose,
> Though full of pain, this intellectual being,
> Those thoughts that wander through Eternity,
> To perish rather, swallow'd up and lost
> In the wide womb of uncreated night,
> Devoid of sense and motion.

Thoughts that wander through Eternity are bound to be conscious, for they require our neurons—our physical equipment—to exert themselves to their utmost power. Here I am, thinking about thinking. About what takes place in my brain electrically and chemically when I do this I of course have not the tiniest idea; but it is plain that such high-level lucubration must be conscious. At a lower rate, however, thinking does not entail consciousness. Thinking, sometimes very intelligent thinking! occurs while we sleep. And it is evident that the higher animals also think, in their own way, without language, in images, sounds, touch and smells, but can one doubt it? their thinking proceeds without rising to consciousness. If I am not mistaken, this same kind of unconscious thinking takes place in infants. Lucidity dawns on us with language and grows as we mature. Be that as it may, our consciousness is not a matter of off-and-on, yes-or-no, black-or-white. There is a gray zone. This is revealed to us when we emerge from sleep or when we are lightly anesthetized in surgery. Perhaps a similar "almost" exists in the highest primates, yet fails to evolve into full lucidity.

This "internal illumination" can also be absent from all cerebral activities other than thinking. We all know that dogs show joy and anger and fear and a gamut of other emotions—have they not obviously felt an itch when they scratch?—but all this without being conscious of these feelings. Similarly, we range through all the emotions while we sleep without their rising into consciousness. And so it goes for the senses. Sight and sound provoke reactions in animals, of course, and we need not posit consciousness for this to happen. And in sleep we too see and hear, but become conscious of what we have seen and heard only when we recall the sights and sounds when we are awake.

So then, our thoughts, even our verbalized thoughts, our emotions, our senses, belong fully to that universe of ours rooted in time, space, matter, energy, causes and effects. All these attach us, evidently, to the animal world, and we are, in these respects, evidently animals as well. But we seem to escape from that world when the happenings of our brains, in their most active phase, thereby become conscious. At that point, we cross into a mysterious otherness which seems to me to escape from the time-place energetic universe. Our thoughts, like our emotions and our senses, are the willing objects of scientific probing—and I do not mean the probing done by psychologists, psychiatrists and psychoanalysts, I mean the men and women equipped with instruments and computers: our tough-minded laboratory scientists of the brain and nervous system. But there is strictly and literally *nothing* for them to measure or record or subject to experiments where consciousness is concerned, just as the astrophysicists and mathematicians have nothing to report to us about that otherness lying "behind" the Primal Burst or "beyond" the boundary, at any moment, of the expanding universe. For our lucidity is an effect—an effect of our animal cerebral activity—but it is not a cause. *It causes nothing.* It has zero energy. A fact that is unique and mysterious. Everything we know of can be a cause of something else than itself, except our "internal illumination." Furthermore, awareness occupies no space, unlike the neurons that think, feel, see, hear. We do know what causes it to vanish— ever so easily, alas—but not what it *is* that is so fragile and so easily fades and dies.

Perfectly and unalterably passive, an effect that cannot cause, it can be flatly ignored by any new Darwin since, living in us without deploying any energy, it can play no role in the survival of our species. And yet (I must repeat!) it is the most important phenomenon of our existence. It is, as I said, our soul. It is the "it is I!" whose survival we so desperately desire.

And our robots? These computer-driven machines which are almost *who* rather than *what* as they become more and more intelligent? Which calculate, reason, translate, recognize, see and hear, walk, win over us at games, and have even learned to correct and improve themselves? Well, they teach us that everything cerebral—almost everything—can happen and be done without a trace of consciousness—without soul, to use the dear old word again. That these devices, whose physical basis is so vastly different from our flesh and bones, can ever acquire lucidity is doubtful. But if they do, they are welcome to it, as far as I am concerned. For the time being, however, we have no need to ask whether the mysterious otherness which seems—*seems* I say—to emanate from our highest cerebral activity can also be produced by inorganic matter.

3

I AM NOT, I think, deviating widely from my subject when I say a few words about a phenomenon I find most mysterious, as if it were produced by an unknown force.

As if! I cannot stress that "as if" too strongly.

Is it not strange, is it not wonderfully strange, that the process of the evolution of life has culminated, in the animals we are, in an intelligence of the universe? An intelligence replete with errors more or less bizarre since people began to speak, and as rife with nonsense as ever in the minds of at least ninety percent of mankind, yet utterly amazing. Life understanding itself, the universe understanding itself. Or trying to. Need *that* have been the landing point of Evolution? Hardly. The orang-utan can no more philosophize about apes, about time and space, about the creation of the universe than does a mollusk, or, for that matter, a stone, a cascade. The highest primate, like the lowliest worm, does no more than eat, sleep, fight, mate, beget and nurture its young, and try to survive as long as possible. "Suddenly" (speaking on a geologic time-scale) a leap takes place and, by way of a wild expansion of the neuronal matter, resulting in grammatical speech, you and I who are organically but one step more complex than the chimpanzee, we become the universe contemplating itself and the brain dwelling on the brain. Need this have happened? Were we not far more likely to become prosaically a more effective species, thanks to our better brain, than our predecessors on the evolutionary ladder? How was it that, in addition to more mere cunning in the hunt, in tool-making, in mating and nurturing offspring, in fighting off rivals and enemies (and so forth), we "suddenly" began to ask questions about the creation of the universe, and questions about asking questions? This was not needed by the creature in order to excel at surviving in forest or steppe. And there was no reason for the universe not continuing blind. To put it playfully, it is as though the cosmos had become bored with no one watching it and talking about it.

They say that the universe is probably or all but certainly a-swarm with life, since, chemically speaking, the leap from lifelessness to life is no great affair, and planets roam the heavens by the billions. It is also thought that intelligent life (without, I hope, the stupidities that accompany ours) must exist "out there" as well, and many an earthling is on the lookout this very day for exotic radio waves and other technological manifestations of fellow-intellectuals. The thought of Oxford Universities sprinkled throughout the galaxies is a charming one, but whether what happened once happened many times does not alter my view—or shall I say my feeling?—that it is *as if* some force (some Force?) had been slowly, and irresolutely, and gropingly, and stumblingly, yet steadily pushing life from its start in muddy water, toward the point at which the universe has become aware of itself, as if that had been, amazingly, the aim of it all.

As if.

4

IN A FABLE called "L'Horoscope," La Fontaine laughs at the stargazers who pretend to read the future. "Considering the present condition of Europe, one of them at least should have foretold it; why didn't he speak up? But not one of them saw it." (Book VIII, Fable 16). This passage tells us that in the 1670's it was still perfectly reasonable for an educated person, a "lettré," addressing other educated persons, to dispute the claims of astrology. The question was still, albeit to some diminished extent, an open one even among the "better people" of the Western world. Today, need one even say it? no person of any intellectual standing would think of attacking astrology when arguing a point. It is beyond grotesque to imagine a writer concerned with, let us say, World War I, invoking the stars when trying to explain how that catastrophe happened. In short, the falseness of astrology has receded, as far as the "sophisticated" are concerned, into the world of subjects educated persons silently take for granted, while those who are still alive to the idea of the influence of the stars on their lives and on history are at once recognized by this elite as belonging to the all too huge world of simpletons.

Now let me guess that, similarly, no intellectual of the Western world will bother, some centuries hence (if not sooner) to take into account, or bother to dispute, the claims of any of the world's religions in his or her discourse on any subject whatever, including religion itself. That the masses will continue to be believers is not in question. In fact, since the unlettered are proliferating at a rate vastly superior to the fertility of the "clerks," religion is bound to keep growing in most parts of the world. But for people like myself and the readers of this essay, the beliefs of Christians, Jews, Muslims, Hindus, Buddhists, (and so forth) will have slipped into the same status as astrology, ghosts, and fairies, the status of "beneath consideration," where serious consideration would register as an embarrassment.

However, writing in my own century, I find that I should probably reiterate that the *otherness* I have been pondering—that otherness which absolutely leaps to the eye, and the existence of which is as certain as two plus two equal four—has nothing to do with mankind's religions (perhaps I should add: unfortunately!). I can make this explicit without sounding as absurd and ridiculous as if I argued against astrology. So, for example, the cosmologist L. M. Krauss who published *A Universe from Nothing* in 2013 found it natural to state, in his preface, "In the interest of full disclosure right at the outset I must admit that I am not sympathetic to the conviction that creation requires a creator, which is the basis of all of the world's religions." It would not have occurred to the writer of these words to disclaim any belief in astrology had he even given this ludicrous notion a thought, but he felt it advisable, and not in the least embarrassing, to take his stand against religion when considering the dismal future of our universe. Thus it is that, in 2019, I feel it is *not yet* absurd to state that my *otherness* has nothing to do (I repeat the phrase) with the creeds that begot Michelangelo's bearded and night-shirted Creator, nor any other creed, knowing that the day will come when the need for such a disclosure will be unthinkable.

TO BE OR NOT TO BE A JEW

1

TO BE A JEW. This infinitive, this "to be," in all its harmless-looking permutations, is in fact a mischief-maker if ever words made mischief in the world. Surely permanence and impermanence are opposites, and surely opposites deserve different words, and yet we will blandly say, "I *am* angry" and "I *am* a man," or "I *am* your God," as if no difference existed. Granted that it is useless to keep chiding language for its notorious deficiencies and delinquencies: language seems to have done its duty whenever it has almost done it. We must take up the cudgels, however, when its laziness becomes outrageous and dangerous; and outrage and danger are ever on duty when the issue is Judaism. What do we really mean when we say, "He *is* a Jew?" As soon as we place ourselves on the alert, we discover that some are interested in giving this *being* its meaning of permanence, and others its meaning of impermanence.

Thus in the first year of Israel's independence, the Knesset defined the Jew as follows: "Everyone who considers himself a Jew is a Jew." This was clearly taking the impermanent view of *to be.* According to it, one might be a Quaker on Tuesday, a Jew on Wednesday, and a Quaker again on Thursday. I do not know in what respect this definition bothered the Parliament, because it could have given trouble for opposite reasons: allowing anyone who wanted in to come in and allowing anyone who wanted out to depart. One can see that either of these alternatives might have displeased. Whatever the reason, the Knesset redefined the Jew in 1978 as follows: "Only a person born of a Jewish mother or who has been converted in conformity with orthodox prescriptions is a Jew." Now both meanings of *to be* were allowed: the permanent one of birth (with the extra caution of specifying the mother), and the impermanent one of conversion and adherence to a creed. This politic duplicity apparently allowed the Quaker to come in if he wanted to (all he needed to do was to satisfy orthodox prescriptions) but prevented the son of a Jewish mother to depart if such was his wish. By implication, impermanence was conveniently attached to every other religion, and permanence, conveniently, only to Judaism.

Not so long ago, race would have been given as the ground of a permanent *being* for Jews. If not race, it was blood. Today it would be genes. The racial doctrine is by no means dead, but professors no longer write treatises to expound it; it has been relegated to the crumbling slums of philosophy. Nowadays, instead, ineradicable Jewishness is simply and undogmatically acquired by birth. "Once a Jew, always a Jew." This true and permanent identity may be repressed into your subconscious, and your thoughts and habits may wear a speciously unjewish veneer, but inspection quickly detects your ineradicable being. Do you love your mother? Obviously a Jewish trait. Are you keen on education? How Jewish! Do you give to charity? Jewish to the core.

The antisemites, of course, detected less attractive racial characteristics: a crooked nose, avarice, and the like. Jewish inferiority being racial and therefore ineradicable, rooting out Jews once and for all became as advisable as killing cockroaches. Interestingly and paradoxically, during the centuries in which most Jews lived in rags, thinkers typically believed them to be ready for baptism and becoming "like us." It is only after the Great Emancipation in Europe, in an age when a child could have seen that a Jewish and a Christian banker resembled each other like the proverbial drops of water that the pseudo-science of races, involving the permanent definition of human *being*, allowed the discovery that the Jewish banker's unalterable racial *being* made him radically different from his Christian partner or competitor.

Different and then inferior. Inferior and then deserving of the gas chamber.

But even today, our intelligentsia regularly discover ineradicable racial traits in Jewish authors they are discussing. Sympathetic traits, of course, for anything else, ever since the attempted final solution, would be cried down as Nazi. I recently read a learned essay on Marcel Proust in which his *verve* was authoritatively traced to the Jewish half of his 5.6 liters of blood. Not very long ago a scholar ferreting among the archives discovered that the great Fernando Rojas had been a *converso*. Presently a swarm of keen critics from the best universities revealed that his immortal *La Celestina* could have been written by none but a Jew (converted or not), an observation no one had thought of launching during the four centuries preceding the happy find in the archives. If a personal experience may be permitted at this point, in *The Hudson Review* some years ago a friendly critic spoke of the "undertones of Jewish self-appraisal" in my verse. If I had signed myself O'Toole, he would have called my negative undertones typically Irish. Is this any better, by the way, than the practice of so many biographers who speak of the "stubborn chin" in their subject's picture in the frontispiece after they have ascertained that he refused to pay his taxes for ten years?

The affirmation of Jewish permanence is thriving today largely because the Jews themselves cannot bear to see the roster of their community depleted. No one dreams of taunting Christians who drop their religion never to give the matter another thought with a sneering "once a Christian always a Christian." But what is singularly terrifying is the fact that Nazi and Jewish fanaticism joined hands across the mass grave to agree that a person's Jewishness is "in the blood."

For myself, it will have been understood that I recognize no innate and ineradicable Jewishness in myself, though born of parents who felt themselves to be utterly Jewish, and who practiced the rites, or rather some of the rites, of Judaism. For

Judaism, if it ceases to be a hard theological creed, can only survive as a set of feelings and loyalties and nostalgia which can be lost, or jettisoned, sometimes easily, sometimes half-heartedly, sometimes wholly, sometimes partially, sometimes quickly, sometimes slowly, like any other "system" social man has devised. Of course I am saying nothing new. Some if not all the fathers of Zionism were convinced that the Jews who refused to settle in the new promised land—Palestine or some Uganda—would cease to be Jews, and merge quietly into Christian Europe.

2

AGAINST THOSE of us who perpetuate this civilized view of free choice, a small army of the scribbling intelligentsia, anxious about losses to the Jewish community, brandish a psychological weapon of which they are astonishingly fond. We who favor dissolution, they cry, are eaten up by "self-hatred." In translation: you are neurotic; you are sick. This "argument" is thought to have a devastating effect on its target. Perhaps, for all I know, it has in fact stopped short several would-be defectors and returned them shamefaced to their kin. A less impressionable subject—someone, perhaps, more responsive to ethics than to the pop psychology of the "well-adjusted personality"—might remind these hardliners that the best theologians, Jewish and Christian alike, have always recommended hating in oneself that which deserves to be hated: where else does salvation lie? So that, if it is true that we hate ourselves, we can retort with some satisfaction that we have found out our sins and meekly hope to mend them. But this is by the way. In serious reality, the "self-hatred" invention is a desperately childish one. No one, it should be noted, ever taunts a Catholic or a Presbyterian with the charge of "self-hatred" when he or she

leaves the Church once and for all. I can assure the implacables and
their allies that the emotion of self-hatred is perfectly unknown
to me. Aversion yes: aversion, that is, toward those who would
enforce upon me an ineradicable *being* contrary to my will and my
convictions. So much for "self-hatred," about which little said is
more than enough

3

THE IMPLACABLES have but a single argument that deserves
serious rebuttal. It takes two, they say, to play the game. Cringe as
much as you like (they sneer); become a Unitarian; change your
name; get a nose-job; tell lies to your children; drop your old
friends. Much good may it do you! The past, my friend, will catch
up with you. Sooner or later the eternal Gestapo will sniff you out.
And since, as far as the *others* are concerned you will always be a
Jew, why fight it? Accept what you forever are.

Recent history, imprinted with the unforgettable hell-mark of
the Nazi, compels one to take this argument—not the puerile "self-
hatred" one—under serious consideration. We must plunge through
a dreadful night of emotions to recover our reason and to grasp
once again that the early Zionists were right: Jews can disappear,
Jews have disappeared en masse, the *others* have again and again
absorbed them instead of sending the Gestapo after them. In short,
opposition of the others is anything but a fixture of history. It has
been, quite on the contrary, an aberration of history. The normal
spectacle of history, pogroms notwithstanding, is one of Christians
begging, cajoling, bribing, or not infrequently compelling Jews
to convert. An example at random, in thirteenth-century Apulia.
This was the period when the Augustinian dispensation—which
tolerated the Jews, though for reasons one may refuse to admire—

was giving way to the missionary craze of the Franciscans and Dominicans, guided by a bull from the quill of Pope Nicholas III:

Summon them [i.e., the Jews] to sermons in the places where they live, in large and small groups, repeatedly, as many times as you may think beneficial. Inform them of evangelical doctrines with salutary warnings and discreet reasoning, so that after the clouds of darkness have gone, they may shine in the light of Christ's countenance, having been reborn at the baptismal font.

Nothing about "Once a Jew always a Jew." The range of actions spread in reality from "discreet reasoning" to solid brutality, but the goal was the baptismal font, not the gas chamber. The impermanent, not the permanent definition of *being* underlay the pressure of conversion. Three centuries later Shylock, cursing all the way, is baptized. His daughter marries a Christian. The audience takes for granted (if it gives the matter a thought) that her children will "dissolve" into the common faith. No Gestapo is dreamed of, looking for foul Jewish blood. Under Oliver Cromwell too, Jews were welcomed back to England by many as fodder for conversion to their vociferous brands of the Christian faith. More centuries pass, and Schopenhauer, in his *Parerga und Paralipomena*, can still quietly and luminously recommend baptism or cross-marriage, innocent of the Nazi future:

I am deeply sympathetic to the sensible Jew who, giving up old fables, humbug and prejudice, makes his exit from a community which (exceptions aside) can afford him neither reputation nor profit, by way of baptism, even if he takes Christian doctrine with something less than high seriousness.... But we can spare him even this step and enable him to put an end to the whole tragicomic mess in the gentlest way in the world, namely by allowing, nay promoting, marriage between Jews and Christians; something the Church cannot object to, inasmuch as it is supported by the authority of the Apostle himself (I Cor. 7:12-16).[17]

Behind these words abides the irrefutable fact that, the historic

---

17 "If a Christian has a heathen wife, and she is willing to live with him, he must not divorce her; and a woman who has a heathen husband willing to live with her must not divorce her husband." A little far-fetched for support?

aberration of racism notwithstanding, it was always evident that
Jews can and do vanish into Christendom or, for that matter, into
any other grouping. Many, for instance, "unjewed" themselves in
the days of Antiochus Epiphanes, as the writer of 1Maccabees
furiously reports, calling them, of course, traitors and renegades,
and rejoicing when Maccabaeus gets to slaughter a pack of them. If
this normal course is easily forgotten—if we can so easily choose to
forget that the *others* have absorbed masses of Jews in the past—a
reason additional to ideological unwillingness to acknowledge the
fact is that no one writes to celebrate the apostate adventure, while
libraries do not suffice to hold the rhapsodies to and histories
of Jewish solidarity, defiance, fortitude, resistance, and spiritual
victory. One finds no words of relief in the commentaries that
the tragic story was over for those who left the fold, no words
of admiration for those who had the strength of mind to cut of
their own volition the "rope of sand" (in George Herbert's phrase)
which tugs so insistently at the common mind.

Quietly or not so quietly, I repeat, populations of Jews have
disappeared a hundred times before and since the fall of Jerusalem.
Nearly everyone you meet in Spain, for instance, is the descendant
of one or more Jews who were baptized (usually under duress) in
the fourteenth and fifteenth centuries, led a precarious existence as
"new Christians," were about to dissolve into the crowd in the late
sixteenth century when a massive influx of Portuguese *conversos*
retarded the natural process, and completed their dissolution in
the eighteenth century. Completed it so well that the term "new
Christian" came to be applied to the gypsies! Again, almost no
one has written the history of this benign solution: hints must
be extracted from all but inaccessible works of erudition, or
casual asides by historians preoccupied with the more glamorous
chronicles of bloody persecution and defiance.

LAST PAGES

4

AFTER THE GREAT Emancipation of the Jews, that is to say throughout the nineteenth century, the unwillingness of most Jews to be thoroughly absorbed meant that they were sailing into dangerous waters. Most evidently dangerous for those who retained their old orthodoxies. Moving from the *shtetel* to the city, the traditionalists kept up a way of life singularly calculated to arouse the fury of the mob, or to make them attractive targets for persecutions inspired by the authorities when they needed a faction to persecute. Intensely tribal themselves, these Jews might have considered that others were as tribally, or almost as tribally minded as they, and that an extravagantly conspicuous minority— conspicuous above all in the trivia of appearance, manners, dress, and language which act, unfortunately, as bright signals to other tribes. For them, so helpless and yet so visible, hatred was an inevitability. We need only reread that famous passage in *Mein Kampf* in which Hitler, shifty, solitary vagrant, genius and idiot, describes the shock he felt when he saw, wandering the streets of Vienna, his first East European Jew. The way of life of the orthodox, perfectly harmless to the Christian world, was a right only in the abstract; it was not a right on the basis of which a prudent family could sensibly raise its children.

But the waters into which the so-called emancipated Jews were sailing were no less menacing, though less visibly so. We know this, alas, only in retrospect. The worldly Jews were about to replay unwittingly a half-forgotten Alexandrian tragedy. While the orthodox Jewish community of that city remained content with its status as resident alien without special privileges, a highly Hellenized minority attempted to enjoy the best of two worlds by keeping the faith of their fathers but demanding Greek citizenship. This aroused an extremist opposition and provoked a brutal pogrom in the year 38. History repeated itself. The liberated Jews of the nineteenth century dressed in the best fashion, learned to speak irreproachable French and German, became plutocrats, physicians, professors, artists, members of decent middle-class families (not to mention the poor)—but remained Jews. They too wanted to dine at two tables, and they entered into a competition for riches and power far beyond anything the orthodox could dream of. Best known, of course, are the numerous Rothchilds, especially those who were at once great financiers in the Christian world and enthusiastic bankers of the Jewish immigration into Palestine. Among the many less famous one might note a man like Moses Montefiore, who began as a modest merchant, became prodigiously wealthy in London, rose to a Victorian baronetcy, all the while proudly maintaining his devotion to the synagogue. This was fine; it was even delightful; it was bold; it was alarming. The situation of these splendid families, which contributed so much to Western civilization (along with those like the Mendelsohn who downright converted), became "difficult and fraught with danger," as Theodore Mommsen wisely warned, though without effect. Like the orthodox, the "assimilated" Jews were displaying—we now know—an unwarranted and perilous optimism with regard to the human species. I suppose that the Age of Enlightenment misled them. A cheerful trust in human—or at any rate in Western— reason and goodness blinded them. They could not, any more than their Christian neighbors and friends, imagine the monsters of the twentieth century who were going to supplant the polite kings and emperors of the nineteenth.

For in those years, one might reasonably predict a century of legal impediments, discrimination in business, the arts, government and the professions, trivial daily insults, social snubs, the occasional Dreyfus Affair, and sporadic violence incited by the lunatic fringe, but hardly a deliberate national program of elimination followed by extermination, and this even while the pseudo-science of racism (permanent *being*) was progressing. Anatole France, so famous in his time, gives a credible account of the situation in his *Lys rouge*, a novel written shortly before the eruption of the Dreyfus catastrophe. A Jewish member of the *Académie des Inscriptions* is complaining about current antisemitism: "Antisemitism is making terrifying strides everywhere. In Russia, my fellow-believers are hounded like savage beasts. In France, civil and military positions are being closed to Jews. They no longer have access to aristocratic circles. My nephew...was obliged to give up a diplomatic career after scoring a brilliant success at the admissions examination."[18] It should be noted, however, that Monsieur Schmoll is in fact speaking his mind in an aristocratic milieu, in which he appears to be at home—he and another Jew, Daniel Salomon, "*arbitre des élégances*" (like Swann) monocled and haughty. It would not have occurred to Anatole France to make Mr. Schmoll express the fear that Jews were threatened with expulsion from the land, much less with extermination by the French or any other state.

Since, racism or no racism, the Christian world was, on the whole, as ready as ever to baptize me and any other apostate Jew, I would probably have done what was needful to liquidate an archaic "being," impatient with the tergiversations of my halfway brethren and unwilling to endure snubs and impediments out of sentimental fidelity to an outworn creed. Or else, lacking foreknowledge of the horror to come, I might have judged that conversion, absorption, disappearance, could wait. Though Jews often had a hard time of it in every circle of human activity, all in all in the Western world they prospered, they made ample room for themselves in society. History proved their optimism mistaken, but that history was invisible.

18 Chapter 3. The *Académie des Inscriptions et Belles-Lettres*, founded in 1663, is one of the five Academies that constitute the *Institut de France*. It is devoted to antiquarian studies.

5

MUST I LOOK upon myself as a Jew because, you say, that is
how the world looks at me? Socrates took himself to be a pious
man. The majority decreed that he was an atheist. Should Socrates
have renounced his own vision of himself? Surely we ought to take
our stand with Socrates. I am, in and for myself, what I choose to
be and not to be. I choose not to be a Jew. Others insist that I am.
To show how serious they are, they throw me into a concentration
camp. I am still not a Jew. They laugh in my face, and to end the
quarrel they shoot me.

Is this an argument?

They call me dog, therefore I bark!

Shall I allow the Nazis to define me? Many, in our times,
have felt themselves to be profoundly Jewish without the slightest
belief in the dogma of Judaism and without practicing any of its
rites, simply in defiance, simply in passionate reaction against
Nazism in particular and antisemitism in general, and in solidarity
with the millions of Nazi victims. I bow before this deeply human
reaction. But I choose not to define my *being* in reaction to what
others call me.

#

I WAS A CHILD when I turned my back on the culture and
religion of my parents—long before I could formulate a single
thought on the subject. My father took me to the synagogue on
the High Holidays in Antwerp's Van Den Nestlei, a short walk
from our apartment in the Belgiëlei. He himself remained all his

life deeply Jewish in all his feelings, loyalties, acquaintances and views, and gave perfunctory but soul-satisfying obedience to ritual. To me, that ritual seemed repellent and downright freakish. I sat deep in the pew-chair, playing with the tassels of my father's prayer shawl—I liked the silky ripple over and under my fingers—or whispered and giggled with the boy who was sitting behind me. In front of the tabernacle, weird bearded personages babbled and dipped their torsos as if possessed. My father showed me the prayer book and made me read the unintelligible words along with him, who understood them no better, but who felt the profound union and unction of faithfulness. The French or Flemish translation on the facing pages (I forget which) edified me little more. The remoteness was absolute. I was bored.

Once a week it was beggars' day in the Jewish world of Antwerp. My mother prepared a cup full of coins and placed it in the vestibule. Every few minutes the doorbell rang. Mother, the maid or I opened the door, and after the bearded beggar had delivered himself of a minimal formality of wailing, we gave him his due. It was a wonderfully organized business of misery. Everyone seemed to regard it as a routine, much like the phases of the moon. For me, in that stage of my life (which could become conscious only many years later), the sheer ugliness of these scenes associated itself, I believe, with every other ugliness pertaining to our religion: the synagogue and its rituals, the Pelikaansstraat in which the diamond business was transacted in a whirl of high gestures, vociferations, and frantic tuggings at lapels, my Hebrew lessons, the dreary black prayer books, and the Passover ceremony over which my dear father presided in our house, leaving me mostly with an impression of inedible food and bedraggled cheer. Can you conceive, my angry reader, the astronomical distance between all this and Verlaine?

In short, looking back, I surmise that an unconscious or preconscious aesthetic revulsion played its part in my discon-nection from Judaism. Not that I was born and raised in an "artistic" milieu. In my family the tone was one of unaffected simplicity. No one talked about Culture. A few books were read, without any clear notion of Literature. For visual gratification, my parents had their glossy furniture (style Art Deco of the nineteen-thirties), a landscape or still life on the walls, and a few trinkets on the mantelpiece, preferably of a sentimental or innocently lascivious character. My sister and I were never taken to museums, castles, or (need I say it?) the famous churches of Antwerp. Recreation consisted in long middleclass walks, respectable hotels at the seaside or in the Ardennes, and many hours on the terraces of cafés. Although the drive to Knokke on the North Sea took us past Ghent and Brugge, it never occurred to anyone to pause for a look at their riches. Now and then my parents went to the opera, and once—once only—I was taken to a matinee in a theatre. A celebrated Dutch actor was performing in *The Miser,* and to this day I see him placing two pinches of snuff into his nostrils, sniffing zestfully away, and then prudently picking the snuff out of his nostrils to replace it in his snuffbox. It would please me to report, in the manner of inspired biographers, that "the enchantment of this first encounter with the theatre had, unknown to the lad himself, marked him for life: he *would* be a playwright." The truth, however, is that I heartily enjoyed myself, but went home the same *petit bonhomme* that had gone in. I do not recollect begging my parents to let me see more plays, or pining away in silence because all I got was Laurel and Hardy at the movies. No one was training me to be an intellectual or an aesthete. On the other hand, my gentle parents were not stopping me. Instead of theatres and museums, I had love—not the worst of foundations, even for an intellectual.

Very likely, a subtler infiltration was affecting the growing boy. I owe much, I think, to the city of Antwerp itself: its old district with its mysterious intimations, the fresh rain rubbing its parks till all the leaves shone, its harmonious avenues valanced with chestnut trees, and the cathedral bells in the distance—all this mingling delicately with the stories and poems of Europe that came my way. Such influences are as hard to capture in words as the quality of a perfume; and if we name them, how do we know why they take hold in one person and not in another?

If only (I hear you say) the mother and father had taken pains to make Judaism intelligible, interesting, and beautiful instead of offering him their half-baked cake, their neither hot nor cold, their both here and there. Who can tell? Would Judaism have won the tug of war against Molière and Hugo, against my Antwerp of streetcars, bicycle rides, parks, coffeehouses, cinemas, cathedral churchbells?

Or else, would a reformed service, stripped of medieval or old Polish trappings, have won over the boy? It would have offered a simulacrum of continuity with the "real world." But here I am peremptory. If the gods have given me indeed the blessing of a clear mind, I know that the man would have quit reformed religion more lightly than orthodoxy. Reformed Judaism is, for me, as vacuous as streamlined Roman Catholicism. When our venerable religions, which were flesh of the flesh of mankind once upon a time, perpetuate inviolate their doctrines and their ceremonies, they are so pitifully archaic that one is tempted to sympathize with inventions to bring them up to date. But the reforms, which ignore as best they can all that is miraculous and morally shocking to the modern mind, are like updating a fish by urging him to breathe good fresh air. Religion is killed when it preaches that one must interpret allegorically the assertions that God created the universe in seven days and that Jesus turned water to wine. It becomes insipidly sociological.

My father had taken steps, at any rate, to make his little son understand prayers better than he. Once a week a Hebrew tutor appeared in our apartment—an advantage which my poor father, who had gone to work in a Viennese sausage factory at the age of fourteen, had not enjoyed. But never did teacher contend with a more mulish pupil. Years went by and I continued to oppose an

inexorable stupidity to the alien language. At thirteen, I stood
chanting in the center of the synagogue, declaring myself, in words
I did not understand, and being declared by the congregation,
a grown-up male Jew. This solemn commitment exhausted all
concerned, I think, for soon afterward my parents rid me of the
Hebrew teacher and substituted an English master. They may
have felt that *their* reputation, at any rate, had been secured by
the irreproachable *bar mitzvah*. Be that as it may, suddenly light
filled my brain. The distinction between "I have" and "I am" and
the conjugations of these two useful verbs were mastered at once,
and I would have conquered the English language in a year if the
German bombs had not interrupted my lessons just as "to run" was
opening to me.

In the meantime I was keeping a small pad arranged in
alphabetical order where I entered newly learned French words
with their definitions. Somehow—memory is so strange!—I recall
looking up and entering the word "*intempestif.*" This miniature
thesaurus meant so much to me that I hastily slipped it into a
pocket on the day of our flight from Belgium and kept it with me
during the entire exodus. Changing my ambition from French to
English proved to be as easy as it is for a rider to leap from one
horse to another when keen on his mission: mine had been, from
the time of my adolescence, to add a posy to the grand Florilegium
of the Western World.

The only object of veneration I kept on my shelves was a
chunk from the hill in the Ardennes where good King Albert the
First had fallen to his death while doing a little easy mountain-
climbing. The authorities had allowed a pious souvenir stand to
be built at the foot of the fatal hill. There citizens could buy the
commemorative stones, each adorned with a tiny photograph of
the king and a couple of flags. How my tears had fallen on the day
of his plunge! And how they fell, shortly after, when the young
Queen Astrid was killed in a car accident! I purchased sentimental
albums concerning my sovereigns, and made my devout, silent

oblations, not to the Maccabees, but to the Saxe-Coburg.

Some of my Jewish school-friends came from homes similar to mine. Others were being brought up within a more earnest orthodoxy. But I do not recall that such matters were ever discussed among us. My evolution in this respect was proceeding alone, unabetted, unopposed, underground. For all I know, I was the only child of that generation to have so decidedly slipped the leash. Again it was alone, without co-plotters, that I "played hooky" so persistently from the Jewish scouts among whom my mother had hopefully enrolled me—I paddled instead to a cinema on the Keyserlei called the Cinéac—that I was brought to trial before the club's leading spirits and deservedly expelled.

In looking for the non-rational elements in myself that led me, ultimately, to refuse my "Jewish heritage," I easily reject the easy and obvious notion of rebellion against my family. I was the darling of the family, coddled and cuddling, and no one was ever less a rebel against his gentlest of parents than I.

A much more likely—if vastly less self-flattering—psychological origin of my departure from Judaism must have been the fact that I was a timid and cowardly child. The force operating on my unconscious mind must have been, banally enough, a desire to elude derision and blows and draw on the strength of the dominant group by becoming one of its members. For although the Jewish minority of Antwerp was substantial, strong, and an excellent mother hen to the young, it was distinctively, even ostentatiously, a minority. Many Jews walked about in their caftans, silk hats, long beards, and curly sideburns, notably in the diamond district, a stone's throw from the grandiose Centraal Station. Certain teachers did not disguise their antisemitism. The Jewish minority very visibly attended the French rather than the Flemish classes in the schools of this most Flemish of cities, another dangerous provocation. Many spoke with "queer" accents (my father's Flemish made my face burn red with shame). Yes, we stood out, and I did not want to stand out except to immense advantage. I did not want to be the member of a bizarre minority.

It takes little wit to guess that this "confession" makes my low moral size in your eyes even lower. So be it. Honesty pays a price. More important: because this is a psychologizing age, you will be tempted to dismiss my arguments concerning Judaism and the reasons for my departure from it on the ground that I myself, poor fool, have thoroughly exposed its dubious origins in my "personal emotional history." But I advise you to drop this weapon. For if it is true that a personal psychological thrust can vitiate an argument, it is equally true that another such thrust may open a person's eyes to realities concealed from others. I might, for instance, be persuaded that Freud brewed his theories from a rancorous desire on the part of this ambitious but humiliated Viennese Jew to avenge himself on the Catholic Austrian ruling class. Yes, he was going to knock the monocles off Count Thun and the rest; or better, he would exhibit them—and by the majestic objective authority of Science at that—with their pants literally down. Did he not all but boast that he would do so, namely in the apparently enigmatic Virgilian epigraph to his book on dreams, his *Die Traumdeutung*? "If I cannot bend the gods, I shall stir up Acheron."[19] Bow to me, you haughty Gentiles, or else! This then is a picture of the man I could readily trust; but how does it help me pass judgment on the truths or errors of his theories? Who shall decide whether a particular psychological pressure is benign or malign to a theoretical body of opinions? "You are misled because you were beaten as a child." "No, because I was beaten as a child, I see a truth concealed from you." Nothing comes, you see, of tracing an opinion back to a psychological source. You must attack me with arguments.

As it turned out, the tribe I finally joined was not precisely that of the dominant majority, but the band of intellectuals who constitute a sort of congregation in itself. Of course it is perfectly possible to be an intellectual *and* a Jew, or an intellectual *and* a Roman Catholic; one recognizes these persons by the intelligent things they say about their religions. Fortunately, in our age it is

19 "Flectere si nequeos superos, Acheronta movebo" (*Aeneid* VII, 312).

also possible to be an intellectual *tout court,* and that evidently has been enough for me. The category Religion simply does not apply to me. Am I Fruit or Vegetable? The category Food does not apply to me in a human circle. My *being* is that of an intellectual; it is a permanent one, unless one day my brain sickens. As such I learned in good time the signs, the language, the things one says, and, even more important, the things one takes for granted and leaves unsaid; I took the decent course of initiation at the universities; learned to grieve when a beautiful monument is razed, to marvel when a scientist drives his imagination into a Black Hole, to commune with a Japanese who loves Bach—and to write an essay on the religion of my fathers. *That,* I repeat, is my being, my being in its permanent sense.

7

What follows is written in grim remembrance of my aunt Helena, my cousins Stella and Dita, and the members of my mother's family whose names are lost to me, all murdered by the Nazis.

HISTORY, as I see it, instructs me that Judaism should have noiselessly vanished from the world about the time of the reign of Caesar Augustus, or else let me put it less specifically, in the Year Zero. An interesting chapter in mankind's history would have closed without bloodshed, like a drained lake whose waters have gone elsewhere. That which the Hebrews had contributed to humanity: monotheism, the immense Writings with some memorable ethical conceptions, pages of beautiful poetry, wonderful tales and personages (has anyone ever written a better novella than the tale of Joseph?)—I mention only the good and beautiful—and whatever else you may wish to add—all this had been contributed, and the Jews could now adopt a safe new home, whether or not they foreknew that the Bible would remain intensively alive during the Christian centuries to come. Over the Temple, shortly to be ruined or already destroyed, the Spirit of History was whispering: *Pass on.*

"Why so?" you protest in anger, "What harm were we doing by keeping the faith? What justice is there in your advising us to convert? All we asked for is a shop or a farm, the right to work hard for a living, our dear Book, and the hope for a return to the Holy Land. What people more innocent? More undemanding? More modest? More unobtrusive?"

Granted, granted, and granted. Justice and Reason are on your side. They should have left you alone. God and Devil know they should have left you alone. So should a tornado leave a house alone. So should a bull leave a man alone. But I am not hardhearted enough to take my stand on Justice and Reason. I take my stand on mountains of corpses and floods of blood. Oh sons and daughters of Moses, you *did* keep the faith, and today you are stronger than you have been in twenty-five centuries: rejoice! You have even become masters again of old Palestine and you have the Bomb. But I say No. I see too many corpses, too much misery. A monstrous price has been paid to pay for keeping the nest in which you feel at home. Or are you telling me that your traditions, your dogma, your rites, your moral life, are so astoundingly superior to anything else the world can offer that a thousand massacres should be endured for their sakes? And that your contributions to civilization have made it all worthwhile?

But now let us ask whether, weighing the contributions of Judaism to civilization since the Year Zero, we should not in fact rejoice that Judaism held firm, despite misery, humiliation, and death. Consider briefly, to begin with, what one might call intramural contributions: Judaism speaking to Judaism, and little said about affecting the rest of mankind. For instance, addressing himself to the "literary creativity" of the leaders of Russian Jewry

as late as 1939, the historian S. W. Baron exclaims: "I was amazed
to note that in less than two years, East European Jews published
more volumes of responsa, halakhic and aggadic commentaries,
homilies, kabbalistic (and hasidic) works than in any two decades
of the seventeenth century, the heyday of rabbinic learning." This
species of learning continues to thrive. I saw it also as a child staring
at the pale faces of young men studying in one Yeshiva or another.
Hurrying along the streets of Antwerp, all seemed to be thinly
pregnant with yet another aggadic commentary, and impatient for
delivery.

I do believe that many of those (and perhaps all) who
perpetuate this particular order of contribution would willingly
if tearfully pay the tragic price: accept the hecatombs, that is, in
order to keep the faith burning in this manner. But the millions
of Jews who live outside this inner circle—inner and, let there be
no mistake, authentic as no other—need to summon the men and
women who poured their works of mind and hand into the stream
of Occidental culture, a culture though fashioned essentially by
Christians, they enriched beyond calculation.

Everyone will admit, I think, that the outpouring that
predates the Great Emancipation is really a trickle. Intellectual
activity in those many centuries was of the intramural kind already
mentioned. Of international figures like Maimonides and Spinoza
the apostate we have not enough to help the implacables' argument.
Nor will anyone claim that the loss of Jewish art of those centuries
(products made by or for Jews) would have dealt civilization an
irreparable blow. Jewish art was borrowed. The best synagogues
were built on general European models, and the aesthetics of
wedding rings, embroidered shawls, silver vessels, book-binding,
and so forth, afford us nothing vitally or remarkably original. For
the rest, we neither expect nor obtain a Jewish Titian or Bach. The
talent, heaven knows, was not wanting; but Jews had survival to
think of, not partitas. Indeed, their really influential inventions
occurred in the fields of finance and marketing, activities close

to the problem of survival. And in the sciences, especial glory of
Western civilization (along with music), *everything* was to come.

The argument becomes genuinely weighty only when we
contemplate the astonishing flood of products of the Jewish mind
and hand without which world history since the age of Napoleon
is hard to imagine. The contention is that if the Jews had converted
along with the emperor Constantine—or before—there would
have been no Einstein (and a thousand others) and no Kafka (and a
thousand others). Let us for the moment pour into the same vessel
contributions that manifest a special Jewish cast (like a painting
by Chagall or a story by Isaac Bashevis Singer); works with no
discernible Jewish character (like those of Modigliani and Soutine
or the symphonies of Felix Mendelsohn or the discovery thàt matter
and energy are interchangeable), and works like Kafka's, into which
one may or may not read Jewish features. Let us call a contribution
Jewish if it has been made by a son or daughter of Jews *and* sent (so
to speak) *extra muros*. There is obviously such abundance and such
importance here that a man would be neither a fool nor a brute
for declaring that the contributions are sufficient compensation for
twenty centuries of hardship, oppression and massacre.

But let me reconsider. I doubt that the disappearance of
Judaism in the Year Zero or any time thereafter would have harmed
or delayed the advancement of science. Even Einstein's discoveries
would have been made sooner or later, if not by one person then
by several a shade less gifted than he. And this is true for all the
sciences. It would be rash to believe that the absence of Jewish
scientists would have prevented our knowledge of the organic and
inorganic universe to reach, by and large, the level it has reached
today, and will be reached tomorrow. Instead, nothing could have
replaced works of art that have owed their being to their Jewish
character or theme. These would have remained unborn; the world
would have had to live without them.

Now for another reconsideration. Directly we think of all
the Jewish contributors to our culture, we need to enter into our

ledger veritable armies of potential achievers since our Year Zero whose field of thought and creation was pathetically shrunk in the ghetto or the squalid village. Thomas Gray said it perfectly, though he was referring to English peasants:

> Knowledge to their eyes her ample page
> Rich with the spoils of time did ne'er unroll;
> Chill Penury repressed their noble rage,
> And froze the genial current of the soul.

Penury, but far more than that: oppression, confinement to squalid ghettos, contempt, pogroms, mass murder. How many "mute inglorious Miltons" are lying in how many graveyards? If the mental forces of centuries of downtrodden Jews had been poured into mainstream channels from the Year Zero, unimaginable works of talent and genius would have compensated for the losses I began by considering. For every living Einstein produced (so to speak) by Judaism, I see another potential Einstein aborted by Judaism, and I make bold to wish that generations of pale youths had turned away from aggadic commentaries to the curricula of Oxford, Paris, or Bologna.

And now, make your choice. Will you preserve mankind from the loss I have sketched out by perpetuating Judaism, or will you accept the loss and cancel the persecutions, the murders, the forced migrations, the ceaseless exactions and degradations, and finally the colossal massacre perpetrated under the reign of Hitler? If I abolish the gas chambers, will you let me baptize the Jews of the Roman Empire? Let the Jewish contribution to our culture be as magnificent as you choose it to be, are you willing to pay the ghastly price? I wish I could put the question to the victims themselves, but the dead are famous for their silence. You have been calling me coldhearted while reading these pages—I know you, sweet reader—but who is the coldhearted one? It was not from a cold heart that I cried, two thousand years ago, "Give it up! It is not worth the blood past, present and future."

Besides, the world is made neither of nor for major achievers and magnificent contributions. Plain families count too. And what does a plain family require? Health, a house, food, schools, work, security, a God to worship. Can these not be found outside Judaism? Are you abjectly "preprogrammed" animals, that you had rather starve or die than change from this church to that church?

One God is as good as another.

If Judaism had been the powerful dominant tribe in our world, I would have cried the cry to the Christians: "Give up your Jesus; he is not worth dying for!" and urged them to file into the warm synagogue.

Today, of course, Jews *are* the powerful tribe in the country they conquered—conquered (by the way) just at the historical hour when they no longer needed it. It is now *their* turn to plague the minority. Unfortunately, advising that minority to melt into the dominant group—in plain words, urging Palestinian Muslims to convert to Judaism—would be what is called in the press a non-starter for three or four reasons, among them, that Israel is hardly willing to embrace hundreds of thousands of converted Muslims, and, more portentously, that the Palestinians, in their suffocating enclaves, remain conscious of the fact that millions of Muslims in a string of well-armed countries round them stand ready to oust the Jews from Israel— or if necessary massacre them—if ever the United States turns its back on what they call the Jewish entity: hardly an incentive to become Jews themselves, however delusional their hope. In short, what I have proposed, so to speak, for Judaism in the Roman and Christian worlds does not apply to the Muslims in Israel.

The struggle in Israel is a fight between nations; it lies outside my argument. Let me return instead to the Western World. Many anxious Jews are heard to say that the bloodletting is far from over. Any time, any place, a storm of violence can fall upon the Jews again, while (short of another "final solution") the old hatred will continue to trigger the old persecutions and the old degradations.

LAST PAGES

If these anxious persons are right, more of my kind should be pleading for the dissolution of Judaism. But in my opinion, the hordes of Cossacks and S.S. troopers will have no progeny. Even in Eastern Europe, I doubt that we shall see another genuine pogrom. I believe, instead, that in the 21st century Judaism stands about where it would have landed if Europe had passed from 1929 to 1945 without the Nazi interregnum. The hatreds of the Dreyfus era would have evolved and paled as they have in our time, and the vexations mentioned by Anatole France, and by Arthur Schniztler in his masterful *Professor Bernhardi* of 1912, would have diminished to the point at which a converted Jew might become archbishop of Paris, as has happened in fact. Antisemitism will probably never die, it was alive in 2017 in North Carolina when a pack of lowlifes marched chanting (rather quaintly) "Jews will not replace us!"—but it will no longer ruin or kill *en masse*.

As a result of this general sense of history, I have responded but sluggishly to my own doctrines. Coming to maturity in the United States just at the time Hitler was expiring in his bunker, I have never made any move to conceal my origins or melt into a safe religion. Unlike Gustav Mahler (if small be allowed to compare with great)—unlike Gustav Mahler, who needed to turn Catholic in order to lead an orchestra, I was not asked to kiss the cross as a condition to becoming a professor at the California Institute of Technology. Furthermore, I feel no need to persuade anyone to abandon Judaism as I have done, on the ground that Jews are still in terrible danger. Free to be safely and rationally what I choose to be, I can see Judaism flourish with equanimity. It will flourish without fretting about one obscure man's desertion.

8

AS I MENTIONED before, modernized, diluted Judaism without hard theological basis is, for me, too tepid for consideration. As for *true* Judaism, my distaste for the thousand prescriptions and prohibitions among which Jews faithful to tradition live to this day derives from something approaching intimacy. My Uncle Heinrich obeyed every detail with touching fervor, admired if not imitated by his younger brother, my father. I have spoken already of my synagogue experiences. Concerning the almost innumerable *do-this* and *don't-do-that* of authentic Judaism Mr. Poliakov, the historian of antisemitism, reproduces an admirable passage from Rousseau's *Considérations sur le gouvernement de Pologne et sur sa réformaion projetée* (1770-1): "To keep his people from melting among alien nations, Moses gave them manners and custom that could not be allied to those of other nations; he overloaded them with rituals and special ceremonies; he cramped them in a thousand ways to keep them unremittingly on their toes and make them forever strangers among other men; and all the ties of brotherhood that he placed among the members of his republic were so many barriers that kept them separate from their neighbors and prevented a mingling between them." Admirable perspicacity! One is free to admire these strategies of survival or to deplore them. Admire them, because they enabled the "nation" to survive through thick and thin; deplore them, because they led the nation *into* thick and thin.

Rousseau's perspective applies to a famous Jewish trait, the love of learning. We have all been treated to emotional descriptions of centers of learning in Babylon, study houses in every Polish village, the veneration bestowed on learned boys and men (women were devoted to imbecility), and so on. But it is clear that the learning imparted by rabbis and other masters amounted to a powerful means of sociopolitical control. The supposedly *spiritual* leaders combined in a single person the monarch, legislature, tribunal, propaganda ministry, and police force. This meant that rabbis needed to provide themselves with something more than a few metaphysical doctrines concerning the nature of God, the modalities of salvation, the hierarchies of angels, and so forth. They must make their God control even daily actions in perpetual danger of gravitating toward the norms of the surrounding Christian communities. This they accomplished by giving religious significance to the most minute particulars of life. One could not rinse a cup without divine prescription; and divine prescription was interpreted and enforced by the rabbis. No wonder study houses were the first dwellings built in every new community! They were the centers of authority, but also the disguised chancelleries and police stations. Thus we understand see why so little interest was shown in the details of the afterlife of the kind that fascinated Dante. Cohesion here below was what mattered; and for cohesion a regulation on hair-clipping was far more important than discussions of Purgatory.

Now the "overload" Rousseau spoke of is probably as dense among obedient Muslims as it is for true-hearted Jews. But the Muslims seem to dwell largely at an earlier stage of history, albeit in the very shadow of their oil wells and their uncanny skyscrapers. Besides, they live in their lands overwhelmingly among themselves. Instead, a Jew who will not turn on his computer on the Sabbath in Manhattan, London, or Sydney is a figure almost farcically displaced in our Occident. I have known a young man—a brilliant physician and musical genius—who refused to open his refrigerator on the day of rest because the open door throws a switch that lights a bulb. At table a few weeks ago a Jewish guest spoke of a professor at Brandeis University who solved the problem of lighting his house on Saturdays by pressing the switches with his elbow, apparently with the blessing of an influential rabbi. Who has not heard of a hundred similar banalities and absurdities that would shame a Papuan? My colleague K. C. is learned, wise, urbane, but she cannot dine at my house because my dishes are polluted. Another colleague of mine, years ago when Stalinism was still alive, was a Russian woman who had fled to Israel with her eleven-year-old boy. The boy died and was refused burial because he was uncircumcised. The mother was compelled to allow the little corpse to be put to the knife before she could get it interred. At the time of the Yom Kippur, rabbis in New York cut the throats of 10,000 chickens in order to fill them with the sins of their congregations. The men and women of a small town in New York state may not walk on the same side of the street. When a pious widower, left with a little boy, remarries, his wife is forbidden ever to touch the child. In short, as many follies pitiful in the context of Western civilization, cover the "ethical beauty" of Judaism as quills on a porcupine's hide. These countless prescriptions and prohibitions diffuse the warmth of tradition and community, and they define the group's identity against all others so that, as Rousseau pointed out, it survives—survives to be preyed upon because so neatly identified, but survives. What is missing, finally, is sense-initself, I mean a present-day moral, intellectual, aesthetic, or at least economic value. A ritual kiss on the cheek among the members of a congregation has moral value. Lighting candles has aesthetic value. Avoiding pork chops has none.

I see once again the boy I was at thirteen, when my father took it into his head to make a mature Jew out of me. I had just completed the ceremony of the *bar mitzvah;* now, if ever, was the moment to make the boy wrap himself every morning in phylacteries. I have forgotten the precise character and importance of this daily ritual, but I recollect a row of voluble prayers, certain ribbons I placed about my arm and head, and a couple of sinister little black boxes, which I suppose contained some incantations or a psalm or two. I contemplate myself at a distance of almost a lifetime shake my head. Why talk about Africans leaping over twenty centuries in a single generation as they cross from animism to heavy industry and computers? Here is the tiny lad in the Avenue de Belgique, the Belgiëlei: outside his window the automobiles and streetcars are rolling by. A short walk down the shaded street, lifted on its trestle over the streets, runs the train, recently electrified, which connects Antwerp to Brussels. He likes to spend hours at the movie houses of the Keyserlei. Now and then he passes by the twenty-four story "skyscraper," Antwerp's pride. His mother takes him for high tea (the Austrian *Jause*, as it was called in my family's German) at the Innovation, Antwerp's grand department store. Two tunnels have been recently inaugurated under the broad-flowing Scheldt. And here I stood muttering incantations to the glory of Deuteronomy's genocidal Yahweh: "Hittites, Girgashites, Amorites, Canaanites, Perizzites, Hivites, and Jebusites...when the Lord your God delivers them into your power and you defeat them, you must put them to death" (7:1-2). It was too outlandish to last. My father struggled from a weak position, for he was not phylacterizing himself. After two or three weeks, he gave up, and the family returned to its peaceful routine.

But the true *rite de passage* happened later. By then I was fifteen and living in New York. When the Day of Atonement came around, I was naturally expected to fast for twenty-four hours along with the rest of the Jewish world. At noon, after an hour of forced prayers in a shabby Queens synagogue, I slipped out to a nearby shabby "luncheonette," sat down on one of its stools, and bought a sandwich. As I ate, I searched myself for the fatal *ayenbite of lnwit,* that is to say, the bitter sting of remorse. I would not have been absolutely surprised if a thunderbolt had fallen on the luncheonette. But oh, what bliss, my conscience was clear. Not a spiculum of reproach stuck in it. On the contrary, I fell into the marvelous elation of a youth who has passed the test of manhood and established his right to selfdetermination. As I was no incipient Spinoza (already notorious in his early twenties), and it was not the year 1656, my departure from the tribe made no noise, got me no excommunication, and only my father grieved.

9

SOMEWHERE IN Germany, Hitler's contemptible dust is aging in some tub or pot. I too, had my family not trembled safe across an ocean, would have disappeared from earth long, long ago. But in those death-camp days, if they had forced me to the ditch under a gun, I would have been liquidated by gangsters for a creed, and in the name of a tribe, that I had renounced two thousand years before, and for an identity foisted on me by the Nazis and the Jews alike in horrid collusion against my true *being*. Like that poor devil in Plutarch and Shakespeare who, when the assassins were looking for Cinna the politician, cried out in vain "I am Cinna the poet, I am Cinna the poet!"

EPILOGUE

EPILOGUE

THOUGHTS
OF A MELANCHOLY
NONAGENARIAN

Qu'as-tu, Rameau? tu rêves. Et à quoi rêves-tu? que tu voudrais bien avoir fait quelque chose qui excitât l'admiration de l'univers.

Diderot

1

IF THEY HAVE lived long enough and have sufficiently "produced" in public view, artists who are destined to endure are always recognized in their lifetime. I say always. There may be exceptions; I don't know of any. Not that they necessarily receive the full measure of the acclaim that will be theirs in time. These men and women are, in their own day, members of a galaxy of living artists who are more or less respected, admired, loved—sometimes immensely, like Goethe and Beethoven, sometimes modestly, sometimes, as it turns out in time, egregiously wrongly. I recently found in a biography of Tchaikovsky that, in 1876, the renowned conductor/pianist Hans von Bülow named as the greatest living composers Tchaikowsky, Brahms, Raff, Rheinberger, and Saint-Saëns.[20] We are less enthusiastic than Herr von Bülow about the last of these, but here in five names is a sum of what I am arguing. Other lists would have given different names, but in all of them the future masters would have figured among the future losers. Those as yet unnamed were unnamed because they had died too young or had not spread their work enough, sometimes not at all.

20 If Bülow's wife Cosima had not run away with Wagner, the latter would have stood in the list as a matter of course, and Brahms probably not.

Still, while the works of the future losers, those of the Raffs and Rheinbergers, crumble into dust, their names remain perforce in the erudite histories of the art at which they labored. I happen to have a poem about this:

> Who's Dìphilos? His works are lost.
> He was a poet time was when,
> Won some prizes, made a dent
> In Greece among the better men,
>
> And got tossed out one time
> Because he wrote a stupid comedy.
> Ten scholars now remember him.
> That too is immortality.

But O humiliation! I am not even a Diphilos, not even a Raff! The historian who will chronicle, many years from now, the lives and works of the famous, less famous, and even the by-then forgotten writers of my lifetime, will probably not mention me at all. I will not even be forgotten.

Here I remember that I quoted a few lines of Wilhelm Müller's "Der Leiermann" ("The hurdy-gurdy man" heartbreakingly set to music by Schubert) in the epigraph to my *Collected Lyrics and Epigrams*—published in 1981 at my own expense, of course. Müller's poem still speaks to me, and will to the end:

> sein kleiner Teller
> Bleibt ihm immer lehr.
>
> Keiner mag ihn hören,
> Keiner sieh ihn an;
> Und die Hunde knurren
> Um den alten Mann.
>
> Und er lässt es gehen
> Alles wie es will,
> Dreht, und seine Leier

Steht ihm nimmer still.

No one listens, his cup remains empty, the dogs growl around him, but the old hurdy-gurdy man grinds on. I was not old in 1981. But I was prophetic.

Let me repeat. To be known and admired to any extent while you are alive guarantees only that the historians will take note of you: it is their business, they must! But it does not guarantee that your work will endure. On the other hand, if your work turns out to endure, it will certainly have enjoyed some notoriety in your lifetime, provided, as I said at the start, that you have lived long enough and have produced work enough for the public to see, read, hear. This was obviously not the case for Emily Dickinson, for Gerard Manley Hopkins, for Vincent Van Gogh. Can anyone doubt, by the way, that Van Gogh would have rivaled the ascent of Monet had he lived a few more years?

To be sure, there is enduring and enduring. The Homer kind and the George Meredith kind. I will not say in what stretch of this very long range it has always been my ambition to be placed by the literate world, but I have never wavered from the longing to stand not laughingly far from the best. There was at any rate never a time when I wrote for any other reason (except the excitement of the act itself)—a reason such as earning a living. I had taken care of the latter necessity by taking up the only profession in America that promised bread and butter and carried with it at the same time the leisure-time I needed. And so, decade after decade, I wrote, wrote as one in love with writing, and wrote in some fair but vain hope of enduring.

As for the excitement of the act itself, excitement, ardor, bliss—that cannot be taken away from anyone who is building something that was not there before: Raff has as much a right to such happiness as Brahms, and I as Raff. To endure may be beyond my reach, but the many rich hours of writing, typing, and "entering text" have had their being-in-the-world; they are not gone, you see, even now: I am hugely enjoying this writing about writing; though without forgetting there is no correlation whatever between the pleasure taken in creating a work and the value of that creation.

2

AS MY DECADES of public obscurity have lengthened, with but a few scattered signals, some personal, some public, bringing hints of light to the obstinate dark in which I have continued to write, it has naturally occurred to me to wonder whether or not I might be a fortunate exception to the rule just mentioned, that no artist who remains unnoticed in his lifetime can possibly endure. No artist, that is, who has "produced" enough to give the public prolonged opportunities to read, see, or hear his work. Such a one is the present writer, for the public has had the opportunity to examine my poetry, drama, fiction, essays, abundance of translations and works of literary history and criticism, over some seven or eight decades. How is it, then, that today, no critic, no scholar surveying the cultural scene of America, would so much as mention me in passing, for the simple reason that this wise person has not so much as heard of me. What explanation can this have other than drastic nullity? What can have driven me to bang the keyboard other than a chronic delusion of talent?

And yet, before I submit to this all too likely verdict, let me exercise my wits in attempting to give possible reasons (more than one reason would be needed, a single one would be too feeble) why in defiance of history, I could be, I might be, one almost miraculously exceptional instance of a writer destined to endure who has remained, over a long, active life, a blank to the public.

3

THE *FIRST* POSSIBLE or plausible reason for my (alas) unlikely fate to be an exception has to be mere chance. Good luck, bad luck. At the end of the last chapter of my *Book of Elaborations*, I tell the story of a play of mine performed at the Pasadena Playhouse in 1965.[21] As bad luck would have it, it was given an enthusiastic review in a newspaper nobody read (it died soon after) and a damning one that everybody read. A twist of chance might have reversed the reviews with who knows what consequences for me.

I have had, to be sure, my share of lucky events, but rarely, and always minor ones that led nowhere. They came and went. I have not enjoyed the chance encounter, the unexpected printed discovery, the significant endorsement "out of the blue," that would have led to the next one, and the one after that, and thus propelled me out of obscurity once and for all. I think that in my *Memoirs of a Loser* (a compilation of documents I put together a few years ago and keep at home)[22] I tell the story of the chance I had, oh so many years ago, when Herbert Blau and Jules Irving ran the Lincoln Center Theater in New York, to see my *General Audax* performed there, thanks to the Morris Agency: it was undoubtedly the highest point of expectation of my sad career; breathless Special Deliveries crowded my house. Alas, the Blau and Irving tenure came to an abrupt end, and my chance was lost.[23] As it was lost when that remarkable writer Guy Davenport had the bad luck (bad luck for both of us) to die—the admirer of my poetry and essays "out of the blue" who introduced me to New Directions and would no doubt have continued to support me.

---

21 If my memory is correct, my play (*Dance To No Music*) was given three week-end performances by a group of Pasadena Playhouse alumni; this was by no means a regular Playhouse production. My tragedy, of which I have lost sight, retold the Paolo and Francesca tale in a heavily Sartrean direction.

22 A photocopy sleeps in the Archives of the California Institute of Technology.

23 A William Morris agent, Sylvia Hirsch, had been present at one of the *Dance To No Music* performances, and evidently admired the play.

It was my bad luck that the Boston publisher who brought out the *Gobble-Up Stories* went bankrupt soon after—not, I hope, through the fault of my little book.

For *Chi Po and the Sorcerer*, a beautifully intelligent appreciation came from my then-friend Burton Raffel, but where? In the *India P.E.N*, whatever that is, and that was as good as nowhere. Bad luck again!

It was also bad luck that Henri Citrinot, whose Editions de l'Amandier published my *Théâtre dans un fauteuil* in 2013 in a very handsome volume that should have made *beaucoup de bruit*—I paid for it, of course—was a politically enthusiastic lover of all the right social and political causes of the day who, I could easily tell, disliked my work. Over two or three lunches (I picked up the *addition*), he never so much as mentioned the book or any of my plays but talked of himself and his family. Hence, having collected my euros, he has done nothing to help the beautiful book live and beget productions. No one in France has remotely noticed its existence.

It was, by the way, Bruno Doucey, the begetter of a charming line of books of bad poetry, who introduced me to monsieur Citrinot in the course of a Salon du Livre at the Porte de Versailles, t I mention this only to reveal that Bruno published my slim bilingual book of poems, *Cette guêpe me regarde de travers*, without a euro of subsidy—an event almost miraculous for me. Mine is probably the only book in Bruno's catalogue which pays no heed to the same predictable causes so dear to monsieur Citrinot.

It was bad luck, finally (I skip many other instances) that Lantana, the fine if modest publishing house in Rome, perished, it too! soon after bringing out my *Essere o non essere ebreo*, translated from the French. I received an e-mail one day informing me that one of the two partners of the firm had dropped dead in the street of a heart attack. Lantana did not survive him.

4

FORTUNE HAS been systematically unkind to me, but truth to tell I have not helped the notorious Dame by living in remote Los Angeles. Isolation is the *second* possible reason I find for my obscurity, other than insurmountable nullity. I happen to be reading these days extracts from the Goncourt brothers' *Journal*. They lived and wrote in a world in which everybody knew or almost knew everybody, for better and for worse. "I dine this evening with Turgenev, Flaubert, and Madame Sand." Instead, I have lived knowing nobody (so to speak), except my famous friend Cynthia Ozick, with whom my connection goes back to her very beginnings as a novelist, albeit that connection has often been fractured because of catastrophic ideological differences. Altogether, I have lacked "useful connections," I have not, as they say today, "networked." I have not mingled with writers, painters, composers, producers, directors, critics, editors, what–have-you. And why did I never join an association, a circle, a professional group? Why did I remain so isolated? Was I waiting for *them* to join me, to court me? Perhaps. So I suspect. Perhaps, had I continued to live in New York.... But never mind the why of the matter. It is so, it was always so. And this persistent remoteness has made it, I do not say inevitably (chance always lurks), but almost impossibly hard for me to emerge from the night.

For instance, I discovered gradually that it is unwise to publish works of an academic nature without being a seasoned member of the sodality concerned with the subject. I leaped so nimbly from subject to subject that I could never make friends in the comfortable world of any of them. Hence it was difficult for me to find renowned publishers to begin with, and it was difficult to be noticed at all, or noticed favorably, by reviewers, since I was not a colleague of theirs, much less a colleague one should befriend—

an alien, an interloper. Let a single instance speak for five or six. Had I been a familiar name and face in the club of Critical Theory specialists, my *Fundamentals of the Art of Poetry* would certainly have been noticed and even talked about. But the outsider I was could find no publisher for it in the best-known houses. I sent it, I don't remember why, to the Sheffield Academic Press in England, which accepted it forthwith, knowing nothing about me. Alas (I return to the *first* reason) luck was again my enemy. Sheffield promptly went out of business. Their list, however, was purchased by Continuum, and later went on "living and partly living" with Bloomsbury. My book has sold a trifling 700 copies since its publication in 1998; these days it enjoys four or five orders a year, not as a book but electronically. In all these years I have never heard or seen so much as a single lonely word of comment on it. I do not belong.

How different the fate of my prematurely deceased friend of old, Professor Murray Krieger! While still in graduate school, Murray made himself an adept of Theory. He quickly advanced in the profession. His publisher was the Johns Hopkins Press, not some pitiable provincial and dying house like my Sheffield one. Out came *A Reopening of Closure; Ekphrasis: the Illusion of the Natural Sign; The Play and Place of Criticism; The Aims of Representation*; and others of the same species. Murray founded and directed the internationally renowned program of Critical Theory at the Irvine seaside campus of the University of California, and presently became one of the few all-university professors in the University of California network. One year, the U.S. State Department sent him and his wife on a tour of China to spread Critical Theory in that vast but benighted country: a strange detail in the history of America's foreign relations, which Murray accepted in good humor and turned into a delightful work-vacation. He was also, I dimly remember, an honored lecturer, perhaps director, on Lake Constance, and no doubt in other agreeable places where Critical Theory flourishes. He enjoyed the friendship and the useful reciprocities of all the brightest members of this especial club, whose members he invited to teach in his program: Jacques Derrida, Paul de Man, René Wellek, J. Hillis Miller, Stanley Fish and other immortals; but he deigned remain my faithful friend as well, although we never talked criticism, no more than a celebrated physicist would have stooped to discuss string theory with me.

Many other colleagues and friends have shown me, or should have shown me, that one had better belong if one wishes to be noticed. A most pleasant instance, coming late in my life, long after Murray's blood-cancer killed him, is that of my very dear friend and lunch companion François Rigolot, emeritus professor of French literature, retired from Princeton to Pasadena. He is and has always been a *seizièmiste*, an undeviating authority in wide demand all along his professional life on that wonderful and terrible French 16th century. François continues research, publication, and delivery of learned papers in the happy years of his retirement. He told me over lunch this week (I write this in February 2018) that he is preparing a work on the poems of Mary Stuart which she dedicated to Ronsard. François is a Chevalier de l'Ordre National du Mérite and an Officier de l'Ordre des Palmes Académiques. Had I met him fifty years ago, perhaps he would have taught me good sense. Cobbler, stick to your last!

5

LIVE IN New York and make the right friends!

Closely related to the theme of belonging to a group is that of "knowing the right people in the right places," whether or not one is member of a circle. Let the absence of this advantage stand as the *third* possible cause of my failures if we forget for a moment plain vacuity of talent. My thoughts now turn to Paris, Paris especially of the *sixième*, heartland of the world of books, where it is nearly impossible to make oneself known without personal relations. How did *Chi Po et le Sorcier* and *La Reine de Patagonie et son caniche* manage to be published—and to be published without subsidy? Well now, I live at the same 27 rue de Bourgogne as Laurence Tacou, owner and director of the Editions de l'Herne, she in the front building, I in the back building. We became friends; she read my work and liked it. Not that she would have published it for friendship's sake. Nonsense! But being friends opened a door that would have remained shut otherwise. I shall never forget (by the way) the day I passed in front of the Palette in the rue des Beaux-Arts and was greeted by Laurence who was having lunch with her then-husband Sandro Rumney (he of the Peggy Guggenheim family): "*Je publie Chi Po!*" she called out to me. *Quelle émotion*!

And I was introduced to Bruno Doucey on the Place Saint-Sulpice during the annual Marché de la Poésie one fine June by a poet of scant talent, Sylvestre Clancier, son of a distinguished traductrice of Emily Dickinson. Clancier was a power and fixer in the little beehive of French poets. He amiably introduced me to the charming Bruno, who consented to read my French poems and then enthusiastically published them. There were no reviews of the little book, and in spite of five or six quite gratifying public readings, it died at birth.

I simplify, of course, but I have hit the heart of the matter. Interesting: when I walk with my writer-friend Serge Koster on or near the boulevard Saint-Germain, every now and then he stops to shake the hand of a Somebody in the literary world, exchanges a few words, and then spends five or ten minutes at *L'Ecume des Pages* to see the owner of that famous bookstore, who faithfully carries and displays Serge's latest. Admittedly, life is not easy even if one is well-connected. Serge struggles, France has yet to celebrate him, even though his works are always commended in the press (he knows the reviewers), and he has broken with his

friend Michel Tournier because the famous writer declined to
recommend him for the pre-list of the Goncourt—in short, I do
not say that "knowing the right people" will open the gates of
heaven to a writer, but at least it brings one *to* the gate.

The failure to make friends with "the right people" proved
even more disastrous for me as playwright. I don't know what
obscure gene turned me into a dramatist around the years 1951-
1952, when I was a civil servant in Philadelphia.[24] I had neither
ancestors (as far as I know), nor relatives, nor friends, nor
professional connections in the world of theatre. But—I wanted
to be a playwright! I wonder (drifting off my theme) if my inability
to compete in the minute descriptions of faces, bodies, clothes,
farm-work and factory-work, home-interiors, flowers, trees,
and so forth which (if I am not mistaken) entered the world of
fiction during the Romantic Age had something to do with my
liking for the barebone nature of drama. George Eliot on village
household-work. Trollope on the fox-hunt, Lampedusa on a great
ball in a palazzo, not to mention Hugo and Zola—and I can't
even name a tree in my garden! Here are two examples of detail-
work from Edith Wharton's *Summer*, which I happened to read
with high admiration a while ago: "The springlike transparent sky
shed a rain of silver sunshine on the roofs of the village, and on
the pastures and larchwood surrounding it. A little wind...." and
so on. And: "She had liked the young man's looks, and his short-
sighted eyes, and his odd way of speaking, that was abrupt yet soft,
just as his hands were sunburnt and sinewy, yet with smooth nails
like a woman's. His hair was...." and so on. Cervantes never told us
what Don Quixote's nails were like! Here instead is Jane Austen
pre-romantically describing Harriet Smith: "She was a very pretty
girl.... She was short, plump and fair, with a fine bloom, blue eyes,
light hair, regular features, and a look of great sweetness." Madame
de Staël gives her heroine Corinne still shorter shrift in 1807: "Her

24 The tragedy I wrote at that time, after much research, concerned the figure of Asclepius,
   punished by the gods for reviving a dead man. This script has mercifully vanished,
   together with my Paolo and Francesca drama.

arms were of a dazzling beauty; she was tall though a little stocky."
I was never able to go farther than this in my novellas. But drama
especially enabled me to by-pass the innumerable specifics of
things and looks which, it seems, novels and stories now demand.

Back to the main road. As it happens, my predilection for
drama didn't look like folly in the next ten or twenty years. A
few of my plays were performed in off-Broadway—or rather, let
me be honest, in off-off-Broadway playhouses, also on radio, in
academic settings, and as readings here and there. My trifle, *The
Fatal French Dentist*, even brought me income (enough for a few
dinners) from amateur theatres throughout the U.S. via the agency
of Samuel French. But I have never enjoyed a genuine mounting
of a play in a normal professional theatre. Now and then, though
least so, mysteriously, in these my last moments on earth, my heart
has ached for some fine ambitious production of a "major" play of
mine in a reputable theatre, and drooped at the thought that I will
not live to see this happen.

I omit any number of comically painful anecdotes about the
piddling stagings of my plays, because what I need to say here
is that a playwright without an agent had better have friends
among producers, directors, fellow-writers or influential actors
in order to see his work on a stage, even a modest one. In order,
indeed, to be read by directors and producers at all. I dare hardly
say it, in these times of formidable unspoken taboos, but being a
homosexual might have helped. In New York I had modest help
from my playwright-friend Arthur Sainer (long since deceased)
and a certain Mario Fratti, a prolifically vacuous playwright and
busybody who managed to have his plays performed in holes in
the wall all over the world. These two found holes in the wall for
me in New York. But all this swiftly sank into oblivion. I have tried
many times in later years to send plays to theatres everywhere in
the States. Naturally, no one has either time or inclination to read
and respond to the downpour on their desks of manuscripts from
agentless unconnected unknowns.

Lacking the right connections, I have had to depend, for my plays, my poetry, my fictions on my purse and the occasional chance acceptance presumably on the basis of perceived merit. It happens. Without the help of friend or agent, my tragedy *Island* (later revised and retitled *The Summoning of Philoctetes*) enjoyed a well-received radio broadcast in the early sixties in New York, San Francisco and Los Angeles, repeated several times, splendidly spoken and backed by a powerful musical score. It was also without "connections" that *Island* found its way for several performances on French radio in 1985 and again in 1986. I had translated the play into French and handed this *Arc de Philoctète* to my helpful friend Jacqueline Lahana. She mailed it forthwith to France-Culture, which to my utter amazement immediately accepted it. I remember attending one of the two or three rehearsals. Several famous actors were in the cast (Alain Cuny, for example). I suppose they made a little easy money by working occasionally in radio when nothing better was at hand. I became forthwith a new adherent of the *Société des Auteurs et Compositeurs Dramatiques* (founded by Beaumarchais), and was royally paid.

This gratifying event led nowhere, surely once again because I knew no one. Two or three years ago, having failed to place any of my plays on a French stage, I stopped my annual *cotisation*— my membership fee—to the *SACD* and thus acknowledged my normal status as Nobody.

. In 2007 I spent 5,000 euros (a pittance) for a production of *La Vierge et la Licorne* in a shabby little theatre of the 11th *arrondissement* of Paris called Théâtre Côté Cour (it boasted a tiny courtyard). Several excellent actors and actresses performed for pennies in a puny production, which my wife and several of my best friends politely ridiculed.[25] As always, since I had no friends in the Press, the reviewers took no notice—scores upon scores of shoestring productions fill Paris—and the public stayed humiliatingly away. Incidentally, I was struck by the complete

25 I thankfully recall the one exception: my brilliant friend Arnaud de la Pradelle, who saw through the dismal production values and the lapses of good taste in order to admire the acting—and my play.

ignorance which my directress, Anne Busnel (delicious, however,
in the role of bitchy Clotilde), displayed concerning the etiquette
of a noble house, medieval or otherwise. In this respect, she might
have been raised in deepest Oklahoma.

I never quite lost touch with Anne, a *bretonne* by birth who
takes a small company on tour in the most remote villages of
her native province. In 2017 my *Vierge* was exhibited (on a half
shoestring) to the good folk of La Bouexière, Domagné, and
Dompierre du chemin, which I defy the reader to find on a map.
All the same, a charming photo of one of these places shows a fine
old church, in front of it four rows of long benches, and in front of
these a humble but honest stage.

This has been the climax of my career as playwright.

I TURN TO a *fourth* possible reason for my failure to be noticed.
I developed it in the chapter "Who is Diphilus?" of my *Book of
Elaborations*. Briefly: the vast number of books printed each year,
added to the staggering number of works of past times which
have more or less endured, together with the huge reading public
compared (in absolute numbers) with the reading publics of the
past, all this thrown against the one immovable tragic constant: the
amount of reading each person can do in any given time, say a year,
whether in print or electronic form. These factors starkly reduce
the chances of any given work to reach a significant proportion
of the literate public and critics, unless the writer has the luck
or the right connections or the wit to write on a "hot" subject—
permanent like provocative sex[26] or some issue of intense concern
for the day. In the past—whether we look into Periclean Athens
or into Victorian England—the combination of fewer books,

26 It was *Lolita* that gave Nabokov his lift in the world.

fewer literate reader, and equal individual capacity of absorption meant (if I am not hugely mistaken in all this) that a given work of literature enjoyed a far better chance of being generally known than its descendants do today. In our times mere unaided quality will easily sink in the flood.

Somehow, in my mind, I see this situation as comparable to the ever-growing dispersal of the stars.

7

DISPERSAL OF EFFORTS might be the *fifth* cause of my inexistence if puny talent is not enough. As my uncharitable Paris friend Jane Desnos once put it, I am a *touche-à-tout*. Poetry, drama, fiction, essays, art history, literary theory, criticism, biography, translation. Well and good if, at the start, one is so well regarded, so famous, that the critics and the public will follow you wherever one goes. I think of Goethe who, after his *Werther* triumph, which came early in his life, could write on anything—a theory of colors!—and be attended to. I, instead, Wertherless, seem never to have stayed in one place long enough to draw anyone's attention. This is as true of my academic as of my original work. I am not known as the Tragedy man, or the Don Juan man, or the Marivaux man, or the Tieck man, or the Kotzebue man, or the Philoctetes man, or the Thomas Corneille man, or the Mérimée man, or the Magnasco man, or the Dutch Art man, or the Poetic Theory man, since as soon as I had published a work on each of these subjects (and others!), I departed to the next topic that beguiled me. I float and bob. How would any innocent reader connect in his mind the Kotzebue scholar I was for three or four years with the author of "The Flattered Hippopotamus"? To be everywhere is to be nowhere.

8

YET THE DEEPEST (and *sixth*) possible reason for my failure
(other than irreparable mediocrity) is cultural. For whom do
I write, if not simply and barrenly for myself and four or five
occasional readers? Perhaps for a Europe that more or less died in
1940 and when reborn surrendered culturally to the United States.
That is inconvenient for a man living at the edge of the Pacific
and beginning to publish in 1955! Speaking now of my tales and
fables, I need to admit at once that I know what transpires these
days in the world of fiction not by reading the novels I should be
studying in order to have the right to pontificate about them, but
by an assiduous attention to book reviews. My impression is that
whatever the quality of my fictions, they lie outside the culture of
our times in both matter and manner, in topics and in voice. Am I
quite mistaken? I can only say that, having plucked a room-full of
examples from the newspapers, journals and quarterlies, such has
been feeling, such has been my opinion. Let me summon a few
witnesses:

> Romeo Puyat, antihero and scourge of Louise's new novel
> *La Rose*, is a cursed man. Addicted to prescription drugs and
> anything else he can get his hands on, he lives in the shadows.
> Decades of ridicule and abuse run through his veins and fuel
> the rage that drives this story to its stunning end.

> The violence that *A Horse Walks into a Bar* explores is not the
> vicious treatment of vulnerable others but the cruelty that wells
> up within families, circulates like a poison in tight-knit groups,
> and finally turns inward against the self.
> Along with drinking beer Miller's characters smoke joints and
> take drugs: "I hoard the pills because I like having them, same

as I like having extra toilet paper...." Entrusted with the care of
battered children, they might steal Adderall from a medical
supply cabinet.

A weightier witness comes from abroad, namely in the
description of Michel Huellebecq's 2019 novel, a major literary
event in France:

> It relates the existence of a man utterly dissatisfied in all
> directions: his professional life is a series of renunciations and
> of betrayal of his youthful ideals, his love-life an accumulation
> of fiascos and an ineluctable march into solitude and mental
> sickness.

If my belief is correct that these voices are typical, perhaps
near-universal, surely I am justified in calling myself, profoundly,
an alien.

My poetry too seems to belong to another culture, alien to me.
Again I ask, am I mistaken? The poetry of our times strikes me as
walking with a demotic slouch. Or, to put it a little more amiably,
its language is casual, informal, relaxed. Most of it is strikingly
indifferent to music, just as the ambitious music of our times has
all but given up on melody. I think that a single instance (taken
from it does not matter which literary quarterly) will do:

> My mother on the phone speaking with
> one of our cousins living in Warri
> where she had lived with her elder sister.

Hundreds if not thousands of poems written in this slouching
manner appear yearly in quarterlies and books. Closely connected
with this "style" is the sense that no event and no experience is too
trivial for poetry, indeed for literature in general. It does not take
acute perception to notice that this is a minor aspect of democracy
triumphant with its all-pervasiveness of casual dress and casual
behavior. T-shirts, shorts, sandals, grungies of all kinds merrily

polluting cathedrals, palaces, museums, concert-halls, anywhere and everywhere: a grand vestimentary leveling. I am remembering just now the moment when, years ago in Basel, during its grand art fair, I very discreetly and successfully hand-nudged the shoes of a Los Angeles art dealer off the low table round which we were chatting in the Victorian hotel's very formal lounge. Stretching his feet on it was the American thing to do, and I was being a retrograde snob. Be that as it may, our poetry puts up its feet just so.

Another innovative aspect of much current poetry is the element of brutality:

> I wonder
> if I should catch
> up, you're drinking
> faster than me, Oh
> I guess I'll get
> another vodka tonic
> and see how the evening
> goes. Clink-Clink.[27]

Yet another is a fondness for the brave use of Henry-Miller language, which, with my prudish sensibility, I find grossly demeaning of the objects and the actions they address.

In short, I have no place to speak of in a culture that revels in such poetry; it has trouble noticing I am alive.

Even more than my fiction and my poetry, the body of plays I have written is flatly alien to the culture that has grown up and spread since World War II: *Living-Room With 6 Oppressions, Of Angels and Eskimos, Agamemnon Triumphant,* and so on: the titles tell the tale. My plays resemble nothing (so far as I know) that is being printed or produced in my time. Again, a pair of reviews

---

27 This is by a poet by whom no fewer than three volumes are admiringly reviewed in the *New York Review of Books* of March 24, 2016. Long ago (quite incidentally) I rid my own poetry of these catch/up enjambments that pervade the poetry of our times (and make it so easy to write), since they are nothing more, in most instances, than code informing readers that it is poetry they are reading.

reveal the nature of what it is I am stranger to:

> Guy is our antihero, "haunted," as he later describes it, by women. He has an Oedipal thing for his mother, Sandy, a former feminist activist who spends all her time and money on beauty treatments and who hopes that he will marry a very thin girl, preferably one with a "pronounced clavicle" [whatever that means].

And:

> In a biology make-up class overseen by empathetical teacher Mr. Mazer, unwed mother Dierdre [sic] trades jovially sardonic repartee with best friend Burbank, born with an 'ambiguous genitalia situation'. Dierdre, who cannot wait to deliver the baby she's intending to give up for adoption, is both curious and tacitly disturbed by Burbank's ongoing medical dilemma.... In turn, Dierdre's condition fascinates Burbank, for whom childbirth will never be an option. Burbank is still a virgin and has no frame of reference or role model for self-discovery. Unless you count Mr. Mazer, who accepts Burbank on the acutely sensitive, uncommonly bright student's own terms.

Endless variations are shown to and expected by the public about the troubles of the mostly humble, with the occasional fling at a manager or a politician. The fashion for dada and its children came and went, leaving no American Beckett or Ionesco as survivors. The culture, it seems, craves plodding, earnest, straightforward worrying about personal worries, expressed in Basic English. How would I interest an American producer in an object like *A Splitting Headache, Conceived During the Memorable War Between Istria and Friuli,* even if it were a masterpiece?

9

A POSSIBLE *seventh* alternative to drastic poverty of talent is the peculiarity of my plays and fictions in that they are ultimately "positive," however tragic on their way to the end. The colossal exterminations of the 20th century notwithstanding, I turned into essentially a cheerful writer, unwilling to leave the reader forsaken in the lowest bolgia after having plunged him into it. My two last plays show this: the resolute departure of Adam and Eve from the Garden of Eden in *The Lord God Planted a Garden* and the reconciliation scene of *Agamemnon Triumphant*. Going back in time: in *The Fall of Numantia*, one discovers, at the end, General Audax, reduced to a weather-beaten slave, biting, after all, into the juice-dripping peach. The grim tale of Sigismund leaves the reader with a whimsical speculation concerning the prince's survival after his vociferous "No more blood!" And so it goes with all else I have written.

That *bonhomie* of mine snubs our high culture. Obligatory gloom begins, I think, in France, in defiance of the despised and detested optimistic bourgeoisie, under the wings of Flaubert and Zola, and reaches Britain with Thomas Hardy. It has been more or less expected, ever since, that the way, in high literature, is ineluctably down—my Huellebecq instance can stand for all of it. Although the horrors of the death camps made this practically an imperative, the beginning, I repeat, had come much earlier. *Buddenbrooks* was never going to depict the *ascent* of a family, as Mann might so easily have turned it. Kafka's rotting bug was not going to be restored to human shape by some act of family love. Beckett's wretches could only become more wretched. The other day I read a review of the fictions of one Juan Gabriel Vásquez which lists "his favorite topics: the breakdown of seemingly solid relationships, the struggle against loneliness, the emergence of sudden, uncontrollable passions, a tendency to act with unwitting self-destructiveness, the unforeseen and unwelcome intrusions of the past," and so on. How utterly In! I exaggerate; no doubt there must be novels and plays of the highest seriousness that end in some hope or upturn or compensation, but my resistance (which was never a decided program—it came to me unconsciously) to the modish despair of our high-culture artistic productions (think Francis Bacon) has set me apart, along with everything else. I may add that I also stand pretty much alone as well in treating my "great men" (leaders like Odysseus, like Scipio) as something else and more than wretches, buffoons, or sordid criminals, as writers inevitably do these days.

10

EVEN THOUGH mere nullity remains the most probable cause of the obscurity that has covered me, I dare believe that I have never been guilty of sinking beneath harmless nullity into the region of contemptible rubbish. Of how many authors, enduring or not, can this be said? Writers write too much (Lope de Vega!): abundance naturally increases the chance that it will spawn some rubbish or even a great deal of it. If only Wordsworth and Browning had stopped in time! My works, instead, are few, a fact that gives me at any rate a chance that my modest claim is a plausible one. Neither do I need to be ashamed of my scholarly work. I am quite sure that it too is free of rubbish. But wait! I do find a bit of dross after all: an article, "Theme in the Drama of Christopher Fry," published in 1957, when I was young in English and silly enough to take that all too voluble poet for a master. What a fall, by the way, the poor man endured in his lifetime! Productions everywhere, applause everywhere, and then obliteration. I prefer my fate to his.

11

TO THOSE WHO, reading these pages, have come to feel that there is something base and shameful in a person's craving for a degree of recognition from the world—or rather, in confessing to such a craving—I reply that, on the contrary, it is a sign and an expression of modesty. No one can despise the human longing, as such, to be something more than a zero in this world; but how is a person to judge, after having done much work, whether he or she stands indeed somewhere above that blank point? Will self-congratulation do the business? Is it admirable to soar far above the supposedly bad taste, the ignorance, the blindness of public and critics who have ignored you, and take your stand on the principle of self-sufficiency? Admirable perhaps, ridiculous more probably, enviable certainly. Be that as it may, I am not there. My modesty forbids it.

Not forgetting, however, the point I made at the outset, namely that the admiration I am speaking of and have missed may, in the course of time, turn out to have been misplaced. I wonder if that thought occurred to Herr Raff and Herr Rheinberger as they breathed the incense they were enjoying.

ABOUT THE AUTHOR

OSCAR MANDEL is a Belgian-born American poet, storyteller, playwright, and essayist. He has also pursued a parallel career as a translator—primarily of classic French playwrights—and has worked as a literary critic and art historian. He is a professor emeritus of literature at the California Institute of Technology.